THE ELIMINATION GAME

CONNIE REEVES

TANNENBAUM PUBLISHING COMPANY
DOWELL, MARYLAND

Published by
Tannenbaum Publishing Company
P.O. Box 117
Dowell, Maryland
20629

First Printing, 2010

ISBN-10: 0978736931
ISBN-13: 9780978736934
Library of Congress Control Number: 2010932217

Printed and bound in the United States of America

This book is a work of fiction. Except for references to the real world meant to situate the fictional story, all characters, places, incidents, and dialogue were invented by the author and any resemblance to actual persons, living or dead, is entirely coincidental.

www.tannenbaumpublishing.com

Dedication

This book is dedicated to all U.S. Army aviators,
but particularly my sisters in flight.

THE ELIMINATION GAME

CONNIE
REEVES

CHAPTER 1

ETLINGEN, WEST GERMANY
5:37 P.M., THURSDAY, MARCH 20, 1980

Chief Warrant Officer Two Crystal Lambert quickly scanned the cockpit panel—all instrument indications were normal. She and First Lieutenant Sandra Boswith were returning from a long day of picking up Special Forces troops at one location and dropping them off at another and they were bone tired. The exertion on the helicopter had been immense, hovering at fifty feet while the Special Forces guys practiced their rappelling. Lambert wouldn't have been surprised to see an overload on the engine, but everything was in the green.

As they headed towards home, Lambert, the pilot-in-command of the UH-I Huey helicopter, began to relax. Although the lieutenant had done most of the flying, as most copilots do, Lambert had retained responsibility for the entire flight—the radios, navigation, coordinating with the Special Forces commander, and ensuring the Huey ended up where it needed to be and when.

Arching her eyebrows at her copilot, Lambert squeezed the intercom on the cyclic and teasingly asked, "So, Lieutenant, how did your big date go this past weekend?"

Everyone in the company was agog that the Operations Officer, Captain Kyle Wittgenstein, had asked Lieutenant Boswith out. Not only were there so few women in the unit to begin with that their every move was scrutinized, but Wittgenstein, who had been in the company for two years, hadn't been known to date a single female in all that time. Boswith had just arrived a few months earlier from flight school.

Boswith turned her head to the right, and Lambert could only see the back of her flight helmet. "It was fine," Boswith said, speaking through the helmet microphone as she squeezed the intercom.

"Come on, Lieutenant," Lambert urged. "Give me some details. We're all girls here!" She turned towards the crew chief in the back, Staff Sergeant Sharon Gregory, and grinned. Gregory gave a thumb's up, but Boswith had her head facing out of the cockpit and didn't see.

"Well," she said, "I hadn't dated a captain before."

"Did you—you know—do the down and dirty?" Lambert smiled lasciviously.

Boswith whipped back around. "Crystal! You know I wouldn't talk about that! Especially in front of . . ." She turned slightly towards the crew chief.

"Yes, I know," Lambert said with a shudder of disgust. "Not in front of the enlisted folks. Got to keep you pure, right, Sharon?"

Gregory keyed her mike and laughed uproariously, "Yes, ma'am!"

Boswith kept on flying, steadfastly looking out of the cockpit and examining the horizon, pretending to ignore her companions.

All of a sudden, a loud beeping sound filled the cockpit.

"What the hell?" Lambert angrily demanded.

The "Transmission Oil Low" light had illuminated. Army doctrine taught every pilot to put the helicopter down immediately.

"I have the controls," Lambert said, grabbing the cyclic and collective.

Glancing over to visually verify this, Boswith then confirmed it by saying, "You have the controls."

From the first day of flight school, pilots are taught to always keep an emergency landing spot in mind while flying, and Boswith had a place in her mind's eye when Lambert took control. Although Boswith was perfectly capable of making the landing, many pilots-in-command are hard put to take a training session that far or to extend that much trust in their copilots. Besides, the helicopter and the safety of its occupants are the responsibility of the pilot-in-command.

As it turned out, Lambert was aiming towards the same landing zone. Simultaneously, she keyed the radio mike and made a Mayday call to the last approach tower they had been in contact with.

"Nuremberg Tower, this is Army 67245, going down at coordinates—"

Boswith was frantically determining the UTM (Universal Transverse Mercator) coordinates off the map. She keyed the radio and said "Lima Mike 9165 4523."

"Got that, Nuremberg?" Lambert asked sharply.

"Roger, Army 67245."

Lambert clicked her mike twice—a way to indicate affirmation or agreement without conversation. "Call out my instruments for me, Lieutenant," she said in a clipped voice. She began to focus all her attention on getting the helicopter down, past a village to a farmer's field surrounded by tall trees. Being West Germany, the whole area was densely populated and heavily wooded, and this was the best choice available. With her years of aviation experience and a couple of other emergency landings under her belt, Lambert felt confident they would come out of it okay, but it was still dicey.

"Your speed's high. Slow it down. You're at two hundred feet. One hundred feet. Still too fast." Boswith nervously kept close watch in and out of the helicopter.

She and Gregory watched the trees come rushing towards them from below as Lambert adjusted the collective and cyclic in minute increments. Barely clearing the treetops, the helicopter began settling into the small open area, with Lambert decreasing speed dramatically while further reducing altitude.

At five feet above the ground, they all breathed a sigh of relief.

"We made it!" Lambert said triumphantly, as she slowly lowered the collective to land the helicopter.

At that moment, the helicopter burst into flames, killing all three women aboard instantaneously.

CHAPTER 2

ETLINGEN, WEST GERMANY
5:45 P.M., THURSDAY, MARCH 20

Villagers—especially children—streamed towards the landing area to get a good look at the Huey and the American pilots. They had just reached the outer edge of the village when the explosion occurred and then, rushing to the clearing, stood transfixed by steel hurtling through the air with arrows of fire. A couple of men darted towards the helicopter to remove the pilots, but the searing heat drove them back.

An older man in dingy overalls rushed to the yellow pay phone at the edge of the village and called *Notfall.* The crowd grew larger as plumes of smoke climbed higher and turned blacker. Gritty soot fell on heads and shoulders. The northwest breeze pushed the acrid fumes of gasoline, burned flesh, and hot metal into nostrils—quickly covered by hands and handkerchiefs. As the scorching heat of the flames drew closer, people in front stepped back, searching for cooler air. When blocked by the individuals behind them, still straining to see the burning hulk, a slight panic ensued.

The familiar siren of *polizei,* firefighters, and ambulances could soon be heard above the fire's pops and cracks as numerous vehicles screeched into the crowd, scattering the bystanders. The firefighters spent thirty minutes dousing the flames of the destroyed Huey, creating a hot, wet steam bath that seeped into clothes. Although some observers experienced breathing problems because of the heavy smoke, no one was inclined to leave. Officials, however, began ordering the crowd to disperse.

Meanwhile, the polizei established a crime scene tape barrier and started interviewing witnesses. *Hauptmann* Karl Gunter had already called his American counterpart, a captain in the military police, and was certain U.S. representatives would soon be on their way. Under the NATO Status of Forces Agreement, jurisdiction for the accident site would rest with the Americans, but until their arrival, the Germans would control the scene.

Gunter suddenly spied an individual with a television camera moving towards the charred wreckage, obviously heading towards the cockpit area and presumably trying to film the dead crew.

"*Halten Sie!*" Gunter yelled. "What do you think you're doing?"

"I work for ZDF!" One of the two major German television stations.

"Get the hell out of here! When we want news coverage, we'll let you know." Gunter gave the cameraman a shove, nearly knocking him down as he tumbled back towards the crime scene tape. The cameraman turned, stared malevolently at Gunter for a moment, and then disappeared into the crowd.

A small helicopter appeared overhead, buzzing annoyingly. As soon as the police recognized the ZDF logo on the side, a spokesperson with a hand-held radio ordered the helicopter to depart immediately. It hovered for another twenty seconds, however, and observers on the ground could detect the glint of a television camera before the aircraft peeled off to the southeast.

Gunter turned to his assistant, *Polizeimeister* Marthe Johannas. "File a complaint with ZDF when we get back. They know better than to fly over an accident site."

"*Stimmt, Herr Hauptmann.*"

Nevertheless, they both knew ZDF would show riveting footage on the evening news of a downed American helicopter, which would only encourage anti-American agitators.

Within an hour after the accident, Major Kenneth Damrow, commander of 17th Aviation Company (Combat), was on the ground. He had diverted from another mission as soon as his operations office had been able to reach him.

Controlled chaos greeted him. American and German aviation accident investigators, police forces, and criminal investigation forces on the ground attempted to cooperate and secure control simultaneously. As the local police chief, Gunter was coordinating all of the efforts, and Damrow introduced himself.

"How long do you think it will be before I can get my soldiers out of here?" Damrow asked.

Gunter shook his head. "I don't know. Right now our firefighters say the metal is still too hot to touch. I'm sure it will be at least a few hours before the bodies can be removed."

Damrow fixated on the helicopter. "I just can't believe three of them are in there."

"*Ja*, it's a terrible tragedy," Gunter concurred.

"I've only got nine women in my unit, and to lose three at once is just . . ."

"These were all women?" Gunter asked in disbelief.

"Yes, two pilots and a crew chief. And it was the first time that an all-female crew had gone out. It was a pretty big deal in our unit today." Damrow shook his head. "This is going to be so hard on my troops."

"*Das tut mir sehr Leid*."

"I've been the commander for a year now, and this is the first fatal accident on my watch. It's something I had hoped would never happen."

Gunter nodded. "I feel like that every day I send my people out." Both men remained silent for a long moment and then turned their attention to the immediate business at hand.

The tumultuous activity at the accident site, as a result of so many people and organizations being involved, allowed several young boys to slip unobserved under the crime scene tape at the farthest end of the clearing and into the woods.

For the next couple of hours, the boys played games in the woods, periodically taking a break to peer out into the clearing and see if they could determine what was happening. The dank, dark woods—with their mildewy smell and rustling leaves underfoot—provided a silent backdrop to the boys' boisterous shenanigans, distracting them from the constant activity around the shredded helicopter.

Every now and then, one would climb a tree and report back. When Josef Bransson announced the bodies were being carried out, they all scampered up as high as they could and solemnly watched. They couldn't really tell what the dead people looked like—some charred, blackened sticks were placed in dark zip-up bags on the ground. Then the bags were placed on stretchers and carried to ambulances that left with their sirens screaming, which seemed rather strange to the boys since they knew the bodies weren't going to a hospital.

After that excitement, the luster of the day began to droop and even these high-spirited young boys began to acknowledge that something serious had happened here and perhaps it was time to head home. As they walked further into the woods, Rolf Pederson tripped on what he thought was a tree root, but, looking down, found he had stumbled over a metal cylinder. Picking up the grimy, still-warm object covered in soot, Rolf quickly realized he now owned a souvenir from the American helicopter. After putting it in his pocket, he wiped his smudgy hands on his pants.

What Rolf didn't know was that it was a small timing device used for explosives, and it would be the only piece of evidence to indicate the accident was sabotage.

CHAPTER 3

WOLFGANG KASERNE, WEST GERMANY
7:15 A.M., FRIDAY, MARCH 21

The air in the pilots' lounge, normally stuffy, seemed exceptionally close. Most everyone found it hard to breathe. No one seemed to have anything to say. The tattered carpet remnant covering the floor looked shabbier than usual. Dust motes floated in the air, particularly near the chalkboard where the safety instructor had clapped the erasers before the meeting, releasing clouds of dry, white chalk. The steam radiators along the hangar walls clanged and whined as they intermittently poured out varying levels of intense heat that clogged pores and then refused to operate, leaving everyone shivering in their flight jackets.

The ZDF cameraman had managed to zoom in for several seconds on the mangled bodies of the pilots through the shattered cockpit glass before Gunter had pushed him aside. In conjunction with the aerial shots filmed by the ZDF airborne crew, television screens across Germany had flickered that night with dead pilots and a ruined American helicopter and dire warnings about an intrusive U.S. presence. Although the Cold War formed much of military and foreign policy for West Germany as well as the United States, it had been going on for several decades, and the younger Germans were less inclined to see a valid threat.

Most American military didn't see these television images because their TV sets could not receive signals from the German television stations. And, even if the Armed Forces Radio and Television Service had been willing to broadcast such graphic images, it wouldn't have done so until the next of kin of the casualties had been notified. Once the bodies were taken to the hospital morgue and dental records were retrieved, positive—meaning official—identification of the individuals could be set in motion. Only then would the Army be willing to tell some parents or a spouse that their loved one was dead. And until that distasteful task was accomplished, no other individual would supposedly hear of it by happenstance.

Nevertheless, plenty of soldiers lived off post and had German TV sets, so they saw the images. Since the accident had occurred after normal duty hours, telephones kept buzzing between unit members all night long as they kept each other informed. By 7:30 the next morning, when they arrived at the pilots' briefing, everyone in the 17th Aviation Company knew what had happened.

Captain Erika Stohlmann walked into the pilots' lounge. As Executive Officer, she usually arrived last, followed only by Damrow. Assigned to the unit for barely a year and the second-highest ranking member, Erika felt all eyes watching to gauge her reaction. As per her usual habit, Erika claimed a spot at the back of the room and leaned against the wall, hugging her sheaf of papers close to her chest. The company headquarters, across the *Kaserne* from the hangar, inspired her to bring work to accomplish before returning to her desk. She seemed to embody the view that work would go on as usual, and people in the room emitted a collective sigh of relief.

The other female pilot remaining in the unit, Warrant Officer One Vicky Dardanelli, slouched in one of the few unsightly couches that ringed the room. A chain-smoker, her nicotine-stained fingers waved hello languidly at her buddies, and her skin, hair, and uniform emanated pungent cigarette smoke that she was never rid of. Vicky's presence could be smelled before heard or seen.

"So, what's the deal-i-o?" she asked her nearest neighbor, Warrant Officer One Walt Cantata.

"Hey, tragic, man."

"Yeah, another one bites the dust." Vicky took a long drag off her cigarette and flicked the ash on the floor.

Alarmed, Walt took a quick look at her and turned away towards the lectern, more to avoid her than because Damrow had just walked in.

The room dropped to a dead silence.

"People," Damrow said, "there's no easy way around this. We've lost three of our own. I can't even begin to express how sorry I am that we lost three fine soldiers yesterday. As your commander, I'm your custodian. As of yet, I don't know what went wrong, but we'll find out. The entire fleet of Hueys is grounded until we determine the cause of the accident. Kyle, fill everyone in on what we know."

Kyle Wittgenstein offered details about the mission that Lambert and Boswith had been flying, the radio call they had made, and the accident itself.

Damrow continued. "Notifications to the families are going out as we speak. I can't stress to you enough not to be calling back to your buddies in the States and telling them what happened." There wasn't much chance of that—phone calls were exorbitantly expensive and the military phone system called Autovon was archaic and impossible to use. "As soon as we can plan a memorial service here, we'll let you know. If anyone wants to help with that, please see Captain Stohlmann." Erika nodded slightly. "Any questions?" he asked.

"Yes, sir," Vicky said, stubbing out her cigarette on the bottom of her combat boot. "Now that your two prized female pilots are dead, are you going to put the two alternates up for another all-female flight crew?"

The intake of air was audible throughout the room. Vicky was audacious, but this was beyond the pale, even for her.

"Miss Dardanelli, that was entirely inappropriate," Damrow commented as he strode from the room, "and unworthy of a response."

The rest of the pilots in the room created a vacuum surrounding Vicky, in which she sat undisturbed and unconcerned.

Erika remained in the pilots' lounge to catch Vicky as she prepared to depart. "Miss Dardanelli, I want to speak to you," she said.

"Gee, ma'am, I can't imagine why."

"People are grieving here today and you're showing no sensibilities whatsoever."

"Screw that!"

"What's your problem?"

"My problem, ma'am, is that this is a dangerous profession, and when we strap on those helicopters and accept that flight pay, we all know we might not come back someday. So big fucking deal. They tried for the brass ring and they lost." Vicky shrugged her shoulders.

"But you and I've also got a responsibility to—"

"Excuse my French, ma'am, but I don't have any fucking responsibility to do anything but fly helicopters and take care of any shitty jobs assigned to me as additional duties. I didn't ask to be a fucking *female* helicopter pilot. I am just a helicopter pilot. And I'm sick and tired of people trying to make a distinction."

Vicky walked off.

"Miss Dardanelli, I did not excuse you!" Although frustrated, Erika knew her complaint was falling on deaf ears and that she would not bring charges of insubordination against Vicky, even though the idea was sorely tempting.

CHAPTER 4

WATERTOWN, NEW YORK
6:45 A.M., FRIDAY, MARCH 21

Chief Warrant Officer Two Tina Loyola stood at her kitchen window that same morning watching the squirrels try, once again, to outmaneuver the plastic lid she had placed on top of the bird feeder. They kept sliding to the edge of the lid and falling to the ground, and their incessant scratching and tiny bounces reverberated in Tina's ear. The bluebird family she had coaxed to enjoy her bird feeder on a regular basis was cowering in various branches of the tall Scotch pine at the edge of her yard. Spring had finally decided to return to New York after an exceedingly dreary winter, but piles of slushy, drippy snow still blanketed the shadowiest corners of her backyard against the weather-beaten fence.

"Hah! Gotcha!" she exclaimed in triumph to the squirrels. "See if you keep eating my birdseed! I'm glad I put that up over the weekend. I think that was worth the ten bucks."

She poured her second cup of coffee, inhaled the fragrant aroma gratefully, and, looking at the clock, judged she had ten more minutes before needing to leave for work. Grabbing a few bobby pins, Tina stuck her light brown ponytail up above the nape of her neck.

Suddenly, the doorbell rang, causing her cat, Eliza, to shriek and race across the kitchen floor, running headlong into her bowl of water and toppling it over.

Through the window panels on either side of the door, Tina could see two Army officers in their Class A uniform—dark green jacket bedecked with ribbons and badges, dark green trousers, light green shirt, shiny black shoes, and green service hat.

Tina's senses began to recoil. The only reason why two Army officers would be at her doorstep so early in the morning would be if—No, don't even think it. Her palms began to perspire and her forehead to glisten. She yanked open the door.

"Tina—" Chief Warrant Officer Two Deirdre Holloway haltingly said.

Tina spun around on her heel and walked into the living room. Captain Owen Nattingly looked at Deirdre and motioned her to follow. They stopped a few feet behind Tina, who had gone directly to the granite fireplace mantel, where she picked up a large, framed photo of a woman in an Army flight suit next to a helicopter. Nattingly, an Army chaplain, didn't know Tina and was confused into thinking the photo was of her. Deirdre knew Tina was looking at a photo of her twin sister—Crystal Lambert.

"How did she die?" Tina asked in a tightly controlled voice.

Deirdre told her all that she knew, which, up to this point, wasn't much since the accident had occurred less than twenty-four hours earlier. Although the role of Casualty Assistance Officer was not one that anyone ever wanted, Deirdre felt that, if anyone could help Tina, she could. She and Tina had been friends since flight school. Tina was Crystal's sole surviving relative, as their parents had died several years earlier on a vacation in Mexico when a landslide hit their tourist bus and knocked it off a cliff-side road into the precipice below.

Although Nattingly offered his ministerial services, Tina gruffly declined. After Deirdre informed Tina what to expect in the days to come and promised to return, she and Nattingly left.

Now that she was alone, Tina, in a state of pent-up anguish and rage, threw the photo of Crystal into the fireplace. Shards of glass poked through the photograph, tearing it into jagged pieces that mixed with the ashes from the winter's fires.

"How dare you leave me!!" she railed. "You promised you'd never leave me! I hate you, Crystal, I hate you!" And then she broke down and cried the tears that Deirdre and Nattingly had expected to see. She sat on the footstool, pressing the backs of her hands into her eyes so hard they hurt, feeling the hot wetness drip down her face and onto her flight suit, where they turned the olive green material into something considerably darker.

FORT DRUM, NEW YORK
9:25 A.M., FRIDAY, MARCH 21

When she returned to her unit, Deirdre felt emotionally spent and called her husband, an Army nurse in the Fort Drum hospital, to see if he had time for coffee.

First Lieutenant Wayne Yarrow was the charge nurse of the emergency room on the day shift this week, so he only had a few minutes. Deirdre drove over to meet him. She could smell the sour mop that had recently been used to clean the hallway floors, and felt overwhelmed by the carts of laundry and supplies she had to dodge en route to the emergency room. Although the ER maintained a coffee pot in perpetuity, the coffee had reached a state of almost solid sludge and burned odor that even Wayne, usually indifferent, disdained.

"What about Crystal's husband?" Wayne asked once he and Deirdre sat down in the hospital cafeteria with their coffees. "Has he been notified?"

"I don't know. They got divorced a few months ago, so the Army wouldn't have sent a Casualty Assistance Officer out to him." Chief Warrant Officer Two Frank Lambert was stationed in Hawaii. "Do you think I should call him?"

Wayne shrugged and looked questioningly at his wife. "If you don't, who will?"

Deirdre sighed heavily. "I can only imagine. But the guy hates my guts."

"Yeah, I remember. He could never get over you beating him out of the Honor Grad spot in flight school. Sore loser."

"Still." Deirdre rubbed her temples roughly. "I'll give him a few hours to wake up, and then give him a call. Even for a louse like him, he shouldn't have to hear news like this over the TV."

CHAPTER 5

WOLFGANG KASERNE, WEST GERMANY
1:05 P.M., THURSDAY, MARCH 27

Over the next few days, Erika Stohlmann immersed herself in planning a memorial service in the post chapel and coordinating with the German community, which had been overwhelming in its response to the deaths of the three American women. The Germans planned two memorial services—one near the post and one in the village where the women died. The services were all on successive days and Damrow gave unit members carte blanche to go to all services if they chose.

One would have thought that Boswith, being new to the unit, had not had time to make deep connections with unit members or German locals, but, apparently, she had quickly won the heart of her landlady, who sobbed ceaselessly and rubbed her red-rimmed eyes with a soiled handkerchief. Moreover, Boswith had made herself immensely popular in the unit by bringing in plates of freshly baked chocolate chip cookies on occasion, not caring that it was an ultra-feminine thing to do that counteracted the macho attitude female helicopter pilots tended to strive for. In contrast to Lambert and Dardanelli, who were quite rough around the edges, Boswith was, according to some, a refreshing change of pace, and seemed to think it was okay to say "please" and "thank you," and who, if she knew any swear words, didn't let on that she did. Just as Dardanelli's presence could be predicted by the whiff of cigarette smoke, Boswith was always preceded by a fragrant perfume. Many people were genuinely sorry to see her young life snuffed out so soon.

A lot of people called Crystal Lambert a friend, because she'd been in the unit a long time and had an extroverted way about her without being too abrasive. She didn't turn people off as Dardanelli tended to do, and was an enormous amount of fun to be with, always laughing and telling jokes, even though sometimes at the other person's expense. Nevertheless, she could make fun of herself as well, which really got people rolling. An extremely competent pilot, she'd made pilot-in-command in record time and was often training the newbies. What hardly anybody knew, though, was that under that tough exterior, Lambert volunteered at the local German orphanage and the local hospital once a week. As a result, the local church near the post was filled to overflowing with people who knew and loved her, especially children.

Gregory's death was the most heartbreaking of them all, for she was a wife and mother of two small children. Her husband, also assigned to the unit, sat in the front pew of the post chapel, with one child on either side of him, bowing his head in absolute and utter anguish as the tears rolled silently down his cheeks. Every now and then, those behind him could see the shudders wrack his body, and their own tears flowed when the little girl looked up at him and said, "Don't cry, Daddy. Mommy's in heaven now." Of course, he only cried harder. Although the highest-ranking female crew chief in the United States Army, Gregory never made a big deal out of it, going about her duties with diligence and pride.

When at last all memorial services were over, Erika Stohlmann sat in her office with her head in her hands, completely exhausted. Not only had German dignitaries attended, but military VIPs as well. The necessary hotel, rental car, and airport pickup arrangements had been enough to drive her mad. But at least it was over. The bodies had already been transferred to Rhein Main Air Base for transport to Dover for mandatory autopsies. Erika felt dreadfully sorry for the poor families at the other end.

First Sergeant Samuel Michaels poked his head in the door. "Captain? Would you like a cup of coffee?"

"Thanks, Top. I'd love one." The first sergeant was the top sergeant in the unit—hence the nickname.

He returned in a couple of minutes with a steaming brew of straight black coffee.

Erika cupped her hands around the mug and sighed tiredly. "So, did we do okay?"

"Seemed okay to me, ma'am. I think it was a good send-off. I think the ladies would have all been proud."

"I'm sorry more of their families couldn't have been here."

"Did I tell you Lambert's ex-husband was here? Made it from Hawaii just in time."

"No, I didn't know. I guess they parted amicably enough. That's one nice thing to know in all of this. Did you get to meet her twin sister?"

"Yeah, it was spooky. Made it seem like she isn't really dead."

"I know. They look exactly alike. I couldn't spot any differing mannerisms or telltale voice patterns. I wonder how their parents ever told them apart."

"You got me, ma'am. Well, guess I better get back to it."

"Thanks for the coffee, Top."

ETLINGEN, WEST GERMANY
1:35 P.M., THURSDAY, MARCH 27

Tina Loyola had taken two weeks of leave. If she hadn't have requested it, her commander would probably have insisted. As soon as she could get on a flight after hearing about Crystal's death, she headed for West Germany. She intended to stay for a couple of days after the memorial services to do her own informal investigating of the accident. Although it would be painful, she absolutely had to make a trip to the accident site.

After arriving at Etlingen, the village where the accident occurred, Tina found the local polizei office. She had been told at the Army post to ask for Hauptmann Gunter, but when he wasn't in, she introduced herself to his assistant, Polizeimeister Johannas—the German equivalent to a police sergeant—and asked for directions to the accident site. Marthe offered to accompany her, and Tina willingly accepted.

"Were you there that day?" Tina asked.

"Ja."

"Is there anything you can tell me?"

Not anything that a family member should know, Marthe thought to herself. "It was very fast. I think your sister lost consciousness quickly, so, hopefully, she didn't feel much pain. I hope not anyway. From what the witnesses told us, the fireball happened suddenly."

Tina whipped around to face Marthe in the car. "Listen, Polizeimeister, I appreciate what you're doing, but I'm not going to faint with vapors here. I'm a tough cookie, just like my sister was. I'd like to know exactly what happened and what it was like that day. You're one of the first people I've met who was actually there."

So Marthe told her how horrible it had been. Tina listened closely and quietly, every now and then blanching from the description, but never interrupting except to ask for more details.

When they got to the accident site, Tina asked Marthe to show her precisely where the helicopter had crashed. Once the area was identified, Tina walked around it, trying to locate any stumps or large rocks that could have hindered Crystal's landing. She examined the tree clearance surrounding the field to determine if tall trees might have affected the helicopter's descent negatively.

She found no power lines that might have tripped up the landing, and the field was level, posing no difficulty or hazards. It should have been an ideal landing zone, whether planned or used in an emergency. Swatting at bees buzzing around the budding flowers growing at the edge of the woods and scrunching her nose as a light wind dropped manure smells into the clearing from a nearby farmer's field, Tina felt that trying to imagine a tragedy in this bucolic location was surreal.

"I don't get it," she muttered. "Crystal was too good a pilot to screw up a perfect landing spot like this. Something had to be wrong with that helicopter."

CHAPTER 6

FRANKFURT, WEST GERMANY
1:47 P.M., THURSDAY, MARCH 27

Before catching his plane back to Hawaii, Frank Lambert stopped off at the Frankfurt Zoo. It was a damp and chilly afternoon after the morning's penetrating rain. Rainwater collected on the sidewalks and turned the dirt paths into muddy rivulets. Teachers were unable to stop their giggling charges from stomping in the puddles and splashing themselves and their friends. Each time Frank passed by another group of schoolchildren, who managed to get him wet as well, he grimaced in annoyance even as he uttered the obligatory "Guten Tag."

Pretending to be a man on a brisk stroll, Frank headed towards the large ice cream restaurant in the middle of the zoo. Being late March, few people partook of the culinary delights offered, but outdoor tables were always available.

Upon his arrival at the restaurant, Frank stopped at a table already occupied by four other men. None of them was eating ice cream.

"Hey, Frank, what's happening?" One of them—a handsome, blond-haired man with a crew cut—jovially said.

"What's happening? I'll tell you what's happening." Frank walked over and rammed his fist upwards under the man's chin, breaking his nose with a soft crunching sound. "That's for killing my wife, asshole."

Mark fell out of his chair and onto the pavement, blood gushing from his nose, joviality gone, and red-hot anger flushing up his cheeks.

"What the hell do you think you're doing?" he screamed. Turning to a tall, gaunt man with short, black hair, he cried out, "Get him, John!"

Frank stood ready with his fists poised for a fight, feet firmly planted apart, eyes blazing. "I'm warning you, John. You know I'm the boxing champ three years running. I wouldn't try it if I were you."

All of a sudden, Frank was rushed from behind by a stocky man with reddish-blond hair, but he swiveled around and cracked his fists into the man's jawbone with resounding thumps.

"Goddamn it!" Cecil cried, holding onto his jaw and stumbling backwards, crashing into the table.

A young family scurried away quickly, leaving their food uneaten on the tables and scattering trash behind them. The father had yanked a toddler off his seat and grabbed the hand of a young girl, urging his wife to hurry with the baby. Outraged that they weren't getting to finish their ice cream, the children emitted a cacophony of cries. Glancing hurriedly and fearfully at the angry group of men, the parents nearly toppled the baby carriage over on the cobblestones as they rushed anxiously to get away.

"You said we weren't going to hurt anyone!" Frank yelled at Mark. "We were just going to scare them!"

"So things got a little out of hand. Those bitches got what they deserved." Mark smirked as he wiped his nose with his sleeve.

The fourth man, who had remained sitting, now tapped his lean fingers rhythmically against the table top. His perfectly coiffed brown hair remained undisturbed in the sudden gust of wind that arose. A sardonic smile appeared on his lips. "Frank, I'm a little ashamed of you. I thought we had an understanding."

"Go fuck yourself, Chad."

"We're all friends here, Frank," Chad said nonchalantly, seemingly undisturbed.

"It's beyond me why I ever got involved with you scumbags, and if the CID finds out what happened—"

Chad lunged across the table and gripped Frank's forearm so tightly that the skin turned white. Although Chad's voice remained low, the threat it carried was unmistakable. "If I hear so much as a whiff that the CID has any of our names linked to this investigation, Frank, I'll be certain it was you who turned us in. And your wife won't be the only dead pilot around here." He threw off Frank's arm and stood up, quietly sliding back his chair as if departing from an afternoon tea.

The restaurant workers had called the polizei, and their piercing siren could be heard a few blocks away.

John grabbed Mark off the ground and dragged him to his feet. "Come on," he beseeched. "We've got to get the hell out of here."

His nose still dripping blood, Mark turned irate eyes towards Frank. "You were in on the plan all along, Frank. Don't come crying to us now, you weakling."

"Not my wife, you fucking idiot!"

"Get moving, guys!" Chad exclaimed as the polizei siren screeched to a halt.

The four men ran away from the restaurant toward the zoo's rear exit, and Frank dashed back in the direction from which he had come.

They'll pay for this, he said to himself. If it's the last thing I do, I'll make sure they pay for this.

CHAPTER 7

WOLFGANG KASERNE, WEST GERMANY
9:30 A.M., MONDAY, APRIL 21

"Come in!" Damrow barked to the person knocking on his office door.

Captain Eugene O'Connell, the maintenance platoon leader, strode into the room with a sheaf of papers. "I've got the results from the aircraft investigation, sir."

Damrow waited patiently.

"Apparently, Lambert put the Huey into a dynamic rollover." A dynamic rollover could shred a helicopter to smithereens in mere seconds and, although fuel tanks were not generally known to explode, flight crew personnel wore flame-retardant flight suits and gloves to protect themselves in that eventuality.

"Do we have any idea what her emergency was?" Damrow asked.

"Yes," O'Connell said. "Nothing mechanically wrong with the helicopter. I'd stake my reputation on it. Its last 100-hour checkup was just a few weeks before the flight. The only red-X condition since then was for a radio malfunction, but that was fixed. Lambert and Boswith were out in the field all day with troops, hot refueling. They probably didn't top the fuel off all the way or they just misjudged how much they needed to get home. Pilot error all the way."

"God almighty, Eugene, I'm going to have people breathing down my neck about this. It's bad enough to lose half the female pilots in our company, not to mention one of your five female crew chiefs, but to have to say it's their own fault—" Damrow shook his head in disbelief. Standing up, he went to the window and stared out at the runway. "Are you sure there's no mistake?"

O'Connell thumbed through the reports. "No, sir," he said emphatically. "The investigation board was quite clear that the responsibility for the accident rested with the pilot-in-command."

"It's already been a media circus here," Damrow sighed, turning back around, "but at least we could then say Lambert and Boswith had done everything they possibly could have."

"Emphasize that pilot error is a catch-all phrase. It's not a disgrace. That's important for the families to know."

"True, true." Damrow was lost in thought.

"Is that all, sir?"

"What? Yes, Eugene. Thanks."

FORT RUCKER, ALABAMA
11:10 A.M., MONDAY, APRIL 21

At the time, fewer than fifty women were flying helicopters in the United States Army. Although each of them tried to be as unobtrusive as possible when they sidled into a unit, the fiery deaths of two at once, along with a female crew chief, caused a reverberation throughout the aviation community.

As soon as he found out that pilot error was the contributing factor to the accident, Major General Horace C. Eckling, Commander of the U.S. Army Aviation Center and School at

Fort Rucker, Alabama, ordered an immediate review of the training records of all female helicopter pilots.

"Dammit!" he said to his executive officer, Lieutenant Colonel William Brannon. "I want to know if those damn women got through on their looks or if they just squeaked by. If the Secretary of the Army so much as infers we passed them willy-nilly, we've got to have our answer ready."

Brannon nodded in agreement.

"I don't want any whitewash of those records, you hear me, Bill? I want to know about every single pink slip those ladies got. If they got set back to an earlier class. If they failed a check ride. And then I want to rate them."

"Rate them, sir?"

"Yeah. We're going to figure out which ones, based on how they did here, are most likely to wind up crashing one of our Army choppers and costing some more lives. We don't need any more deaths, Bill, and I'm going to do everything to prevent that. I don't care who I make unhappy."

"General, I know this was pilot error, but a great many Army aviation accidents are blamed on pilot error. We all know that, and we don't rush around examining the flight school training records of male pilots."

"Dammit all to hell, Bill! Don't you think I know that? That's the whole damn point! We got these crazy women out there flying our expensive Army helicopters and they're crashing them all to hell. We got to do something to stop that!"

"With all due respect, sir, if it gets out that you're treating female pilots as a group so differently from male pilots, I think you could have a hurricane on your hands. Not only the media, but people like Congresswoman Melinda Tonnelli. She would bite into you like a pit bull and never let you go."

"Bill, you let me worry about the media and Congress. That's why I get paid the big bucks." Eckling smiled. Generals' salaries were capped at a ridiculously low rate by Congress.

"Yes, sir."

"I want that report on my desk by the end of the week."

THE PENTAGON, WASHINGTON, D.C.
2:30 P.M., MONDAY, APRIL 21

Just as Eckling had suspected, the Secretary of the Army was also deeply mired in explaining away the accident involving two of the service's few female helicopter pilots. Since women had been flying helicopters for just a few years, and only one had died in a crash almost at the beginning of the "experiment," the deaths of Lambert and Boswith were an entirely new experience for the Army to deal with. The glamour of flying always attracted attention. Coupled with female pilots and an unexpected tragedy—the media was having a field day. The entire situation brought the whole "women in the military" question back to the forefront again with naysayers and proponents vehemently arguing their positions all across America. The Army itself was not immune.

Secretary of the Army Reginald Maloney not only approved of Eckling's review of female training records at Fort Rucker—he decided to order a review of the unit training records of all female aviators out in the field as well. Once they graduated from flight school and were assigned to a unit, they still had to become qualified in that unit's mission and had to maintain specified proficiency levels.

Lieutenant General Carl Nigelson, the Deputy Chief of Staff for Operations and Plans in the Pentagon, refused.

"We can't do this, sir," he said. "This would be blatant discrimination against the women. There is absolutely no cause to examine their records. The women who were at fault in the aircraft accident died. No other female helicopter pilots have been so much as involved in a scrape. If any records would need to be examined, it would make more sense to examine the training records of everyone in that unit."

"Eckling's doing it down at Rucker," Maloney gruffly remarked. "What's the difference?"

"And as soon as I got wind of it I ordered him to stop. It was the most ridiculous thing I'd ever heard of. He'd only gotten through about twenty percent of the records when he quit."

"And?"

"And what, sir?

"What did he find?"

"Absolutely nothing to corroborate any valid reason to single out female helicopter pilots for examination."

"There must be something we can do," Maloney said.

"Put out a statement saying we support our female helicopter pilots, they're well trained, and this accident is a tragic example of how risky this profession is that they've chosen."

"Alright, Carl. I'm going to trust you on this one, but I don't like it."

When General Eckling had gotten off the phone with Nigelson, he had turned to Lieutenant Colonel Brannon and said, "That son-of-a-bitch DCSOPS thinks he can run my shop for me."

"Sir?"

"Nothing, Bill. Don't worry about it. I want that report on the female helicopter pilots on my desk tomorrow."

"Yes, sir."

CHAPTER 8

FORT DRUM, NEW YORK
5:30 P.M., WEDNESDAY, APRIL 23

"That is such a load of crap!" Tina said to Deirdre when she heard the results of the investigation. They were having a beer at the Fort Drum Officers' Club after work. "I saw that LZ. There is no way that Crystal rolled that helicopter. The only reason you get into that position is if you're landing on a slope. And that field was flat as a pancake."

"Maybe she put a skid down wrong—"

Tina glared at Deirdre. "And maybe you've forgotten about what a great pilot she was, Deirdre. Better than you or me, remember?" Crystal had aced every single check ride in flight school, never getting less than a 99 percent while making it appear effortless. Even though she and Tina were identical twins, Crystal's flying emanated a natural grace. To reach similar levels of performance, Tina and Deirdre both had to exhibit more perseverance.

"There's something else I don't understand," Tina muttered.

"What's that?"

"Well, the report says she ran out of fuel, right?"

"Yes," Deirdre said, still not following.

"First of all, most pilots don't autorotate just because they have a low fuel warning light, and there isn't a mention of one here. So, let's assume she had no warning of low fuel. I see a disconnect here. All of a sudden she has to land and then blows up. What sense does that make? How could there be a fireball of such magnitude in a helicopter with no fuel? And how likely is it that she'd flip a helicopter in a flat field with no slopes to begin with? Why aren't these questions addressed in here?" Tina waved the report.

"Tina, I know it doesn't make sense, but it's all been investigated. Don't you think that if the dots couldn't be connected, the Army would be digging up the answers?"

"Yeah, I suppose so," Tina said disgruntledly. "I just don't understand how this could happen. It blows my mind."

"If it had happened to my sister, it would blow my mind, too. I'm sorry, Tina, I wish I had some answers for you."

Just then, two other members of their unit, the 33rd Aviation Battalion (Combat), appeared at their table with another round of beers.

"Ladies," Second Lieutenant Mark Andreason said as he sat down, holding up his beer. "Salut!"

"Salut!" They all said as they clinked glasses and smiled at each other.

"So, when's the packaging coming off your nose?" Deirdre asked Mark. Mark had returned from a ski vacation in Colorado with a broken nose.

"It'll be a couple of weeks yet, I think," he grinned. "Doc says I can't fly yet."

"You should have seen him come flying down that mountain," First Lieutenant Cecil Boniface said. "It was pure daredevil!"

"Yeah. That tree came out of nowhere!" Mark laughed.

Tina shook her head. "Sir, you were damn lucky."

"And don't I know it. But I can't wait to get on the slopes again!"

They all laughed. Mark Andreason was known for his wild ways. Not too long before his ski trip, he'd gone moose hunting near the Arctic Circle in Canada. Didn't catch a moose, but he did find himself staring down a polar bear. According to Mark,

"The bear blinked first." No one ever believed his stories, but they made for good tall tales.

"So, Tina," Mark said, running his finger along the rim of his beer glass, "it really sucks that the Army's pinning pilot error on your sister's Class A accident."

"Yeah, thanks, sir. That's what I think. It really does suck. I hate to see her reputation tarnished."

Cecil interjected, "I know a lot of guys who've served with her. They thought she was a great pilot, for a—"

"For a girl. Right, sir. Thanks for the recommendation. Deirdre, are you ready?" Tina threw her napkin on the table and stood up quickly.

Deirdre looked apologetically at the two men, shrugged, and said her goodbyes quickly.

"Man, you know what, Cecil? That's what I can't stand about these damn chicks. They're too feminist. You can't give 'em a fucking compliment."

"No kidding. There's no pleasing them. That's why we're on the right track."

"We got to hang tough, buddy. Things are going to get rough, but it'll all be worth it in the end."

The two men slapped each other on the back, guffawed loudly, and stayed in the club drinking until Happy Hour was over and the beer nuts and chicken wings were all gone.

CHAPTER 9

ETLINGEN, WEST GERMANY
10:20 A.M., THURSDAY, APRIL 24

Rolf Pederson's mother was extremely weary from the long night of tending to the baby, who had croup again and couldn't be comforted. That dry, hacking cough really worried Nadina Pederson and she knew she needed to call the *Kinderarzt* as soon as the office opened. Perhaps the doctor would have a new medicine that might work this time.

At long last, the baby had drifted off to sleep, but Nadina's rest had remained interrupted. After getting Rolf off to his *Grundschule*—he was in the fourth grade—she was finally able to turn her attention to the piles of dirty laundry that seemed to crop up every time she turned her head.

Nadina picked up a few things from the baby's room and then dragged her laundry basket into Rolf's room. *O Gott,* she thought. Couldn't he even try to keep his room neat?

Rolf's room was a pigsty and had been for the last couple of years. It was a constant battle between Rolf and his parents—their desire for order and cleanliness, and his total disregard of it.

Resigning herself to extra work to uncover Rolf's clothes that needed washing, Nadina quickly collected them into one pile. She steadfastly ignored everything else, although it took an enormous effort. I don't have the time today to clean his room for him, she said to herself. And besides, he wouldn't appreciate it if I did.

Turning his pockets inside out, because Rolf always left things in them that were likely to ruin her washing machine, Nadina set aside her little boy's treasures. Every once in a while, she found a few pfennig pieces—mostly 10 and 25—and even a one-mark coin. She was quite surprised to see that Rolf had been able to hold onto as much as a mark and not spend it, and then seemingly even forget he had it. The boy was quite a spendthrift. His pockets held gum wrappers, candy wrappers, marbles, a movie ticket, caps for his cap-gun, a filthy metal cylinder, and what looked suspiciously like a used condom.

O Gott! Nadina clasped her hand to her mouth. My Rolf is only ten years old. Please, God, don't let him be having sex. Where did he get this condom? I know that young boys sometimes ... She shuddered to think of all the possibilities.

Her washing forgotten for the time being, Nadina sat down heavily on Rolf's stale, unmade bed. Please, God, she prayed. Don't let anyone have touched my little boy.

When Rolf came home from school that afternoon at 1:30, he was unpleasantly surprised not to see his usual soup and sandwich waiting for him. His mother and father were sitting on the couch in the living room, looking decidedly uncomfortable. Rolf's stomach turned somersaults. It was completely unheard of for Oscar Pederson to be home from the factory in the middle of the day.

Deciding that someone must have died, Rolf asked tentatively, "Vati? Why are you home?"

"Your mother and I need to talk to you, Rolf."

Not Oma! Rolf thought with rising panic, his throat beginning to constrict with tears. Nadina's mother hadn't been well for the past year, but Rolf didn't think she was—

"Has anyone been touching you, son?" Nadina asked gently.

"Touching me?" Rolf asked, creasing his forehead in a frown.

"A man, or a woman, or even an older boy?" Oscar asked.

"It could have been a teenage girl, too," Nadina hurriedly pointed out.

"Why are you asking me this?" Rolf's voice began showing his fear. "I don't know what you're talking about."

Oscar pulled out the dirty, limp condom. "Have you ever seen this before?"

Rolf took a quick look. "No." He knew where it came from and he knew what it was but he wasn't going to discuss sex with his parents. He already knew more than they thought he did.

Oscar stood up and slapped Rolf across the face. "Don't lie to us, Rolf. Your mother found it in your pocket. Now tell us where it came from!"

Deciding it was best to tell the truth, Rolf rapidly said, "I found it in the woods, by the helicopter accident."

Rolf's parents looked at each other in alarm.

"What do you mean 'by the helicopter accident?'" Oscar demanded.

"Where the American helicopter crashed," Rolf said stubbornly.

"What were you doing there?" Nadina cried unbelievingly. "That's five kilometers from our house. How could you be so far away and I didn't know it?"

Oscar gave Nadina a withering glance, and said to Rolf. "I don't believe you. You're lying again. You were never there at the accident site."

"I was, too!" Rolf exclaimed. "I was there with Josef and Stefan and Willi."

"How come I never heard about this from any of our friends. Plenty of them were there that day, you know," Oscar said.

"I saw them," Rolf retorted. "We scooted under the tape and played in the woods. Nobody saw us, so we got to watch everything when the polizei sent everybody home."

"O Gott," Nadina threw up her hands. "Our boy is becoming a heathen."

"Don't get all worked up, Nadina," Oscar warned. "I'm still not convinced."

Rolf went running off to his room while his parents sat there stunned. Nadina had left all his treasures on his bed, and he quickly pawed through them until he found what he was looking for. He returned and thrust something into his father's hand.

"There! That'll prove I was at the accident!" Rolf said triumphantly. "It was part of the helicopter! I found it in the woods."

Oscar looked at the metal cylinder and turned it over in his hand, feeling its sharp edges. When he had served his obligatory tour of duty in the German Army years earlier, he had been an explosive ordinance disposal specialist, and he recognized what he was looking at. Although it was primitive, Oscar knew he held an explosive timing device in his hand.

"Nadina," he said. "I believe the boy. And if this is what I think it is, I need to go see the polizei."

CHAPTER 10

FAIRBANKS, ALASKA
1:15 P.M., THURSDAY, APRIL 24

The flight to Fairbanks had been bumpy due to extreme turbulence, but it still didn't prevent First Lieutenant Vanessa Robison from getting thrilling glimpses of the Alaskan topography. She had just graduated from flight school at Fort Rucker, followed by maintenance test pilot school at Fort Eustis, Virginia, and was reporting to the 1311th Aviation Maintenance Battalion at Fort Wainwright for her first aviation assignment after a thirty-day leave.

The Alaskan Waterway had been gorgeous—what little she had seen of it. The big jumbo jet flew over a heavy cloud layer for most of the trip from the States and, when it popped out of the clouds, was over verdant land and mountains reaching to the sky.

No one ever told me Alaska was this beautiful, Vanessa thought, with her face pressed up against the airplane window. *And I'll be here for three years. I just can't believe it!*

Her sponsor, First Lieutenant Dale Dykstra, had told her in a letter he would meet her at the airport. She could hardly contain her excitement. Only ten more minutes until landing!

Habitually late to all of his appointments, an extremely poor character trait for a military officer, Dale Dykstra had been rushing every step of the way and trying to cut out precious minutes of the trip so as to arrive before the new officer. It would reflect badly on him and the unit if he wasn't waiting there for her, and his company commander had already formally reprimanded him once on his tardiness.

Preoccupied with the clock and the passing minutes, Dykstra failed to notice the small economy car darting in and out of traffic, driven by an individual who looked too young to drive. When he first noticed the car, which was zipping in front of him from the right at seventy miles an hour with only a foot to spare, Dykstra yanked his wheel to the left. Unfortunately, a large semi created an unmovable barrier, dragging Dykstra's car along for several hundred feet before throwing the passenger's side against a railing. By some incredible circumstance, Dykstra was able to walk away from the accident with only a broken arm and some ugly bruises, after spending several hours in the vehicle waiting for the Jaws of Life to slice open the crunched metal.

When the plane landed, Vanessa walked eagerly across the tarmac, inhaling the fresh scent of Alaskan pine trees. Snow was still on the ground in patches. Although a brisk breeze stirred the air, the warm sunshine belied the myth that Alaska was only a cold place.

After thirty minutes, when no Dale Dykstra showed up, and after Vanessa had collected her numerous pieces of luggage and flight gear, she sat down, opened her briefcase, and searched for the phone numbers to her new unit.

Damn! She thought. All they've given me are the Autovon numbers. Although she could eventually find the civilian telephone numbers, it would have helped to have them from the start. I'll just take a cab to the post, she decided. No point in calling anyone to come pick me up.

Having made her decision, Vanessa loaded her bags onto a trolley and headed for the taxi stand outside the terminal. Within minutes, she was on her way.

Once she arrived at Fort Wainwright, Vanessa directed the taxi driver to take her to the BOQ—bachelor officer quarters—where she would be living temporarily until she could find an apartment off post. As she tipped the driver, Vanessa looked approvingly at the modern, two-story building with mountains in the background.

"Hey, there!" Someone called out. "Can I give you a hand with those bags?"

Vanessa whipped around and, spotting a male captain heading towards her, saluted smartly. "Why, yes. I'd appreciate that."

"I'm Earl Thornton," he said, reaching out to shake her hand as the taxi took off for the main gate.

"Vanessa Robison," she replied.

"Are you with the 1311th?" he asked, eyeing her helmet bag.

"Yes. I'm a maintenance test pilot. And you?"

"MI." Military intelligence. "I work in the headquarters building. I'm the general's aide."

"So I guess you're out of the intel business right now."

"For a while. It's a two-year assignment working for him and I've got one to go."

They had reached the front door of the BOQ. "Do you like it?" Vanessa asked.

"It's not all glamour, I can tell you that. I pull a lot of long hours. But I get to meet the most interesting people. And, as they say, it'll be good for my career." He grinned as he opened the door.

After Vanessa settled into her room, she headed over to the 1311th to report in to her company commander. Major Maurice Petrovich's huge office contained an executive desk, conference table with seven padded leather chairs, two leather sofas, and an assortment of coffee tables, end tables, and bookcases. It looked as if the room belonged to a general officer instead of a mere major. Petrovich enjoyed the finer things in life because he had a most enterprising supply sergeant. Although the office overlooked the runway, it was at the far end of the series of aircraft hangars that constituted the bulk of the 1311th's working spaces. Thus, Petrovich could rotate himself in his executive chair, smoke one of his smelly cigars, and gaze through the leafy branches of numerous trees and shrubs dotting that end of the runway.

Petrovich never shut his office door, completely believing in the "open door" policy. He believed he had no secrets, and, therefore, neither did any of his soldiers. When Vanessa knocked on the door, she interrupted Petrovich in one of his frequent mid-day musings out the window, cigar in hand and feet up on the windowsill.

He turned at the noise. "Come in! Come in!"

"Lieutenant Robison reporting for duty, sir," Vanessa said crisply, coming to attention in the middle of the room and snapping a salute.

Petrovich idly returned her salute, maintaining his comfortable pose, and motioned her to sit down in a chair adjacent to his desk.

"How late was Dykstra?" he demanded.

"I beg your pardon, sir?"

"Dykstra. How late was he in picking you up?"

"There wasn't a problem, sir. I took a cab."

"Are you ready to get to work?"

"Oh, yes, sir!"

"Alright then. I was going to have Dale take you around, but since he didn't show up, I'm going to assign someone else." Petrovich pushed a button on his intercom. "Sally, tell Lieutenant Emerson to get in here."

While they waited, Petrovich asked Vanessa a few questions about her recent training and about her flight, all perfunctory and nothing too personal, just enough to fill the time.

"Here he is!" Finally, Petrovich swung his legs off the windowsill and stood up. "Vanessa, this is Chad Emerson. Chad, I want you to take Vanessa around for the next few days and show her the ropes. She's our new maintenance test pilot."

"Nice to meet you, Vanessa," Chad said. Turning to Petrovich, he asked, "What happened to Dale?"

Petrovich shrugged. "Your guess is as good as mine."

"At any rate, welcome to the 1311th and to Alpha Company," Chad said. "Now, we better get cracking, because I've got a test flight in a couple of hours."

"Thanks, Chad," Petrovich said. "Glad to have you, Vanessa. You couldn't be in better hands than Chad's."

CHAPTER 11

SCHOFIELD BARRACKS, HAWAII
12:30 A.M., THURSDAY, APRIL 24

Back in Hawaii, Frank Lambert nursed a rage so deep and hidden that his colleagues took his after-hours drinking to be strictly related to grieving for his ex-wife's death. Frank was one of the cowboy pilots, one of the hot-shots. He didn't always do everything the right way or by the book, but he always got the mission done. His commanders loved him even while they kept a close eye on him.

As a young enlisted man, before he had ventured off to flight school, Frank had been the Army's top middleweight boxing champion. He'd grown up in Brooklyn and learned to use his fists the hard way—on the streets—protecting his young brothers and sisters from the toughs who were always hanging around. Right after graduating from high school, barely squeaking through, a grizzly old boxing promoter had seen Frank working out at the local Y and started training him for the "big time." He thought Frankie had a lot of potential with those fists, but Uncle Sam wanted Frank for Vietnam.

Drafted into the Army, Frank was rushed through infantry training and found himself in the Mekong Delta before he could blink an eye. Like a lot of kids in that war, he was only nineteen years old when he arrived and, though he was young in spirit at the beginning of his tour, he had aged an eternity by the time his twelve months were up. None of the fighting or boxing he had done had prepared him for the experience of seeing dead and maimed women and children, and never knowing if they were enemies or not.

He hated going out on patrol into the bush where the chance of encountering the Viet Cong could be instantaneous as they popped up out of their underground tunnels and barely showed their heavily camouflaged bodies. The numerous ways the Viet Cong had prepared for him and his buddies to die kept Frank in a constant state of tension every time he went out into the jungle and was probably the reason he was one of the few to come back alive and unscathed.

When his tour was over and he returned to a safe job in the States, Frank was at loose ends. He felt as if he no longer had a purpose. Although he despised the Vietnam War and the bloody idiots who kept it going, he volunteered to go back, because it was the only place where he felt completely alive. He didn't try to explain it to his family. He just told them that the Army was sending him back and he listened to his mother wail and watched his father tighten his lip. Back in Vietnam, people looked at Frank like he was crazy when they found out he was serving his second tour, so he quit telling them.

The end of hostilities coincided with the end of Frank's second tour, and he was posted to Fort Hood, Texas. While participating in the often-benumbing peacetime Army training and the transition to the All-Volunteer Force, Frank found an outlet in boxing outside the base in Killeen. A couple of retired Army sergeants ran a boxing hall—and a somewhat illegal betting operation—that many of the enlisted personnel from Fort Hood frequented on Friday and Saturday nights. Frank became one of the most popular boxers in their repertoire and was soon being asked to perform out of town. When his first sergeant learned what he was up to and came to see him box, he recommended Frank for the Army's Boxing Team. Frank made the team and won the championship for the next three years in a row.

For his next assignment, Frank asked to go to flight school. In Vietnam, he had ridden many times in the Hueys that crisscrossed the skies dumping supplies, scooping up wounded, and dropping off soldiers. He admired the tenacity and bravery of the pilots who went into hot LZs regardless of the danger to their own lives, often in overloaded aircraft. As a warrant officer candidate at Fort Rucker, Frank had to bite his tongue many times at the sheer stupidity of the requirements to keep his bed and uniform just so. His wartime experience and older age were vastly different from the "high school to flight school" set that comprised most of his class.

Deirdre Holloway had been one of the two women in his class, both of whom were straight from high school, green and wet behind the ears. Nevertheless, Deirdre applied herself to her studies, her warrant officer requirements, her flying, her check rides—and damned if she hadn't done better than he had. Frank couldn't believe that that slip of a girl had bested him in three categories, while he had only bested her in one. The accolade of Honor Graduate was awarded to Deirdre and his pride recoiled with revulsion whenever he thought of it. He was certain that somehow she had manipulated the minds of the instructors or her grades because he just didn't deem it possible that a Vietnam vet could be considered a lesser pilot than a young girl, which was all she really was.

Halfway through Frank's flight school class, the Loyola twins arrived as warrant officer candidates, creating a sensation on the post. The Army hadn't trained twins before, much less female twins. Although each flight school class was pretty much a closed entity, and the warrant officer candidates had most of their hours accounted for, the one or two women in each class managed to create a female network stretching backwards and forwards several classes. Deirdre became fast friends with Tina and Crystal Loyola.

Tough and sassy, irreverently funny, Crystal immediately attracted Frank's attention and they began dating. Within months, they were deeply in love, but Frank was scheduled to graduate and depart for Hawaii. Desperate for the Army to assign them together, they opted to marry quickly. Despite the Army's avowed promises to station married couples together whenever possible, Crystal was sent to West Germany. For the next two years, they lived apart and tried valiantly to keep their relationship alive through expensive long-distance phone calls, letters that took two or three weeks to plod across the vast ocean distances, and two or three visits per year. By the end of that time, Crystal had had enough of trying to flog a dead relationship back to life and asked Frank for a divorce, which he grudgingly consented to give.

Somehow, Frank had always been able to keep separate in his mind the fact that his wife, Crystal, whom he still loved, was an Army aviator, because, as a general rule, he detested female Army aviators. Along with many of his compatriots, Frank held these women in scorn because he knew that when push came to shove, when the balloon went up, when the rubber hit the road—these women weren't going to be anywhere near combat. The Army had a strict rule against women in combat and every man knew what it was, or certainly believed he knew what it was. That nowhere, nohow would a woman be involved in combat operations.

It was completely nonsensical in Frank's opinion for a woman to be flying a helicopter that was, to all intents and purposes, a combat tool. Helicopters were used for flying soldiers to the very front edges of the battlefield, for taking them their meals and supplies and rations, for bringing out their wounded and their dead, and for providing machine-gun fire and laying mines. He could just see the enormous confusion that would result in a new Vietnam-like situation if female helicopter pilots were assigned to units but couldn't be sent forward by their operations officers. Not only would it be pandemonium, but the male pilots would be forced to fly all the dangerous missions, while the virtually useless women would be occupying seats and flying only safe missions. The scheduling problems alone were enough to give anyone nightmares.

Wives of male helicopter pilots were, of course, in an uproar because they did not at all fancy the notion that their husbands might be in such close proximity as to be flying in a cockpit right next to a woman, maybe breaking down in a helicopter and having to "RON" (remain overnight) somewhere with her, and go on field exercises with her. No one would voice the thought, but it was obvious the wives were threatened not only by the female aviators' femininity but also by their professional competence. After all, these women could do what the wives did and what the husbands did—a double whammy.

Male aviators found themselves threatened as well. They didn't like their territory being encroached upon. Being an Army aviator was akin to being the cream of the crop. It wasn't grungy like the infantry, or hot and heavy like armor, or mind-numbing like artillery. Aviators had the right stuff, even if flying helicopters for the Army was on the lower end of the spectrum compared to astronauts. And throwing women into the mix was certain to destroy one of the last bastions of male pride, where men could be men, especially if any of the female aviators refused to go along with the status quo. The bawdy jokes, girlie magazines, constant stream of profanities—men resented having to clean up their act when a female came into their midst as one of their colleagues. And, if a female pilot decided to act like one of them and tell the same jokes and use the same language, they slapped her on the back and acted as if she fit in, but behind closed doors, they derided her as a slut and a whore. For, in the man's world, they expected men to be men and women to be women, and crossovers were not allowed.

As female graduates from Fort Rucker began to filter onto posts throughout the Army, rumblings began to assert themselves among groups of men who were more vociferous than most. Some officers began to discuss the idea of getting rid of this scourge of female helicopter pilots, with the most common suggestion being to flunk them on check rides in their units, to downgrade them on their officer evaluation reports, or, better yet, to ensure they didn't even graduate from flight school. Such was the level to which Frank had agreed and was the limit to which he had been involved.

The scumbags at the Frankfurt Zoo, though, had different, more evil motives, and had made other plans that he knew nothing about. He had no idea when their plan to kill female pilots had arisen. Somewhere along the way, they had left him and others of a non-violent nature out. How they discerned the difference he didn't know. And he figured they had to have a leader, because those bozos couldn't lead their way out of a paper bag. Now he lived in horror that men he knew, and with whom he had made plans, had gone so far as to kill women in their quest to remove them from flying. In addition to the all-consuming rage that made him want to seek revenge for Crystal's death, Frank was terrified that these maniacs would strike again.

CHAPTER 12

ETLINGEN, WEST GERMANY
2:40 P.M., THURSDAY, APRIL 24

Oscar Pederson rushed to his car to drive to the polizei station, holding the grimy explosive timing device clutched in his hand. He could scarcely believe the enormity of the information he had to impart to Gunter. Oscar and Karl Gunter had both grown up in Etlingen. They had been childhood friends for most of those years and had had a brief spat when both had wanted to marry Nadina, but had reconciled in the last few years.

"Na, ja," Oscar said to himself. "This is big, really big. Karl told me the Americans had decided the pilots crashed the helicopter by accident. This will prove it was no accident."

Imagining the amazement on Karl's face when Oscar showed him the device, Oscar forgot to slow down on the cobblestone bridge over the Eisel River. Although it was afternoon, the bridge was in continual dark shadow from the huge oak trees overhanging the riverbank. The freezing rain that had settled as ice during the freak winter storm the night before had not melted. Oscar's light compact car spun crazily around on the cobblestones, seeking to find a foothold, and, finding none, careened around a sharp curve, flew off the bridge onto the river bank, and smacked into the broad trunk of a tree. Oscar—who had failed to fasten his seatbelt because he was only going less than half a kilometer—was thrown into the windshield, suffering contusions, a broken arm, and a concussion.

The explosive timing device flew out the open passenger window and into the Eisel River.

CHAPTER 13

FORT RUCKER, ALABAMA
9:55 P.M., THURSDAY, APRIL 24

Lieutenant Colonel Bill Brannon felt extremely uncomfortable about the report on the female helicopter students who were currently in training at Fort Rucker. Something didn't add up. He sat at his desk until late in the night, rubbing at the tension in his neck with his left hand while turning pages with the pencil eraser in his right.

One of the problems was that there were so few female graduates to judge past experience by and so few current students. A new flight school class started every two weeks and they didn't all have female students. Those that did almost always had two, but rarely more. All in all, Fort Rucker wouldn't have more than thirty or forty women in flight training at one time.

In Brannon's current experience at Fort Rucker, which amounted to fifteen months now, he had seen about the same percentage of female students set back to the next class or "washed out"—thrown out of flight school entirely—as male students. They weren't coddled and they weren't treated harshly. As far as he could tell, the female students at Fort Rucker were treated fairly, which was astounding considering the huge bias that existed against female pilots in general.

Flight school consisted of several distinct phases—learning to fly the TH-55, learning to fly the Huey, the instrument phase, night flying, and tactical flying—and students had to pass each phase or they would be set back to an earlier class to revamp their weaknesses. And some students, of course, were just a lost cause altogether and were thrown out of flight school for fear of flying, color blindness, or because they simply couldn't make the grade.

Every day of flight school, when a student went out flying, the flight instructor filled out a form at the end of the flight, grading the performance for that day. A white slip meant a passing grade—a pink slip, a failing grade. The student didn't get to keep a copy, however. It simply went into the individual's training record, to follow the person around from one training phase to another. The instructor didn't get a copy, either.

Because of the nature of the grading, there was no way an instructor could expect to remember what grade he gave an individual student on any given day in the past, even with these white and pink slips. Each instructor taught several students per class, gave them five grades per week, and had numerous classes of students every year. It would have been impossible for any of them to resurrect a particular memory about any white or pink slip.

So only one copy existed, and that was in the student's folder. Most students, of course, accumulated white slips most days or they wouldn't be allowed to continue to stay at flight school, or to graduate. Some students never received a pink slip during their entire tenure at flight school. Too many pink slips in a given phase meant that a student was having difficulty mastering that particular phase of instruction and needed to repeat it.

What niggled at Brannon, however, was that a higher proportion of the student training records in front of him purported to show that the female students had a greater incidence of pink slips. If this were so, he thought, then the women should have been set back during that phase of instruction. Brannon couldn't understand why the women wouldn't have been set back or washed out if they had had so many pink slips. Having served previously as a flight instructor himself at Fort Rucker, he knew that accumulating too many pink slips was the kiss of death and automatically sentenced a student to being set back.

Continuing to puzzle over the quandary, Brannon shuffled the papers into a folder, turned out his light, and went home.

CHAPTER 14

ETLINGEN, WEST GERMANY
4:38 P.M., THURSDAY, APRIL 24

Nadina opened her door, surprised to see a polizei officer standing there.

"Hallo, Nadina." he said, tipping his uniform hat and holding it nervously with both hands.

"Ja, ja." She peered around behind him. "Did Oscar come with you?"

Gunter frowned, obviously confused. "With me?"

"Yes, he was going to the police station. I don't know why you would need to come back here, but come in, please." She held the door open and waved him in before her.

Looking behind him momentarily, Gunter wavered, then stepped inside the apartment, stopping just inside the door.

"Nadina, I'm terribly sorry, but Oscar has been in a car accident and he's in the hospital."

An audible gasp escaped from Nadina's mouth before she covered it with one hand in a gesture of shock. As she clutched her sweater with the other hand, she stood there dumb, waiting to hear more.

"He's in critical condition on account of a concussion. Other than that, only a broken arm and some bruises. The doctors think he'll be fine. I'll take you there if you like."

Nadina stood transfixed.

"Nadina," Gunter said gently. "Would you like me to take you to the hospital?"

At precisely that moment, he spotted Rolf hanging back near the kitchen.

"Come here, son," he coaxed. "I'm sure your Vati will be fine."

"No!" yelled Rolf. "I never should have given him that stupid thing. It's all my fault!" Tears streaming down his face, Rolf ran out of the open door, slipping through Nadina's outstretched arms.

"Rolf! No!" she cried. "Come back!" She chased after Rolf down the stairs and would have followed him down the street and wherever he was going, but she couldn't leave the baby home alone. Resigned to let Rolf deal with his hurt on his own, Nadina sobbed as she dragged herself back up the stairs.

Gunter looked at her questioningly.

"Yes, please," she said. "Take me to the hospital. Just let me get my baby."

As Rolf ran down the street, sobbing and clenching his fists, he pumped his legs up and down, trying not to trip over the many fissures in the cement sidewalk. Trying to mimic the older boys, Rolf didn't tie his shoelaces in the mornings, and their flapping constantly threatened to halt his forward motion.

It's all my fault! It's all my fault! Rolf repeated the endless refrain to himself in a monotonous litany that was rising to a panic mode. *If I hadn't gone to the crash site, if I hadn't picked up that filthy piece of metal, if I had kept my room clean, if I had thrown the metal away, if I hadn't shown it to Vati—*

Sobs kept escaping from his open mouth as Rolf ran and tripped, always catching himself before his shoelaces or the sidewalk cracks could throw him headlong onto the ground.

Vati wouldn't have been driving off to the polizei station if it wasn't for me, he thought to himself. *And that's the only reason he's now in the hospital. He's probably going to die and it's all my fault!*

Rolf could only think of one place to go where his mother was sure not to find him, at least not for a while. And he needed to be able to think. His head was whirling. Everything was out of kilter. He had to fix things and set them right, and he needed some time alone to be able to just think about it.

After running along the suburban streets of his quiet neighborhood, Rolf halted short of a stop sign at the bottom of the hill. If he turned right, he would be at his Grundschule with a ten-minute walk. If he turned left, he would pass the local bakery, butcher's shop, and florist. Thinking quickly, Rolf skirted around the stores using the alleyway behind them so that no one who knew him or his mother would see him. When he came out on the other side, he crossed a busy four-lane road, and entered the forest.

Once inside Oscar's hospital room, Nadina stopped dead still. She looked at the nurse. "Can he speak?"

The Krankenschwester replied, "So far he's been under a great deal of pain. We've given him morphine for relief. He hasn't spoken to us yet."

"Will there be a problem with him talking?" Nadina's terrified eyes were wide open and staring straight ahead at her husband lying helpless in the bed.

"It's too early to tell at this time, Frau Pederson. The doctor will tell you more," the nurse said as she quietly left the room.

Nadina sat beside Oscar and stroked his wrist, the one not covered with an IV insert. "Oh, Oscar! Oscar!" she cried.

Just then, little Maria, the baby, woke up from her nap and needed nursing. Thankful to be distracted by a normal activity, Nadina tended to her maternal duties, watching over her husband with a mournful air.

The woods were too manicured a place for hiding, and Rolf knew that well. Hikers, joggers, dog-walkers—all sorts of people would be walking the groomed and ungroomed trails at all hours, and without a lot of ground shrubbery, he wouldn't be able to camouflage himself very well. No, Rolf couldn't count on staking out a place in the forest, at least not for a long period of time. Besides, it was still too cold at night.

During his many explorations of the woods, however, Rolf had found the perfect hiding place—a small cave set into the bank above the Eisel River. He hadn't been there in several months, but he was sure he could find it, especially since it was still daylight. He just wished he'd been able to bring a little food with him. But Rolf believed in bravery and courage and he wanted to prove he was capable of spending the night in a dark cave with no food. It was certainly easier than what his Vati was going through.

After a few false starts of leaving the trail, Rolf finally located the cave. It was a bit trickier than he remembered, getting himself down the bank and into the tiny opening. There was just enough room in the cave for him to sit upright if he was careful to stay on the right-hand side. He could stretch out his legs and look out the cave's hole over the rushing water—sparkling in the sunshine that sprinkled through the tall pine trees—as it tumbled over a few large boulders below. Rolf could also see that as the night grew longer and he got sleepy, which he knew he would, there was enough room for him to lay down his head and curl up in a fetal position. The wet soil beneath him and the slick rock on the walls made him realize that it was likely to be an uncomfortable night, but this only bolstered his intent to be courageous.

Until the sun went down, Rolf sat and looked at the tree leaves blowing slightly in the gentle wind, listened to the distant sounds of people in the woods, disregarded his hunger and thirst pains as best he could, and reflected that the smell of the cave was not unlike that of the woods surrounding the crashed Huey, where all his troubles began.

Although the hospital staff offered to let Nadina spend the night, which she would have wanted to do under other circumstances, Nadina urgently wanted to get home and find out that Rolf had returned. Even without her concern over Rolf, Nadina would have found it difficult to keep little Maria overnight in the hospital.

Feeling her loyalties stretched in several directions, Nadina whispered in Oscar's ear, "I have to go now, Liebchen. I'll be back in the morning." She kissed him goodnight on the cheek, gathered up the baby and left. Forgetting until she reached the lobby that she didn't even have a car to get home, Nadina sighed in frustration. It would be too far to walk with Maria. The only solution was to catch the next bus. Checking at the information desk, she found that it wouldn't come for another twenty minutes, so she settled herself and the baby down to wait.

When the bus dropped Nadina off two blocks from her apartment building, she walked briskly up the street, but her spirits flagged when she saw no lights burning in their second-story home. Rolf had his own key and, even if he'd run out without it, there was a spare hidden under the large plant in the hallway.

Once inside the silent, dark apartment, Nadina settled the baby into her crib and then started to make phone calls to all of Rolf's friends, to their neighbors, to anyone who might have seen her little boy. No one knew where he was. Certain he would return home any minute, Nadina sat in the dark and waited, looking out the window at the street, willing Rolf to come dashing up the hill. But she waited all night in vain.

CHAPTER 15

FORT RUCKER, ALABAMA
6:15 A.M., FRIDAY, APRIL 25

The next morning, Brannon appeared in General Eckling's office and presented the essential facts of the report.

"Goddamn it! I knew it!" Eckling exploded. "Somebody is letting these women just waltz on through."

"Sir, it's not as simple as that."

"Bill, it's as plain as the nose on your face. You've explained it to me quite clearly. These young ladies haven't got the wherewithal to be Army aviators. I have half a mind to kick them out of flight school altogether."

Brannon took a deep breath. "General, first of all, the facts I've presented don't apply to all the female students here, just some of them."

Eckling peered at his aide. "Didn't you say forty percent?"

Wincing, Brannon said, "Yes, that's what the report implies."

"Then I don't understand why the hell we're advancing about ninety percent of all the female students to the next phase, if forty percent are getting so many goddamn pink slips, Bill!" Eckling yanked out a desk drawer, pulled out a cigar box, selected a cigar, snipped off the end, lit up, and puffed heavily, filling the room with pungent smoke.

Sinking into an armchair, Brannon said wearily, "I don't understand it either, sir."

Chomping on the cigar, Eckling demanded, "Get me every goddamned training battalion commander in my office by noon today, along with the brigade commander. And tell them they better have met with their flight instructors and have answers to these questions before they come!"

"Yes, sir."

When Bill Brannon had gone home the night before, perplexed over the incongruities in the report facing him, he had talked it all out with his wife, Stefania. The daughter of a well-heeled Italian diplomat, Stefania had been carted around the world from one posting to another. As a result, she was not only well-rounded and well-educated, but extraordinarily well-connected. She often didn't let her husband know what she was up to, particularly if she thought overt moves might adversely affect his military career. Militantly feminist in her beliefs, Stefania's diplomatic upbringing taught her to keep her innermost thoughts and feelings to herself, sometimes even from her husband.

Having been married to Bill for fifteen years, she knew that when he was concerned about a situation, he wouldn't rest until it was resolved. At the same time, Stefania had no doubt that, despite his legitimate questions, he wouldn't go behind Eckling's back and suggest to anyone up, down, or outside the chain of command that something seemed out of kilter. Stefania, on the other hand, had a sixth sense that something untoward was going on. And she knew a thing or two about male hostility towards women in the workplace, or at least in their favorite venues.

In her early twenties, Stefania had tried to break into the world of car racing, a sport that was almost impenetrably closed to women. Despite her family's money—and she came from a long line of Italian vintners and restaurateurs—she came across obstacles everywhere she turned. When she finally gained a sponsor at the age of twenty-five, the effort it took to keep everyone's focus on her driving and not on her gender was enormous. Her competitors and the men on their teams were merciless in ragging her and her abilities, finding fault with whatever she did, emphasizing all her weaknesses so that her strengths became invisible to the casual observer, and even, some suspected, playing dangerous games of subtle sabotage. After six years of car racing, Stefania was recognized as one of the top twenty drivers in the world. That was before she barreled into a concrete wall at 140 miles an hour and lost her right leg. Fitted with a prosthesis that could run her through the same paces as her old leg, Stefania continued to race, fitting it in to her husband's military lifestyle.

Almost as soon as Bill left for work the next morning, Stefania ran her mind among the various people in Washington whom she knew might be able to influence what Bill thought was happening. Having made her decision, she picked up the phone and made her calls. Luckily, Bill didn't know all of her contacts.

CHAPTER 16

ETLINGEN, WEST GERMANY
3:48 A.M., FRIDAY, APRIL 25

Rolf hadn't walked in his sleep in a long time, but that night in the cave, he sat bolt upright in the middle of a dream. He thought he was at home and, being thirsty, decided to walk to the kitchen to get a drink. He kept hitting his head and didn't know why, as there was nothing to impede progress from his bedroom to the kitchen, but he kept envisioning the ice-cold milk slipping down his throat—that refreshing coolness—and persisted on his way.

Although his eyes were wide open, they were completely unseeing, as they had always been when he was sleepwalking, unnerving his parents whenever they came across him during the middle of his night-time sidling through the house. So when he hit the icy cold water of the Eisel River, Rolf gasped with shock, taking in large gulps of brackish liquid. His clothes and shoes weighed him down, especially since he had taken the time during the night to double knot his laces. Before Rolf's brain could wake out of its sleepy torpor, the swiftly moving current pushed his small body up and down among the boulders, keeping him underwater for long seconds at a time. When he finally began to realize he was in danger, it was too late. He had entered a deep eddy, thrashing wildly in the dark, not knowing which way was up, and, swept along several feet below the surface, was tossed against the sharp, protruding ledge of an underwater rock formation where his neck received a crushing and mortal blow.

For the rest of that night, Rolf's limp body floated, bounced, careened, and dove in the Eisel River as it made its way towards the North Sea. Before sunup, the poor little boy was kilometers from home when he finally came to rest against an old, scarred rowboat tied up beneath some gnarled cherry trees along a muddy bank. Vegetable gardens belonging to city-dwellers, each on small adjacent patches of ground with their own quaint shed or cottage, were nearby but looked deserted at this time of year.

By the time Rolf's body was discovered several days later, Nadina was beside herself with frantic worry. She had been to the polizei first thing the morning after Rolf had run out of the apartment, stoically enduring the policemen's penetrating stares as to why she hadn't called them the night before. She told them Rolf had run away twice before, but each time he had returned within several hours.

When she opened her door to Gunter and another ashen-faced policeman, Nadina took one look at their nervous faces and let out a blood-curdling cry. "No!" she screamed. Of the four apartments in her stairwell, two of the doors immediately opened and Frau Besser across the hall rushed over.

"Nadina! What is it?" Glancing at the policemen and then at Nadina, Frau Besser grabbed her neighbor before she fainted dead away. Frau Besser was astonished, however, by Nadina's strength, twisting out of her grasp and running headlong into the back of the apartment, slamming a bedroom door behind her.

As the policemen imparted the tragic news to Frau Besser, she vowed to stay as long as needed to help her friend and little Maria, playing in the sunshine on the floor beneath the window.

Oscar was still in the hospital and incoherent. Due to his concussion, he had no memory of the accident. The doctor advised against telling him about Rolf until he was in a more stable condition. Receiving such horrible news could set him back irretrievably. Nadina went through the funeral of her little boy alone—with other relatives and with friends, but without Oscar.

No one had yet to mention the explosive timing device to the polizei. The moment Nadina had heard of Oscar's accident, the device had left her mind. With Rolf's death, nearly everything else had fled from her thoughts.

CHAPTER 17

FORT RUCKER, ALABAMA
10:30 A.M., FRIDAY, APRIL 25

Colonel John Buehlankamp strode into the conference room looking rather smug. "Bill," he said, nodding his head towards Brannon.

"Sir," Brannon acknowledged as Buehlankamp made his way towards the head of the long mahogany table in the center of the room. The table was ringed with twenty executive-style padded leather chairs in deep burgundy, studded with nails and rolling on casters. As brigade commander of all the training battalions, Buehlankamp traditionally sat at the right-hand side of Eckling, who presided over his meetings from the far end of the table. Eckling particularly enjoyed having all eyes looking at him seated beneath the gargantuan oil portrait on the back wall that depicted Army Aviation heroes in previous wars.

For the next ten minutes, the room bustled with activity and loud conversation as training battalion commanders and their executive officers entered the room and greeted each other before settling into seats and adjusting their paperwork. From long experience, the executive officers knew to take their positions in the less desirable seats along the walls and windows directly behind their respective battalion commanders, ready to answer a question at a second's notice. Although the conference room was luxuriously endowed, it had the misfortune of being in an old World War II building, as were many structures on Fort Rucker, and hence, not air-conditioned. Being the end of April, the air inside the room was stuffy and stale. Several individuals glanced longingly at the windows as if to open them up to let in a fresh spring breeze, but no one dared.

As soon as Eckling marched into the room, everyone rose without a preceding need for anyone to call out "Attention." The general waved them all to their seats, sighed wearily, stuck an unlit cigar in his mouth, and turned to Buehlankamp.

"Okay, John, hit us with it. What the hell is going on down there? Bill tells me that up to forty percent of the young lady students have a multitude of pink slips in their files."

"General, I'm sorry to say it's true—"

Eckling slammed his fist down on the conference table, causing innumerable flinches among his subordinates. "This is entirely unacceptable! How long has this been going on? Why have I not been informed?"

Buehlankamp looked down at his report, breathed in and out, and then looked Eckling in the eyes. "Sir, it seemed politically expedient not to fail these women."

"By whose opinion?" Eckling's neck and face had become beet-red. The men around the table were afraid he was going to become apoplectic.

Almost in a whisper, so quietly that the commanders at the end of the table, and the executive officers at the back of the room, had to lean forward and strain to hear, Buehlankamp said, "Your predecessor, General Richards."

Eckling exploded. "I have never in all my goddamned life heard anything so absolutely fucking ridiculous. Do you mean to tell me that the former commanding general of this fine institution actually ordered you to pass along women who were literally failing?"

Buehlankamp sadly nodded his head.

"And I've been in this position now for over three months and you've never brought this to my attention?"

"I presumed General Richards would have briefed you on that, sir."

"That goddamned son-of-a-bitch!" Eckling looked around the conference table. "From this moment on, I want to make my policy absolutely clear. There will be no coddling of anyone who gets more than the acceptable number of pink slips. I don't care if it's the President's son or daughter. The person's gone. Washed out. Set back. You battalion commanders are going to make it happen. You are going to go through your training records of every single student, male and female—we're not going to be accused here of discrimination—and you are going to immediately set back or wash out those that do not belong. Do you understand me? Do I make myself clear?"

Nods of assent and understanding occurred around the table.

Eckling added. "And you're going to make this happen by the end of next week. I want a full report from each battalion commander, through you, John, as to how many pink slips each student has had, in each phase of their training, and which students have been set back. And those that need to be sent back or washed out had better be, or there will be hell to pay."

CHAPTER 18

WOLFGANG KASERNE, WEST GERMANY
12:05 P.M., TUESDAY, MAY 13

Damrow was out on a training flight to Pirmasens with one of his new flight instructors when a call came in on his line. Erika Stohlmann waited for First Sergeant Michaels to answer the phone, but apparently he had stepped away from his desk. Sighing, she punched the flashing button and picked up the receiver.

Gunter was at the other end. "Hallo, Frau Hauptmann," he boomed. "I need to speak with your commander, please."

"He's not here. He won't be back until sometime late this evening."

"I have something very delicate to discuss with you in person, since your commander is not there. You are the second in command, nicht wahr?"

"Yes, I am"

"This is of the utmost importance."

"It can't wait until Major Damrow gets back?"

"No. I shall want to speak with him again myself, of course, but I need to speak with someone in authority from your unit immediately."

"Okay. Where would you like to meet?"

"Can you come to the polizei station in Etlingen?"

"Yes, of course."

"I'll expect you in about an hour." Gunter seemed assured that she would leave right away.

"I'm grabbing my keys as we speak," Erika said.

Driving along the two-lane back roads that connected Wolfgang Kaserne to Etlingen, Erika had to pass through several medieval rural towns, each no larger than a blip on a map and containing fewer than a couple hundred souls and several hundred farm animals. Since it wasn't summer yet, the manure smells hadn't begun to overpower the country air. Despite widespread belief in America that driving in Germany was done at an unlimited speed, that was only on autobahns. On these tiny roads, not only was Erika limited to driving at a hundred kilometers an hour on straight stretches and sixty kilometers an hour in towns, she could barely manage that with the constant curves, hills, farm machinery, horse-drawn carts, and animals on the road. The distance of fifty kilometers to Etlingen was bound to take an hour, and be fairly stressful en route, albeit bucolic and beautiful with fields stretching out on all sides of the road. The small villages she drove through were filled with half-timbered houses, most likely several centuries old, surrounding courtyards where the farmers kept their wagons and implements and loaded up their produce for market day. Except for Meisingen, which had a couple of restaurants and a small hotel, the other hamlets consisted only of houses and an occasional gaststube where locals could gather for a beer and schnitzel after a hard day's work.

Arriving in Etlingen, Erika found her way to the polizei station, located on the main road. She was ushered into Gunter's office, where he quietly closed the door behind her.

"Coffee?" he asked, holding up a thermos.

She shook her head no.

Unswiveling the stainless steel lid, Gunter started talking in a low voice as he poured himself a cup. "A local man was coming to see me a few weeks ago when he had a car accident."

He replaced the thermos lid and took a sip of the steaming black liquid. Holding his coffee cup, Gunter's eyes held Erika's. She waited patiently.

"He suffered a concussion and then, very tragically, his son died the next day. It took the man a while to regain his senses and then, to overcome his grief sufficiently to remember what he wanted to tell me. He came to see me this morning. It appears that his son found something in the woods by your crashed Huey that indicates it might not have been an accident."

Gunter raised his eyebrows in a questioning way. When Erika didn't comment, he continued. "This man, who knows explosives from personal experience, by the way, believes that his son found an explosive timing device. He was bringing it to me when his car hit a tree. Unfortunately," Gunter shrugged, "the device flew out the window and into the river." He shook his head in disbelief. "So I have no proof to show you, but this man and I are old childhood friends and I completely trust him."

Erika rubbed her forehead, lost in thought. "But the accident investigation report said—"

"I know," Gunter replied in a gentle voice. "It was all attributed to pilot error. We provided our input and received draft copies and the final copy of the report."

"But surely if the helicopter had exploded, that would have been completely noticeable?"

"Surely," Gunter nodded. "I have no doubt that the investigative team would have recognized the telltale marks of an explosion."

"Then I can't understand at all why it wasn't mentioned in the report."

"I think there can only be two reasons." Gunter held up the index finger of his right hand. "One, there was no explosion because there was no explosive device, and the report was correct that it was pilot error. I don't believe this is true because I know my friend. He was an explosive ordnance disposal specialist in the German Army for several years. He's an expert on these matters and he has absolutely no reason to lie. For me, he is a completely credible source."

"And the second reason?" Erika found her hands had tightened on the arms of the chair.

"The second reason," Gunter said very softly, leaning over his desk, "is because someone decided to keep it out of the report." He looked intently at Erika, waiting for her reaction.

Erika was stony-faced. Her entire personality was wrapped up in being an officer in the United States military. She completely believed that officers do not lie, cheat, steal, or tolerate those who do. Her father had been a colonel in the Vietnam War and both her grandfathers had been enlisted men in World War II—one of them on the Pacific front and one in Europe. Her mother's lineage stretched all the way back to the Revolutionary War and her grandmother was a member of the Daughters of the American Revolution. A great-great-great uncle had served in the Civil War under Ulysses S. Grant. Erika did not brook anything that smacked of treason. It was totally against her nature to believe that an officer could commit violence against another officer or cover up an official government report. Therefore, she could only believe that Gunter was lying.

"I can't believe that anyone in the United States Army would do that," she proclaimed. "What you're implying is absolutely outrageous. The investigators on that board are Army officers, sworn to uphold the United States Constitution. I would stake my life on the fact that they turned over every rock in that accident to try and figure out what happened and found nothing untoward. Why, our maintenance officer himself said the helicopter was fine. If what you're saying is true, then there would have to be a conspiracy among them. And that's impossible."

"I understand this is upsetting—"

"I'm not going to sit here a moment longer and let our military be insulted. You have no evidence, no proof, nothing to go on except what someone else has said. I can't even believe you brought me out here for this." Erika rose stiffly to her feet and grabbed her flight cap and handbag.

"Frau Hauptmann, will you please pass on this information to your commander?"

"Oh, yes, you can be sure I'll do that." Erika's eyes blazed with righteous anger as she stormed out of the room.

Driving back to the Kaserne, Erika muttered to herself—in a thousand years I'll tell Major Damrow. As a matter of conscience and military propriety, she knew she had to keep her boss informed, but she was going to be certain to spin it in such a way that Damrow knew she didn't have any faith in Gunter's wild accusation.

CHAPTER 19

CAPITOL HILL, WASHINGTON, D.C.
8:45 A.M., THURSDAY, MAY 15

"How in the world could they suddenly decide that seventeen women were unfit to stay in the same flight class with their colleagues?" Congresswoman Melinda Tonnelli angrily demanded as she threw *The Washington Post* onto the corner of her desk. "I've been receiving phone calls all morning with people ranting and raving about unqualified female pilots flying our national assets and asking what am I going to do about it? I'm going to tear my hair out, that's what I'm going to do." Statuesque at nearly six feet tall, the congresswoman was a powerful figure on the House Armed Services Committee, having served on it for the past twenty years and in a senior position for the last five.

As the congresswoman leaned forward heavily on her desk, brushing a lock of curly jet-black hair away from her pale gray eyes, her assistant, Lydia Porterhouse, said, "When Stefania Brannon called you, it was extremely prescient that you phoned your contacts in the media right away. I mean, your action was only based on her husband's gut feeling."

Tonnelli clicked her pencil against her teeth, a habit she'd never been able to break since her boarding school days in Switzerland, where she'd first become friends with Stefania. Also the daughter of an Italian diplomat, who was married to an American Southern girl, Melinda had lived in numerous places around the world before requesting to attend, and having her parents agree to let her go to, a school for girls in the Swiss Alps near Zurich. Skiing, hiking, swimming in alpine lakes and waterfalls, mountain biking—Melinda loved the outdoors, but she was also extremely adept at foreign languages and math. When she first arrived at St. Albans on the Mount, her roommate was a lovely, sweet girl from Greece whom she adored, but who had to return home after the first term when her family ran out of money. By then, Melinda and Stefania had become best friends and begged the headmistress to let them become roommates. Although the move caused some ill will among Stefania's former roommate, the change was allowed, and the two young girls forged a bond that lasted for the rest of their lives.

Immediately after graduating from Stanford University, Melinda married Congressman Paul Acheson, who had represented that congressional district for fifteen years. They had met while skiing at Lake Tahoe a couple of years earlier and, although he was thirty years her senior, sparks flew at the beginning and only grew more intense as time went on. In addition to her instant role as a stepmother to two grown children from Paul's previous marriage, Melinda and Paul quickly had two children of their own in the next few years. With one house in California and one in Washington, D.C., two toddlers, and life as a congressman's wife, time was never empty in Melinda's hands.

Her life radically changed at the age of twenty-five, however, when Paul suffered a brain hemorrhage and died within a few short hours. Thinking she would refuse with two young children, the governor was reluctant to ask Melinda if she would serve the remainder of Paul's term, but she was adamant that she would like to do so. The nation saw her sworn in with little David and little Ricky holding hands beside her, and many eyes swelled with tears. When the eight months of Paul's term were up, Melinda decided to stand for election and the Democratic Party supported her. She had proven herself in the House as an ardent supporter of women's rights, civil rights, and foreign policy. Although the election was close, she won and was returned to Washington for that and subsequent terms.

"What I need to know, Lydia," Melinda mused, "is what is really going on at Fort Rucker. I'm glad the media are reporting what the brass are saying and doing, but I think Stefania's right. Something fishy is going on down there, and we need to get to the bottom of it."

The *Army Times* was filled with letters to the editor about keeping unsafe women out of the cockpit. Most of the letters were from pilots who now felt extremely threatened about who they might be flying with—not knowing whether the female they were assigned to as their copilot or, even worse, horror of horrors, their pilot-in-command, should have actually failed flight school. They were demanding that the Fort Rucker training records of all female pilots be checked from the beginning to be sure that "no one slipped by," and sounded dire warnings about the future of Army aviation if women with shady qualifications were allowed to fly. The wives who wrote in were almost hysterical with fear for their husband's safety and demanded to know what the Army was going to do to ensure that their loved ones were not going to be exposed to any unnecessary danger.

In aviation units around the world, male pilots now looked at their female colleagues with greater suspicion than they ever had before, wondering whether each particular female pilot had made the grade legally and had qualified without any undue number of pink slips. Every female pilot felt the huge number of eyes boring into her back and straight into her forehead every time she walked into a room. No longer could the female pilots even think that there were just a couple of bad apples in the bunch—they had all seen the news. Close to forty percent of all the female flight students currently in class at Fort Rucker had been set back or washed out altogether in one fell swoop.

None of the female pilots even wanted to be associated with other female pilots, because who knew who the bad ones were? It was a time to stake out one's own circle, draw a line in the sand and say, "Don't anyone come near me or you'll contaminate me. I'm a good pilot, but I'm not sure you are. Until I have proof that you are, I will presume, just like everyone else, that you aren't." Most female pilots yearned to belong to the group of pilots, who were predominately male, and not to a group of females. When push came to shove, they would do anything to assure their peers—the male pilots—that they were nothing like the rest of the female pilots, if those female pilots were found to be unworthy. Unlike the attitude of the Women's Airforce Service Pilots, who had trained together in World War II and so had bonded as friends and colleagues, female Army aviators tended to be loners and "gut it out" rather than try and network with other women. Besides, most units only had a couple of female pilots to begin with—a warrant officer or two, and maybe a couple of commissioned officers. And the smaller the post, the more likely there was to be only one aviation unit at that location.

The feeding frenzy between the media, families, and Congress was astounding. A new headline would send family members across the country to their telephones to call their senators and congressmen, demanding to seek change. The families were especially outraged by what they saw as a cover-up by the Army—that apparently for several years unqualified women had been made Army aviators and were out flying Army helicopters, and what was Congressman so-and-so from my district going to do about it and why do I pay my taxes anyway? The esteemed representatives and senators were deeply concerned, not just because they had to answer to their constituents, but because they feared the Army had tried to hide what now seemed to be out in the open. The media would report on the family responses and the congressional reactions, and the battered congressmen and women would beat on the doors of Fort Rucker, who would issue new public releases, and the cycle would begin again.

Melinda said to Lydia. "Get me that commanding general down there. What's his name?"

Lydia perused some papers. "Eckling. Major General Horace Eckling."

"Get him on the line. Now. He and I need to talk." Melinda slumped down onto a black leather couch piled high at one end with briefing packets, and crossed her slim legs. She looked across the room and out the window, where she could partially see the dome of the Library of Congress across the street.

When Lydia snapped her fingers twice, Melinda picked up the phone. "General Eckling. Hello. This is Congresswoman Melinda Tonnelli."

Eckling drew in a sharp breath. That bitch, he thought. "What can I do for you, ma'am," he drawled in a honeyed voice.

"You've created quite a maelstrom recently with suddenly deciding that seventeen young women don't belong in the class they started out in."

"Don't we know it," Eckling said with a sigh. "It has been bedlam down here. Reporters all over the place. News cameras. Parents calling all the time. Young women at my door crying for second chances. Their male colleagues angry that it wasn't found out sooner. I tell you, I'm thankful we found out about it when we did."

"That's just it, General. Why now?"

"What do you mean, why now?"

"Well, it's come to my attention that you only looked into these training records after the accident in Germany that killed an all-female flight crew."

"That's absolutely correct, Congresswoman."

"Doesn't it seem rather coincidental, General, that no one on your staff thought there were any significant numbers of female flight students who were failing before the accident, but now, all of a sudden, there is a multitude of them?"

"It would if it hadn't been explained to me that it had been my predecessor's policy not to fail them."

"You know, General, something doesn't sit well with me. And as a senior member of the House Armed Services Committee, I just want to let you know that I think we're going to be looking into this very closely."

"I welcome the opportunity, Congresswoman Tonnelli. We have absolutely nothing to hide. You send your people down here and we'll treat them well."

Exasperated by the conversation when they hung up, Eckling slammed the receiver down, bit his cigar in half, and threw it against the far wall. "I will not let those sons of bitches in Washington dictate to me how to run my school! This is the Army, for Christ's sake, and no mealy-mouthed civilian puke is going to poke her ditzy broad's nose in my business."

CHAPTER 20

ETLINGEN, WEST GERMANY
2:40 P.M., FRIDAY, MAY 16

Gunter ushered Marthe into a booth at the back of the dark gaststube across from their polizei station. On the way in, he had held up two fingers and pointed at the silver tap for the darkest brew. While he and Marthe sat facing each other across the scarred and sticky table, he played with the stack of beer coasters, building small pyramids and refusing to talk until their drinks arrived in tall slender glasses. Being mid-afternoon, the place was mostly empty, but their table was near an open window and the constant motor traffic on the main road through Etlingen would serve, he thought, to keep prying ears away from their conversation.

The waitress flitted by from the kitchen with a platter of sizzling sausages and potato salad, and Gunter felt his stomach contract and his mouth water. He had forgotten to eat lunch, as usual, since he had been out on a case that had lasted all morning and then had returned to catch up on paperwork. As the officer-in-charge of an area that included a number of small towns and villages, Gunter's jurisdiction was quite wide-ranging and it seemed that his responsibilities were never ending.

Following his futile pursuit of Nadina, Gunter had married once but the marriage failed after three years. His wife claimed, as many wives of police officers do, that he was married to his job, but he also knew that he was emotionally remote as he did not love her as she deserved to be loved and he willingly let her go when she asked to be freed. He felt a bitter pang, however, when, two years later, she remarried—this time a Scotsman—and took their young daughter, Katrina, away from him for good, although he was able to see her periodically, whenever he could convince himself to break away from his work and take a holiday across the English Channel.

Taking a sip of the dark, bitter beer, Gunter said, "Marthe, I need your help." He drummed his long, lean fingers on the table, and gave her a piercing glance.

Marthe leaned back against the banquette, which was completely uncomfortable as it was not even padded, and prepared to listen. This was the most unfashionable bar and restaurant in town and they only frequented it because it was closest to where they worked.

"Do you think that something that's been tossed into the Eisel River could be found a few weeks later?"

"Like what, sir?"

"A small metal object."

"How big?"

Gunter described the circumstances of how the explosive timing device came to land in the Eisel River after Oscar Pederson's car accident and how Erika Stohlmann had adamantly refused to believe the helicopter had been sabotaged.

"I'd like to go to Herr Major myself and present him with the evidence, but I need that explosive device. Otherwise, it's just Oscar's word against the Army's, and that won't go over very well," he said.

"No, it won't, will it?"

"So, what do you think? As a scuba diver. Do you think it would be possible to find something like this?"

Marthe shook her head slowly. "Really, sir, I just don't think so. The Eisel River flows fairly fast. Especially at this time of year. And you're talking about something small."

"Would you be willing to give it a look?"

"What?" Marthe pushed her hands against the table as if in alarm. "Sir, I don't mean to be disrespectful, but are you crazy?"

"We both know I can't order you to do this. It's outside of regulation police business. You're not a trained police scuba diver. So, if you got hurt in the line of duty—"

"Herr Hauptmann! I've been a scuba diver since I was twelve years old! And you know that! You're trying to insult me to egg me on!"

"Well, is it working?" Gunter flashed his associate a smile.

Marthe scrunched up her face and rolled her eyes. "Alright, sir. I'll do it, but I can't promise anything. I think this is looking for the proverbial needle in the haystack."

"Great, Marthe! I knew you wouldn't let me down!" Gunter raised his glass to Marthe's and clinked, saying "Prost!" With a few more sips, they finished their drinks and returned to work.

CHAPTER 21

FORT WAINWRIGHT, ALASKA
10 P.M., THURSDAY, MAY 22

The side door to the maintenance hangar clanged shut with a loud boom. It was ten o'clock on a Thursday night and Vanessa was in her tiny office on the ground floor. The last person in the 1311th had gone home a couple of hours ago and she hadn't expected anyone to be coming in. She found the noise somewhat unnerving, even though lights were blazing throughout the hangar. Vanessa was putting together the monthly maintenance report for the battalion meeting the next morning and had to get it finished. Since it was the first time Major Petrovich had given her the total responsibility for the report, she was already jumpy and on edge, wanting to ensure she got it right. She also knew she would have to present it to the battalion and brigade commanders the next morning at the briefing and that pressure was weighing on her as well.

Who was out there in the hangar? Her door wide open, Vanessa waited for someone to come to her office. But no one came. She could hear footsteps along the far wall of the hangar getting further and further away from her. Getting up, she stood outside her door, peering into the depths of the hangar, but couldn't see anything.

"Hello? Who's out there?" Her voice echoed eerily in the cavernous building, rising nearly a hundred feet to the steel girders at the top of the roof and bouncing off the many plate-glass windows in the immensely tall sliding hangar doors. Despite the shining fluorescent lights, the numerous helicopters arrayed in various levels of repair and maintenance appeared as silent hulks.

Vanessa heard some metal against metal noise and the scraping of a tool. A flicker of fear crept down her spine. "Who is it? Who's out there?" She took several steps towards the noise. She looked around for some sort of implement to protect herself with. Dashing back into her office, she grabbed her baseball bat—she had joined the post baseball team shortly after arriving—and continued stealthily towards the far right corner of the hangar. She no longer called out to whoever was there.

The 1311th, at that moment, had a mixture of helicopters in its maintenance hangar, and Vanessa was rounding the tail rotor of a UH-1H when she came upon Chad Emerson peering inside the cabin with an open logbook beside him and a few tools spread out on the cabin floor.

"Whoa, Vanessa!" Chad exclaimed. "What are you doing skulking around here with a bat over your shoulder!"

"I've been working. Writing up the maintenance report. What are you doing here?"

"Oh, I realized I had signed off something incorrectly on the maintenance log and I wanted to get in here right away and get it done before I completely forgot."

"But why didn't you answer me when I was calling you?"

"I didn't hear a thing," Chad said breezily. "You know how it echoes in here. I didn't know you were in here until you nearly hit me with that bat. You would have had some 'splaining to do, Lucy."

"Yeah, right, Ricky. But I also heard some other noises—"

"Oh, that. What you probably heard was me finding a couple of things that needed tightening. One of my crew chiefs missed something and I just happened to notice it as I walked by. No big deal. I'm not even going to mention it to him. It wasn't a safety measure, just a tiny thing. Nevertheless, he'll be embarrassed if he knows he missed it, so I'd rather you didn't say anything."

"Sure, Chad." Vanessa appeared distracted.

"Say, aren't you about ready to go up for your ARL I exam?" Every aviator arrived at a new unit in Aviator Readiness Level, or ARL, 3 status and had to be checked out by an instructor pilot to move up to ARL 2 and then I. The process ensured that the unit taught the aviator about its training area, combat mission, and helicopters, as well as ensuring that during the move the aviator didn't get too rusty with flying and had the opportunity for refresher training. There was always a rush, however, by unit commanders and their higher-ups to get aviators up to ARL I status within ninety days to prove the unit's mission-ready status.

"Yes, it was going to be tomorrow, but we've got the monthly meeting, so I think it will be Monday."

"I think your instructor pilot is probably going to be Chief Nelson. She has really amazed all of us since she got here. I mean, out of flight school, to test pilot school, instructor flight training, and all of it within a few short years. It's nothing short of miraculous."

"Anything I should know about her?"

"Don't think that just because she's a W2 she's inexperienced. She grabs flying hours whenever she can and she knows the insides of helicopters like you wouldn't believe. As far as testing you, she loves to make commissioned officers squirm. Don't call her Miranda. She hates that. She likes to be called Chief."

"Okay, that's about her. What about the test?"

"She's a real stickler for procedural details, for meeting maintenance deadlines, the endless paperwork, but she'll also make sure you know every monotonous boring facet about every helicopter we service."

"Great. Thanks for narrowing it down for me."

"Hey, no problem!"

"Well, I guess I'll get back to my report."

"Sure thing. I just have a tad bit more to do here and then I'm out of here." Chad waved a tool around in the air.

Vanessa said goodnight and went back to her office, finishing up her report in thirty more minutes.

After watching Vanessa disappear out of sight, Chad ventured to the farthest corner of the hangar and made a few minor adjustments, not on the helicopter he was responsible for test-flying, but the one Vanessa would test-fly on Monday.

CHAPTER 22

WATERTOWN, NEW YORK
5:35 A.M., FRIDAY, MAY 23

Tina awoke out of a sound sleep. The jarring ring of the telephone was set exceptionally loud as she had always had a hard time being roused out of bed. She rolled over onto her stomach, lunged into the darkness for the phone, and, misjudging, grabbed the tail of her cat instead. Eliza shrieked and jumped off the bed howling in protest. Tina cursed and slid further towards her nightstand, wondering where was the damn phone, hoping it would quit ringing. She flipped on the lamp, saw the previous day's newspaper strewn all over the top of the bedside table, hiding her phone. Tossing the paper aside, Tina whipped the phone off the cradle.

"Hello," she said breathlessly. "Who is this? What time is it, anyway?"

"'Lo, Tina?" said a slurrily drunk voice. "Tina, I miss her so much." The caller started crying. The background noise indicated he was calling from a noisy bar.

"Who is this?" Tina said sharply.

"It's me, Tina. I loved her. You know, don't you?" he sniffled and sobbed.

A sick feeling began to dawn on Tina and settle in the pit of her stomach. "Frank? Is that you?"

"Yes. Oh, God, I miss her so much. Why'd she want to divorce me?"

"Oh, Frank. You know why." Why do we have to go through this now, Tina thought.

"No, I don't," he wailed. "I never understood why. We loved each other. You know that."

"Yes, I did," Tina said impatiently. "But it didn't work out, Frank."

"Why?" Frank cried. "I loved her. Didn't she know that?"

"She knew that, Frank, but it was just too hard for her. She couldn't live that way, being separated all the time."

Tina could hear Frank wiping his nose with his sleeve. "But it wasn't going to be forever."

"I know, Frank, but it was too long for Crystal."

"It's been so hard for me, Tina."

She was silent.

"First the divorce, and now this."

Highly irritated now, Tina said, "It's been hard for me, too, Frank. She was my sister, you know."

Frank stumbled all over himself, "Yes, yes, I know, Tina. God, I'm sorry. I'm a pathetic mess and I'm drunk as all get out. I'm only thinking of myself and not of what you lost."

"Yeah, well, forget it."

An awkward silence ensued. Tina heard clanking glasses and loud laughter in the background and Frank slurping down a beer. "Haven't you had enough to drink, Frank?"

"Nope. I drink to forget. Can't forget."

"Go home, Frank. Come on. It must be—what time is it there, anyway?" Tina peered at her alarm clock now blinking red since it was freed from the newspaper. Five-thirty a.m. in New York meant it was—

"I don't know. Hey, bud!" he yelled to the bartender. "What time is it?"

"Time for you to hit the hay, Chief. And we're closing up shop soon."

"Yeah, yeah, Smitty. Come on, I'm talking to my dead ex-wife's sister here, and she wants to know what time it is in Honolulu. So give me a break, okay?"

The bartender shrugged, threw a towel on the counter and looked at his watch. "It's close to midnight, Frank. And you really ought to get home. Didn't I hear you tell your pals you're supposed to be flying some general tomorrow morning? You've got to get that alcohol out of your system. How many hours from bottle to throttle?"

"I know, I know. Did you hear that, Tina? It's midnight. I'm about to turn into Cinderella and I gotta go home."

"Okay, goodnight then, Frank."

Tina was about to hang up the phone when she heard a hoarse whisper. "They killed her, Tina." Frank's words were becoming harder and harder to understand as the alcohol took hold of his brain.

Tina's hand froze in midair. She gripped the phone tightly with both hands and brought it back up to her left ear. "What did you say?"

"I'm going to kill 'em myself, Tina."

"Who? What are you talking about?"

"That was no accident."

Goosebumps suddenly appeared on Tina's bare arms and legs.

"I know who they are," Frank continued in a low voice.

"How? What do you mean?" Tina wanted to jump through the phone and tear the information from Frank's throat.

"It was a conspiracy."

"A conspiracy." Tina felt the worst dread she had ever known. Could this possibly be true? Had Crystal and the other two women in the helicopter actually been killed by a conspiracy? It was impossible. The accident investigation report had claimed pilot error. But Tina had seen the accident site and she knew Crystal. In her gut, she knew Crystal didn't cause that accident.

She had known from the very beginning that the Army was hiding something. She didn't know what it was, but she didn't expect this. This was too horrible for words.

"And now if you'll excuse me," Frank drunkenly said, "I have to go to sleep."

"No, Frank!" Tina yelled. "Wait, you have to explain!" But it was too late. Frank had dropped the phone and she could hear him shuffling in his combat boots away from the pay phone She clung to the receiver for about ten minutes, hoping he would come back, but all she heard was the distant noise of a military bar in Honolulu until the bartender finally placed the receiver back on the hook.

CHAPTER 23

FORT WAINWRIGHT, ALASKA
5:20 P.M., FRIDAY, MAY 23

"What do you mean, you don't know how it happened?" Major General Sherman R. Tucker paced slowly back and forth in front of his desk, pausing from time to time to look at the glowing embers of the fire set by his secretary each morning. Throughout the day, Tucker's secretary or aide would add a couple of logs to keep the room toasty warm. The division headquarters building at Fort Wainwright, although in a renovated World War II building, was still rather drafty. The building did have central heat, but the general's office, a remnant of the old days, had a stately fireplace at one end with a comfortable seating group facing it. There Tucker had his morning coffee, held his important meetings, read all his documents, and greeted his visitors. Just about the only time he wasn't seated in front of the fireplace was when he had to talk on the phone—like now. The phone wouldn't stretch very far as the outlet was behind the mammoth executive desk that faced the fireplace at the opposite end. Red velvet drapes, looking as if they had seen better days, hung from ten-foot high ceilings, revealing windows that opened out onto a vista of snowy, craggy mountains in the near distance.

Tucker took a sip of his afternoon tea and listened to the irritated voice at the other end. "I don't know how it happened. That's what I'm trying to tell you, Dad."

"Iris, honey, they can't just toss you out of your class for no reason. The Army doesn't do things like that."

"But, Dad, that's exactly what they did."

Captain Earl Thornton walked in to throw another log on the fire. Tucker shook his head no. It was getting too late in the day, and time to let the fire die out. He motioned to Thornton to take a stack of signed papers from the desk.

Thornton riffled through the papers and said, "Excuse me, sir."

"Just a second, honey," Tucker said to his daughter, covering the receiver. "Yes, Earl?"

"Did you notice that Congresswoman Melinda Tonnelli has changed her plans and instead of coming next month, she's coming next week?"

"Yes, I did. We'll have to talk about that when I get off the phone. It doesn't give us a lot of time. But we had most of her visit planned already."

"Yes, sir. I just wanted to make sure you were aware of it."

"Thanks, Earl." Tucker turned his attention back to Iris. "So tell me again, sweetie, when did you find this out?"

"Just yesterday, Dad. And I can't tell you how furious I am. I was told I had too many pink slips."

"I thought you told me you hadn't gotten any pink slips."

"I haven't! That's what's so outrageous about this!"

"You're sure about that?"

"Absolutely."

"There's obviously some mistake then. You need to go ask to see your file."

"I've already done that. When they brought it out, there were pink slips in there I'd never seen before."

"Aren't those pink slips supposed to have your signature on them?"

"Yes!" Iris cried out in frustration. "And these do! But I swear to you I never signed them."

"So how did pink slips with your signature get in your file, Iris?" Tucker asked sternly.

"Dad, you always seem to have the answers. I thought you could help me figure it out."

"This just makes no sense at all. Either you're forgetting something—"

"Which I swear to you I'm not, Dad." Iris was adamant. Her memory in the family was legendary.

"Or something is rotten in the state of Denmark," he mused. "But that just isn't possible."

"What should I do?"

"Let me think about it over the weekend, honey, and then I'll give you a call. How's that? Now, let me tell you the family news."

When they got off the phone, Second Lieutenant Iris Tucker felt a little better, but not by much. She still had to face her new class and restarting the instrument phase on Monday, without the slightest understanding of why she was being set back. More than humiliated, she was incensed. For the moment, she would rely on her father. If he couldn't come up with a good game plan, she would have to figure something out for herself, and soon. Preferably before Monday.

CHAPTER 24

NEAR THE DEMILITARIZED ZONE, SOUTH KOREA
10:07 A.M., FRIDAY, MAY 23

"You have to be extremely careful flying around up here," Chief Warrant Officer Two Charlotte Driver, the pilot-in-command of the UH-60, said.

"It's gorgeous," Sergeant Lucy Abraham said from the back, clicking her mike as she scooted over to the left-hand side of the helicopter to get a better view of the valley they were flying over. The grey ribbon of the river wound around below them with lush vegetation on the mountaintops and rice paddies terraced in between. All along their route men and women rose from their back-breaking work, holding onto their cone-shaped straw hats, and waved at the helicopter as it whirred past them.

Driver, from the 92th Aviation Company, was taking her new copilot trainee on her first orientation flight up to the demilitarized zone between North and South Korea. It was one of the most essential elements that any pilot stationed in South Korea had to become familiar with. A pilot who inadvertently ventured into the area and strayed into North Korea, or vice versa, could be shot down. Knowing the terrain and how it fit the political boundaries was crucial to staying alive.

While Warrant Officer One Stella Rodriquez studied the map and compared it to the land features outside the cockpit, Driver continued flying. She loved the mountains and valleys of Korea. Although they presented enormous challenges to flying—particularly in winter and on blustery, windy days—they created spectacular scenery. Today, however, was a lovely spring day. The sky overhead was brilliant blue with the sun, whenever it peeped through a dip in a mountain pass, providing welcome warmth through the cockpit glass. Patches of white cloud drifted lazily overhead in the slight breeze, causing occasional shadows to darken the ground momentarily and then disappear again just as quickly.

For the next hour, Driver flew the Blackhawk along the designated route, ensuring that Rodriquez understood the key checkpoints on the map and what they corresponded to on the ground. After checking and double-checking her copilot's understanding of the demilitarized zone, Driver decided it was time to head home. They would conduct this type of flight several times before she signed Rodriquez off as competent to fly it on her own.

The radar operator in the air defense artillery battery nearest the demilitarized zone spotted a blip on the screen.

"Sir!" he called out. "An unidentified object is flying around out there."

"Alright, Sergeant. Make radio contact on the emergency frequency and try to ascertain who it is."

Sergeant Juan Fuentes made several attempts to induce the aircraft to identify itself, to no avail. He slowly turned towards his battery commander in dismay. They were on the front line between North and South Korea, and tensions were extremely tight. North Korea had been rattling its sabers and threatening its southern neighbor. For several weeks, the battery had been under a weapons-free environment and knew that at any moment it could be required to shoot down an aircraft that came across the border. Every single soldier in D Battery, 1st Air Defense Artillery Battalion, no matter how many times they had conducted the drill, hoped they would never have to do so in real life. Unfortunately, it looked as though the time had come.

Captain Roger Whitman turned towards his missile team and ordered them to lock onto the target and fire. The rest of the battery members steeled themselves for the disappearance of the aircraft from the radar screen. It only took a few seconds.

During that period of time, Whitman had already picked up the radio to transmit to his battalion commander that a North Korean intruder had entered South Korean airspace, refused to respond to calls to identify itself, and had been neutralized by a D Battery antiaircraft missile.

"Ma'am?" Abraham clicked her mike from the back. "I just saw a small burst of fire from the ground and it looks like it's heading our way. About ten o'clock. Maybe five klicks."

"Goddamn!" Driver exclaimed. "That looks like a missile launch! Surely no one's firing at us!"

She jammed her finger and held the mike open to the emergency radio frequency.

"Mayday! Mayday! What the hell's going on out there?" Driver stared at the ball of fire barreling towards them, trying to maneuver the helicopter out of the way.

All she heard through the radio was a burst of static. "Rodriguez!" she barked. "Change the frequency!"

"To what?" Rodriquez frantically asked.

Driver threw a book with radio frequency codes at her. "Quick, look up the 92nd ADA. That has to be who that is. We've got to get them off our tail."

"I can't find it!" Rodriquez wailed.

"Here, take the controls and keep twisting the helicopter—" Driver glanced over to be sure Rodriquez was flying and then grabbed the book back.

As soon as Driver had found the frequency for the 92nd, she looked up, just in time to see the missile shatter the cockpit window and take off Rodriquez's head. The missile exploded inside the helicopter, causing it to break apart into hundreds of pieces a thousand feet above the ground. Driver's last vision, as her seat broke away from the cockpit and she hurtled to her death, was of Abraham screaming, her face seared with burns as she rode pieces of the helicopter down to the ground.

CHAPTER 25

ARMY OPERATIONS CENTER, THE PENTAGON
4:13 A.M., SATURDAY, MAY 24

Lieutenant Colonel Jean-Pierre Manitou gazed at the casualty report that had come across the telefax. Three young women had been killed in a helicopter and by a U.S. missile. It was an absolutely tragic event. Casualty assistance officers would soon be arriving at their loved ones' homes to tell them the news of how the Army had completely fucked up. Of course, it wouldn't be phrased that way. "Mr. and Mrs. so-and-so, the Army regrets to inform you . . . Your daughter was a credit to her nation and to the U.S. Army . . . Her service will be highly missed . . . We will do everything we can to uncover what happened." The parents and spouses would be lucky to ever find out the truth behind what really happened.

Taking another drink of the bitter, dark liquid called coffee in the Emergency Operations Center—the only thing that helped Manitou stay awake during his twelve-hour shifts—he looked around his subterranean hole in the depths of the Pentagon. Blazing with lights that never went out, this small space was the heart of communication for the entire Army. Anything of significance that went on around the world would be reported here and the officer or noncommissioned officer on duty knew how to get in touch with the most senior members of the Army at any time, day or night, wherever they might be. Behind Manitou on the wall were bookshelves filled with binders that he and his NCO could pull that provided standard operating procedures for them to follow in various incidents. Their two desks were separated from the rest of the room by an L-shaped counter. While they were on duty, other members of the Army Operations Center would come to them for assistance and information, but Manitou's primary responsibility was to maintain contact between the Army outside the Pentagon and the Army's senior staff in Washington, D.C.

As the officer on duty in the Army's Emergency Operations Center, he dreaded making the call in the middle of the night to Maloney, but when the call came in to his center from U.S. Forces Korea, he knew he had no choice. Casualty reports came across his desk frequently that required informing the Secretary or the Chief of Staff of the Army, but as sad as they were, they were usually due to vehicle accidents. Occasionally, deaths occurred as a result of the rare homicide, suicide, or illness. Not only was it extremely rare that friendly fire took place, but the ramifications of such an event were enormous.

"Oh, my God." Secretary of the Army Reginald Maloney slumped into his chair. He wiped the last vestiges of sleep from his eyes, brushed a coil of steel-gray hair off his forehead, and poured himself a strong whiskey. He had no time to bother with ice. He took a quick swig and said, "When did this happen?"

Manitou replied, "It was about ten in the morning Korea time. Of course, the aviation unit realized fairly quickly that their pilots were overdue, but they didn't match that up with the reported shoot-down of a North Korean aircraft until some investigators got out there and could see it was one of ours."

"Oh, God, what a disaster." Maloney rubbed his forehead and took a long drink. As a young Army captain, he had served in Korea and well understood the pitfalls facing the military there.

"Yes, sir."

"Alright, Colonel. Thank you very much. Keep me informed if anything else comes in," Maloney said.

Just then, Maloney's wife, Kaneesha, walked into his study, tightening her vibrant silk kimono around her waist. She sat down beside him on the arm of the chair, stroked his neck, and leaned her head against his.

"What it is it, Reg, honey?" she asked. "What did they call you about this time?" After thirty-one years of marriage, including the past two with him serving as the Secretary of the Army, she was used to calls in the middle of the night. She was not accustomed, however, to seeing him looking so downtrodden. Reginald Maloney, who had been one of the first black lawyers in the Judge Advocate Corps, had a reputation of being tough and grizzled, even more so as he grew older. It had been an especially difficult time to be black in the Army during the civil rights era, but Reginald Maloney had done it with verve, class, and a great deal of spirit. He had taught a lot of people, white and black, about the Constitution and the Rights of Man, and had helped many young black soldiers defend themselves against harassment. An extremely principled individual, he was rarely wrong, unless he refused to follow good advice.

Maloney shook his head. Kaneesha got up and went to the kitchen. She came back with an ice bucket filled with ice and a pair of ice tongs. She quietly plopped a few cubes of ice into her husband's drink, refilled it with whiskey, and fixed herself a drink.

She handed him the drink and gently urged, "Now, Reg, tell me. What's wrong?"

"There's been another helicopter accident, Neesha. This time, we shot it down thinking it was a North Korean aircraft, but it was one of our own."

Kaneesha's eyes widened in horror.

"What seems inexplicable," Maloney said, "is that there were three women onboard."

"Were they all killed?" Kaneesha asked.

"Yes."

"Those poor girls."

"And their families," Maloney added. "I wish we could go back in time and make it all disappear."

"What an amazing coincidence, Reggie, that there were three women killed in that accident in Germany and—"

"Yes." Maloney sat, staring down at the ice silently swirling around in his glass.

"That just seems unbelievable to me," Kaneesha went on, prodding her husband.

"It is rather remarkable." Maloney suddenly lifted his glass and drained the last of his drink.

"So what do you think about it?"

"I don't know what to think," he admitted.

"The other accident was pilot error," Kaneesha reminded him.

"I know."

"So this is totally different."

"Yes, so one would think. There will still be a full investigation, and, trust me, Kaneesha, it isn't going to look pretty. The Army's going to look really bad on this one. Parents can usually forgive us if their children die for a good cause, but not when we kill them ourselves. This is inexcusable. I'll be chafing at the bit until we get to the bottom of it."

"But you will find out, Reg. I know you will."

CHAPTER 26

ETLINGEN, WEST GERMANY
7:20 A.M., SATURDAY, MAY 24

Marthe knew it was outrageously ridiculous to even think that a small metal object could be anywhere near the accident site, but she had promised Gunter that she would give it a try. In the early morning hours after sunrise, and before many people were whizzing by, she had pulled her Volkswagen Jetta off to the side of the road and parked. After opening the trunk and collecting her gear, she walked over to a cluster of trees where she could prop up her buoyancy compensator and air tank. Once she had struggled into the dry wetsuit, which included a warm hood, she sat down and put on the BC, underwater socks, and underwater gloves. Checking her gauges and blowing air out the respirator, she was convinced her equipment was in working order. Grabbing her mask, snorkel, and fins, Marthe picked her way carefully down the bank, shrugging off the thought that she needed a buddy for safety's sake. With her mask strung around one arm, she entered the icy water with a shiver, shaking at first as her body grew accustomed to the temperature while she slipped the fins on her feet. Finally, she swished water around inside the mask and suctioned it to her face, placed the respirator in her mouth, breathed slowly in and out, and descended to the river's bottom to begin her exploration.

Although the day was sunny, Marthe had a flashlight attached to her weight belt to help her see around underwater foliage and into shadows. She had studied the river's current and thought she had a good idea of where she would most likely find a projectile thrown from a car that had hit a particular tree. If it wasn't where she thought it would be, then she was quite certain it would have been washed downstream weeks ago.

At the point where Marthe had entered the Eisel River, just below the cobblestone bridge that had iced up the day of Oscar Pederson's unfortunate accident, the riverbed was about twelve feet deep and comprised mostly of smooth rock and boulders. An object might lie on the bottom if wedged tightly enough against some rocks rather than being forced downstream.

For the next hour, Marthe cruised back and forth from bank to bank, aiming her light at all the crevices in and around the many obstacles on the river's floor. Despite her gloves, socks, and wetsuit, she was beginning to lose body warmth and was going to have to give up her search. She had only covered about three-quarters of the area that she thought an object could reasonably be in, if it were still there.

Heading away from her vehicle, towards the far bank, on what she had decided would be her last go-around, a dazzle of sunlight illuminated the riverbed in a wide circle in front of her. A glistening pool of diamond droplets seemed to have entered the quickening river. Marthe caught her breath involuntarily at the beauty, causing her to take in a little river water, cough, and have to readjust her respirator. Breathe in, breathe out, and return to normal. As she did so, her eyes strayed over the scene and lit upon a large boulder to the right that she had already passed. The sun's rays, refracting as they were throughout the water, and the direct aim of her flashlight, glinted off of something that wasn't bumpy and natural and that had not previously been noticeable.

Gliding to the boulder, Marthe noticed a large crescent-shaped hole in it about one foot above the riverbed. Tucked into the back was something manmade. She reached in and, giving it a sharp tug, pulled it out. If this wasn't the explosive timing device, it wasn't going to be found, because she was now done.

CHAPTER 27

FORT RUCKER, ALABAMA
11:15 A.M., SATURDAY, MAY 24

Bill Brannon and his wife, Stefania, had just returned to their home on Fort Rucker from a trip to the commissary when the phone rang. Brannon's face blanched. He barely said a word, just nodded his head, and kept saying, "Yes, sir," "I understand, sir."

When he hung up, Stefania, who had been putting away groceries in the small kitchen, walked in with a bag of carrots still in her hand and said, "What is it, Bill? You look like you've seen a ghost."

"A helicopter with three women was shot down in Korea yesterday. They're calling it friendly fire."

Stefania's free hand flew to her mouth. "Oh my God! What a tragedy! Did anyone survive?"

"No. They're all dead."

She shook her head and closed her eyes. "This comes so close on the heels of that other accident. It's almost as if women pilots are cursed."

Brannon narrowed his eyes. "Well, Eckling is worried about other things."

"Such as?"

"What their training records were." He uttered a heavy sigh.

"But what would that have to do with—"

"Exactly. Nothing. He's ordered me to get the records so he can peruse them."

"And?"

"I want to see what's in them first."

"What do you expect to find?" Stefania asked.

"Stefania, darling, I don't really think I'm going to find anything. That's why I'd like to see the records before anyone else. Eckling seems to think there's some correlation between there being two female pilots on the crashed helicopter and their training records, that maybe they didn't do so well here. I maintain that, since they died of friendly fire, how they fared here has nothing to do with their crash."

Stefania ruffled his hair. "You're a good man, Bill. Just be careful, will you?"

CHAPTER 28

SCHOFIELD BARRACKS, HAWAII
9:15 A.M., SATURDAY, MAY 24

Frank picked up a copy of *The Stars and Stripes* Saturday morning on his way to the barber shop. As he sat in a chair awaiting his turn, he glanced at the headlines. "Friendly Fire Destroys Helo in Korea" caught his attention immediately. Scanning through the article, he gathered the gist of the events very quickly, until he reached the last paragraph where the information moved like a slow ricocheting bullet into his brain. Two female pilots and a female crew chief had been aboard the aircraft, just like Crystal's accident. Although Frank felt that his blood was running ice cold, he broke out into a flaming sweat, staring at the words on the page, no longer seeing them.

Just then, the barber snapped his towel across the seat of his chair and called out, "Next!" He looked questioningly at Frank. Frank looked up at him with a dumbfounded expression, threw his newspaper on the floor, and dashed out of the barber shop. His head was pounding, he had to get away. In his haste, he nearly tripped over a stroller parked outside the entrance to the florist shop but he recovered and made it to his car before his mind exploded into a million pieces.

He sat in his old Audi 5000, gripping the worn leather steering wheel and then smashing a fist against the dashboard over and over. "Goddamn it! Goddamn it!" He cried. "They did it again.

I know those fuckers did it again. Ohmigod, I should have stopped them. I should have gone to someone."

Frank fumbled around in his shirt pocket for his cigarettes, and, after grabbing one and stuffing it in his mouth, threw the pack on the passenger seat beside him. He angrily jammed the cigarette lighter in several times until it would stay in, and, since it never popped out on its own, he yanked it out when he thought it was probably hot enough. Of course it wasn't, which also irritated him, so he had to endure sucking down some nauseating-tasting smoke until the cigarette caught a good light.

"These guys are fucking assholes," Frank muttered. "I've got to come up with a plan. My God, my God, my God, I could have prevented this."

Looking around at the parking lot outside the PX, Frank thought it was inconceivable that such a horror was taking place inside the United States Army. Innocent families were conducting their Saturday shopping—little children were skipping along, holding mommy or daddy's hand, begging for sodas or toys. Soldiers were going in and out of the exchange, picking up their dry cleaning, getting haircuts, and taking care of errands they couldn't get to during the week. The post elementary school had set up a bake sale by the main entrance to help buy new books for their library, and children were gleefully trying to get passersby to buy brownies and cookies. It was an ordinary day on an ordinary post, and the scene appeared idyllic, but there was no longer anything ordinary about the Army for Frank.

All of a sudden, Frank and the Army had become opposed to one another. He knew there was a conspiracy—he just didn't know how far up it went or how wide it extended. He felt completely helpless in one respect—he didn't think anyone would actually believe him if he tried to tell them some officers were killing off female pilots. They would think he'd gone off his rocker and, hell, Frank thought, might even try to put him in the loony bin. Then where would he be? He'd be of no use to anybody.

The one thing Frank could do, and the one thing he would do, was eliminate each member of the conspiracy that he knew before they killed anyone else. It was what he should have done before. But he'd been feeling too sorry for himself, grieving too much about Crystal, to really give a shit about what those fucked-up assholes might do. God almighty he was such a fucking idiot himself! If only he'd—

But it was too late now to be crying over spilt milk. He'd go fly the mission he had to do today and then ask for emergency leave. He'd get his dad to call the unit and say his grandmother was dying or something and that he needed to get home right away. He had a shitload of leave saved up, and he'd say he'd be gone for thirty days. That should give him ample time to take care of the four guys he knew about—John, Mark, Chad, and Cecil—and anyone else they clued him in on. He wouldn't take thirty days, though, because he planned to take them each out damn fast. But before he did, he'd make sure they squealed like stuck pigs.

CHAPTER 29

WATERTOWN, NEW YORK
6:30 A.M., SATURDAY, MAY 24

Tina had been unable to sleep anymore after being awakened by Frank's drunken call, so she padded downstairs with Eliza scampering at her heels and made a pot of coffee. As she sat at her kitchen table and looked through the glass doors at her backyard, she agonized over what Frank could possibly have meant.

"Who would have wanted to kill Crystal?" Tina asked out loud. "And the other women? What point did that serve? Why? What could they possibly gain? And how did they do it? The investigation report says pilot error. I saw it myself. Of course, I never believed Crystal was at fault, but still, I can't believe that anyone deliberately caused that accident. That's murder."

Despite the warmth of her kitchen as the morning sun flooded in, Tina shuddered. "Think, Tina, think." She pushed her brain to recall all the people she'd ever known in the Army who had ever had any contact with Crystal who might have had the slightest reason to wish her dead. But even though she could think of some individuals with whom her sister might have had conflicts, her imagination couldn't take her as far as thinking they would inflict harm. Moreover, since there were many other people who had come into contact with Crystal whom Tina didn't know, it was basically a useless mental exercise.

After half an hour of pondering, Tina retrieved the investigation report and pored over it for an hour or more, trying to find something she had missed before that might trigger suspicious questions this time around, but she could find nothing. The report looked genuine and flawless. Tina sighed heavily and went upstairs to shower.

Having dressed, Tina went outside to get the newspaper, laid it on the kitchen table, and fixed herself a light breakfast of toast and orange juice. Because Watertown, New York, was adjacent to Fort Drum, military events were not given short shrift in its newspaper. The helicopter accident in Korea was on the front page.

Shrilly, the headline proclaimed "Female Pilots Killed by Friendly Fire."

Tina's toast turned to mealy mush in her mouth and she stopped another slice mid-way in the air. She couldn't imagine this was a coincidence, not on top of Crystal's crash and Frank's accusations.

The one thought electrifying her brain was, "Frank was right. And they've done it again. This can't be happening." She felt like vomiting.

Tina pushed her plate of food away. "What can I do? I have to be able to do something. I can't just sit here. I have to get in touch with Frank." She glanced at her clock. It was now only eight o'clock. Middle of the night for Frank, whom she knew was flat out drunk. She'd have to wait a while to call him.

Deirdre Holloway and Wayne Yarrow lived only a few miles away and, since they had an infant, Tina suspected they would be at home. She grabbed her car keys and slammed the door on the way out. She had to talk this over with a trusted friend, and Deirdre was as close as they came.

CHAPTER 30

CAMP VANGCHON, SOUTH KOREA
4:00 P.M., SATURDAY, MAY 24

After hearing that one of the 92nd Aviation Company helicopters had been shot down by friendly fire, Sergeant Lindley Ochiotto, like everyone else, had felt an immediate frisson of horror. He had known the pilot-in-command, CW2 Driver, ever since she had been in the unit, and he had worked periodically with the crew chief, Sergeant Abraham. The copilot trainee, WO1 Rodriquez, was new, but had made a favorable impression in her short stay. Other than professional associations with the women, he had had no personal dealings with any of them, for the 92nd maintained strict delineations between officers and enlisted, with no fraternization occurring at social functions. Although it sometimes irked the personnel that their company commander was so punctilious, no one could deny that the morale in the unit was better than what they were accustomed to experiencing elsewhere, so perhaps there was something to be said for it.

Once the shock had worn off about a U.S. Army air defense artillery unit shooting down one of its own helicopters, Ochiotto began to think about the IFF equipment—the Identification Friend or Foe equipment that pinpointed U.S. aircraft as friendly. He was one of the electronics technicians for the 92nd and had just repaired and tested the IFF on Driver's UH-60 before she left on her flight. They had gone out on a thirty-minute test flight together before she took off for the

DMZ and he knew, beyond a shadow of a doubt, that the IFF had been working perfectly fine.

Ochiotto also knew how investigation reports were supposed to work. Blame was going to be placed somewhere. Right now it was being placed on the artillery unit, but friendly fire was so beyond the pale of what anyone in the Army wanted that extreme pressure would be placed on everyone to get rid of that explanation. If it could be proven that the IFF wasn't working, and that the fault, in fact, lay with the equipment, then the maintenance of the equipment would be to blame and the artillery unit could be held, so to speak, blameless. The parents and other relatives of the dead women might not feel any better, but the artillery unit could say it wasn't their fault.

The only thing was, Ochiotto wasn't going to be anyone's fall guy. He only had three months left on his tour in Korea and three months left in the Army. Moreover, he had pride in what he did and he knew that the IFF had been working when Driver took off. There was no way that it could have failed all of a sudden. Something had to have happened. He just didn't know what. He also knew all of her radios had been working properly, because they had also been checked out.

Knowing that the investigators might put a different spin on things, Ochiotto decided he wanted someone to know the truth, so he sat down on Saturday afternoon and wrote a letter to Lieutenant Vanessa Robison, his cousin, serving in the 1311th in Alaska. Although Lindley and Vanessa were enlisted and officer, they were very close and he knew she wouldn't think he was distorting the truth regardless of how the investigation report made it sound. Besides, depending on when the investigators came to question him, Lindley thought Vanessa might be able to provide him with sound advice based on her position as an officer and a maintenance test pilot.

CHAPTER 31

FORT RUCKER, ALABAMA
10:15 P.M., SATURDAY, MAY 24

Wearing a pair of dark brown pants, a black shirt, and black shoes, Lieutenant Iris Tucker had put her long, blonde hair in a bun and hidden it inside the hood of her black windbreaker. She parked her midnight blue Corvette close to the base theater, and walked to the unit where her training records were kept. She spotted no lights on and no CQ—charge of quarters. When she had asked earlier in the week to see her records, she had noted what room the clerk had gone into to retrieve them. Now she was determined to get those records herself. She hadn't yet decided what she would do with them once they were in her hands, but the first thing was to get the records.

The room with the file records was at the back of the building, which, Iris thought, was a stroke of luck since the front of the building was lit up like a Christmas tree. The back of the building was pitch black and Iris found herself tripping over large rocks and small bushes as she made her way to the third window, which was the one she thought should be the right room.

The only problem, she perceived, was that the window ledge was about six feet off the ground. A downward slope had occurred from front to back of the building and now she had to figure out how to propel herself up to the window, a feat she had never been very good at. As her eyes adjusted to the blackness, she suddenly spotted a water faucet standing about three feet tall just a foot to the right of the window.

"If I can totter on that," she thought, "maybe I can reach the window ledge." After several unsuccessful tries, she just managed to grab hold of the ledge. With her right foot on the faucet, left foot scraping against the wall, and left hand on the ledge, she managed to open the miraculously unlocked window with her right hand after a number of strenuous attempts. Her strength having failed her at this point, she fell from the faucet, but quickly clambered back up again and flung herself through the now open window. Luckily, she wasn't impeded by the many file cabinets that adorned the walls and, instead, fell hard onto the linoleum floor.

Rather than turning on a light and risking detection, Iris had brought a penlight with her. Using this, she flashed her tiny pinpoint on each file cabinet's label, looking quickly for the Ts. When she found the right one, she tried to yank the drawer open, but the cabinet was locked. Rapidly moving to the inner room, where two battered wooden desks were located, Iris thrust open the middle drawer of the closest one, sweeping the belongings around in a heap, rejoicing when she found a tiny silver key on a metal loop.

"Yes!" she exclaimed under her breath. Taking the key back to the file room, she quickly opened the cabinet, thumbed through the files, and found her record. As she was pulling the record out of the filing cabinet, she heard a key turn in the lock of the outer door of the company's main office. She froze. Almost immediately, lights came on in the front rooms. Iris looked at the window and at the door leading to the clerk's room, but before she could move, Lieutenant Colonel Brannon had breezily waltzed into the clerk's room, turned on the light, and now his bulk filled the door of the file room.

"What are you doing here?" he demanded.

Iris couldn't speak. Her guilty face answered for her.

"How did you get in here?" Brannon's eyes flitted towards the open window. "I see," he dryly commented.

"What have you got there?" Brannon grimly nodded towards the file Iris had half out of the cabinet. Iris hastily pushed the file back into the drawer and closed it, standing with her back against the cabinet.

"I see," Brannon said impatiently. "This is going to be a cat and mouse game. That is not going to work. You're going to have to answer some questions. And you're going to have to answer them from me, or you're going to have to answer them from the police. Now, which do you choose?" He moved towards the telephone in the clerk's office.

"Wait! Please!" Iris called out.

Brannon turned back around. "What's your name?"

"Lieutenant Iris Tucker."

"What are you doing here?"

"I—" Iris faltered. She looked at Brannon and looked around at the filing cabinets. Then she straightened her shoulders and stated quickly, "I've been set back to another flight class. To a new instrument phase that starts on Monday. I have no idea why. I was told I have a lot of pink slips. They showed me my training records. There are a lot of pink slips. But I never received any pink slips. Never. So I came here to get my records."

"Why?"

Iris shrugged. "I hadn't figured that part out yet. I just know I don't want to be separated from my old class. It isn't fair and I didn't do anything wrong."

"Let's see your records."

Iris reluctantly moved away from the filing cabinet and retrieved her file. Brannon opened it up and saw the numerous pink slips in there. He looked down at her questioningly.

He pointed to one in particular. "What about this one? You say you didn't receive this one?"

"No."

"Is this your signature?"

"It looks like it, but it can't be. I have no idea how that got in there."

Brannon appraised the young lieutenant's demeanor and snapped the file folder shut. Ordinarily, he knew her actions should have required him to turn her in to the authorities. After all, she had committed a serious crime of breaking and entering and trying to steal government documents. But her explanation to him rang true. He had already found himself questioning the wisdom of Eckling's demands to review only female student training records, even though male training records were eventually included, as well as the general's insistence that women were crashing too many helicopters. Although Brannon knew that what Lieutenant Tucker had done was wrong, he could understand her frustration when backed up against a system that seemed unfair. Usually one to follow the rules, Brannon did know how to bend them on occasion, if a situation warranted it and, in his opinion, this one did.

He closed the cabinet drawer and placed an elbow on top of the filing cabinet. "I'm not entirely sure whether I believe you or not, Lieutenant, but I have a gut feeling you're telling the truth."

Iris remained silent.

Brannon continued. "I could use your help."

"Sir?" Iris suddenly looked quizzical.

"I didn't exactly come in here trying to find an intruder," Brannon said with a disarming smile. "I had a job to do."

"Yes, sir."

"By the way, I'm Lieutenant Colonel Brannon, General Eckling's XO. I'm on a hunt for the training records of the pilots in that helicopter accident in Korea."

"What can I do?"

"Help me find the archived records for students who graduated in the last few years." Brannon smiled again as he turned towards the filing cabinets.

It took the two of them half an hour to narrow down their selection to two rather dusty, steel gray cabinets in the farthest corner of the room. Having removed the files he needed on Driver and Rodriquez, Brannon locked the cabinets, shut the window, turned off the lights, and closed the door. He handed Iris the key to put away, and they left the company offices.

As Brannon walked towards his car, he turned back around and said, "Oh, Lieutenant Tucker."

Iris filled with dread. "Yes, sir."

"Come here a moment, please."

She stepped closer towards his car and Brannon handed her one of the files. He said, "I have no idea if I'm doing the worst thing I could possibly be doing by giving you this, but something tells me I'm not."

By the streetlamp, Iris could see her name on the file. "Thank you, sir," she said. "I'll never forget this."

"Believe me," he said, "I'll never forget this, either!"

CHAPTER 32

ETLINGEN, WEST GERMANY
6:10 P.M., SATURDAY, MAY 24

After finding the metal device in the Eisel River, Marthe stripped off her scuba gear and wetsuit, dried herself with a rough towel, and drove to the polizei station to find Gunter. Unfortunately, he had a rare training seminar in Stuttgart that day and wasn't expected back until 5 p.m. She went home, showered, and returned to the station.

When Gunter finally returned at the end of the day, dispirited and exhausted after a long, grueling day of doing nothing but listening, Marthe knew that the first order of the day would be a quick beer at the gaststube. Marthe, thirty-three years old, had never been married and knew that on a Saturday evening she was not at all interested in preparing herself something to eat. The wienerschnitzel and pommes frites they both ordered, though not good for the waistline, were perfect at the end of a frazzling day, especially when eaten in the comfort of a familiar bar with a colleague, talking over the events of the day while sipping down a cool brew.

Before heading over to the gaststube, Marthe had quickly shown Gunter the metal device she had found, and they spent a good portion of their time in the bar discussing whether it could possibly be the explosive timing device or not.

"I'll call up Oscar," Gunter said, "and we'll take it over to him. See if it's the same thing his son found."

"Do you think that's a good idea?" Marthe asked.

"Why not?"

"It might be better to have him come to the station, don't you think? Because of their son?"

"Na ja. O Gott. What was I thinking." Gunter slapped his forehead. "Seeing that, if it is what Rolf found, would throw Nadina off the edge. Thank you, Marthe." Gunter patted Marthe on the hand, not noticing her blush as he motioned to the waitress for another round of beers.

Gunter and Marthe had worked together for seven years, during which time Gunter's marriage had faltered and fizzled, and Marthe had grown attached to Gunter, but he had yet to notice. Marthe was Gunter's right-hand woman in the office, his second in command. In the small polizei station, three other individuals also worked full-time—a secretary and two other policemen. Of medium height, Marthe would never stand out in any crowd—a good characteristic for a policewoman. Her mousy brown hair, pale skin, and watery blue eyes often led people to the inept conclusion that she was someone who could be easily tangled with and who had little intelligence, which was far from the truth. Moreover, Marthe had as much inner strength as she had compassion. One of her finest characteristics was her tenacity to stick to a problem and see it through to the end. Another was her intense loyalty to her friends. She didn't have many, but Gunter, she had decided, was one of them.

As soon as they returned to the polizei station, Gunter rang up Oscar and told him what they had found.

"I'll be right there," Oscar promised.

"You don't have to come today," Gunter explained. "Monday will be fine."

"No," Oscar said. "I'd like to come now. I want to know now."

"I understand," Gunter acknowledged. "Right, then. I'll be here."

Marthe and Gunter were the only ones left in the station when Oscar arrived, and Marthe greeted him at the door, ushering him into Gunter's office. The two men shook hands and fell into their respective seats. Gunter brought the metal device out onto the top of his desk and pushed it over towards Oscar. Oscar rose, staggered towards Gunter's desk, picked up the device, and handled it for what seemed a few very long moments.

He sighed and put it down. "Nein," he said. "This isn't it. I don't know exactly what you picked up out of the river, but it's not what my boy found." Oscar's voice nearly cracked under the emotional pressure.

Gunter stood up. "Danke sehr, Oscar. We can only imagine how hard this has been for you and Nadina. We appreciate you coming in. We wish it had been the device. That would have been something anyway."

"Yes," Oscar said. "It's what started it all." As he left the building with his shoulders sagging, Marthe and Gunter looked after him with pitying glances, then locked up and went home to their separate weekends.

CHAPTER 33

FAIRBANKS, ALASKA
11:50 P.M., SATURDAY, MAY 24

Chad draped his arm over the top of the pay phone and hissed into the black transmitter, "What the hell were you thinking, John?"

Second Lieutenant John Datterly, a pilot in the 92nd Aviation Company in Korea, wasn't too keen on being chastised at the other end. "I was only doing what we agreed on. It was time to take them out."

"You fucking numbskull!" Chad drew in a long breath, and looked around the parking lot behind him at the bowling alley to see if anyone was paying attention. It was nearly midnight and most of the patrons were inside still getting drunk, except for the youngsters who had been picked up long ago by worried parents. A piercing wind was blowing debris along the pavement. Chad pulled the collar of his windbreaker closer to his neck to try to keep warm. The smell of burnt pizza and oily hot dogs permeated the air.

"What's your problem, Chad?" John asked angrily. "I got done what needed to be done. Just because you don't have the—"

"Let me remind you, John, what the schedule is," Chad said bitingly. "Germany, then Alaska, and then Korea. You were supposed to wait until after my operation. What was going on in your head?"

"Sometimes plans go awry. You know that. We're on different continents. A moment of opportunity arose and I took it."

Chad wanted to scream. "But I'm now set up for another accident!" he said through gritted teeth. "There is no way we can let another accident take place right now."

"What's the big deal?"

Chad could just imagine John shrugging his shoulders. Although John was loyal, he wasn't the brightest bulb in the chandelier.

"Because, John," Chad said ever so slowly, "we can't afford to bring suspicion upon ourselves. And if there are two more accidents within days of each other in which three women are killed, then everyone will know it was no accident. More than a few people will jump to the immediate conclusion that something is afoot. We have to prevent that."

John pondered for a few minutes. "So what do we do?"

"We shouldn't have deviated from the plan, you idiot!" Chad felt better as soon as he said it, but then realized that his outbursts weren't going to get him anywhere. "Alright, alright," he said, "what we have to do now is regroup. I've got to deconstruct this accident-waiting-to-happen before it actually takes place. Has the Colonel called you?" he asked.

"Do you think he will?" John sounded a bit nervous.

"John, of course he will. You've fucked this whole thing up. I don't know how you could have gotten the timing sequence off, but you're going to hear from him. Trust me. I'll make sure of it."

"Gee, thanks, Chad. You're all heart."

"Don't mention it, John. Anything to help a fellow aviator."

"Go fuck off, Chad."

CHAPTER 34

WATERTOWN, NEW YORK
8:30 P.M., SATURDAY, MAY 24

After having spent the morning with Deirdre and Wayne, Tina had been absolutely exhausted, especially since her sleep had been interrupted by Frank in the early morning hours. She ran a few errands that couldn't be put off and then went home and took a short nap, lying on the couch in her living room.

When she awoke around 3 p.m., slightly groggy and with a parched throat, she got up, drank some orange juice, stared at the television set for about five minutes, and then decided to go for a drive. Tina loved the area around Fort Drum—the St. Lawrence River, the Thousand Islands, Sacketts Harbor, Cape Vincent, and especially the Adirondacks. She decided to cross the bridge into Canada and take a spin through the beautifully restored Victorian homes in the resort areas lining the river. The grace and dignity of those old homes always helped to bring a measure of peace to her soul, especially the quietude of the streets that she drove up and down as she looked at the wide porches and gingerbread trim and vivid colors.

By the time she returned home several hours later, Tina had managed to calm herself considerably, enough to be able to go out to dinner with some friends and think about something other than Crystal. When she got home that evening, however, she decided to call Frank to talk some more about his disturbing allegations. Deirdre and Wayne had urged her to get as much information from him as possible before she took any other steps. As they pointed out, she had been talking to a complete drunk, and, in his state of inebriation, he most likely could have been making baseless claims with no facts to back him up.

Dialing Frank's number in Hawaii, Tina took a deep breath.

After about five rings, a click came on the line, and Frank's voice said, "Hey. This is me. I'm on emergency leave for thirty days. Don't leave a message. You'll fill my box."

Tina looked down at her handset astounded. Between midnight and 4 p.m., Frank had gotten word about an emergency and was already gone? This was too strange. Having been in the military, Tina knew it happened, but still, it didn't usually happen that fast. Especially when someone lived overseas. Especially on a weekend. Especially when someone had been drunk the night before and presumably woke up with a serious hangover. Well, maybe not, since he was accustomed to it.

Slowly hanging up the phone, Tina sat down on an ottoman. She wouldn't be able to talk to Frank now for thirty days.

CHAPTER 35

FORT RUCKER, ALABAMA
4:35 A.M., SUNDAY, MAY 25

"Sir, what are we supposed to do now? John went off like a cowboy, all cock-eyed, and has thrown our whole plan out of kilter."

Buehlankamp sat in his buttery leather chair, chewing on his cigar. "Chad, my boy, I understand you're a bit riled. But remember, son, flexibility is the key. In this mission, as in all things, we have to be ready to roll with the punches."

"You can't approve of John stepping out of line like that, Colonel! Surely not!" Chad's incensed tone came through the long telephone line clearly.

"Sometimes, Chad, overstepping boundaries has to be overlooked when achieving the ends is what matters. And you must agree, dear boy, that the end result is what we all wanted, now don't you?" Buehlankamp took a long sip of the scotch-and-water at his side and continued. "John saw an excellent opportunity that might not have presented itself again for a long time. Yes, it was a hazardous risk, and, yes, it could have played devilishly against our hand. But we can correct what's in motion up in your neck of the woods. Can't we, Chad? You can undo what you've done."

A bit sullenly, Chad said, "Yes, I suppose so. I just don't like a renegade running amok. It smacks of unprofessionalism and everything unmilitary."

"Yes, yes, Chad. Well, you'll have your chance to run your show, but the important thing is, we're getting these women out of the helicopter, aren't we? Isn't that our main goal? We're planting in the minds of their colleagues and others that perhaps female aviators shouldn't be flying. I can tell you for a fact that here at Fort Rucker the plan is going swimmingly."

"Is it really?"

"Oh, yes. You've seen the papers, haven't you? Young women being set back in droves because of their poor training records or washed out of flight school altogether. Men are up in arms about having to fly with them. Their families are nervous for them. Congress has been besieged to provide explanations. In fact, as I understand it, General Eckling's going to have to suffer a congressional investigation sometime in the near future. The previous commanding general, as I told him, allowed women to graduate under the guise of political correctness. They weren't equipped to graduate and their records were altered to pretend they were good pilots."

"And that's exactly one of the reasons why we have to get rid of them."

"Exactly so, son. It's a blot on Army aviation. Because of all the feminists running around out there, we have to do it surreptitiously. But we're simply correcting a wrong that shouldn't have been allowed to happen in the first place."

"You don't have to convince me, Colonel," Chad said fervently. "I've been with you since Day One, and I'll be with you to the end."

"I know that, Chad. I know I can count on you. Now, we need to figure out when the best time for your little action is going to be."

After hanging up with Chad, Buehlankamp called John, who was understandably a bit nervous when he heard who was on the other end of the line. "John, John, calm down, it's only me," Buehlankamp said.

"Yes, sir. Well, sir, Chad told me you'd be very upset with me, sir." John sat on the edge of his couch and twirled the coiled telephone line around his index finger.

"Actually, John, I'm rather pleased that you took the initiative to seize the moment."

"You are, sir?" John straightened his back and preened slightly.

"Yes, it takes some of the pressure off of the other operations. And I have to say, John, it was extraordinarily clever to come across an opportunity in which friendly fire could be found to be the culprit."

"I know I should have talked it over with you first, sir, but with the time difference and all—"

"Say no more, my boy. I'm sure you only had a few split seconds of time to decide."

Buehlankamp waited for John to agree that was true. When he didn't, Buehlankamp was convinced that John had made his decision in sufficient time to have informed his superior, but for some unfathomable reason, decided not to do so. "Or perhaps, John, you were just a tiny bit afraid that I might veto your plans? Is that it, John? Since we already had Chad's operation underway?"

John was silent for a moment. "Everything was lined up perfectly, Colonel, and I knew it was going to work. I know it was wrong of me, but I operated under the principle of act now and ask for forgiveness later."

"You're entirely forgiven, John, under the circumstances. After all, look at the results. I'm practically giddy! Now, tell me how it all came about. I want every detail."

For the next fifteen minutes, John explained to Colonel Buehlankamp how he had set the so-called friendly-fire helicopter accident in motion. By the time they got off the phone, Buehlankamp was in great spirits and extremely congratulatory.

"Well done, my boy! Well done! If something like this comes up again, though, I want to know about it beforehand and not afterwards."

"Yes, sir. You have my word."

CHAPTER 36

ENTERPRISE, ALABAMA
11:45 P.M., SATURDAY, MAY 24

After breaking into the training records room, Iris Tucker sat in her apartment in Enterprise, just outside of Fort Rucker, with several friends, trying to figure out her next course of action. First Lieutenant Mary Ann Tate had already been set back, and had quietly, albeit resentfully, accepted her situation, while Second Lieutenant Samantha Ellison was in the class behind Iris, and was supposed to be set back. One of the lucky ones who hadn't been tapped was First Lieutenant Tatum Richards.

After Iris told them all about her break-in, they applauded her verve and exclaimed how they would have been her apprentices had they only known.

"Girl, I would have boosted you up on my shoulders and thrown you in that room!" Tatum exclaimed.

"I wish I'd thought of this," Mary Ann said wistfully.

"Well, I still don't have a solution. If I don't think of what to do, I'm set back Monday morning and my stealth attack doesn't mean a thing," Iris pointed out.

All eyes dropped to the folder in the middle of the coffee table. Tatum exclaimed, "I think this calls for another bold action. Just take out the pink slips, go to your old class, hand them your folder, and dare them to set you back."

Samantha demurred. "I don't think that's going to work. They're going to claim she took the pink slips out. Which she would have done. We have to come up with something better than that."

"Well," Tatum said, "you'd want to make a copy of everything in your folder before you handed it over, pink slips and all, just in case."

"Just in case of what?"

"I don't know. In case they're trying to pull something over on you."

Mary Ann interjected, "Maybe they are."

"What do you mean?" Tatum asked.

"Do any of us remember getting all of these pink slips?" Each of the girls shook their heads. The others had also gone to see their files and, although they hadn't been as fortunate as Iris in being able to claim zero pink slips, they were astonished to see a far greater number in their files than they remembered receiving.

"The question we all have is—how did they get there? What if someone is trying to frame us?" Mary Ann said excitedly.

"Why would anyone try to do that?" Samantha asked.

"I don't know. That really doesn't concern us right now, does it? We just want to stay with our classes and we need to prove we didn't get those pink slips, or at least not all of the ones they say we did. So, how can we do that? We need to take the ones we have, and get someone to examine them. What do you think?" Mary Ann looked around anxiously at the others.

Tatum jumped up and hugged Mary Ann. "Brilliant!! That's it! That's exactly it! It must be a forgery! Someone's been forging pink slips. Or maybe lots of people have been forging them."

"But how will we find out?" Samantha asked. "Wouldn't we have to have instructors' writings to compare them to?"

"Maybe, but I would think the most important thing, and the easiest way would be to prove that we didn't sign the pink slips," Mary Ann said with a triumphant grin.

Now Iris got up and gave Mary Ann a hug, and soon all the women were jumping up and down and hugging each other with glee.

"All we have to do is find a handwriting expert," Tatum said.

"Before Monday," Iris pleaded.

"That really isn't necessary," Tatum explained. "You see, you can go to the company commander and tell him you believe the pink slips were forged, you have them in your possession, and are turning them over to the proper authorities for authentication. He has to let you return to your class."

"You think so?" Iris asked.

"I'm sure of it," Tatum said. The other girls nodded.

"It has a ring of success to it," Iris said, "but I don't know if I'm that comfortable with the idea."

Mary Ann interjected, "I think it would work best if you had already turned your pink slips over to a handwriting analysis expert before you went to the company commander."

"How can she do that?" Samantha asked. "This is already Saturday night, and she's supposed to report to her new class Monday morning."

"I'm going to call my dad and see if he can help me out," Iris said. "How about you, Samantha? Do you want to go back to the training room tonight to get your record and do the same thing?"

Samantha grinned. "You bet."

Tatum and Mary Ann howled, "Not without us!"

CHAPTER 37

WATERTOWN, NEW YORK
10:45 A.M., SUNDAY, MAY 25

After a sleepless night and restless morning, Tina again dropped by Deirdre and Wayne's house.

"He's gone on emergency leave, Deirdre," Tina said as she burst into their house.

"Who?" Deirdre said, cuddling the baby, who had been up since 4 a.m. with a cold that had begun sometime in the middle of the night. As much as Deirdre loved Tina and sympathized with her problems, she and Wayne hadn't gotten much sleep and were worried about Zach. With their house currently in disarray, dishes not washed, showers not taken, and a baby in distress, Deirdre felt a bit irritated at the presumption that she could drop everything and deal with Tina's life. Wayne was trying to catch a catnap and, later on, it would be Deirdre's turn, but for now, she was walking around in her houserobe and tending to a warm baby who didn't want to suckle. Normally placid and empathetic, Deirdre had enough to take care of at the moment in her own household. Nevertheless, Tina was a dear friend, so Deirdre sighed inwardly, shifted Zach more comfortably onto her hip, and wiped his nose softly with a tissue. With luck the medicine she'd given him a little while ago would take effect and he would soon fall asleep.

"Frank! I called him last night and he's left a message on his machine that he's gone on emergency leave for thirty days! Now

I can't even reach him to find out anything more about his cockamamie story," Tina exclaimed.

"So call his family," Deirdre tiredly said, looking down at Zach.

"What?"

"His family. His mom. Don't you have her number?"

Tina appeared to be stopped in her tracks for a moment. "No, but Crystal's things were sent to me, and I bet her address book is in there. I'm sure she had it."

"That's the most logical place to call, isn't it?" Deirdre finally looked up at Tina, trying valiantly to keep the impatience off of her face and out of her voice.

Tina left shortly thereafter and whipped through the few boxes of Crystal's possessions that had arrived from Germany. She had stored them in the basement and hadn't looked at them other than to stack them neatly one on top of the other. Now she quickly and methodically tore into the detritus of Crystal's life, trying like hell to do so without emotion as she came across jewelry that had once been their mother's, a perfume bottle that had sat on a grandmother's dresser, photos of Crystal in Germany, audiotapes Frank had sent from Hawaii, letters to Crystal from friends, plaques from military courses Crystal had attended, gifts Tina had sent her sister, Crystal's collection of rock music, a notebook of poems Crystal had written in high school, Frank and Crystal's wedding album, and much more. It was all Tina could do to set everything aside and not pore over it—to keep searching for an address book. After a couple of hours and into the fourth box, she found the address book, but there was no entry for Frank's parents. Crystal had apparently started this address book sometime after the marriage dissolved and felt no need to include her former in-laws in her future correspondence or phone calls.

Tina slumped on the basement floor. "Oh, hell's bells!" Within a few minutes she gathered herself together, went back upstairs, and sat down at the kitchen table with the phone, a piece of paper, and a pen. She found the area code for the Bronx and started dialing information, hoping to find the phone number for a Lambert living in that vast area. The problem was, she didn't know the name of the street or the parents' first names.

After an hour of what seemed like hopeless, useless phone calls to Lambert families in the Bronx who had no son named Frank and didn't know anyone named Frank, a bright light finally occurred to Tina. She ran back down to the basement, grabbed the wedding album and rushed back up the stairs to the kitchen. Turning the pages, she searched quickly for anyone who could conceivably be Frank's parents and, when she found them, found their names. Crystal had been very good about labeling her photos.

Alistair and Margaret Lambert still lived in the Bronx and, as it happened, were home that day. Once Tina knew their names, it only took seconds to obtain their phone number.

"Hello? Mrs. Lambert? This is Tina, Crystal's sister. I'm looking for Frank. I understand he's come home on emergency leave. I wonder if I could speak to him."

"Crystal? Oh, dear. Tina, I'm so sorry about your sister. Did you get our card, dear? She was such a lovely girl. We were so sad to hear about it, even though we hadn't seen her in such a long time. We're just so sorry for you."

"Card? Yes, oh, yes, Mrs. Lambert, thank you." Tina realized now that she had had their address and names all along, tucked into the box of condolence cards in her office, if she'd only been thinking.

"I'm calling about Frank, Mrs. Lambert. Is he there?"

"Frank? No, dear. He's in Hawaii," Mrs. Lambert said patiently.

"I thought he was coming home on emergency leave."

"No, there's nothing wrong here. We're all in tip-top shape, aren't we, Alistair?" Margaret tinkled merrily. "Knock on wood."

"So, he isn't coming home then," Tina said in a wooden voice.

"No, dear. Why don't you call him in Hawaii? Do you have his number there? I'd be glad to give it to you. Just let me grab my address book."

"I've got it, Mrs. Lambert. Thank you," Tina said tiredly.

Tina hung up. Son of a bitch, Tina thought. What the hell is going on?

CHAPTER 38

FORT WAINWRIGHT, ALASKA
9:20 A.M., SUNDAY, MAY 25

"Iris, sugar, please don't tell me you really did that!" General Tucker was appalled. His daughter had just related to him the escapades of the night before, both her entry into the records room and her encounter with Lieutenant Colonel Brannon, and then her subsequent return with her accomplices. With lookouts posted on the front and back of the building, they had managed to obtain the training records of every single female they knew who had been set back or washed out of flight school in the recent uproar, amounting to twelve of the seventeen women the school had decided didn't measure up.

"Dad, I'm sorry, but we couldn't think of anything else to do."

"You were the instigator, Iris!"

"Well, that's true, but I warned you I had to do something before Monday."

"Oh, honey, this is tampering with government records. Breaking and entering. I understand your motivation, but I can't in good conscience—"

"Dad, give it a rest, would you, please? I don't need your general-speak now. I need you to be my dad."

General Tucker sighed. Iris could wrap him around his little finger and then some. His wife, God rest her soul, had died when Iris was two years old, and they had had no other children. Even before Sylvia had lost her battle with breast cancer, Sherman had become enraptured with the delight that the tiny baby and then the little toddler had brought into his life. Although his soldiers always perceived him as a gruff, tough infantry officer, his heart melted completely at the sight of his little girl's blond curls and green eyes. Whenever he walked in at the end of the day, she cooed endlessly as an infant to get his attention, and, later, she toddled over to the door and cried "Da-da!" When Sylvia died, Sherman thought his heart would break, but each time he looked at Iris, he knew that Sylvia lived on in their child and that he had been given the most solemn of responsibilities and the greatest of joys to be her father.

The tiny Tucker family moved around from post to post, and, as the years flew by, Sherman grew in stature in the Army. Iris adored her father, and the adoration was mutual. Regardless of his military duties, Sherman always took time out to attend her softball games, soccer games, school plays, concerts, and, of course, he had to be mom and dad. Sherman's single parenthood helped him in later years to understand the conflicting demands of military and family once female service members were allowed to have children and stay in the military.

"Alright, Iris, what do you think you can do with these files you now have in your possession?" General Tucker asked with resignation.

"What we were thinking is that we need to have a handwriting analysis expert take a look at our signatures and verify that we, the women students, didn't sign these pink slips."

"I suppose that sounds reasonable."

"Do you know anyone?"

"Anyone what?" Her father was startled.

"Any handwriting experts?"

"Oh, Iris! Please don't get me involved in this."

"Dad! You have to know somebody. You're a general, for pete's sake!" Iris exclaimed.

"I thought you weren't talking to me as a general," he muttered.

"Okay, forget that, now I am."

"Iris, you drive me crazy."

"I know, I know, but you love me anyway. But who can we get to look at these pink slips, Dad? Don't hold out on us. Pretty please?"

The magic words. Iris had always used them to get what she wanted. She knew it and he knew it. Here he was, a general in the United States Army and his daughter could still manipulate him like putty.

"Okay, it isn't going to be easy. I'll have to make a couple of phone calls. The person I have in mind lives in Jacksonville, Florida."

"I'll drive there today. Can you call now? I have to get this done so that I can be back for class tomorrow morning."

"I'll try. She owes me a couple of favors."

"Thanks, Dad. You're a peach! Love ya!" Iris blew her dad a couple of kisses and hung up the phone. General Tucker smiled with a grimace and then prepared to make phone calls on his daughter's behalf.

CHAPTER 39

WOLFGANG KASERNE, WEST GERMANY
9:25 A.M., MONDAY, MAY 26

Major Damrow was utterly perplexed. Hauptmann Karl Gunter had just called and announced that he needed to chat with him, but asked if they could meet outside the post.

"I'm up to my eyeballs right now, Gunter," Damrow had said in an irritated tone.

"Ja. That's understandable. Always on a Monday morning. But this is extremely important. And I shouldn't have waited so long."

"What's it about?" Damrow asked impatiently.

"I need to talk to you about that helicopter accident."

"I can't tell you much more than was in the accident report."

"Ach, ja. Well, the thing is, Herr Major, I have something to tell you."

"Can't you tell me now?"

"I'd rather not." The two men were silent while Damrow pondered what information Gunter could possibly have of significance to tell him.

Damrow sighed and said, "How about lunch? Could we do this over lunch?"

"As you wish. I often skip lunch anyway and this would be a good way to—how do you say—kill two birds with one rock?"

"With one stone."

"What?"

"Kill two birds with one stone, not rock."

"Oh, danke sehr. I'm most grateful. I'm always trying to improve my English," Gunter said.

"Your English sounds great to me," Damrow acknowledged a bit testily.

"Is there a restaurant around your post you'd like to meet at?" Gunter asked. "I can be there at noon, if that would work."

A couple of hours later, Damrow arrived at the gaststube on the edge of town. He felt a bit uncomfortable wearing his Army flight suit and combat boots into a crowd of convivial Germans, who stopped their lunchtime boozing and eating to stare at him as he looked around for the person he remembered from the accident site. Gunter, however, was already seated in a booth, looking towards the door, and waved at him. Both men looked strikingly similar—tall, slim, blond, chiseled features—as if brothers from different nations and different, but similar, professions were sitting together. As was his nature, Gunter played with the beer coasters after they placed their orders, while Damrow remained relatively still and poised.

"I presume your XO told you my suspicions about the accident," Gunter began.

Damrow narrowed his eyes, but said nothing.

Gunter looked up at Damrow sharply. "Frau Hauptmann did say something to you, didn't she? I expressly asked her to convey my message to you."

By very briefly shaking his head, Damrow managed to show that she had not done so. Gunter could tell that Damrow was not going to divulge any more than that and show disloyalty to his XO before he obtained any more information. It was no more than Gunter would do for Marthe.

Spreading his palms upward in the air, Gunter said, "Let me start then at the beginning." He explained how he had called the company, urged Erika to come to the polizei station, and told her his suspicions.

"I had very good reason to believe that your helicopter had been sabotaged by an explosive timing device, but I didn't have the proof. Frau Hauptmann, good Army officer that she is, refused to believe me without any evidence. She did agree, however, to tell you about our meeting and my suspicions. In the meantime, my assistant, who is a scuba diver, has scoured the Eisel River where the car went into the water and was unable to find the timing device. It was truly an unlikely event that we would be able to find it, but it was worth a try. Now that we've given it the last effort, I had to come and tell you what I know."

"Why have you come to me?" Damrow asked. "Why didn't you go to the military police?"

"I suppose," Gunter said, "it's because I think the accident report is crooked. And because those were your people who died. Someone is trying to cover up that they were killed. That's what I think. I don't know who is trying to cover it up. Whoever wrote the report, maybe. Whoever signed off on it. Whoever ordered it. Whoever ordered the helicopter sabotaged. Frankly, Herr Major, you're even a suspect in my book."

Damrow whitened with anger and nearly jumped off the booth seat to leap over the table at Gunter.

"But, Herr Major, I don't see you as a suspect because I saw you at the accident site that day, and no one could have faked the true loss you felt when those women died. So, no, I don't believe you're involved. And I've been fighting crime for a long time. Every now and then, I've been fooled, but I don't think you're fooling me. You're not the one."

Calmed as a result of Gunter's words, Damrow sat back in his seat. The waitress brought their platters of food just then, and both men busied themselves with forks and knives and napkins.

Gunter continued. "Since I'm convinced you're not involved, and I have no idea who is involved, that's why I had to tell you. Besides that, I knew you would want to find out the truth, and to bring justice for your young women. That is what any commander would want to do. Isn't it?"

Their eyes locked, and Damrow nodded. "This is pretty hard for me to get my mind around at the moment," he said. "The accident report said pilot error, which is normal. So, first I have to try and comprehend who would have been behind manipulating a false report. It's inscrutable to me. I also can't understand why my XO didn't breathe a word of her visit to me. I certainly would have thought she would have felt some camaraderie with the female victims, being a woman and all, and that she would have been outraged."

"She was outraged, ja, but as an Army officer, that I was making this accusation."

"So," Damrow said, "where do we go from here?"

"I'll help you all I can," Gunter said. "I have no idea how much more help I could possibly be, but if you need me, all you have to do is ask."

CHAPTER 40

FORT RUCKER, ALABAMA
7:05 A.M., MONDAY, MAY 25

"Sir, I'm not going to allow myself to be set back to another class," Iris announced to the company commander on Monday morning.

Captain Walt Gibson leaned back in his gray swivel chair and put his left hand on his gray metal desk and his pencil behind his right ear. Not for him the luxuriously appointed office. His walls were basically bare, except for a paper calendar issued by the government turned to the previous month and a cheaply framed photo of a Revolutionary soldier in military garb, standing with musket at the ready.

"I beg your pardon, Lieutenant—?"

"Tucker, sir."

"Would you like to tell me what this is all about?"

"I have reason to believe my training records have been forged, sir."

"I beg your pardon?"

"And I refuse to be set back until I ascertain that is not the case."

"What in the world are you talking about, Lieutenant?"

"I never received so much as a single pink slip in the entire time I've been here at flight school. Somehow, my training records now have pink slips in there with my signature on them. I think someone has forged my name and I'm going to find out."

"And how are you going to do that?"

"I've handed over the pink slips to an investigator."

"You've what?" Captain Gibson jumped out of his chair. "To whom? How did you get them?"

"Sir, I refuse to answer those questions. I'll have the results shortly. If the investigator somehow says it's my signature, which I doubt, then I'll go to a new class. Until then, I demand to be reinstated to my old class."

"Or what? You can't make demands here, Lieutenant. This is the Army. Or have you forgotten that?"

"Sir, I grew up in the Army. Or have you forgotten that?" Iris's eyes bored into the captain. Upon arrival at Fort Rucker, every new student had to fill out a card informing the administration whether or not they were related to a general officer, so it was common knowledge that Lieutenant Tucker was a general's daughter. Gibson hadn't known Iris by sight, but he certainly knew her by name. He had cringed at Eckling's demand to set back or wash out anyone, no matter their connections, especially when Iris's name popped up. But orders were orders.

"You're under orders to report to a new class, Lieutenant Tucker."

"I haven't seen them."

"I'm giving you verbal orders."

"I'm considering them illegal. I'm showing up to my old class, and you can have the MPs haul me out of there bodily if you want to. That's the only way you'll get me out of the class. In addition, I have press releases ready to go to *The Washington Post*, *The New York Times*, and *The LA Times* the instant I'm pulled out of the class. An anonymous source will be sure they're sent." Iris smiled brightly. "Sir?"

"You think just because your father's a general you can pull rank like this?" Gibson asked bitterly.

"My father has nothing to do with this," Iris said calmly. "And you can make your own decisions, just as I'm doing. I'm asking you to do the decent thing, to let me go back to my class, while I try to resolve what I believe is some kind of smear campaign against my reputation. I don't know why and I don't know how. If you won't do it of your own free will, then I have my back-up plan, that's all I'm saying."

"Alright, Lieutenant Tucker. I'll give you one week. After this week is over, you better have some proof. If you don't, you're out on your ass, because my goose will be cooked. I don't like being threatened, but you've left me no choice. I'm doing it for the good of the school, not necessarily because I believe you, do you understand me?"

Smiling thinly, Iris replied, "Yes, sir. It doesn't matter why. I appreciate it anyway. Thank you."

Iris left in a rush, afraid he would change his mind and hurried to the building a few blocks away where her old flight class was scheduled to meet. Although her fellow students were startled to see her, they easily accepted the explanation that she'd been given a second chance after pleading her case. After they had all exchanged a few hearty back slaps and hellos, the instructor walked in and the class settled down to instrument training.

CHAPTER 41

WOLFGANG KASERNE, WEST GERMANY
2:55 P.M., MONDAY, MAY 26

Damrow drove back to the Kaserne weighing all of his options. Each time he thought about Erika Stohlmann, he felt incensed that she had kept information from him, and then, just as swiftly, he regretted thinking that this highly competent and capable officer could have done such a thing.

As soon as he returned to his office, Damrow called Erika in for a conversation.

"Close the door, Captain Stohlmann," he said calmly. "Have a seat."

Erika slipped into the gray padded chair in front of his desk where she often sat when they had their conversations and made herself comfortable. Without preamble, Damrow asked, "When were you going to tell me about your trip to Etlingen?"

Color began to inflame her face. "Sir—" she started to say.

"Erika, I'm very disappointed. I just met with Hauptmann Gunter and he presented me with an extremely disturbing story. But before I even get into that, what distresses me as well is that he tells me you went out there to talk to him, on my behalf, and promised you would convey certain information to me, but failed to do so. Is that correct?"

Simply by looking at her, Damrow could see that Gunter had been telling the truth. "Erika, you're my XO, for God's sake! I trust you to run this company when I'm not here. You can't meet with German officials, representing me and this unit, and then not let me know what the outcomes of those meetings are."

Erika lowered her eyes, and the reddening warmth crept down her neck, as visible to Damrow as it felt to Erika. "I'm sorry, sir," she uttered quietly.

"Why didn't you tell me, Erika?"

"I just … It just … It just seemed too preposterous, sir." Straightening her shoulders, Erika raised her eyes and challenged Damrow to disagree with her.

"I understand your feelings, Erika. Yes, it does seem rather out there. I agree with you. But we can't take allegations of sabotage lightly. And I'm the company commander. I have to know about things like this. When a law enforcement officer of our host nation has taken the time and trouble to tell us that he believes our own Army has sabotaged one of our helicopters, I have to take that seriously. I cannot afford to stand on principle and loyalty and stick my head in the sand and say it can't be. This is too serious and too delicate."

"Yes, sir."

"I just can't believe that you decided on your own, Erika, to keep this information to yourself. How am I going to trust you again in the future to carry out responsibilities for me?"

"Sir, I truly thought I was acting in the best interests of the unit and the Army."

Gently, Damrow said, "I know that, Erika. But you weren't exercising mature judgment. You have to look at the bigger picture. Now, I have lives at stake here. If there is someone who sabotaged that helicopter, then I need to know who, and I need to stop them. If someone falsified the investigation report, then that has to be found out, too. And this is going to be a very risky business, knowing whom to trust. Do you get my drift?"

"Yes, sir. I'm so sorry, sir. It's just that I've been taught that the Army is always right."

"Welcome to the real world, Erika. I think you've just grown up. Now, can I trust you to help me in this? I know I can trust Gunter, because the Germans had nothing to do with the report. So far, I don't know exactly what avenues to take, but Gunter's going to help all he can. I think I want to avoid the official Army as much as possible because I don't know who all is involved. Because of your refusal to inform me, one might think I should suspect you—"

"Oh, no, sir! I didn't have anything to do with it!"

Damrow smiled. "I know, Erika. You wouldn't hurt a flea. Your problem is you're too tied to the rules most of the time. I couldn't imagine you going outside of the rules. That's why it was such a huge surprise that you didn't tell me about your meeting with Gunter. But I also could understand how loyalty to the Army could trump the idea that someone in the Army would kill their own."

"Yes, sir."

"Okay, Erika. You can get that hangdog expression off your face now. We're partners again. Get back to work. I'll let you know what happens."

Erika gave Damrow a tremulous smile, and, opening the door to his office, slipped across the hallway to her own and tried to concentrate on her paperwork. She felt rather ashamed that her boss had, for the first time, expressed disappointment in her. Although she made a point of never crying in front of others in the Army, now that she was in her private office, a few tears slid down her cheeks while thinking of how she had let Damrow down. Vowing not to do so again in the future, Erika wiped the tears away slowly, cupped her face in her hands for a few moments, and then, finally, turned to the work at hand.

CHAPTER 42

FAIRBANKS, ALASKA
10:35 P.M., SUNDAY, MAY 25

Snowstorms in Alaska were not uncommon at any time of year, but this one at the end of May was a monster. Beginning early on Sunday morning, before dawn broke, the huge, soft, wet flakes that drifted slowly down from the dark sky fell onto peoples' lawns, their cars, their fences, their backyard toys and grills, and, of course, all the roads. Throughout the day, children delighted in being able to play in the snow, which continued to fall heavily without stopping and built up to several feet by nightfall. The quiet gloominess cast over Fairbanks and Fort Wainwright created a lethargy that kept most grownups indoors, beside their flickering television sets and blazing fireplaces, to create the warmth they couldn't find outside.

One person, however, had intended to go out, but found himself stuck at home because of the road conditions. The snowplows had to wait to get to Chad Emerson's secondary road until most of the snow had fallen, and it was still coming down late Sunday evening. Chad felt rather impatient, as he knew he needed to get to the maintenance hangar to undo what he had done to Vanessa's helicopter. There was no way he could let her go up on Monday morning to test-fly that aircraft after the crash in Korea on Friday. It would be too suspect. The timing was too close. Even though he was certain that nothing could be traced back to him, he didn't want any fingers of suspicion lurking about and certainly no questions arising. There needed to be a proper sequencing about these things and because of John's rush—even though Chad grudgingly had to admit his mission was a success—Chad's operation was going to have to wait.

Not being able to get out to the post was making Chad anxious, however, especially since Vanessa's ARL exam was scheduled for the morning. Chad stood in front of his living room window and watched the snow fall, and fall, and fall. There was nothing he could do about it. He lived ten miles from the post. He couldn't walk there if he tried. Most likely, however, the post would be closed the next day, and Vanessa's flying exam canceled. Focusing his mind on that possibility, Chad was able to breathe a bit easier.

In the morning, the snow was still coming down. The post was closed except for all emergency personnel, which did not include Chad. Now he just had to concern himself with how and when he could access the helicopter once the snow quit. It wouldn't do to show up during daylight hours when maintenance personnel were around. He could only attempt to touch the helicopter and do what he had to at night once everyone had left work. *Damn it!* he thought. Waiting out the weather put him on edge. For most of the day, Chad sullenly sat in his recliner, flipping through channels on the television and alternately looking out at the constantly falling snow, sipping away at a whiskey-and-Coke. By the time he went to bed, the snow had finally stopped, but a good six feet of snow had piled up in the parking lot, and Chad knew he wouldn't be leaving his apartment the next day, either.

CHAPTER 43

CAMP VANGCHON, SOUTH KOREA
5:10 P.M., MONDAY, MAY 26

Frank got off the plane at Kimpo International Airport in Seoul and, although he'd never been to Korea before, scarcely looked around. He was single-mindedly focused on his newly hatched plan. Walking briskly into the terminal with his carry-on bag, he quickly passed through customs and grabbed a taxi. After arranging for a cheap hotel room in the environs of Seoul, Frank paid the taxi driver to drive him to the outskirts of Camp Vangchon, twenty miles to the east, where the 92nd Aviation Company was located.

After the taxi driver let him off near the front gate, Frank sat inside a crowded, noisy bar, squeezed on all sides by people intent on having a good time—Koreans, Americans, customers, prostitutes, military, civilians—he found himself nearly shoved into the street through the open window while sitting on a bar stool downing a couple of beers. The cacophony of sounds from inside the bar combined with that of the other bars on the street to completely overwhelm the senses. Being so close to June, the temperature was nearly unbearable. Frank could feel the sweat dripping down his back as the heat rose in the room with bodies pressed so closely together. The thick make-up worn by the Korean women made him uncomfortable with the sheen of bright rouge and red lipstick. He could feel the women's skin pores being clogged, screaming for air, and he tugged at his own collar and loosened it in response.

Food smells caused a tightening in his stomach. He hadn't eaten since he left Hawaii, but he didn't know what he dared to eat on this street—what would be safe. Roasted chicken filled the air, along with a pungent smell that he knew could only be the famous kimchee. He could see a number of stalls on the street outside the bar at which old shriveled men and women sold their wares from mobile kitchens, but Frank knew he'd rather starve than buy something from one of them. Back in his Vietnam days, he'd been able to eat food off the carts, but he'd paid a price, and it had been a long time since then. His body was now used to more conventional fare. Plus he had a job to do and couldn't afford the gastrointestinal consequences that might come with giving in to hunger pains.

Frank had left in such a rush that he hadn't really thought his plan out very well. He had merely decided to go to Korea first, because it was the first flight he could get out of Hawaii. Now he had to figure out how to carry through his plan since he was here.

After about an hour, Frank drained the last of a third beer, and shoved himself off the stool. He showed his identification card to the gate guard and walked on post. Briefly eyeing the post map board to see where the officers' quarters were, Frank then headed in that direction. The building had a worn front door with a corroded metal strip, propped open with a red brick. Frank easily let himself in. The officers' names were all listed on a registry on an inside wall, and Frank quickly vaulted up three flights of stairs to John Datterly's room at the end of the corridor. No one had seen him come in and no one was in the corridor. Frank slipped a credit card between the door and the door jam, and the door popped open. Easy as pie.

The apartment was similar to many other bachelor officers' quarters—small rooms, functional—living room, bedroom, kitchen, and bathroom, furnished with drab government pieces.

Datterly wasn't the neatest person, Frank noted, but then, neither was Frank, so he wasn't judging. A few clothes were strewn over a chair in the bedroom, newspapers and books were piled on the couch in the living room, several unwashed glasses sat on the coffee table, and a number of dishes remained dirty in the sink. It seemed pretty much like a normal bachelor's pad—a single guy who went off to work in the morning, came back in the evening, and didn't much care what his surroundings looked like.

Frank swept the clothes off the bedroom chair and sat down to wait for John's return.

CHAPTER 44

FORT RUCKER, ALABAMA
6:35 A.M., TUESDAY, MAY 27

"So tell me again what you saw in those girls' files, Bill. The ones killed in Korea," General Eckling said abruptly. Brannon had been sifting through early morning paperwork at his desk, drinking his second cup of coffee of the day when Eckling had arrived, trailing an aura of discontent through the hallway and into the large reception area in which Brannon's desk and Eckling's secretary's desk were located. Eckling marched into his grandiose office to the right of where Brannon sat, while Milly, Eckling's secretary, scurried to fix his morning cup of hot water and lemon. Milly placed the fragrant, steaming cup on Eckling's sideboard, along with a vanilla wafer, his favorite treat, and then, glancing pityingly at Brannon, glided out of the room and quickly shut the door behind her.

"Well, sir, as I mentioned yesterday, there didn't seem to be anything significant about either of the pilots in their records. Stella Rodriquez, the new pilot in country, was a fairly average student here. She held her own in every phase, although she seemed to be a bit over her head in the instrument portion of the course, but nothing to be overly concerned about. The pilot-in-command, Charlotte Driver, was above average, but not in a particularly exceptional way. Nothing that really stood out. There were no red flags about either one, nothing that would indicate that either one had problems with flying or being in the course."

"In other words, Bill, what you're telling me is that these young ladies graduated from Mother Rucker honestly and as they should have."

"It seems very clear to me, sir," Brannon affirmed. "Besides that, if I may, sir—" Brannon paused for a moment. Eckling frowned. Brannon knew he was on shaky ground. His boss didn't appreciate frank opinions, only the bare facts, and those only when he asked for them.

"Yes, Bill?" Eckling's voice had an edge of frostiness to it that Brannon was quite familiar with, but he rolled on.

"I don't understand at all what their training records have to do with their deaths. The accident was friendly fire. That was admitted immediately by the artillery unit."

"Because, Bill," Eckling now exhibited a level of patience that one would have used with a four-year-old or someone of limited intelligence. "If these female pilots had in any way not been properly trained or somehow had been improperly granted their aviator wings, then is it not conceivable that they might have been in the demilitarized zone incorrectly? I maintain that it might very well be their fault that they were in the wrong place, hence giving our ADA unit the mistaken impression that a North Korean aircraft was coming across the border. Since I am responsible for training all Army aviators, I believe it is incumbent upon me to determine what the training of these young women had been so that I can answer that question when it is posed to me, as it surely will be. Doesn't that make perfect sense to you?"

Brannon shrugged his shoulders and nodded. "When you put it that way, sir, then yes, I guess it does."

Eckling slapped Brannon on the back and laughed heartily. "I knew you'd see it my way, Bill! You're a man of great intelligence. So we can lay this matter to rest now and I have my answers for whoever may ask the questions."

CHAPTER 45

WATERTOWN, NEW YORK
6:45 A.M., TUESDAY, MAY 27

"Hello? Hello?"

"*Hallo? Ist jemand da?*"

"Don't hang up! Please!" Tina could hardly hear the person on the other end. "Is this the polizei station in Etlingen?" After making phone calls to the international operator all morning, Tina wasn't optimistic about her chances of reaching the tiny place she had visited in March.

"*Polizei? Ja. So sind wir.*" Oh, for a little German. Tina wished she could express herself in this language, but all she knew how to speak was English and she wasn't even particularly good at that.

"Does anyone there speak English?" Please, please understand me.

"*Ein moment, bitte.*" Silence on the other end for so long that Tina thought the line had gone dead.

Just when she was about to hang up, a voice said, "*Hallo,* may I help you, please?"

"Oh, thank you, thank you!" Tina cried. "Do you speak English?"

"Yes, I do. Not so well, perhaps, but we can try. What do you need?"

"This is Tina Loyola, I came to the station in March. My sister was killed in a helicopter crash—"

"Yes, Frau Loyola. I remember you very well. I took you around to the accident site. This is Polizeimeister Johannas."

"Oh, I'm so glad it's you!" Tina breathed a sigh of relief.

"How can I help you? This must be in relation to your sister's death, I am guessing."

"I've received some very disturbing information and I've been thinking it over for a couple of days. I just haven't known where else to turn."

"What kind of information?" Marthe probed.

"It's very delicate, and I don't know if it's even reliable. It was told to me in a drunken stupor by my sister's ex-husband and it's so outrageous, that I just can't even believe it. But the thing is, you see, I can't get it out of my head."

"What is it?"

"Before I tell you, I have to tell you also that I can't corroborate it. I've tried to get in touch with my ex-brother-in-law, but now he's disappeared, right after he made this wild accusation. I have no idea where he went, so I can't get any more details from him. All I know is just this one thing that he told me. And it's so crazy that I really feel ridiculous even mentioning it."

"I understand, Frau Loyola."

"But, if what he says is true, then I don't know where to go with the information. That's why I'm calling you, because the Germans are the least likely people to be involved."

"What do you mean?"

"What he said—" Tina hesitated, and Marthe could hear the visible break in her voice, "was that someone meant to kill my sister and that her accident was no accident. That it was a conspiracy."

"Frau Loyola, I probably shouldn't tell you this, but I would want to know if it were my sister. I think you may have just provided corroborating evidence."

"I don't understand," Tina said.

"There was a young boy here who said he found an explosive timing device at the accident site. Unfortunately, his father lost the timing device in the river and then the boy died tragically a few weeks later, so we don't have that evidence. We tried to recover it but have been unable to do so. My police captain attempted to tell the Americans that we suspected the helicopter had been sabotaged, but the executive officer didn't believe it was possible and apparently never informed her commander. Gunter just met with the company commander yesterday and told him what we knew. We don't know what the outcome of that is going to be. This information from you will go a long way, I think, in convincing the American commander that something has been covered up."

"How do I know he can be trusted?" Tina angrily demanded. "It was on his watch that my sister got killed. And the accident report said it was her fault. That's why I'm calling your office, because I don't trust the Army right now. And now that you're telling me that there really was sabotage, I don't want to have anything to do with the Army or anyone from her unit."

"Gunter, my boss, has a good feeling about him. He thinks that Herr Major isn't involved. As you say, though, that's just my boss's hunch. He could be wrong. I'll tell you, though, that Gunter usually isn't wrong about character assessment."

Tina said abruptly, "I'm coming over there."

"I beg your pardon?" Marthe asked.

"I want to come over there again, now that I know the whole situation has changed. I want to talk to you and your boss. It felt like total crap before, excuse my language, saying that the accident was Crystal's fault, and now that I know it wasn't, I need to explore everything again and figure out what happened."

"I don't know if that's such a good idea," Marthe countered. "There really isn't much you can do here without arousing suspicion."

"I can at least talk to you and your boss, can't I?" Tina asked. "And, if need be, I can make my own determination about Major

Damrow. I'd also like to find out who wrote the investigation report and figure out how that got by people. Maybe I could scour the accident site. Maybe there's something there that was missed. If a little boy found something there, maybe something else was missed."

Marthe softened. "Yes, I'm sure I would react exactly the same way."

"So, will you help me?"

"Yes. What else can I do?"

CHAPTER 46

CAMP VANGCHON, SOUTH KOREA
4:00 A.M., TUESDAY, MAY 27

Frank awoke with a start. He had fallen asleep despite his best intentions. The room was still dark, meaning that it wasn't yet morning outside, as best as he could tell. The heavy drapes hanging listlessly at the one window on the far bedroom wall obscured any light that might come through the opening, making the room as pitch-black as a tomb.

What had caused Frank to awaken was the sound of the door to the outdoor hallway slamming shut. He bolted upright, looked at his watch, and saw that it was 4 a.m., Korea time. What in the hell was someone doing coming home on a work night that late? Staying in his chair, Frank eased the kinks out of his neck and shoulders and listened intently to the noises in the other room. He heard the refrigerator door open and could see the chinks of light. John hadn't bothered to turn on any lights when he came in. This would make it even easier, Frank thought.

Just as Frank was preparing to stand up and accost his victim, he heard another voice say, "Come on, John, I haven't got all day." A woman was in the room. "You promised me a drink and then you know I've got to get back home and to beddy-bye. I go back on shift at seven. I have to get a couple of hours of sleep." The sultry voice sounded oddly familiar but Frank couldn't place it at the moment. At this point in time, he was only concerned about extricating himself from this delicate situation.

"I'm coming, hold your horses." Frank could hear John's voice moving across the room until he plopped down onto some furniture, presumably the couch. "There you go, drink up. I brought you a beer. Ice cold."

"Oh, honey. You know I prefer wine."

"Sorry, toots. It's all I have. And at this time of the morning, we can't exactly go out shopping, now can we?"

For the next few minutes, Frank didn't hear any more discussion and was quite certain that the couple was engaged in a more intimate form of conversation, considering the sounds emanating from the room. He began to wonder what he would do if they headed into the bedroom. With luck, they wouldn't turn on the light and he could ease out past them in their moment of passion. He would have to return to deal with John when he was alone.

No sooner had Frank begun to consider his options in this scenario, however, than the woman in question apparently decided it was time to leave. "Well, John, I've had a lovely evening, but I have to go now."

"Come on, honey, not yet." Frank could hear the pleading in John's voice.

"No, John, some other time. I told you I've got to go." The woman was obviously sitting up and straightening her clothes.

Irritation in his voice, John acquiesced. "Alright then, go ahead. See if I care."

"Come on, John, don't be like that. You knew I couldn't stay."

"Ah, get out of here." John was dismissive.

"See you later, John. Call me." The door opened and closed in a matter of seconds.

John sat in the living room for a few minutes longer, apparently finishing his beer, then trundled slowly into his bedroom. When John walked past the doorway, Frank tripped him onto the floor, dug his knee into John's back, quickly tied John's hands behind him, slapped duct tape over his mouth, tied his feet, and then handcuffed one of John's ankles to the bedpost.

Leaving John lying on his stomach on the floor, Frank said, "So, John, I've come a long way to deal with you. I couldn't believe what all of you did to my wife, but I didn't do anything about it. I just wallowed in my own grief. Then I heard about the other accident. Accident, my ass! I know who's behind it. Friendly fire. Bullshit! How many women are you going to kill, John? How many will be enough? What will it take to satisfy your bloodlust? You and your compadres? You don't deserve to be Army officers. Hell, you don't deserve to be Americans. And I'm here to take care of that. Do you hear me, John?" Frank kicked John in the side with the hard heel of his cowboy boot. John grunted, and Frank grinned.

"Now, what I want to know is who is leading your dirty little pack of heathens. Whenever you think you're ready to spill the beans, you let me know and I'll figure out some way for you to tell me. I don't think we'll be taking the tape off your mouth or undoing your hands because, well, that just wouldn't do, now would it? But I'll come up with something. Maybe you can tap Morse Code with your fingernails. That might do it. We did learn Morse Code, didn't we, John? I also want to know what other little tricks like this are planned and where, and don't think you're going to get away without telling me, because you know what, John? I don't have anything to live for anymore. You're in a room with a dead man, John. I don't care whether I live or die. And that ought to scare you to death, John. I am willing to go to the limits of the earth with you—no matter the consequences—if you get my drift." Frank leaned back his head and laughed bitterly. He could smell the fear emanating from John.

CHAPTER 47

NEAR WOLFGANG KASERNE, WEST GERMANY
12:15 P.M., TUESDAY, MAY 27

"So," Damrow said as he threw his flight cap onto the gaststube table, "is this going to become our favorite watering hole?"

Gunter reached across the table and shook hands. "Hallo, Herr Major," he said. "I'm pleased to see you brought Frau Hauptmann with you. *Wie geht's*?" Shaking hands with Erika, Gunter exhibited only friendliness and charm, with no hint that their last meeting had ended in rancor.

"I'm fine, Herr Hauptmann, thank you." Erika's eyes looked swiftly toward Marthe.

"Herr Major, Frau Hauptmann, please let me introduce you to my extremely important second-hand assistant, Polizeimeister Johannas." More hand-shaking and smiles ensued. "I've asked you both to meet with us today because Marthe spoke yesterday with Tina Loyola, the sister of Crystal Lambert, and she has something significant to impart that I think you must know."

Quizzical, Damrow and Erika turned to look at Marthe. "As you can imagine," Marthe began, "Frau Loyola remains very disturbed about her sister's death. She came to meet with me after the memorial service and walked around the accident site. She wanted to know everything she could about what happened. I could tell then she felt uneasy about accepting that her sister had somehow crashed the helicopter into what seemed a logical landing zone. I didn't hear anything from her again until yesterday. It seems that her brother-in-law—excuse me, her ex-brother-in-law—has had a conversation with her that has raised some serious questions for her. She was quite reluctant to voice what he told her. Apparently, it was under the influence of alcohol and he wasn't all that coherent. Nor did he give her many details. But the gist of what Frau Loyola was told is that her sister's helicopter was sabotaged and that there was a conspiracy out there that did it."

All the time she had been speaking, Marthe had held her hands in front of her on the table joined together, somewhat nervously pulling at her fingers as if even she couldn't believe what she was saying. As she finished, her hands stilled, and Erika and Damrow sat in stunned silence for a moment.

Erika was the first to speak. "Hauptmann Gunter, I owe you an apology. I had blinders on as far as the Army goes. I hope you can forgive me. I know you know that I didn't tell my boss what you went out of your way to tell me, and that was wrong. I was wrong to do that. I wasn't thinking beyond the Army's reputation. I can see now that this is much more than the Army's reputation. This is the Army's soul."

Smiling at Erika, Gunter reached over and patted her hand. Marthe drew her hands out of the way and blushed slightly. Damrow noticed and thought to himself that Gunter was unaware that his assistant might have romantic feelings for him. "It's quite alright, Frau Hauptmann," Gunter said reassuringly, "I'm sure I would have reacted the same way if someone had made similar accusations about the German police." Everyone at the table doubted it, but it was a kind thing to say.

"So now we have two sources telling us that someone tried to kill my pilots," Damrow said angrily. "And I'm hearing that it was a conspiracy? This is completely outrageous. Of course, how can we believe a drunk guy? And the husband of one of the pilots, even if they were divorced? It seems natural that he would have a bone to pick, doesn't it? I mean, he isn't exactly an objective source."

"You have a point there," Gunter acknowledged. "Still, the two stories are too closely similar, don't you agree? We have a young boy here in Germany who found an explosive timing device in the woods, or so his father says—a man whom I can vouch for. And then we have another man across the world, who doesn't know this German man, who also says the helicopter was sabotaged. He calls his ex-sister-in-law. He doesn't know she's going to call us. That just happens in the sequence of events. Two separate stories claiming sabotage, and one of them alleging a conspiracy. There is, of course, still no proof, and as a law enforcement officer, I need proof. At the same time, this is an extraordinary coincidence and in the criminal business, as we say, there are no coincidences."

"What do you think we need to do now?" Damrow asked.

"I don't have the authority, because it's out of my jurisdiction," Gunter pointed out, "but I'm happy to advise you, unofficially, of course. What I would do, if I were you, is find this ex-husband and find out what he knows."

"Which is a bit of a problem," Marthe interjected, "because he suddenly went missing, and Frau Loyola has no idea where he is. She's planning to come here, by the way. She wants to meet with us and you, Herr Major, and go over the accident site again."

"Maybe the best thing she can do is help us find her ex-brother-in-law," Erika suggested.

"Right now that looks like the first clear path for us to take," Damrow agreed.

The four finished their meal and agreed to meet again once Tina Loyola had arrived in Germany or if they acquired additional information.

CHAPTER 48

FORT WAINWRIGHT, ALASKA
8:05 A.M., WEDNESDAY, MAY 28

The freak Alaska snowstorm abated on Tuesday night, and the runway crew worked feverishly to open the airport to commercial traffic for the following morning. One of the first flights to arrive carried Congresswoman Melinda Tonnelli, making one of her usual rounds to inspect U.S. military bases. She had visited Alaska three years earlier and was hoping to see improvements, particularly in living quarters for junior enlisted married personnel.

General Tucker and his aide, Captain Thornton, were waiting on the tarmac as Tonnelli departed the plane, with Lydia Porterhouse deplaning behind her. After introductions were made, Captain Thornton led the way to General Tucker's sedan, where an enlisted chauffeur opened the doors for the general and congresswoman, and, once they were seated, drove them to Fort Wainwright. Meanwhile, Lydia procured the bags from baggage claim. After Captain Thornton helped her carry them to an idling military van, they were transported to the VIP Quarters to drop off the suitcases and then to General Tucker's office.

"You would not believe the snowfall we've had here," Captain Thornton remarked to Lydia as they were en route. "It's been unbelievable. The post was completely closed on Monday to everyone except essential workers and mostly closed yesterday.

A lot of the secondary roads out in the suburbs still haven't been plowed today. Some Army people can't make it in to work yet."

"I thought that kind of thing didn't happen in Alaska," Lydia laughed. "Don't you see snow here all the time?"

"Yes, but this is so late in the season. It was unexpected. It caught everyone by surprise. And having snow wasn't so much the problem as the amount of snow. We had up to six feet in a very short time. The city just couldn't move. Even for Alaska, that's too much snow to shove around."

"I'm glad Congresswoman Tonnelli wasn't scheduled to come in before today, then," Lydia said.

"Yes, you're quite lucky in that regard! Okay, here we are," Captain Thornton said as they pulled up in front of the headquarters building.

Inside General Tucker's office, Congresswoman Tonnelli scanned the scheduled activities proposed for her visit.

"I like this bit about having lunch with the troops in their dining facility, General," she said. "Thanks for doing that. Now, how about the child care facility? I expressly mentioned that I wanted to see the child care facility here. I don't see that on the schedule."

Looking over his own copy, Tucker spotted the child care facility visit on the following morning and pointed it out to Tonnelli.

"Good," she said. "How long of a waiting list do your active duty people have to be on to get their children into the facility?"

"It's not that long. That's always been a priority of mine. I was a single dad," Tucker explained. Tonnelli raised her eyebrows. He continued, "So I know first hand how important it is that our folks have that resource to rely on or else they won't be able to focus on their jobs."

"But how long is not that long?" Tonnelli persisted.

"I'd say about a month."

"That's a very good record, General." Tonnelli's appraisal of Tucker instantly went up a notch.

"We try to pay our child care providers the most allowable, they're treated well, they know they're valued, there isn't the high turnover that you see in a lot of facilities. I think those are all reasons why we have enough child care providers and can then keep the waiting period so low. Plus, of course, we give our active duty members the highest priority."

"Which is, I think, as it should be."

Pointing to her schedule, Tucker said, "If you notice there, Congresswoman Tonnelli, we have you scheduled to go up in a helicopter if you're interested."

"That's tomorrow afternoon? Yes, I would love that. As you can imagine, General, that's one of the perks of this job, getting to go about in all of the great equipment!" Melinda leaned back her head and laughed, and Sherman Tucker found himself suddenly dazzled by this vibrant, lively woman.

CHAPTER 49

FORT RUCKER, ALABAMA
7:10 A.M., WEDNESDAY, MAY 28

"Goddamn it, Bill! I thought you told me there was nothing wrong with those women pilots shot down in Korea!" Eckling demanded as Brannon came into his office.

"Sir, this newspaper article is totally out in left field," Brannon said. "We have no idea where this came from."

"This is a serious allegation, Bill," Eckling exclaimed, waving the newspaper in his hand. "Some wife is claiming that her husband slept with Charlotte Driver and that's the only reason why she graduated from flight school. Do you know what that does to the credibility of this school?"

"But it's an anonymous source. There's no way to prove or disprove it," Brannon disputed.

"That doesn't matter. The public perception is going to be that female students here sleep their way to get their wings. And if some of them do, I'm going to wring their necks and those of their instructors. I'm going to make sure this is a stellar institution. This is not going to be a hotbed of sex exchange!" Eckling was clearly worked up.

"I can't believe that female flight students would risk their standing here like that, General. They know they live in a fishbowl. With only two of them to a class, their every move is monitored. If we had to be concerned about anyone, it should be the older, wiser, more experienced, and dare I say, lascivious male instructors."

Eckling pointedly raised his eyebrows but said nothing right away. Finally he said, "Not all the male instructors are like that, Bill."

"Right, sir. And not all the female students are like that, either."

"Point well taken. What about this article, Bill? What the hell are we going to do about it?"

"I guess the only thing we can do is look more closely at Driver's file, and interview her instructors, the married ones. Although I'm supposing it's a red herring, we have a moral obligation to look into it, even though it is an anonymous allegation."

CHAPTER 50

CAMP VANGCHON, SOUTH KOREA
4:45 A.M., WEDNESDAY, MAY 28

On Tuesday morning, Frank had called up John's work, muffled his voice and croaked out an excuse that he was home sick with the flu. Frank didn't want to risk doing it again and he didn't want to stay in Korea longer than necessary. Moreover, he wanted to get out of the BOQ while it was still dark. If he didn't take care of John before another workday began, however, the possibility began that someone would come looking for him.

Apparently some of the BOQ residents had maid service. Frank could hear the Korean women tapping on the doors down the hallway, asking in their halting English if anyone was home, then inserting their key and slipping inside. From the state of John's apartment, it was apparent he didn't engage maid service. Nevertheless, after leaving John alone long enough to slide the top bolt closed on the hallway door, Frank breathed a sigh of relief.

Frank was running out of patience with John. The bastard had been lying on the bedroom floor now for nearly twenty-four hours. Of course he had had to piss on himself a couple of times and the stench had become nearly unbearable. Frank didn't dare take the tape off John's mouth for fear he would let out a bloody scream and nosy neighbors would start running. The walls in the BOQ were thin enough. All day and night Frank had been listening to the sounds of footsteps, showers, people greeting each other in the hallways, televisions, and even the occasional nocturnal snoring and sexual pairings.

At the moment, John was sleeping. It had been a rough night. Frank had dripped cold water in John's ear over and over again, trying to get the idiot to understand that he meant business, but the stupid shithead just shut his eyes and grimaced. Each time that Frank asked him if he was ready to say who the head honcho was, John violently shook his head no. Frank had wrenched John's arms up backwards nearly to his head, and could see the tears spilling out of John's eyes, but still he couldn't get any results out of him. When the pain finally subsided, John would shudder and coil into a fetal position, as much as he could with his hands still tied behind his back, sweat streaming down his face. From time to time, Frank held the handgun that he had purchased on the black market against John's neck and pulled the trigger, watching intently as John arched his back in fear, never knowing if a bullet was loaded or not. In all the hours, however, John only looked at Frank with anger and hate, but never with pleading, and never gave the indication that he was ready to talk.

Considering his boxing skills, Frank could easily punch John to death, but that was too simple a way out for these scumbags. Flying from Hawaii to Korea, Frank had had to consider some other measure, and he wanted it to be something that would cause a bit of fear and reflection for John while he was waiting for the final moment.

During the brief periods when John had fallen asleep exhausted, Frank had roamed the small apartment with his penlight flashlight and searched John's papers. He found a phone bill with some numbers indicating that John had made a few long distance calls in the recent past to some wide-ranging places. Frank stuffed the bill inside his shirt. Other than that, Frank discovered no clues that would help connect John to anyone beyond the conspirators he already knew about.

It was time for the final action. Rising from his chair, Frank tied a blindfold around John, swiftly undid the handcuffs from his feet, grabbed John tightly from behind, and lifted him in one fell swoop. Disoriented upon being awakened, John's resistance was feeble as he didn't know what was happening. Taking advantage of the few seconds of surprise, Frank dragged John a couple of steps to a chair waiting in the middle of the room. Hopping onto the chair first, Frank hoisted John onto the chair with him. By now, John was beginning to flail violently, but Frank had his left arm wrapped tightly around John's chest. Earlier, Frank had attached a rope to an exposed pipe in the ceiling and fashioned it into a noose. Now, with his right arm, he tightened the noose around John's neck.

Feeling the coarse rope around his neck, John began to panic. Frank ripped the blindfold from John's eyes and jumped off the chair. "So, buddy boy. Have you guessed how your end is coming?" John's eyes showed that he was truly terrified. The anger and hate had dissipated. "Interested in a little talk, are we?" Nodding assent, John cast wildly about the room, looking for salvation.

"Too late, Johnny boy. You had your fucking chance. You didn't give my wife that chance, and you didn't give those women here in Korea a chance. I'm off to find our other so-called friends, and I'll see if they prove to be more cooperative."

The pleading in John's face was now pathetic.

"Oh, just so you know, Johnny boy. After your death, everyone's going to think you were a raging faggot." Throwing down a few male porno magazines he had bought outside the post, Frank laughed with delight at the horror on John's face when realization dawned that his reputation was going to suffer. He would never have the opportunity to tell anyone, least of all his mother and father, that it was all a lie.

"So, sayonara, John." With those last words, Frank kicked the chair out from John and watched with deep satisfaction as the hanging man thrashed around, convulsed, turned color from living pink to dying purple, and suddenly was still. When Frank was certain John was dead, he untied his ankles and hands, removed the tape from his mouth, and cleaned up any other vestiges of his own presence in the apartment. Over the course of the twenty-four hours, Frank had been careful not to handle John's things, and now went around wiping down the few surfaces he had touched. Within ten minutes, Frank sidled out of the apartment, locked it behind him, quickly walked to the front gate, and caught a taxi back to Seoul. Within a few hours, Frank was en route via a commercial flight to Alaska.

CHAPTER 51

FORT WAINWRIGHT, ALASKA
2:50 P.M., WEDNESDAY, MAY 28

On Wednesday afternoon, Major Maurice Petrovich decided to test-fly one of the helicopters that hadn't gone up yet because of the snowstorm. So many off-post unit personnel had stayed home because of closed roads that the maintenance schedule had backed up. It was imperative to get things back on track and, besides, Petrovich needed to keep his hand in the business of test-flying as well as checking out the maintenance of his personnel.

When Petrovich walked into the maintenance office and looked at the blackboard, he saw that several helicopters needed test-flying.

The maintenance technician, Chief Warrant Officer Three Adam Kinney, said, "Lieutenant Robison was scheduled to fly 693 with Nelson on Monday before the storm broke."

Petrovich said, "Yeah, that's a shame. I was hoping to get her up to ARL 1 by now. You know how I hate for my new aviators to stay at ARL 3 for very long."

"Too bad you can't take her up today yourself."

"I would if I were an instructor."

"Right. Nelson's still stuck out there in the suburbs. Can you believe the snowplows haven't made it out there?"

"Lucky thing we live on post, right, Adam?"

"I suppose that's the helicopter you want to take up, right, boss? The one that Nelson and Lieutenant Robison were going to test-fly?"

"Exactly."

"Here you go." Kinney handed over the aircraft key and logbook. "Have a good flight."

Sergeant Julie Estavez was in the immediate vicinity of the helicopter. "Good afternoon, sir. Are you taking her up instead of Lieutenant Robison and Chief Nelson?"

"Yes, I am. If you'll just help me get her out of the hangar, then you can take a break until I get back."

"Yes, sir!" Estavez grinned. Most of the enlisted loved it when Petrovich decided to test-fly their helicopters because he usually liked to take his test flights alone. Only on rare occasions did he ask the enlisted personnel who had worked on the aircraft to go up with him. Once in a while he took the maintenance technician with him, but Petrovich usually liked to hear the roar of the engine and the wop-wop-wop of the rotors by himself.

A couple of other maintenance personnel helped push the helicopter out of the hangar. Luckily, no other aircraft were in the way at the time and it only took about fifteen minutes until the helicopter was situated about fifty feet in front of the hangar.

Petrovich ran through his preflight check outside the helicopter, seated himself inside the aircraft, and ran through the cockpit checklist. Within a short period of time, he was hovering down the taxiway and asking the tower for permission for takeoff.

As soon as he lifted off the ground, Petrovich began to closely monitor all instruments and gauges and listen carefully for any unusual telltale signs of distress. This particular helicopter had come into the maintenance bay to have its generator replaced. There didn't seem to be any problems with the new generator and everything seemed to be functioning fine.

All of a sudden, Petrovich felt the tail rotor controls go slack and the helicopter began to spin wildly. The aircraft was only two hundred feet above the ground, too low to provide enough time for corrective action when the tail rotor controls wouldn't respond. A seasoned aviator who knew what to do and didn't panic, Petrovich rapidly attempted the emergency procedures for a tail rotor failure at low level, but to no avail. The helicopter was swiftly falling to earth like a rock.

As the helicopter smashed into the ground and broke into hundreds of pieces, Petrovich's last words were, "Son of a bitch! Done in by a tail rotor."

CHAPTER 52

JACKSONVILLE, FLORIDA
7:30 P.M., WEDNESDAY, MAY 28

Cynthia Hailey, the handwriting expert, had called Iris on Tuesday evening and told her she could come discuss the results with her on Wednesday. Luckily, class was being dismissed early that day, around 2 p.m., and Iris parked in front of Cynthia's residential office later that evening.

"I know I already told you over the phone that these are forgeries, but let me show you why."

For the next hour or so, Cynthia painstakingly compared the actual signatures of Iris and the other women with the signatures on the pink slips, giving Iris more technical detail than she was interested in receiving.

Iris looked down at the pink slips spread before her. "But who in the world would be doing this?"

"I can tell you this, Iris. Even though it looks like a lot of different papers, different inks, and has a bunch of different dates on there, it's only one person."

"You can tell that?"

"Oh, sure. There are all kinds of telltale ways. The average individual wouldn't be able to tell, but someone like me knows. The person who did this is a pro. He knows exactly what he's doing. He knew how to fool all of his colleagues at the Aviation Center—that was easy enough, so it's obviously someone who works there. He went to great lengths to make it appear as if different instructors had written the pink slips, and he knew how to forge separate documents to do that, so that means this guy is a master forger."

"How could that be?" Iris asked.

"Well, there aren't too many ways that happens," Cynthia mused. "Either he's a criminal running loose who's somehow also managed to get access to Army records, or he was trained by the FBI."

"The FBI trains people how to forge documents?" Iris looked aghast.

"Not exactly, but we learn a lot about it when trying to catch forgers. Having done what I've done for so long, I've managed to incorporate so much knowledge I could probably be a pretty good forger myself. Do you understand what I'm saying?"

Still a bit confused, Iris slowly nodded. "I think so."

"You find out who at Fort Rucker used to work for the FBI and I think you'll have your man."

"Oh! Thanks, Cynthia!"

"I'll do a little quiet sleuthing myself and see if I can rustle up any information. I'll give you a call if I find out anything." Cynthia handed Iris the pink slips. "Good luck, Iris, and tell your dad we're even!"

"I will, Cynthia. Now I owe you."

"No you don't, Iris. It was my pleasure. Now, be off with you. You have a long drive ahead of you."

Iris spent the long night hours driving back to Fort Rucker trying to figure out how to uncover the mysterious man who used to work for the FBI and who was now forging student records.

CHAPTER 53

WATERTOWN, NEW YORK
2:15 A.M., THURSDAY, MAY 29

In the middle of packing for her trip to Germany, Tina could barely hear the phone ringing over the noise of the television set in her bedroom. Rushing to turn down the volume on the television and search for the phone, which this time was placed on the floor by her bed, Tina breathlessly picked up the receiver on the fifth ring.

"H'lo? Tina?" The voice sounded tinny and far away. Although she could tell Frank had had too much to drink again, Tina was so glad to hear from him, she didn't care.

'Frank? Frank? Can you hear me?"

"Tina? I got one. I got one of 'em."

"Frank! You have to tell me what you know! Now! Where are you?" Tina was determined to get as much information out of him as she could this time.

"I'm in Alaska! Whew! Cold country. Did you know that a big snowstorm hit here? I mean, big snowstorm. Snowdrifts all over the place. Plane almost couldn't land today. I was lucky. I'm not always lucky, Tina." Moroseness was threatening to seep in.

"Yes, I know, Frank. Why are you in Alaska, Frank?" Tina tried to remain patient.

"Got to get Chad."

"Who's Chad?"

"One of the conspirators."

"What do you mean by conspirators, Frank? How many people are there?"

"Shhh. I can't tell you. People might be listening. I know who they are, and I'm going to get them all. I already got John." Tina could detect the pride and smugness in his voice.

With a bit of fear, she asked, "What exactly do you mean, you got John?"

"I mean, he won't be bothering anyone anymore."

"How exactly, Frank?"

"Just watch the papers about Korea, Tina. You'll see what I mean." Suddenly, Frank sounded completely coherent. Tina felt a shiver go up and down her spine.

"But why, Frank?"

"Because they killed my wife." Frank's angry tone was resolute.

"No, I mean why is there a conspiracy?"

"They don't want you women in the cockpits." Tina's stomach fell to the floor.

"What?" she whispered. "People are killing female pilots because they don't like us?"

"I'm afraid so, and now that I know it, I'm going to stop them."

"How can you stop them, Frank?" Tina cried. "That's as crazy an idea as a conspiracy to kill female pilots. I can't believe what I'm hearing."

"Tina, like I said. One down, at least three more to go."

"Who are the other two?"

"You have to watch your back, Tina."

"What do you mean?"

"Two guys are at Fort Drum. Mark and Cecil."

"Oh, my God! I know those guys. They wouldn't hurt anybody!"

"It's only a matter of time before they have you in a helicopter with other women, and pull the plug, Tina. That's why I have to get to them first."

"I can't believe what I'm hearing. This is crazy! You just can't make these kinds of accusations against people."

"Believe it, Tina. There's someone else pulling the strings, though, and I have to find out who it is. John didn't give it up. Maybe Chad will."

"I'm going to Germany, Frank. For a week. Later today."

"Okay, kid. At least you'll be away from those bastards for a while."

"How can I get in touch with you?"

"My dad will know."

"But I talked to your mom and she said you were in Hawaii."

"Tina, listen to me. I said, my dad. My mom is clueless. Here's his work number." Tina hurriedly copied it down on a scrap of paper she yanked out of her nightstand drawer.

"Frank, be careful. I don't know what you're doing, but it sounds dangerous. If you're really dealing with a conspiracy of men who want to kill female aviators, well, I don't know what you're up against. Why don't you go to the authorities?"

Frank laughed. "They're not going to believe me, Tina. I haven't any proof. Besides that, now I've committed murder. I can't go to them now."

And now I'm an accessory to murder, Tina thought to herself. Aren't I? Should I turn Frank in? I have no idea. If he's helping to bring my sister's murderers to justice, I don't care what he does.

CHAPTER 54

FORT WAINWRIGHT, ALASKA
8:15 A.M., THURSDAY, MAY 29

"I'm sorry I can't accompany you today, Congresswoman." General Tucker stood up from his couch by the fireplace as Melinda entered his office. He poured her a cup of coffee from the silver service sitting on the cherry coffee table, and handed it to her to prepare as she wished.

As she stirred in a few drops of cream, Melinda objected, "Oh, no, General, don't mention it. I completely understand. Your duty today is to take care of the tragedy. If there's anything at all that I can do, I'd be glad to help. I feel as if my visit here is a complete imposition."

"I wouldn't call it that. Of course, having any member of Congress on a post causes a certain level of high activity, but that's good for us. It forces our units and activities to gear up and put on their best face. We're not supposed to admit that, but we all know it's true." Tucker smiled disarmingly. "Walls get painted, papers get filed, equipment gets repaired, you know the drill."

"Not first hand, I don't. I only see the results. I sometimes fear that my presence is too much of a burden on our young military members. But I appreciate your putting such a positive spin on it. I've heard the tales of first sergeants keeping their troops up until the wee hours of the morning spit-shining floors and cleaning trucks. It makes me want to scream with frustration because

I can only figure that those poor enlisted will resent my face the moment they see me."

"Some of them will, but most of them consider it an honor that their unit gets visited. That's how we talk it up to them, that's how we see it, and, in the end, we know you're going to do great things for us." Tucker smiled at her again and she couldn't help but smile back. His enthusiasm was contagious.

"I'd love to go out with you to the flightline, if that's alright," Melinda suddenly said. "I know that will disrupt the schedule, but under the circumstances—"

"Congresswoman, I think the troops would be greatly heartened to have you out there. Major Petrovich was a gruff, rather domineering commander, but his people really took to him, and I understand they're quite stunned by his death. He was a top-notch test pilot, which is another reason why this accident has caught everyone so off guard. It's one of those things that just shouldn't have happened."

"Shall I meet you out there then later?" Melinda consulted her schedule. "When were you going to go?"

"I was planning on going around eleven this morning," Tucker said. "You can follow through with your schedule, and then have your driver drop you off here about a quarter til and ride with me. How's that?"

"That would work fine." As Melinda rose to leave Tucker's office, she noticed a photo of a young Army officer on his desk. "Is that your daughter?"

"You're very perceptive," Tucker said. He picked up the silver frame and handed it to Melinda. "Yes, Iris had just graduated from the University of Alaska and I had sworn her in as a second lieutenant here in this very office."

"You're obviously very proud of her."

"Isn't every dad?" Tucker took the photo back and replaced it on his desk.

"Where is she now?"

"She's at Fort Rucker going to flight school." His forehead wrinkled imperceptibly in a frown.

"Has she been caught up in any of the—" Melinda began to gently probe.

"Any what?" Tucker asked sharply.

"I've received numerous phone calls from constituents and reporters about young women being set back down there at Fort Rucker. Some seem to think it's justified and some seem to think the exact opposite. It's been such a firestorm that I'm leading an investigation to go down there and check it out. I thought it was extremely ironic that the commanding general suddenly found numerous female students who didn't fit the bill after the helicopter accident in Germany when three women were killed."

"I didn't realize there was that connection," Tucker mused.

"Well, you haven't been getting all my mail," Melinda said sardonically.

"Yes, Iris is one of those," Tucker admitted.

"And what does she think?" Melinda asked. "Does she feel that she deserved to be set back, that her training was somehow lacking?"

"Not hardly. She hasn't had a bad day of flying since she got there. She's mystified by the whole thing. But my daughter," Tucker sighed, "isn't going to wait around for a congressional investigation. She's already taking matters into her own hands."

Melinda laughed. "Good for her! I promise you I'll be looking into the whole thing as soon as I get back from this military jaunt. Tell your daughter for me, and she can spread the word to her friends. They're not alone. Fighting the system can be a pain in the butt when you're down in the trenches."

Tucker grasped Melinda's hand and said, "Thanks, Congresswoman. I'm glad we've met. Now, I see Lydia waving your schedule and Earl motioning that we need to get going, so I'll see you back here later. Have a good morning."

CHAPTER 55

FORT WAINWRIGHT, ALASKA
10:57 A.M., THURSDAY, MAY 29

Frank hadn't been so drunk the night before that he'd failed to hear about Petrovich's crash and burn. After arriving at Fort Wainwright, he had managed to bum a ride off post in one of the few taxis operating during the snow emergency and had secured a room in a local low-rent motel. Having spotted a bar en route, Frank had made his way there in the evening, finding to his delight as he nursed several beers into the late night that it was apparently one of the main hangouts for members of the 1311th Aviation Maintenance Battalion, to which Chad Emerson belonged, Frank's next prey. On the main drag into Fort Wainwright and not too far from the front gate, the bar was a convenient place for the guys and gals to drop in and have a few when the day was done.

Coming from Hawaii, Frank hadn't been well-equipped with winter gear and had been shivering from the short walk to the bar through the windswept snowdrifts on the sidewalk. His regular athletic shoes had been no match for the wintry mix, and the snow that had seeped into the eyelets and crevices had worked its way in rivulets into his socks. He had dreaded the walk back to the motel and had known that only hours of warmth in the comfortable bar would make it worth his while. Having taken off his thin gloves and windbreaker-like jacket and set them on a table in the farthest dark corner, Frank had gone to stand before the roaring fire at the opposite side of the establishment. During his stride to and from the cavernous fireplace, Frank had been able to surreptitiously determine that Chad was not one of the customers enjoying the conviviality of peers.

While sitting in a booth, hunched over one beer after another, thinking of how to find and annihilate Chad, Frank had begun to catch the conversation about the accident that day that had killed Maurice Petrovich. As the evening wore on and more individuals had become increasingly loquacious, Frank had heard numerous details. Of course, many of the speakers had their theories as to how the accident had occurred, but the overriding opinion was that it shouldn't have happened. Frank had heard that loud and clear. Petrovich had been an outstanding pilot. According to the general consensus, something had clearly been wrong with the helicopter, and it was bound to come out in the accident report.

Frank kept his ears peeled the next day for activity pertaining to the 1311th and to the accident. He figured Chad would have to be around for whatever was taking place. When he learned that General Tucker was going to be addressing the unit at the flightline in the morning, he decided to show up incognito. The piles of snow that had been such a problem for the post and city all week had been alleviated and everyone was finally able to return to work.

Members of the battalion were outside in formation, waiting for the general and congresswoman, so Frank slipped inside one of the now-vacant hangars and peered through one of the dusty windows. He had a decent view and could vaguely hear what was being said, although the general's remarks weren't what really concerned him. Frank was searching for Chad. Although he strained his perfect eyesight as hard as he could, Frank couldn't find anyone who looked like Chad in any of the company formations. Of course, with everyone wearing identical flightsuits and ballcaps, they all looked pretty much the same from a couple of hundred feet.

All of a sudden, a liquid smooth voice from behind drawled, "Looking for me, Frank?"

Frank spun around.

Chad slowly smiled. "I heard you were in town."

Frank backed into a corner. Chad advanced a few paces. He said, "You should learn to keep your mouth shut on public telephones, Frank. At least look around you and see who might be listening."

Frank cast around in his mind to the previous night and could vaguely remember calling Tina. What did he tell her?

"Once again, Frank, I'm very disappointed in you. You've betrayed our trust. We were a band of brothers. Now you've gone and spilled the beans to your ex-sister-in-law. You've told her our names, Frank."

Now Frank felt quite frightened. Not for himself, but for Tina. He knew he had put her in a position of imminent danger. Somehow someone had overheard him talking to her when he told her about the conspiracy. The damn alcohol that loosened his tongue also weakened his brain so that he didn't think. He should have known better than to call Tina right from the bar where people from the 1311th were hanging out. God, he was stupid! But he'd been whispering and he thought no one had paid any attention to him or knew who he was. After five or six beers he just didn't think! He'd been sitting in that corner all alone, no one had approached him, and he thought he'd been safe. What a fool he was! What an idiot! And now Tina was going to have to pay.

But first, he was going to take out Chad. At least Chad had shown his face and presented him with the opportunity to do some serious damage. Without saying a word, without showing any emotion, Frank yanked his right fist back and shoved it forward into Chad's face, breaking his nose. Then he shoved his left fist into Chad's stomach, seriously impaling some inner organs. While Chad was instinctively protecting his face and stomach, Frank then kicked Chad in the groin, knocking him to the ground.

Chad, however, had come spoiling for a fight and didn't intend to be the one going down for good. He grabbed Frank by the leg and pulled him to the ground, crashing Frank's head hard on the concrete floor of the hangar. The two men grappled in hand-to-hand combat, breathing heavily and trying to tear each other apart limb from limb. At the same time, they both remained aware that an Army formation was taking place just feet away from them outside the hangar. It wouldn't do either of them any good to be embroiled in a scuffle with so many witnesses. That is, if they wanted to get away with the death of this particular enemy.

Frank realized he needed other tools to kill Chad. His boxing skill alone wasn't going to do it, and he'd been taken by surprise. With blood dripping down the right side of his face and a large knot forming on the back of his head, he broke away.

"Watch your back, Chad," Frank hissed. "I'm not leaving until there's nothing left of you to piss away."

"And you tell that pretty sister-in-law of yours to watch hers," Chad said in a silky voice. "There's only one of you. How well can you protect her?"

Frank left the hangar with Chad's thin smile leaving a bad taste in his mouth. Chad was now as determined to kill Frank as Frank was to kill Chad.

CHAPTER 56

ENTERPRISE, ALABAMA
8:15 P.M., THURSDAY, MAY 29

Iris gathered together as many of the affected female flight students as she could into her apartment and told them what she had learned from the forgery expert. The women sputtered with outrage.

"Why would anyone do this to us?" Mary Ann Tate demanded. She'd been set back in the night-flying phase, which was hard enough the first time around. Truth be told, she hadn't been aceing it, but she hadn't thought she was failing. She didn't relish having to go through it a second time, even if it would make her a better pilot. The humiliation grated on her every time she walked into the classroom and saw the eyes of her new peers boring into her, knowing she hadn't been with them from day one. Even though male classmates had also joined the group along the way, she felt more conspicuous for being female. But knowing now that she was never supposed to have been set back—that someone had deliberately set her back for some unknown and malicious purpose—sent her senses reeling.

Samantha Ellison clutched her file and stared at the expertly forged pink slips. At the first meeting in Iris's apartment, Samantha had been expecting to be set back but had been secretly hoping it wouldn't take place. Unfortunately, she hadn't had the courage to do what Iris had done, and a week later found herself in a new class undergoing UH-1 training. She was still trying to come to grips with how she had been ripped out of her old class, because she thought she had been doing well enough. Now, it seemed, she was right.

"The bastard." Samantha muttered. "Whoever he is. We have to find him. We have to make him pay for this."

All of the women in the room readily agreed. The question was how.

Iris said, "I have to tell Captain Gibson what I know. He gave me a week to come up with information or he'd kick me out of my class."

Mary Ann asked, "What happens if the forger finds out that you know about him?"

"That's a good question," Iris said. "I did tell Captain Gibson that I suspected my pink slips had been forged and I was going to have an investigator take a look at them."

"Iris," Tatum Richards said in alarm, "if Captain Gibson told anyone that that's why he didn't set you back, then the forger could know about it."

"That's true, Iris." Samantha added. "And if he thinks someone is closing in on his identity, he could turn out to be dangerous. Remember, this is a person who has an Army career to uphold and maintain. He's not likely to let that go lightly."

Iris laughed. "Come on, ladies! I think you're making too much of this. It's one thing to set us back in flight school. It's another thing to go all cloak-and-dagger. Besides, I got the impression that Captain Gibson wasn't above making up some other reason as to why he wasn't setting me back. That's just my gut feeling. He doesn't strike me as the kind of guy who would want to tell his superior officers that he was caving in my demands. He would present my staying in the course as a decision that he had made. So I don't think the forgery possibility has raised its head yet among the Fort Rucker folks."

"Is there anyone who can help us at Fort Rucker?" Mary Ann asked.

"It sounds risky when we don't know who was changing our records in the first place," Tatum said, shaking her head.

"How else are we going to find out information about someone on the permanent party staff?" Mary Ann continued.

"I suppose that's one way of going about it, but how in the world would we know who to trust?" Iris asked.

"Yeah, we're pretty much going blind in this department, wouldn't you say?" Samantha interjected.

"What about that lieutenant colonel who helped you with your training record, Iris?" Mary Ann suggested.

"Brannon?" Iris asked in an undecided tone. "I don't know."

"He didn't have to give you your file, you know," Mary Ann said.

"True," Iris said in a low voice.

"He could have turned you in, Iris," Mary Ann pointed out. "But instead, he brought your file out of the records room and handed it to you. Now why would he do that?"

"I don't know." Iris felt confused. She hadn't really thought about Brannon's actions until now. She had simply felt so grateful to get away from him unscathed and to have her file in her hands that she hadn't considered that he had any motives of his own.

"He was trying to help you, Iris," Mary Ann said gently. "Maybe he can be trusted."

"If we go to him and tell him what we know, perhaps he'll help us find the forger," Samantha pressed.

Iris looked around the room. "Is this what everyone thinks we ought to do?" All the women nodded. "Alright then. But I think it might be better if just I meet with him. Too many of us might raise suspicion, don't you think?"

Nods of assent went around the room. Iris breathed a sigh of weariness and said, "Okay, I'll see him just as soon as I can. Wish me luck, ladies."

CHAPTER 57

FRANKFURT, WEST GERMANY
8:35 A.M., FRIDAY, MAY 30

"Ach, so Guten Tag, Frau Loyola. How was your flight?" Gunter said as Tina came through security. Marthe had pointed her out to him, and he had briskly walked to the gate without another word, flashing his police badge so as to get past the queue of waiting family and friends.

Without waiting for an answer, he continued, "I'm Hauptmann Gunter. Polizeimeister Johannas works for me. She's just back there." Gunter stretched out his right hand, shook Tina's, motioned with a quick nod of his head where Marthe was standing among the crowd, and grabbed Tina's carry-on bag with his other hand. "Shall we?" he asked politely, waving her ahead of him. Unused to such attentiveness, Tina was caught off guard for a second but quickly recovered and made her way towards Marthe.

"Hallo, Frau Loyola," Marthe said warmly. "It's nice to see you again, although I'm sorry that we meet under such circumstances."

"Thank you for picking me up. Both of you." Tina looked from one to the other. "It really wasn't necessary. I could have rented a taxi."

"Absolutely not!" Gunter replied. "It's a long way from the airport to Etlingen. It would have cost you a fortune."

"I know. It did when I came here before." Everyone fell silent, remembering why Tina had come to Germany in March—for

Crystal's memorial service. "I probably should have rented a car. That way I could move around more freely and not have to bother either of you."

"You can still do that at any time, Frau Loyola," Gunter said. "But at the moment, let it be our privilege and honor to escort you back to our hometown. I have taken this flight across the Atlantic a couple of times myself and I know it is no picnic. I'm sure you have better things to do than stand at a rental agency desk and figure out our strange driving rules. Now, tell me I'm right."

Tina felt herself relax for the first time in days. "Yes, Hauptmann Gunter. I couldn't get any sleep at all on the plane. A family with a young boy was sitting a few seats behind me and the poor little thing cried most of the flight. So, you're right, I would probably drive a car right into a ditch. The first thing I need to do is get to a hotel and get a few hours' sleep."

"You know you're supposed to stay awake to avoid jet-lag," Marthe advised.

"I know," Tina said. "But it's only eight in the morning now and if I can just sleep until noon or one, I'll be okay. All I have to have is about three hours and then I can last the rest of the day. Can I have that?"

"I think we can let her do that, don't you, sir?" Marthe asked Gunter with a smile. "She's not going to be of much use if her head is falling in the soup."

"You're right, Marthe. I think we have to let her check into the hotel and catch a few winks while we twiddle our thumbs."

Tina looked up guiltily. "I'm sorry. I don't mean to disrupt your plans."

"Herr Hauptmann !" Marthe exclaimed. "That's not nice at all. Here she's come all this way and you're giving her the wrong impression. Frau Loyola, please don't worry. I know all of Herr Hauptmann's business, and he has plenty of other things to do to keep him busy. We'll drop you off at your hotel and then pick you up again at noon. I think we should take her to lunch then, sir, and we can talk about our plans. What do you say?"

"Well, Marthe, I would say one might think you're the boss and not me." Gunter looked amused.

Marthe rolled her eyes. "Sir, clearly you are the superior officer here, but it still takes a great deal of effort on my part to keep you in line."

"And a fine job you're doing of it, too, Marthe. Now, here we are at the car, so it's off to the hotel we go."

CHAPTER 58

FORT RUCKER, ALABAMA
9:35 A.M., FRIDAY, MAY 30

Milly gingerly poked her head into General Eckling's office and said, "Sir, the DCSOPS is on the line." She tiptoed out of the room and quietly shut the door. Even through the heavy wood, she could hear General Eckling's booming voice as he picked up the receiver and said, "General Nigelson, to what do I owe this distinct pleasure, sir?"

"Cut the crap, Horace." Eckling and Nigelson had been competitive colleagues in the Army for their entire careers. They had entered infantry officer basic together decades earlier and had risen through the ranks virtually simultaneously, first one and then the other being the shining star. From their very first interaction at Fort Benning on the obstacle course, as second lieutenant wanna-bees, they had taken an instant dislike to each other. Even then Eckling was inclined to lord it over people while Nigelson took the attitude that teamwork and persuasion would win hands down. Almost everything Eckling did disgusted Nigelson, and Eckling thought Nigelson was a weak-kneed namby-pamby.

A complete rupture, however, took place when they both served in Vietnam in the late sixties during the most intense period of the war. Both men were battalion commanders—Eckling of an aviation unit and Nigelson of an infantry unit. Eckling had become an aviator shortly after infantry basic. Part of Nigelson's battalion had gone on a mission in the mountainous region near the Laos border and became encircled by the Viet Cong. Eckling's unit was tasked to bring in supplies and take out the wounded. For two days, Eckling's subordinate commanders insisted that the area was too hot to infiltrate, and Eckling didn't overrule them. By the time relief arrived, the Viet Cong had breached the perimeter and thirty percent of the unit was dead. Nigelson never forgave Eckling for the deaths of his men. Although no mention of this ever went into Eckling's file, it apparently slowed down his promotions and he knew that two stars were the most he would ever see. When Nigelson was selected for DCSOPS and lieutenant general, Eckling had gritted his teeth as he made the congratulatory call.

Eckling removed the false pleasantry from his voice. In a decidedly icy tone, he said, "Go ahead, General, I'm all yours."

"The Secretary of the Army just called me up, Horace. It seems that a Mrs. Driver is quite upset. Does that name ring a bell with you?"

"No. Why should it?" Eckling said angrily.

"That's the mother of the pilot killed in Korea."

"What the hell does that have to do with me, General?" Nigelson flinched at Eckling's not-so-subtle insolent and insubordinate inflection on his title, but he let it pass. Little minds played little games.

"You do read the paper, don't you, Horace?"

"What?" Eckling felt confused for a moment. "Oh, that. You mean, the notion that Driver slept with a flight instructor to graduate?"

"Yes, that, Horace. Her mother is quite upset about the allegation. Can you imagine what that's done to the family?"

"She called the Secretary of the Army?" Eckling was aghast. He couldn't believe that the arm of a bereaved mother would have thought to reach quite so far when she should have been grieving. The woman clearly wasn't in her right mind.

"No, she called her local congressman—they happened to grow up in the same hometown—and he called the Secretary of the Army. The congressman and the secretary are good old boys from their military days together."

"I've got my XO looking into it," Eckling muttered.

"Thank God."

"I got to tell you, General, I had my XO pore over those ladies' training records to see if they were at fault in the accident—"

"You did what?" Nigelson's voice rose several notches.

"Take it easy, sir. We didn't find anything. They were average students, but there wasn't any indication that they shouldn't have passed."

"What is the matter with you? Why do you keep thinking that female pilots need to prove themselves? Isn't it enough that they've graduated from one of the toughest academic institutions in the world? Doesn't that say enough for their caliber?" Nigelson was nonplussed.

"It just seemed too coincidental to me that one helicopter accident full of women had come upon the heels of another," Eckling said defensively in a loud voice.

"My God, man! You are the epitome of what feminists hate," retorted Nigelson, growing increasingly agitated. "You can't accept that women can do the job. How many accidents have there been in the past in which all three crewmembers killed have been men?"

Total silence persisted for some seconds before Eckling said, "Sir, if you have nothing else, I'll keep you apprised of our investigation."

Nigelson said, "You do that, Horace. And remember, the Secretary of the Army and I are watching you like hawks."

After slamming down the phone, Eckling yelled for Brannon to get into his office on the double.

CHAPTER 59

ETLINGEN, WEST GERMANY
11:40 A.M., FRIDAY, MAY 30

Tina awoke groggily from her jet-lagged sleep and splashed some water across her face. After searching through her garment bag for clothes that looked the least wrinkled, she dressed and went downstairs to wait outside the small gasthof for Marthe and Gunter.

At noon, the people of Etlingen swarmed through the streets with purpose—housewives stopping at the butcher's and purchasing the day's dinner meat, construction workers buying Greek gyros for lunch from a walkup window, customers going in and out of the town post office and bank directly opposite the gasthof. The light summer sun drifted down between the buildings that had defined the main street of Etlingen for centuries, warming Tina's shoulders as she sat on a green iron bench. Huge pots of spring flowers hanging from decorative streetlamps perfumed the air and gave a festive mood to the day. Tina felt her spirits lift despite her reason for being in Germany.

Within a few moments, a white Renault pulled up to the curb and Marthe jumped out of the passenger's side. Smiling broadly, she said, "Guten Tag, Frau Loyola. Did you sleep well?"

"Like a rock," Tina said. "I'm ready to go for hours now." She didn't protest the front seat offered by Marthe, who quickly moved into the back, and the Renault zoomed away.

Gunter said, "We're taking you to meet with Major Damrow and his assistant, Hauptmann Stohlmann."

Tina didn't say anything.

Gunter continued. "We know this will be difficult for you, but we understand this is what you wanted."

"Yes," Tina said. "I have to meet with them to find out exactly what they know. Where are we going?"

"I thought it best that we go back to the accident site. Reconstruct what happened. Marthe has copies of the investigation report for each of us. First, we'll have lunch at a local gasthaus near the crash site, go over the report and the photos, and then walk over the site. We can tell each other what we know, to put the pieces of the puzzle together, so that we're all starting from the same place."

"That sounds fine to me," Tina said. "I'm still distrustful of anyone in Crystal's unit." She looked out the passenger's window at the rolling countryside.

"I don't blame you," Gunter said. "But Herr Major seems, in my estimation, to be a man of integrity. I don't get the feeling from him that he had anything to do with this crime, with killing his own people."

"Do you really think this is what happened?" Tina asked.

"It's hard not to think so," Gunter said. "I'm sure you've heard it said that police officers don't believe in coincidences. The facts are that someone here in our own town says he held in his hand an explosive timing device—regardless that it has since been lost—and then you reported your brother-in-law saying a known conspiracy exists that sabotaged the helicopter—well, this is too bizarre to be coincidental. When you throw in that these pieces of knowledge occurred among people who didn't know each other, were in separate parts of the world, and that at least one of them had no motive to come forward—then it really bears close scrutiny."

Gunter pulled up in front of a gaststube and parked. "I see a car with American plates on it, so I'm guessing they're here already," he said. Unlike the dark gaststube across from the polizei station that he and Marthe normally frequented, this one was fairly new—at least built in the last two hundred years. It was set into a small clearing with its back to the woods, and the summer sun flooded the many open windows. Since it was such a lovely day, the gaststube was serving lunch on the raised wooden deck out front, with customers seated at plastic tables under white umbrellas advertising the local beer.

All three would have enjoyed basking outside, but they continued into the interior of the gaststube to locate Damrow and Erika, whom they found seated at a long table in an airy corner.

"Hallo, Herr Major," Gunter said with gusto as he approached and shook hands. Introductions were made, hands shaken, and orders given for drinks and lunch. Then everyone got down to the business at hand.

"I actually have more information than I did when I last talked to Marthe on the phone before coming here," Tina said.

Everyone waited.

"My brother-in-law called me again. He said two of the conspirators are in my unit. He told me to watch my back. I just can't believe what Frank is saying."

Gunter asked, "Frau Loyola, do you know where your brother-in-law is?"

Tina hesitated. "Not exactly."

"But you know more than you want to tell us," Gunter said.

Tina stared impassively at her beer.

Gunter continued, "Frau Loyola, I appreciate your concern for your brother-in-law, but you said you want to get to the bottom of who killed your sister."

"I do," Tina said.

"Then you're going to have to be more forthcoming with the information you have."

Tina sighed. "He's in Alaska. I don't know exactly where. I do know he's on a revenge quest."

Damrow asked sharply, "What do you mean?"

"He told me he's going to kill off the conspirators one by one."

"Oh my God," Damrow said slowly. "What's going on here? Do you know the names of the men in your unit? We can't allow your brother-in-law to get there and kill those guys."

Tina set her face stubbornly.

Gunter asked her quietly, "Has he already accomplished part of his mission?"

Tina looked Gunter straight in the eye and didn't blink. "I don't know."

Damrow asked her, "What's the name of the person in Alaska that he's going after?"

"He didn't tell me," Tina said.

Marthe quickly said, "Obviously, Frau Loyola knows very little about her brother-in-law's plans. Perhaps, though, he explained why the conspiracy exists in the first place."

Tina nodded. "He said these men don't like women helicopter pilots and want to kill us off."

Damrow's face turned bright red. "Those sons of bitches! I have a mind to kill them myself." He clenched his fist and quietly pounded it on the table. "Crystal Lambert was one of the finest pilots I have ever come across and Sergeant Gregory—well, she was an absolutely superb crew chief. The loss to our unit is incomparable. I can't comprehend the Neanderthal thinking in this process that doesn't want women flying or in the military."

Tina looked startled at Damrow's outburst, while Erika had obviously heard it numerous times before. "Sir," Tina said, "I'm glad you feel that way about Crystal. I knew she was a great pilot. That's why it's confounded me as to how this could have been pilot error."

"I know, Tina," Damrow said. "And the investigation report was so cleverly written. We're going to have to unravel that. Someone had to have been involved at that end. I just don't know who. If we can break everything out some other way, we can come at it in another direction. I'd rather not have to be asking questions through Army channels because I have no idea right now who to trust."

"I completely understand, sir," Tina said, for the first time giving him a tiny smile.

For the rest of the afternoon, the small group discussed the accident and the investigation report, then drove out to the accident site, dissecting how the sabotage could have occurred and how it could have been covered up.

CHAPTER 60

FORT RUCKER, ALABAMA
1:20 P.M., FRIDAY, MAY 30

Brannon hadn't been in his office all morning, and General Eckling had become more and more agitated. Finally, after lunch at the club with one of his old friends who had come in for the weekend from Fort Ord, Eckling arrived back at the office to find Brannon at his desk.

"Goddamn it, Bill! Where the hell have you been?"

"Sir?" Brannon looked up quizzically. He had been sitting at his desk ever since he'd seen Milly's urgent note, but Eckling hadn't returned from lunch, so he was taken aback at Eckling's cogitation.

"I've been waiting around for you all morning."

"I was at the—"

"It doesn't matter where the hell you were. I'm sure you had a damn fine excuse. It's just that I needed you here."

Eckling walked to the window behind Milly's desk and looked out over the parade ground. It was early June and the grass was still a vibrant green, lush to look at and a relaxing color against the deep blue of the Alabama sky. He quickly turned around, hands clasped behind his back, and said, "The DCSOPS called here and reamed me out, Bill. I didn't like that."

"No, sir. I suppose you didn't." Brannon waited to hear the rest, pen poised above his paperwork.

"He'd just read about the allegations against that female pilot who was killed in Korea. What was her name?"

"Charlotte Driver, sir."

"That's right. That's the one. He wants to know what we're doing about it. I told him we're investigating it. We are, aren't we, Bill?" Eckling peered intently at Brannon.

"Of course, General. You told me that was the highest priority."

"What have you found out?"

"Well, of course, not all of her instructors are assigned here anymore. It's taken me a while to get hold of them all. As you can imagine, the whole subject is a bit sticky to get into. And quite a few were offended that they might be accused of taking advantage of a student."

"Screw their sensibilities. Follow me." Brannon got up and the two men walked through the reception area and into Eckling's office. After motioning for Brannon to take a seat, Eckling demanded, "So tell me, did anything seem out of the ordinary?"

Brannon took a deep breath. "I really didn't uncover anything. Everyone appears to be clean. Of course, sir, I'm not exactly a CID investigator." He smiled. Eckling didn't.

"Bill, why on God's green earth would someone make an accusation about a dead pilot like that if it wasn't true?"

"Good question, sir. I've been asking myself that."

"So? What have you come up with?"

"The logical answer, of course, is that it could be true."

"Or?" Eckling prodded.

"Or someone could be trying to smear Driver's reputation."

"Now why the goddamn hell would someone want to do that?" Eckling demanded.

"Sir, I haven't a clue. Maybe someone had something against her. Perhaps she had just enough time in the Army or in Korea to make an enemy. I don't know. It could be a professional jealousy thing."

"What do you mean professional jealousy?"

"Well, sir, you know there are quite a few men out there who don't really care for female pilots."

Eckling rolled his eyes and jumped out of his chair. "I cannot believe my own XO is giving me this load of bullshit."

"Sir, I'm not saying that I believe this."

"You just said it, Bill."

"General Eckling, please listen to what I said. I said some men think so. There are some military men out there, as you well know, who don't think women should be in the military."

"What the fuck does that have to do with Charlotte Driver?"

"I guess it's just a supposition on my part. But there's always the possibility that some disenchanted military guy could put out a rumor that takes wing that she only made her way because she slept her way there. That discredits her and makes him happy."

Eckling's blood began to boil and it showed in his face. "I'd like to crush the guy, if that's the case."

"Sir, I have no idea if this is what happened. I'm just putting it forth as one possibility," Brannon said.

"Alright," Eckling decided. "I've already heard enough. You're satisfied with your investigation?"

Brannon nodded.

"You've talked to every instructor she had?" Eckling looked Brannon full in the face. "Don't backslide on me, boy. I find out you so much as missed one person, I'll string you up so fast you won't know what happened."

"Yes, sir. I talked to them all." Brannon prayed that Eckling would never find out about the one instructor who adamantly refused to answer his questions and railed obscenities at him on the phone. But, strictly speaking, he did talk to him. Brannon had a slightly uneasy feeling about the guy, but not enough to think he would have discredited Driver and the aviation school in the process.

Eckling leaned back in his leather chair and pulled out a cigar. He snipped off the end, lit it, and breathed in deeply. As he exhaled a plume of smoke, he said, "I'm not going to let any son-of-a-bitch destroy this school just because he's got some inferiority complex about women. I may not be too crazy about them flying helicopters, either, but I'm going to be dead certain that any decisions I make are based on absolute fact. You got that, Bill?"

"Yes, sir."

"So I want you to put out a press release that says this has been investigated and there was no, none, nada, untoward sexual activity between Driver and her instructors. And you can quote me on that." Eckling looked at Brannon. "What the hell are you waiting for? Get the hell out of here and snap to it!"

CHAPTER 61

FORT WAINWRIGHT, ALASKA
7:45 P.M., FRIDAY, MAY 30

Vanessa Robison had had a grueling day. The much-delayed ARL upgrade exam with Chief Nelson had taken place in the afternoon. Chad Emerson hadn't been kidding when he said that Nelson was absolutely anal about details. Vanessa felt as if she'd been put through a wringer and squeezed tight several times. She was looking forward to getting to her BOQ room and settling in for a quiet Friday night.

Considering Petrovich's death and the huge snowstorm that had immobilized the post for days, Vanessa was amazed at how quickly the unit could return to normal. The acting commander, Captain Steve Cantone, had held a formation early Friday morning with all of the unit personnel, grieving with them over the loss of their commander but letting them know that the best thing for everyone considered would be to get back to business as soon as possible. Cantone urged anyone who felt they couldn't fly to see him or the flight surgeon and they would be taken off flight status temporarily, but otherwise all missions, training and support, would go on as scheduled. Most people breathed a sigh of relief for they didn't relish sitting around the pilots' briefing room and staring at the dingy walls with nothing to keep them occupied but their thoughts of Petrovich's crash. For if Major Petrovich, one of the best pilots any of them knew, could die in a fiery crash immediately after takeoff, their own demise seemed a bit more likely. And no confident pilot wanted their thoughts spinning in that direction. Action was far preferable to introspection.

Nelson approached Vanessa shortly after the formation and informed her that, indeed, she would take her up that day for the ARL upgrade. Vanessa had been expecting it and, in fact, had spent some of the previous days since she should have taken the exam, boning up on the emergency procedures and specifics of the aircraft. So she wasn't taken by surprise. They wouldn't start the process until after lunch, when Nelson would first administer an oral exam in her office, so Vanessa spent the morning conducting regular maintenance officer business.

Vanessa was surprised, however, to find out just how terse and businesslike Nelson was. She'd rarely encountered anyone, male or female, who used so few words. At first, she found it extremely unnerving. Vanessa had attempted a bit of chit-chat, but when it wasn't returned and only silence reigned, she gave up. Nelson didn't smile or acknowledge when Vanessa had done something well. On the other hand, she also didn't sneer or make nasty comments when Vanessa goofed up. After a little while, Vanessa became accustomed to flying with someone who seemed virtually robotic and she discovered that, in a sense, it gave her the freedom to concentrate on flying rather than what the reactions of her instructor pilot were going to be.

Nevertheless, Nelson asked so many questions about the helicopter, about emergency procedures, and about the unit's area of operations that Vanessa could almost scream in frustration. As soon as Vanessa had the aircraft recovered from one emergency procedure or situation, Nelson would put her into another and make her explain or demonstrate what was going to happen next. By the time the exam was over, although Nelson assured Vanessa she was upgraded to ARL 1, Vanessa felt her brains jumbled into one big mess. She was completely relieved and didn't object one iota when Nelson took the controls and flew the helicopter back to the airfield from the company's training area.

When Vanessa picked up her mail, she noticed a letter from her favorite cousin, Lindley Ochiotto. Oh, how wonderful! she thought. What a special treat! I'll save this to read in my bubble bath.

Lindley's father and Vanessa's mother were brother and sister and they came from a large Italian family in Brooklyn. Their grandparents had opened a small bakery when they first immigrated to America, selling fragrant fresh bread early in the morning as people left for work and to housewives who were just beginning to think they didn't want to make their own bread. Soon, the Ochiottos had little bakeries all over Brooklyn. One of their specialties was Italian cakes, which immigrants clamored to buy for weddings and other celebrations. The family wasn't rich, but it was a way to employ the numerous members of the Ochiotto clan. A year apart in age, Lindley and Vanessa grew up in houses across the street from each other. Vanessa had gone off to college, which hadn't interested Lindley in the least, but he stuck around home for a year after high school and then enlisted in the Army. Since Lindley had been in Korea for nearly a year, none of the family had seen him in a long time and he wasn't a very good correspondent. Vanessa was thrilled to hear from him.

She went into her BOQ room, ran herself a hot bubble bath, and took a bottle of wine and a long-stemmed wineglass into the bathroom. She was extraordinarily lucky because she happened to be living in a modern BOQ in which she had her own private bathroom. She was well aware that many officers still had to live in World War II buildings, sharing bathrooms down the hall or, at best, with another officer, often with only showers available. Having an actual bathtub was a true luxury and she took advantage of it whenever she could.

Vanessa slipped into the bubbles and breathed a sigh of contentment. She poured herself a glass of wine, took a long sip, then another, and set her drink down on the floor. At last, she picked up Lindley's letter and broke the seal.

My dearest cuz,

Vanessa smiled.

I don't have much time. I suppose you heard about the UH-60 that went down in Korea. That was my helo. I was the electronics tech on it. I swear to you, Vanessa, that the IFF was working when the Blackhawk went down. I had just repaired it and then the pilot and I did a test flight right before her accident. I know there was nothing wrong with it.

I'm afraid the artillery unit isn't going to take the whole friendly fire accusation lying down. I'm worried someone's going to try to put the blame on the IFF not working. Which isn't true. All of the radios were working, because we checked those, too. So, if any of this comes up in the accident report, something's gone haywire. I don't want to be the fall guy.

No doubt investigating officers will come to me soon, and I need to get some advice from you as to what I should tell them. CW2 Driver was a great pilot, from everything I heard, so I don't think she made any crazy mistakes like have been alluded to.

I'm sorry to dump this on you, cuz, but you're the brain between the two of us. I find this all really confusing. Why did Driver's helo crash? Why did the artillery unit fire on it? My mind keeps going around in circles because I KNOW the IFF was working.

Take it easy, cuz.

Love, Lindley

Vanessa's smile faded and she dropped the letter to the floor. She immediately began brushing the bubbles off her skin and turned on the shower, wincing at the cold water that rushed out before the water heated up. Think! she said to herself. Think!

The closest friend Vanessa had made since arriving at Fort Wainwright was the first person she had met—Captain Earl Thornton. Maybe I'll talk to him, she thought. At least he'll be a good sounding board.

CHAPTER 62

ELTINGEN, WEST GERMANY
7:20 P.M., FRIDAY, MAY 30

Gunter had arranged to pick up Tina for dinner Friday evening. Marthe, as much as she would have liked to join them, had long had prearranged plans to be at family festivities for her grandmother's hundredth birthday party in Rorstadt eighty-five kilometers away. Her father would never forgive her if she begged out and besides, she shared a special bond with her Oma, and Marthe looked forward to the evening despite the bitter pang of feeling left out of what Gunter might learn from the American.

Instead of driving somewhere, Gunter escorted Tina a few doors down the street from the gasthof to a quietly elegant, unobtrusive Chinese restaurant. Somehow, Tina had presumed they would eat nothing but hearty German food. Pink linen tablecloths and candlelight created a romantic glow against the warm wood walls, helping Tina to relax as she slipped into a comfortable armchair.

After ordering a bottle of ordinary table wine, Gunter gently began to press Tina for the details she wouldn't reveal earlier in the day. "Frau Loyola—"

"Please, call me Tina," she said.

"Danke sehr," he said, smiling. "That's a great compliment in Germany, you know, to be asked to call people by their first names. We don't often get to that in the first decade of knowing someone."

Tina laughed. "And your first name?"

"I don't know if I even remember it."

"Come now," Tina said. "That sounds like a stickler for tradition if I ever heard one."

"No, not really. I'm just not crazy about it. It's Karl."

"What's wrong with that?"

Gunter shrugged. "Okay, Tina, now we're introduced on a first-name basis," he smiled again. "I don't know if you realize you could be in very serious trouble."

"What do you mean?"

"If there's a conspiracy to kill women helicopter pilots and two of the men are in your unit, what in the world makes you think you're safe?"

"I'm not there now, am I?" Tina asked.

"Tina, I think that's a very naive view of the world. At the moment, we don't know how these perpetrators sabotaged the helicopter that killed your sister, nor do we know who they are. As a law enforcement officer, I know that the best way to operate is to collect all the clues possible. And you're hiding something."

Tina had been looking down at her wineglass, but jerked her head up to look at Gunter. "Why would I do that?" she asked. "More than anyone, I want to find out what happened to my sister."

"True," Gunter acknowledged. "But I think you're protecting your ex-brother-in-law. I think you know more about him than you told us."

Tina dropped her eyes to the table.

"Tina, I can understand your desire for revenge, if that's what it is—if you think your brother-in-law, in his quest for justice, can take out these conspirators faster than the Americans can find them and take them to trial. But what if … just what if … he can't get to them fast enough and they keep on with their mission and sabotage more helicopters and kill more female pilots, including you?"

"I'm already warned," Tina said.

"Okay," Gunter agreed. "Perhaps you are. Perhaps you won't be caught off guard. But what about your female friends? What about your female colleagues? I suppose you can warn some of them. Have you warned any of them?" Gunter noticed a flicker of confusion pass across Tina's face. "I thought not. How are you going to feel the next time you hear about a so-called accident of female aviators and know that you could have helped prevent it?"

"Screw you!" Tina said angrily.

"Ja, I understand that American saying all too well," Gunter said. "But, Tina, you can't possibly think that these conspirators are going to let your ex-brother-in-law roam around the globe knowing what he knows, spilling information to you, do you? They're going to come after him and then, my guess is, they're going to come after you. Don't you think so?"

Gunter waited for reality to set in.

"I'll think about it," Tina said.

Gunter sighed. "I guess it's true what they say—the Lord helps those who help themselves."

CHAPTER 63

FAIRBANKS, ALASKA
2:18 A.M., SATURDAY, MAY 31

Chad awoke from a deep slumber in his recliner, his TV set still blaring. In the recesses of his mind, he thought he had heard the click of a door lock, but the memory outline was so faint and the urge to sleep so strong, that he shifted to a more comfortable position, threw his head back, and began to snore anew. In the course of the evening he had consumed nearly an entire bottle of Jack Daniel's, not a particularly unique feat, but one that he didn't often indulge in. His encounter with Frank Lambert the previous day, and the resultant aches and pains, had seemed appropriate license to get drunk at the end of a difficult and disappointing week.

The flight surgeon had told him his nose was indeed broken and he wouldn't be able to fly for several weeks. Chad lived for flying and didn't know how else to spend his time. Come Monday, he would have to start spending all his time in the maintenance hangar and that was going to be such a bore. As soon as Chad had left the flight surgeon's office and turned in the slip recommending he be grounded for a while, he went straight home and started drinking. Somewhere in the late afternoon he had a sandwich and some chips to stave off hunger, but other than that, it was just Chad and old Jack, with a bit of Coke thrown in to sweeten the taste.

By 9 p.m., Chad was off to dream world, with just a few ounces of whiskey left in the bottle on the end table beside him.

Every now and then, he would rouse himself long enough to change position and consider moving to his bed, but his eye would wander to the television or he would take another sip of his drink, and then slump back to sleep in his recliner, deciding that getting up and walking down the hall wasn't worth the effort.

While Chad was in his living room, sleeping peacefully, TV covering all the usual noises a house makes, an unwanted intruder picked the lock of the kitchen door, turned on the gas, and left as quietly and quickly as he had entered. As Chad's dreams continued to flit from one alcoholic scene to another, the invisible but lethal gas stealthily made its way around all the corners and crevices of the house, entering his nostrils, his lungs, and his body, invading his life and ending it at the same time. For a person who had vowed violence and was ready to do violence, the total lack of violence in Chad's demise would have been ironic had he only known.

CHAPTER 64

ETLINGEN, WEST GERMANY
11:37 P.M., FRIDAY, MAY 30

After returning to her gasthof, Tina did think over the ramifications of what Gunter had said. Suddenly, the horror of her selfishness overwhelmed her as she thought of Deirdre flying around unsuspectingly in a helicopter while Cecil and Mark were allowed to do God knew what to the equipment. Thinking, I've got to warn her! Tina flew out of her room in search of an international pay phone.

She stopped at the front desk to inquire in her halting German where she might find the nearest phone, and found that one of the bright yellow booths was located on a street corner two blocks down. The clerk, who spoke excellent English, which Tina found to be a relief, explained how to dial the United States, and exchanged some dollars for convenient five-mark coins so she could operate the phone booth. With tools in hand, Tina set out on the balmy night to dispense bad news to her good friend.

She knew Deirdre would probably be at work. But she could be flying as easily as she could be near a phone. Or she could have gone home. After all, it was Friday and end of the workday. Should Tina risk calling her at the hangar? What if she reached Cecil or Mark? What would she say then? She certainly couldn't leave a message. Not what she needed to say, at any rate. And what about needing to keep her own whereabouts a secret? Tina's leave form did state where she'd gone, so that was a moot point. She hadn't really thought that out when Frank told her to watch her back. She'd only been thinking that she was safe since she wasn't at Fort Drum. Now that she thought about it, if they were intent on finding her specifically, it wouldn't be hard at all. A shiver ran up her spine.

Somehow, Tina didn't think it would be a good idea to leave a message on Deirdre's home phone, either. What if Cecil or Mark—and what if there were more of them—had tapped their phones or something? God, she was becoming paranoid! Tina decided to try Wayne at work. It might not be his shift at the hospital, but if it were, he would at least be easy to find. And she knew she could trust him beyond a shadow of a doubt.

The phone only rang twice before it was picked up in the emergency room and Tina was astonished by the clarity of the call. "Emergency room, Fort Drum." Tina asked for Lieutenant Yarrow, was told just a moment, and before long, he was on the line.

"Oh, Wayne!" Tina said with a burst of emotion. "I'm so glad I was able to reach you."

"Tina! Aren't you in Germany? Have you found anything out about Crystal's accident?"

"Yes! Yes! Wayne, that's why I'm calling. This is so important. Listen to me. I'm calling you because you have to tell Deirdre. Frank told me that—"

At that moment the glass doors behind Tina opened and rough hands yanked her out of the booth. The receiver fell, dangling from its cord.

Wayne said, "Tell Deirdre what, Tina?" He heard a scuffling noise. "Tina? Tina? Are you there?"

After a few seconds, Wayne shrugged and replaced the receiver in its cradle. To the nurse behind the emergency room desk, he said, "I guess our reception was lost. She said it was important, so I'm sure she'll call back."

As Friday afternoon turned into Friday evening and the emergency room filled with dire cases, Wayne completely forgot Tina's fifteen-second phone call.

CHAPTER 65

FORT RUCKER, ALABAMA
8:15 A.M., SATURDAY, MAY 31

Stefania, answering the phone hanging off the kitchen wall, called out. "Bill! There's a Lieutenant Tucker on the phone for you."

Enjoying his second cup of coffee and the Montgomery paper in the living room, Brannon furrowed his brow and looked up. "Lieutenant Tucker? I don't know a Lieutenant Tucker."

"Come get the phone, Bill," Stefania said. "She specifically asked for you. I certainly don't know a Lieutenant Tucker."

Brannon tossed his paper onto the sofa and strode into the kitchen. "Hello? This is Lieutenant Colonel Brannon."

"Hello, sir," Iris Tucker began. "I don't know if you remember me. But I met you the other night when I was trying to get my training record."

"Oh, yes," Brannon said. "That Lieutenant Tucker. Of course! The cat burglar."

Iris blushed to the roots of her blonde hair. "I'm sorry about that, sir."

"Yes, yes. I'm sure you are. Nevertheless, you got what you went after, didn't you?"

"Yes, sir," Iris admitted.

"Although my appearance nearly put the kibosh on that, didn't it?"

"That's true, but, actually, that's why I'm calling you."

"You going to clarify that, Lieutenant?"

"Yes, sir. You see, I—I mean, we, a bunch of us—really need the help of someone here at Fort Rucker. And since you helped me out that night, I—I mean, we—thought that maybe we could trust you and that you might help us out."

"What's this all about?" Brannon felt a sinking feeling in the pit of his stomach, as if the next words he heard were going to change things irrevocably and he wouldn't be able to go back to the way things were.

"I went back to the records room with some of my friends and we got the files of everyone we knew who had been set back, washed out, or was going to be."

Brannon remained silent.

Iris continued. "Then I took the files to a forgery expert from the FBI and she informed me that all of these pink slips have been forged."

"You have to be kidding me."

"No sir."

"You're telling me that there's some big scam here at Fort Rucker to set women students back, to not let them graduate, to—to what?"

"We don't know, sir. That's part of what we have to find out. But the forgery expert was able to narrow it down in one respect."

"What do you mean?"

"It's apparently not a big scam. This is apparently all the work of one person."

"Unbelievable." Brannon was stunned.

"Based on her examination of the forgeries, and her knowledge of how the FBI works, she thinks this was done by someone who used to work for the FBI in handling forgery cases and now works at Fort Rucker, perhaps in the Army or for the Army."

"And what you want me to do is–"

"Sir, we have no way of knowing who might have worked for the FBI, but you have all kinds of knowledge about the permanent party personnel at Fort Rucker, and we thought you might be able to gain the inside track a lot faster."

"What made you think you could trust me?"

"Well, you did give me my file and didn't turn me in. There weren't a whole lot of officers who would have done that."

"Alright, you have me there," Brannon said. "That doesn't mean, however, that I necessarily believe what you're saying about someone forging documents for a number of flight students. That's just too bizarre to be plausible."

"Colonel Brannon, I know it is. But if you could just do one thing for us, we'll take care of the rest. Perhaps you could find out if there is, in fact, anyone on the staff at Fort Rucker who used to work for the FBI."

"That won't prove anything," Brannon pointed out.

"No, sir," Iris agreed. "It won't. But it would at least give us a direction in which to search. We wouldn't ask you to be involved more than that, sir."

Brannon thought to himself, Like hell you won't. "Alright," he said reluctantly. "I'll see what I can find out."

CHAPTER 66

WATERTOWN, NEW YORK
5:05 A.M., SATURDAY, MAY 31

After the long red-eye flight from Alaska, Frank was absolutely beat. The taxi driver had obliged and dropped him off two blocks from Tina's house. Although dawn was breaking, Frank still created a shadowy figure as he flitted along the sidewalks under the protection of tall pines and sprawling oak trees. During his quick jaunt, in which he attempted to look as unobtrusive as possible while carrying a small suitcase, Frank spotted only one lone individual leaving a residence a few houses down, ostensibly going out with a dog for a walk, and that person set out in the opposite direction.

As soon as Frank reached Tina's house, he quickly veered into her backyard, set his suitcase down on her deck, and searched in all the likely spots for a hidden key. During his marriage to Crystal, Tina hadn't been living in this house, but if she was like Crystal, a house key would probably be hidden under a plant or a rock somewhere. Crystal liked the idea that she would never be locked out of her own house, and he suspected that her twin sister would have the same habit. It only took Frank two minutes to find Tina's supposedly secret key, taped underneath the deck behind one of the posts. He unlocked her sliding glass door and let himself in.

Knowing that Tina was in Germany for at least a week had convinced Frank to make use of her place. One, it gave him an anonymous place to hole up in where, hopefully, no one would see him. Two, he would be able to keep an eye out for any suspicious activity taking place against Tina that she might not notice, especially if something was being put into place before she returned. Three, Frank grinned to himself thinking about the jump he would have on those creeps if they tried to get into Tina's place and found him there.

The first thing he needed to do, though, was get a good night's sleep. He hadn't been able to sleep on the plane, at least not much. In addition to the usual discomforts and crying baby or two, he'd been busy congratulating himself on how easy it had been getting into Chad's apartment. Frank laughed out loud.

"I can't believe the shithead didn't even hear me come in there," he said to himself. "I wish his death could have been painful, but no matter. It's better that everyone thinks it's an accident or suicide."

Frank had had a few misgivings about the way he had orchestrated Chad's death, the primary one being that it could still go wrong and Chad would live. But he had decided the odds were in his favor and, if he found out later it didn't work, he would go back. He still had most of his leave to burn and Chad wouldn't have known that a murder attempt had been made on his life. The way Frank figured it, he needed to get on with his plan before more women were killed, especially Tina.

That was something else that had kept him awake on the plane. His stupid, stupid drunken revelations to Tina in a public bar. Why couldn't he ever keep his mouth shut? Why did he have to drink so much? He was such a damn fool. When had he started to drink constantly? Frank couldn't remember. It seemed that his slide into alcohol had been inexorable. He didn't think he had been drinking excessively when he and Crystal were together. Sure, they had had a lot of fun going to bars, having parties, throwing back a few beers. But it wasn't this morose and steady drinking night after night that he'd been doing now ever since—ever since when? Ever since Crystal had left him? In the gut of his stomach, he knew that was the answer and now that she was dead and could never come back to him, it was even worse.

Frank looked in Tina's refrigerator to pull out a beer. It was the tonic that soothed every frayed nerve, the antidote to every bad day, the cool elixir that went down smoothly. He saw a six-pack of Heinekens gleaming on the bottom shelf in their bright green bottles. Salivating, Frank reached in to grab one, maybe two, because he knew he could drain one walking up the stairs and finish the second while getting ready for bed. But something stayed his hand and he pulled it back empty, puzzled.

I don't think I want a drink, he thought to himself. Maybe it's time I don't drink quite so much anymore. Without deliberating too much over this startling revelation, Frank grabbed some orange juice, swigged it out of the carton, and went up to bed.

CHAPTER 67

FORT RUCKER, ALABAMA
9:00 A.M, SATURDAY, MAY 31

"Melinda, I don't have much time," Stefania said breathlessly. "Bill has just left the house for a few moments."

"How nice to hear from you, too," Melinda Tonnelli said sarcastically. It always amazed her how Stefania could find her no matter where she was. That woman had a sixth sense or just an excellent set of contacts. Melinda was still in Alaska and about to set off to tour Fort Richardson on a daunting itinerary of activities that would last all day and into the evening. "What is so important that you have to track me down at—" Melinda peered at her watch. "—five o'clock in the morning? I know I have to get up early, but even for me this is ridiculous. And you know I need my beauty sleep."

Stefania smiled. When they were in school together, Melinda had nearly always overslept, craving those last few minutes in bed, and Stefania had always had to yank the covers off of her.

"I'm sorry, Melinda. Truly I am. You know I wouldn't disturb you if it wasn't important."

"Alright, out with it. I'm finally awake."

"Remember when I called you before about the female students here at Fort Rucker?"

"Do I ever! Believe me, since then, I heard about it from my constituents. I even talked to the commanding general down there and promised him I'd be looking into it."

"Great! Alright, there's this young girl here. A flight student. They tried to set her back but she didn't take it lying down. She got hold of her records because she didn't believe she deserved to be set back. Furthermore, she demanded to stay in her regular class."

"Good for her," Melinda applauded.

"Then she went to see a forgery expert."

"And the other women just took it?"

Stefania continued, "Not exactly. They're all in this together. This one student took the records of everyone to the forgery expert who determined that someone at Fort Rucker has forged their records to make it look like they're failing."

"Oh my God, Stefania. How do you know all this?"

"Lieutenant Tucker called up Bill and asked for his help."

"What did you say her name was?" Melinda said very calmly.

"Lieutenant Tucker."

"Do you know her?"

"No, but apparently Bill met her one night while she was retrieving her records. She climbed into the window of the records room. He's now calling her the cat burglar."

"Stefania, she's the daughter of the commanding general here at Fort Wainwright."

"Oh." Stefania was silenced for a moment. "I don't think Bill knows that. At least, he hasn't mentioned it."

"It doesn't surprise me that she has the chutzpah to take matters into her own hands, considering who she's grown up with. Her father is one impressive man. He raised her by himself," Melinda explained.

"Sounds like you two have something in common," Stefania commented.

"He's also quite unlike most men I usually come across," Melinda said.

"Ordinarily, you know, we could make an hour-long conversation out of that tidbit alone. But, Melinda, I thought perhaps you could look into this somehow."

"You bet I will, sweetheart. This is absolutely untenable. I'll also let General Tucker know what's going on. I would think his daughter has filled him in already, but it wouldn't hurt to let him hear from me again. Then, maybe she's trying to handle everything herself."

"Well," Stefania said, "not exactly by herself. She wants Bill to find out who the forger is."

"I see," Melinda said. "So that's where Bill comes in."

"Right," Stefania said. "She said that's all she needs. She and her friends wouldn't know how to find the person."

"How is Bill supposed to find him?" Melinda asked.

"Supposedly he used to work for the FBI, helping to catch forgers."

"Good luck to Bill. Is he already off on that mission?"

"I don't think so, but I just wanted to give you a call and tell you what I knew."

"Oh, Stefania, you and your little subterfuges. Trying to save the world behind the bureaucracy. If only you would trust the government," Melinda said, shaking her head with amusement.

"Unfortunately, Melinda, the government often lets us down, so I need to give it a push. You will do what you can, won't you?"

"Of course, Stefania. Give Bill my love."

CHAPTER 68

SOMEWHERE IN EAST GERMANY
9:30 A.M., SATURDAY, MAY 31

The unknown assailant had clamped his arms around Tina in the phone booth and dragged her quickly away in the dead of night into a van idling at the street corner. An individual sitting in the back of the van grabbed Tina and forced her down onto a makeshift bed. Even in the midst of her panic and confusion, Tina sensed that they wouldn't physically harm her because of the care they had taken to provide her with a soft place to fall. But that was the last thought in her mind before the man in the back of the van injected her with a powerful sedative and she fell instantly asleep.

The van had lumbered on through the night, eventually stopping at one of the least well-guarded East German border crossings. This team had accomplished this crossing a number of times before and knew exactly which border patrol guards were on shift at this time of night, which ones could be trusted, and which ones could not. They had no difficulty slipping across into East Germany and continuing on to their destination, a safe house in the woods about two hours away from the border.

When Tina awoke in the morning, lying on a thin mattress and clean sheet under a warm featherbed, she had no immediate recollection of where she was. Feeling groggy, she first attributed that sensation to jet lag. The aroma of coffee aroused her and she raised herself on one elbow to look around, finding a tray of coffee, hard rolls, butter, and jam beside her on a chair. At first grateful that her gasthof hosts would provide room service, then feeling her privacy had been invaded without her request, Tina peered around the small room, which had one small window. The thought occurred to her that it didn't resemble her gasthof room in the slightest and, suddenly, the memory of the night before returned in full force.

Tina sprang from the bed, knocking the tray over as she did so, spilling coffee on the hard cement floor and breaking crockery in the process. The outside door to the room burst open and a man with an AK-47 rushed in.

"*Was ist denn los*?" he bellowed. He waved the machine gun at the mess on the floor.

"What am I doing here?" Tina cried out. "Where am I?"

"*Ich spreche kein Englisch*," the man said. "*Sie müssen mit jemanden anderen sprechen.*"

"Please, I don't understand you. What is going on? Get someone to help me! Please!"

Tina watched helplessly as the man turned his back, stepped outside, closed the door, and locked it. She raced the few steps to the door, yanked on the doorknob and pulled as hard as she could.

"Open the damn door!" she yelled. "Get me out of here! I'm a U.S. citizen! I'm an Army officer! You can't do this to me! I have rights, you know! Just what the hell do you think you're doing?"

Tina kicked the door over and over, and then she remembered the window she had spotted from the bed, but when she flung back the curtains, all she saw was plywood that had been nailed up from the outside. Searching around the room for anything that could break the glass and then pry the plywood away from the frame, Tina could see that her captors had left very little in the room of tool value. The chair could possibly work, but the window was five feet off the ground, and Tina didn't know if she could hoist the chair that high.

Just as she was picking up the chair to give it a try, the door opened again, bringing with it a breath of fresh air. Tina was amazed at how stuffy the room could become in such a short time once she realized she was locked in.

Expecting the man with the AK-47, Tina was surprised to see a new individual and even more so to hear a man speaking English with a Russian accent.

"I see you did not care for your breakfast this morning," he said, looking at the remains of her tray on the floor.

"Where am I?" Tina demanded. "Who are you and what the hell is going on?"

"All in good time, Miss Loyola, all in good time." Taking only two steps to cover the room, the tall, lithe man with dark hair picked up the chair, turned it around so its back was facing her, and sat down straddling it, crossing his arms over the back.

"I trust you had a good night's sleep?" he asked. "We provided a little something to help you out in that regard."

"I have no idea what you're after!" Tina said vehemently. "What is this all about? You can't possibly think you'll get away with this."

"Oh, but my dear, I do and we will." The man smiled. "Unfortunately, you have begun to poke your nose into places where it doesn't belong."

"What do you mean?"

"The untimely demise of your sister is best left to the findings of the official report. It is in your best interest that her death be known to be an accident."

Tina sputtered, "But I believe otherwise."

"Tut-tut, Miss Loyola. You're not hearing me. I'm trying to convince you what is in your best interest. Please listen to me closely, because that is exactly why you are here. What were you doing when we apprehended you?"

"I was in a phone booth—" Tina said.

"Yes, and who were you calling?" the man asked.

"Don't you know?" Tina asked angrily.

"As a matter of fact, we do. Your best friend's husband, First Lieutenant Wayne Yarrow." Tina's face drained of blood. "Ahh, like so many people, Miss Loyola, you can't help but give yourself away. No matter, we already knew the answer anyway."

"What do you want from me?" Tina's voice was barely above a whisper.

"You were, I believe, about to divulge information about a so-called conspiracy. And, Miss Loyola, we can't have that. We've worked too hard and too long to get where we are to have our plans wrecked by someone like you."

"I don't understand. What are you up to?"

"That isn't really for you to know, now is it, Miss Loyola? Just as in your intelligence agencies, we also deal in the need to know. And I would say, unequivocally, that you don't have a need to know." The man pointed the tips of his fingers together as if he had come to a decision. "And so, we will keep you here until our mission is done."

"What do you mean?" Tina felt her insides cave a little and nausea begin to rise.

"We don't intend to harm you, Miss Loyola. We just need to be sure you can't communicate with anyone. That's all. We have to complete our mission. Isn't that what your army says? The mission comes first?"

The man stood up from the chair, placed it next to the bed again, carefully avoiding the broken crockery and said, "I'll send in another breakfast tray. I'm sure you'll be hungry again before too long. It was nice chatting with you, Miss Loyola."

CHAPTER 69

FORT WAINWRIGHT, ALASKA
3:45 P.M., SATURDAY, MAY 31

It was Saturday afternoon before Iris got hold of her dad. "I feel like I'm treading water, Dad."

"What's going on, pumpkin?"

"I would have called you sooner, but I had to work some things out first."

"That's my girl, taking matters into your own hands as usual. What's this all about?"

General Tucker was at home in his quarters for a change. Although Congresswoman Tonnelli was still in Alaska, she was touring Fort Richardson for the day and wouldn't return until late that night. He had no obligations or responsibilities for her or her entourage until the next day. After the week he'd had with the snowstorm, Petrovich's death, and Tonnelli's visit, he didn't mind relaxing for a few hours. Tucker settled back into his old beat-up leather recliner that had followed him from post to post, put his feet up, and prepared himself for a long chat.

Spunky, Iris's Dalmatian, hurried from across the room, circled around the chair twice, sniffed the floor, and then laid his nose onto his paws. Tucker had brought Spunky home from the pound for Iris on her tenth birthday and, not only had they been inseparable, Tucker could swear that Spunky now knew when Iris was on the phone and insisted on being as close as possible.

Iris brought her dad up to date on Cynthia Hailey's analysis of the pink slips and her suggestion that a former FBI agent was responsible, as well as letting him know that she had approached Lieutenant Colonel Brannon for help in identifying the forger.

Tucker sighed. "I find this so disheartening, sugar," he said. "If this is true, I feel someone's got to let the commanding general know. Do you want me to give him a call?"

"No, Dad, thanks. I want to give Colonel Brannon a chance to work on finding the guy first."

"I don't know if that's wise, Iris. If this were happening on my post, I'd want to know right away."

"Yes, well—" Iris wasn't sure why, but she didn't want her dad to get involved. She felt she had to solve this problem on her own. She was really only using him as a sounding board, just as she'd done all her life. In earlier years, true, he'd help her solve problems, but she was an Army officer now and this was her problem, not his.

Tucker decided to change course. "So is everything alright in your class?"

"Yes. I let Captain Gibson—the company commander—know right away that my pink slips had in fact been forged. So there's no problem with me staying with my class."

"But Iris, surely Captain Gibson is going to report this up the chain of command. If he didn't, he'd be derelict in his duty."

"You know, Dad, I got the feeling that Captain Gibson is the kind of officer that just wants problems to go away. I showed him the pink slips, I showed him Cynthia's analysis, I told him they had been forged, and he looked at me with a bland face."

"Are you saying he didn't believe you?" Tucker asked.

"No, I think he probably did believe me. I just don't think he really cared all that much. I didn't tell him I was going to look into it anymore. As far as he's concerned, all I really cared about was staying with my group. He promised to let me do that if I could provide proof that I shouldn't be set back. I've done that."

"But what's he going to tell his higher-ups when they ask why Lieutenant Iris Tucker wasn't sent back to another class like she was supposed to be?" Tucker posed to his daughter.

Iris thought for a moment. "Well, first of all, I don't think anyone's going to be asking. Second, if anyone does, and he hasn't reported that I'm still in my class, all he has to do is give some plausible explanation. I don't think he's going to tell them the records were forged, though, because that would bring all kinds of questions about how he found out, credibility, etc. That just sounds like too much work and something he probably doesn't want to go through. Finally, Cynthia's done us all a favor."

"What's that?" Tucker could only imagine what his old friend had done.

"She gave us new forged white slips to replace the forged pink slips in our files."

"Kudos, sweetheart!" Tucker applauded.

"She called Thursday evening and I was able to drive there last night and pick them up."

"That's brilliant, Iris!" Her dad was more impressed than he'd been in a long time—and it took a lot to impress Sherman Tucker.

"We think so. So the girls and I have another rendezvous with the records room tonight. Our training files will soon have a clean slate and then each of us can go in, request to see them, and demand to find out why we were washed out, sent back, etc."

"And the forger will be running around like a chicken with his head cut off, unable to vocalize that your records aren't clean or he'll incriminate himself. What a twisted web you've woven." Tucker laughed. Then he became somber. "But you girls better be careful, Iris. If someone has gone to this much trouble, he could be dangerous. And you don't even know why he's done it yet."

"I'm not worried, Dad. If things get too hot, I can always count on you, right?" She smiled.

Tucker felt the warmth of her smile through the thousands of miles of phone lines. "Yes, dumpling. But, unfortunately, I might not be able to fly to your rescue immediately, so I'm ordering you—yes, ordering you, Lieutenant—to be careful!"

"Yes, sir!"

CHAPTER 70

ETLINGEN, WEST GERMANY
12:20 P.M., SATURDAY, MAY 31

Gunter and Marthe had cleared their personal schedules on Saturday to escort Tina wherever she would like to go. When Gunter had left Tina at the gasthof the night before, they had arranged to meet again at noon. Just as before, the two police officers had pulled up in Gunter's Renault and waited at the curb for her to exit the building. Since they were early, Gunter opened up the newspaper and propped it on the steering wheel to while away the time. Marthe popped out of the car for a few moments to get each of them—and Frau Loyola—a *Limonade* and pretzel from the *Café-Konditorei* down the block. She and Gunter devoured their treats and drank their ice-cold Limonades, and still Tina had not appeared.

Gunter looked at the large round clock hanging from an iron post in front of the post office across the street. Tina was twenty minutes late.

"Perhaps she misunderstood the time," he said. "I'll go in and call up to her room." He brushed crumbs off his lap, looked behind him for oncoming traffic, opened the door, and got out.

Inside the gasthof, a small lobby to the right offered a welcoming seating area for tired travelers as they waited to check in, look out the window for a taxi they had ordered, or sit with their baggage until their tour bus arrived. Gunter spotted a shelf with a house phone just a few steps past it, but, realizing he didn't know Frau Loyola's room number, stopped first at the reception desk.

After obtaining her room number, Gunter patiently dialed her extension not one, but three times, thinking that perhaps he had made a wrong connection. After the third try, he was convinced she wasn't in the room as he had let the phone ring a considerably long period.

Before returning to the car, Gunter stopped at reception again. "Excuse me. Have you seen Frau Loyola—the woman from Room 319—go out today?"

The young clerk behind the desk looked up from her paperwork and said, "Frau Loyola? I'm not certain I'm familiar with her."

Gunter described her. "She's an American—tall, thin, dark hair. Arrived here yesterday."

The young woman, whose nametag proclaimed her to be Susanna, said, "I wasn't here yesterday, sir. I have seen a few women with that description leaving this morning, though. I'm sure that isn't of much help," she shrugged.

"Have you been on the desk all morning?"

"I came on at eight, and I was only gone for ten minutes at nine-thirty."

"Does anyone else work on the desk with you?"

"Yes, José."

"Would you kindly ask José to step out here for a moment, please, Susanna?" Gunter asked pleasantly.

Susanna nodded, stepped away from the desk, and walked a few paces to a room behind a closed door. She tapped lightly on the door, opened it immediately, poked her head in, and returned without waiting for a response. Within a moment, a young man with perfect bone structure, dressed in a white silk shirt and impeccable black trousers, glided to the reception desk.

"Guten Morgen," he said briskly in perfect German. "How may I be of service?"

Gunter was momentarily taken aback. He realized he had expected a young man with the name of José and with tightly curled black hair and golden olive skin to speak only passable German—and that with a heavy accent. Quickly recovering his wits, Gunter explained, "I'm Polizei Hauptmann Gunter, and I'm looking for the American woman in Room 319, Frau Loyola. Have you seen her this morning?"

José stared intently into Gunter's piercing blue eyes, and Gunter could sense the truth emanating out of José's warm brown eyes. "No, Herr Hauptmann, I haven't seen her."

"You do know who she is, though?" Gunter specified.

"Absolutely. I make it a point to know who all our guests are."

Gunter slid a quick view over to Susanna, but the young clerk was oblivious. It was apparent she wasn't nearly as conscientious about the hotel trade as José.

"Were you here then when she checked in yesterday morning?" Gunter asked.

"No, actually, I worked the night shift last night," José said matter-of-factly. "From eleven to eleven. I'm technically off-duty now. I just haven't left yet," he smiled.

"So, you saw her when?" Gunter felt confused.

"She wanted to make a phone call last night and came to the desk for help. I explained how to use the phone booth on the corner and gave her some five-mark coins for dollars."

"And what time was this?"

"I think it was around 11:30. Yes, it had to be, because it was right after I'd come on duty and before the big church bells ring at midnight."

"How long was she gone?" Gunter asked.

Now it was José's time to look perplexed. "I never saw her come back in the building."

"What do you mean?" Gunter's voice raised two octaves.

"Herr Hauptmann, our desk is never left unattended. You also see behind me here, in our cubbyholes, that we have the old-fashioned brass keys. Very heavy. We ask our guests to leave them here when they go out. Frau Loyola did that at my request when she left to make her phone call."

"And you're certain she never returned?"

José turned around, ran his fingers along the wooden cubbyholes built into the wall, found the plaque marked 319, and pulled out a key. Laying it on the countertop at chest-high level, he said, "There you are, Herr Hauptmann. Frau Loyola never came back to ask for her key."

Gunter thought for a moment. "Perhaps she left her door unlocked, since she intended to return quickly, and simply forgot she needed to pick up her key."

"I don't think so, because we lock the outer door at midnight. She would have had to ring the bell and have us buzz her in. Last night, no one came in after midnight."

"You're certain about that?"

"Absolutely," José said confidently. "I was here all night. If I left for a moment to go in the other room, I could still hear the buzzer, and I never heard it."

"Was anyone on the desk with you?" Gunter asked.

"Not until eight o'clock this morning, when Susanna arrived," José said. "I don't know where your American lady went, but you can be certain she didn't return here."

"Would it be possible to check her room?"

"But, of course."

"Do you mind if my assistant comes with us?" Gunter asked.

"Not at all," José said.

Gunter went outside, imparted the disturbing news to Marthe, and the two went back inside the gasthof, where José was waiting beside the stairs with the key to Room 319. As the three trooped up the winding stairs to the fourth floor, they all remained silent, wondering where the American woman could possibly have gone on her first night in Germany. Each in his or her own way was hoping to find her sacked out in her room, recovering from jet lag.

José first knocked on the door to Room 319 politely, then a second time, loudly. When these two attempts engendered no response, he called out and said, "Frau Loyola, I'm here with the police and we're going to enter your room. Please don't be alarmed."

With that, he unlocked her door and the three went inside. Instead of a rumpled room and a young woman in bed, they found all of Tina Loyola's possessions in the room, indicating that she had gone out and intended to come back in just a few moments. Her television set and bedside lamp were on. The bed had obviously not been slept in. Her belongings were strewn about the room. The most revealing and startling item was her purse, seemingly tossed casually upon the bed. She hadn't taken it with her. It was clear she had not intended to go far or be away long. And yet now she'd been gone for more than twelve hours.

Marthe said, "What do we do now?"

Gunter commented, "We have to wait a bit, to see if she shows up."

"I don't like this, sir," Marthe said, shaking her head.

Nor do I, Gunter thought. Something seems to have gone terribly wrong. But what?

CHAPTER 71

NEAR FAIRBANKS, ALASKA
12:30 P.M., SUNDAY, JUNE 1

General Tucker and Congresswoman Tonnelli were scheduled to have brunch on Sunday. Rather than take her to the Officers' Club, which did have a fabulous spread, Tucker decided to take her to one of his favorite haunts on the outskirts of Fairbanks. The Silvery Pine Lodge was set in the woods and could only be reached by driving several miles along back roads. A person had to know where they were going to be able to find the place, and even then, at night, it was perilously difficult to locate. Upon arrival, though, bursting out of the last strand of tall firs and pine trees, one came suddenly upon the old lodge, built in the 1890s, in a small clearing. Its worn wooden logs, wide porch, steep roof, and hand-split railings were a welcome sight in the day, particularly if sunlight were glinting off freshly fallen snow or dewy grass. But it was its most spectacular at night, when white orbs of incandescent light draped the restaurant from front to back and top to bottom and created a beauteous vista of enchantment as travelers broke free from the frightening darkness that threatened to envelop them in the dark woods. They scurried to the lodge, drawn to its light and promises of warmth. The Silvery Pine Lodge also enraptured the palate so that people who knew how to find it were inclined to keep coming back, though most tried to keep the place a secret except from the most deserving.

Either Tucker decided that Congresswoman Tonnelli had fallen into the category of most deserving, or he decided that it was a good secluded spot to take her where the two of them might be able to converse without their entourages or busybody onlookers. Another good thing about the Silvery Pine Lodge was that it was not an "in" place, and its clientele was comprised of primarily local folk. That meant Tucker knew they could both be more relaxed during the meal and with each other. Tucker hadn't examined his motives too closely when he'd asked her to join him for brunch and had suggested the Silvery Pine Lodge. For her part, Melinda had been only too pleased to accept when he had told her a little bit about the place.

Rather than having his driver along, Tucker decided to pick Congresswoman Tonnelli up himself. It was a bit out of the ordinary, but somehow he didn't think she'd mind. She struck him as a very down-to-earth woman. He had been impressed with everything he'd learned about her in the past few days. She was smart as a whip, beautiful, intensely motivated about the military, and crazy about her kids. He was amazed at how much he had learned about her two sons—both in their early twenties—in the short time he'd spent with her. Dave had just graduated from the University of Texas Law School, fluent in Spanish, and was currently in Venezuela with a nonprofit organization helping to build hospitals before he started with a law firm in Dallas. Having graduated from the University of Chicago with a degree in journalism, Rick had managed to get a foot in the door at the *Chicago Tribune* as an overseas correspondent and would soon be showing up all over the world. Congresswoman Tonnelli was understandably proud.

Once they were seated at Silvery Pine Lodge, Melinda Tonnelli reached over and patted him on one hand, saying, "Please do stop calling me Congresswoman. Since it's just the two of us, I'd much prefer for you to call me Melinda."

General Tucker actually blushed. "I'd love to. But only if you'll call me Sherman."

"I'd be delighted, Sherman."

"So, Melinda, are you looking forward to getting back to Washington?" Tucker asked.

"Yes and no. You know I'm leaving tomorrow for my trips to Korea and Japan. It's been quite a while since I've seen any of the military installations out there, so those are of keen interest to me. I'm hoping there will be some improvements there."

"I can tell you take a sincere interest in our men and women in uniform, Melinda," he said.

"Absolutely. As do you. It's our job, isn't it?" Melinda looked him in the eye and shrugged. "It's what we swore an oath to do. I take it very seriously. As a matter of fact, there's something I want to bring up to you before I forget."

Tucker grimaced. "I hope your report isn't going to make our post or some of our other Alaska installations look bad."

"No, Sherman. You already know my thoughts in those areas. No, this is personal."

Tucker looked at Melinda, with his eyebrows raised. "Go on," he said.

"My best friend in all the world is married to someone at Fort Rucker," she said. "And it seems that a young lieutenant down there has come to him with a problem. Her name is Iris Tucker."

Melinda paused and looked closely at Tucker for his reaction.

"I know," he said. "I talked to Iris yesterday, but I'd like to hear the rest of what you have to say first."

Letting out a sigh of relief, Melinda said, "Thank goodness! I was hoping I wouldn't be bringing bad news to you. My friend says that Iris has had her records examined by a handwriting expert and that someone has apparently forged the records of all the young women who were recently set back or washed out. My friend's husband has been tapped to help Iris find this forger."

"Yes, that's basically what Iris told me. Although there is one thing more. They're replacing the forged papers in their files with new forgeries. The handwriting expert has given them training slips that say they've been passing, and they supposedly were going to sneak into the records room last night to put these into their records."

"I get it!" Melinda said. "That way, no official person at Fort Rucker can go back to their records and claim these women are failing again without making a big stink about where the old forged records were. Or at least without it being a big mess."

"Right."

"You might think that as a congresswoman I would have a problem with what these women are doing, but it seems to me they're simply rectifying an injustice. Their true and original training records were falsified; they found that out, and now they're replacing them with a facsimile of the originals. Do I have a correct understanding of the situation?"

"Yes." Tucker smiled. "I've had a pang of guilt wondering about the whole thing myself, but have come to the same conclusions. Those young women should never have been put in the predicament they're in. I don't think I would have solved it the same way as Iris—"

Melinda grinned. "I probably would have and might have been a ringleader just like your daughter. I already told you I've been receiving tons of calls every which way from constituents as soon as the whole flap at Fort Rucker came about. Wives upset that their husbands were going to die because they were flying with incompetent female pilots, men upset that women were getting over in flight school, female pilots upset that their reputations were being shattered, female students at Fort Rucker who didn't know which way to turn, parents calling on behalf of their children in the military, and, of course—"

"The ever-present, incorrigible, never-satisfied press?"

"Yes. Always wanting a statement about this comment or that from so-and-so or so-and-so. Well, I called up General Eckling down there and told him that as a senior member of the House Armed Services Committee, I intended to investigate this very thoroughly."

"How did he respond?"

"Oh, very cordially. That's how all of you generals act," Melinda said with a smile.

"We've learned our lessons. It doesn't take too many times to realize that a congressperson wields a lot of power. For most years in uniform, a military officer believes that a civilian isn't all that important. When we're suddenly faced with people in Congress, we quickly, and graciously, I might add, have to change our tune."

"Let's backtrack a little. I have encountered some of you generals who might not be considered all that gracious," Melinda countered.

"That's because they still make the mistake of thinking the stars on their shoulders outweigh the zero stars of a congressperson. Just because you can't see the stars on a congressperson's suit or dress doesn't mean they don't have a zillion of them zipping around in the daylight."

Melinda laughed. "And we know how to pull them out to our advantage!"

"Don't you, though! So what do you think about all this at Fort Rucker?"

"I've told my friend to keep me apprised, and I've got contacts that can start looking into this. It's a bit more difficult to get the ball rolling while I'm hurtling along from one country to another, but I'll do what I can."

"Is there anything I can do?" Tucker asked.

"Well, I hate to get you involved," Melinda said.

"Actually, Melinda, I am involved. My daughter is one of the young women down there. So, aside from being an Army officer who finds this all totally abhorrent, I'm also a very concerned parent."

"Touché, Sherman. Maybe the best thing you can do is stay in touch with your daughter. Persuade Iris to get her friends to talk and come forward with as much information as they can about time, dates, circumstances. Hopefully, they didn't destroy the forged documents they had. Perhaps you can check on that with your daughter the next time you talk to her. We might have to build a case against someone."

"Sure thing. This is, as I'm sure you're aware, a very sticky wicket to be involved in. It's hard to know what side of the fence we're going to find the right people on."

"Yes, I know. So, we have to be careful, and it might be best if you take my lead. Just keep me informed about Iris's doings."

With that settled, Tucker and Melinda proceeded to enjoy their brunch, surprised to find nearly three hours had passed in each other's company and neither felt like a moment had gone by without having something to say. Each found the other so easy to talk to that it was almost disappointing to break up the meal, but all the other diners had left and they could see the wait staff eyeing their table and wanting to clear away their dishes. Reluctantly, the two left the restaurant, dashing out into a sudden rainstorm.

With no umbrella, Tucker took off his suit jacket and held it over Melinda's head as they ran towards his four-wheel-drive vehicle. As they reached the passenger's door, both their hands reached for it at the same time. Melinda had noticed he hadn't locked the door, which was why she had tried to open it herself, but Tucker was trying to be a gentleman. With both their hands slippery from the rain, they collided on the door handle, and Melinda lost her balance and fell in the muddy parking lot. Watching her lying on the ground and laughing, Tucker realized at that moment that he could easily fall in love with her. He helped her up and invited her to his quarters where she was able to wash her filthy clothes in comfort. He gave her some of Iris's athletic clothes to wear, and the two sat around for the next couple of hours getting to know each other even better than they would have imagined possible a few days earlier.

CHAPTER 72

WATERTOWN, NEW YORK
8:20 P.M., SUNDAY, JUNE 1

Just as the sun was setting, Frank had awakened and heard a noise in the house. Steeling himself against an intruder, he crept down the stairs, keeping his back to the wall and gliding noiselessly down the carpeted steps to the living room, from which he had an obstructed view of the rest of the house. Pausing to hold his breath, he looked quickly around the room where lengthening shadows promised to hold a possible threat.

All of a sudden, a blur of movement in the kitchen caught his eye and Frank tensed. He could hear someone moving beyond the dining area.

"Who's there?" he called.

Hearing another scuffle in the kitchen, Frank rapidly moved from the stairs across the width of the living room and dining area to the kitchen opening. Keeping his body protected by the wall and showing only as much of his head as was necessary to obtain line-of-sight into the kitchen, Frank could finally see the intruder.

Eliza had spent the day outside and had entered through the cat door, starved and thirsty after her long hours of play. She might have been in and out while Frank was asleep, but he wouldn't have noticed—he had been dead to the world.

"You gave me a fright, you stupid cat!" Frank mumbled.

Tina had left Eliza with a two-week supply of cat food and water in automatic feeding systems and, as an outdoor cat, she didn't need anyone to come in and change a litter box.

Watching Eliza lap up her water, which was sloshing onto the floor as much as into her mouth in her frantic desire to drink, Frank realized he was also parched. In addition, he felt like he was burning up. Yanking open the refrigerator, he grabbed one of the cold Heinekens and rubbed it across his hot forehead. Thinking about drinking the beer, though, made him nauseous. Instead, Frank filled a tall glass with icy water from a pitcher in the refrigerator and drank it straight down. Not yet quenched, he grabbed another full glass of cold water and walked into the living room, drinking more slowly as he went.

I need to take care of Cecil and Mark now, he thought, but first, I need to warn Deirdre. I don't know how much she knows. Tina is gone, so I better make sure her friend knows what's going on.

As he sat down in one of Tina's easy chairs, Frank thought, damn, I'm hot. I feel like I'm sweating from the inside out, but all I have on are my boxer shorts. What the hell is wrong with me? What's the temperature in this place? Maybe Tina turned her air off before she left.

Frank got up and checked the thermostat, which he was astonished to see was still set at a comfortable 72 degrees. Tina obviously wasn't in the habit of changing the temperature when she left for a considerable period of time. So what the hell is wrong? he asked himself again. Maybe the vents are closed. After checking a few of them, Frank realized nothing was wrong with the air conditioning in Tina's house and he began to understand something was going haywire with his own air conditioning system.

God, I feel like shit. Beads of sweat began to form on Frank's forehead. I better go lay back down, he thought. Maybe I should take a shower first. That might cool me down. But the bed linen is cool. The shower is too much work. I'll do that tomorrow. If I feel better. Right now I just want more sleep. I need to get in bed.

Frank dragged himself out of the chair, leaving the half-finished water on the glass coffee table. Feeling weaker in the legs by the minute and recognizing that his body ached and wasn't simply sore after many hours of sleep, he hauled himself back up the stairs and down the hall to Tina's guest room. Plopping himself onto the bed, Frank found the strength to pull his legs all the way up and was asleep the instant his eyelids closed.

Throughout the night, pneumonia raged to gain control over Frank's body and, by morning, his lungs were pierced through, forcing him to gasp while breathing. His temperature hovered at 105 degrees. Barely at the edge of consciousness, each time Frank awoke he had no idea where he was or what he needed to do. Then he drifted off again to a dream world where he was absolutely of no use to anyone. He needed to get to a hospital, but he didn't have the wherewithal to recognize the extreme danger he was in.

CHAPTER 73

FORT RUCKER, ALABAMA
7:25 A.M., MONDAY, JUNE 2

Colonel John Buehlankamp stared at the casualty report in front of him. He couldn't believe what he was reading. First Lieutenant Chad Emerson had been found dead in his apartment Sunday afternoon. An apparent suicide or accidental death—it hadn't been determined yet. He'd been intoxicated and died of asphyxiation. So it seemed likely that he'd accidentally turned the gas on and forgotten about it while he lay in an alcoholic stupor.

Stupid, stupid kid! Buehlankamp railed at Chad. How could you be so idiotic?

Buehlankamp crumpled the paper and threw it in the trash can. He had no idea what was going on. First John had died, and now Chad. Buehlankamp had seen the casualty report on John Friday morning. There was no question that John had committed suicide. He had done a pretty bang-up job of doing it the old-fashioned way—kicking the bucket. And if he really was queer—well, Buehlankamp could understand why John might not have been able to take the dichotomy anymore of being an Army officer when it wasn't tolerated. Hell, he wouldn't have been able to look John in the face once he'd known, so it was simply better that way.

But Chad? There was no clue as to why Chad would have committed suicide, so it had to have been an accident. But,

Buehlankamp asked himself, why two of my key guys in one week? Yes, that's the question. Exactly!

Buehlankamp became excited, stood up from behind his gray executive desk, and started pacing. Pounding his right fist against his left palm, he walked back and forth from the American flag in its pedestal to the battered leather couch against the opposite wall. Buehlankamp's office was filled with memorabilia from his tours in Vietnam, Germany, Fort Benning, Korea, and elsewhere.

Something doesn't seem right, Buehlankamp thought. His eyes narrowed. He had tried to contact Chad after seeing the casualty report on John, but hadn't been able to get in touch with him. Of course, now he knew why. Buehlankamp had been traveling for several days during the week, and had just returned to Fort Rucker late Thursday night, so if any of his men had tried to get in touch with him, they wouldn't have been able to find him.

How likely is it, Buehlankamp wondered again, for two of my officers to commit suicide? I don't think it's likely at all. He frowned. If there's a possibility that Chad's death is a result of foul play, then perhaps John's death wasn't a suicide, either. He rubbed his right temple in a circular motion several times while he pondered the thought.

Buehlankamp sank down onto the leather sofa and propped his legs onto the coffee table, nearly knocking over a crystal box given to him by a Korean counterpart a decade earlier. Agitated, he quickly sat up, reached over to the trash can, pulled the casualty report back out, and smoothed the paper along his knee.

Looking at the bold, hard facts of Chad's death, and thinking back to the circumstances of John's death, Buehlankamp began to shake off the notion that either one was a suicide at all.

Someone is knocking off my men, he decided. I don't know who it is, but I'm damn sure going to find out. Whoever it is thinks they're pretty smart, but they've got to go a long way to fool me.

Buehlankamp decided to call Cecil that evening and convey some instructions. It was apparent that they needed to shift some plans. Other people were moving in too close.

CHAPTER 74

ETLINGEN, WEST GERMANY
11:45 A.M., MONDAY, JUNE 2

In Etlingen, the summer sun was beginning to warm the back office of the polizei headquarters. Gunter was in conference with Damrow, and had just filled him in on Tina's disappearance. It had taken until Monday morning to find Herr Major, as apparently much of the American Army in the region had been called out on an alert over the weekend and was unreachable. Gunter hadn't dared to discuss it with anyone else in the Army at the moment, although he had reported it up his own chain of command.

Damrow slumped in his chair and dangled an unlit cigarette.

"Would you like a light, Herr Major?"

"What? Oh, no. I'm trying to quit. I just carry it around with me. Makes me feel better."

"I am reluctant to call her unit in the United States, you understand."

"Because she said her ex-brother-in-law reported two of the conspirators are assigned there."

Both men nodded an understanding.

"Frankly, this is way out of my league," Damrow said. "Conspiracies, disappearing Army officers—I don't know what I'm expected to do here."

"I felt I needed to let someone in the U.S. military know and, after all we've learned, I didn't know who else to turn to."

"She isn't even a member of my unit."

Gunter shrugged sympathetically. "I completely understand. This is a burden for you. I wouldn't know what to do in your shoes, either. A foreign country, a missing officer—" He shrugged again. "But I feel we must do something. There are only a few of us who know what is going on."

Damrow suddenly leaned forward. "But do we know what's going on? I haven't the foggiest idea. Here I am in the Army and I feel as if the institution I know has been kidnapped."

"Sir, I'm sure it is only a few—how do you say?—bad apples."

"I hope so. Women in my unit have been killed in what you've suggested was an intentional helicopter accident. Now the sister of one of them is missing. This doesn't seem like a coincidence to me."

"Nor to me," Gunter said quietly. "I'm afraid it's very ominous."

"Are you thinking someone was watching her?"

"It seems to me the most likely explanation, Herr Major. We are not a country in which kidnappings or disappearances normally take place, especially not of Americans, and particularly not in the middle of our towns. Since we knew that she knew about a possible conspiracy, we can only conclude that others must have known it, too, and wanted to shut her up."

"My God!" Damrow exhaled slowly. "This is a nightmare. It's making me less trustful of my own people."

"It could have been anyone. At the moment, we have no clues."

"And you weren't able to find anything out over the weekend."

"No. And no phone calls. No messages. No proclamations of responsibility, kidnap demands, or anything of that sort. It's as if she vanished into thin air," Gunter said.

"I'm sure you checked out witnesses from Friday night."

"We've had a notice up and we went to the nearby stores and residences, but no one noticed anything. We're still hopeful that we'll get some information. But as time goes by, the trail gets colder. Trust me, Herr Major, we're working on it."

"I still don't see how I can be of any use."

"I suppose by telling you, I feel I've fulfilled my obligation to let the U.S. military know. Now I leave it in your hands as to where it goes from there."

Damrow sighed loudly. "Hauptmann Gunter! You're putting me in an impossible situation!"

"Perhaps you could contact her ex-brother-in-law, or her best friend in New York."

"From what Tina said, I don't know that her brother-in-law would be so willing to hear from the unit commander where his ex-wife was killed—not that I had anything to do with it."

"I think he knows that. He knows who the conspirators are. That's the point. If you can find him, perhaps he'll talk to you."

"You're the police officer. Why shouldn't you be doing this?"

"Because, Herr Major, you have the special Autovon phones and you know all the military installations. It sounds very efficient to me for you to find this Frank Lambert. I also think that perhaps Frau Loyola went out to call some friends at her post in New York—maybe some other female officers she's assigned with."

"What makes you think that?"

"Because Friday night when we had dinner I urged her to think of her female aviator colleagues. Frau Loyola knew of the conspiracy and that men were out there planning to kill off female Army helicopter pilots, but other women didn't. I asked if she wanted that on her conscience."

"So you're thinking that's why she went to the phone booth so late at night?"

"It's crossed my mind, yes. If you could start by calling her female friends in New York, maybe that would get us somewhere. Maybe we'd at least know who she called."

"Can't you do it from your police end?" Damrow asked incredulously.

"You don't know a lot about police work, do you?" Gunter asked. "It really isn't like you see in the movies. I wish it were."

"Alright, Gunter. You've got yourself a partner in crime." Before Damrow could change his mind, Gunter tossed him Tina's address book, which he had found in her hotel room.

CHAPTER 75

CAMP VANGCHON, SOUTH KOREA
1:15 P.M., MONDAY, JUNE 2

Monday was the first day Lydia Porterhouse had been able to get in touch with most of Congresswoman Tonnelli's important contacts. Considering that Lydia and the congresswoman had been flying from Alaska to Korea and then considering the time difference, there wasn't much that most people were able to do that day once Lydia made the connection and handed the phone over to the congresswoman.

Melinda was dispensing tidbits of information to the hungry press, intimating that something was going on at Fort Rucker that journalists and television media might like to look into, not playing her own hand too much nor tipping the scale as to her own belief of what might have happened. Having played the Washington game for two decades, Melinda was keenly aware that the ravenous press corps could uncover facts faster and oftentimes more accurately than anyone else. She just hoped some of them might feel loyal enough for the tip to give her a head's up and let her know before printing or airing their stories.

Arriving in Korea, Congresswoman Tonnelli specifically asked to be able to go to the two units involved in the friendly-fire shoot-down of the Blackhawk—both D Battery, 1st Air Defense Artillery Battalion, and 92nd Aviation Company. It took some scrambling on behalf of the itinerary planners, but they arranged it for that afternoon.

Melinda knew she had royally ticked everyone off by ripping their itinerary to smithereens and, more importantly, insisting on showing up at two units that weren't expecting her at all. She rarely ever pulled rank in such a way but she found it completely moronic that the general's aides hadn't put themselves in her shoes and figured out ahead of time that, of course, she would have wanted to go to the scene of the most significant fratricide incident in Southeast Asia in years. These military minds sometimes stuck their heads in the sand and it took someone like her to yank them back out, spitting unpalatable granules fitfully all along the way.

At D Battery, Congresswoman Tonnelli initially felt pity for the poor battery commander, Captain Roger Whitman. When the artillery regiment commander had knocked on the door of the tracked vehicle containing Whitman, a young enlisted man had opened it. But the vehicle was so small that Whitman had no time to hide his surprise and utter dismay that he was having to face—without any preparation or warning—his big boss and a member of Congress. Looking scared and pale, but certainly aware of why they were there, Whitman rose from behind his tiny station, came to the door, and firmly closed it behind him. Within seconds, though, his fear had disappeared and he regained the confidence and bearing of an Army officer—a leader prepared to go to battle.

"Captain Whitman," Congresswoman Tonnelli said, "I'm interested in finding out, unofficially, of course, why your unit fired on the Blackhawk."

"Yes, ma'am. We've been asked that a lot already. My radar technician noted an unidentified aircraft that didn't respond to our calls to identify itself. Our orders were to shoot such aircraft down when they were in or near the DMZ."

"Just like that?" Although Tonnelli asked the question, she didn't sound incredulous.

"Yes, it's called weapons-free. It means we don't have to get permission. That would take too long. The aircraft could be gone by then."

"Do you have many aircraft that enter the DMZ or come that close to it?"

"There have been a few close calls since I've been the commander. I've been here about a year now. But we've never had a problem before with anyone using their IFF."

"And the IFF works all the time?"

"It's supposed to. It's supposed to be a fail-safe system."

"But nothing is fail-safe, is it?"

"I'm sorry, ma'am, but I don't think I know how to answer that."

"So what do you think now, Captain Whitman? Now that you know it was a friendly-fire incident."

"Obviously, it was tragic, but I don't think my men are at fault, ma'am, if that's what you're after." Whitman shook his head. "I don't know why the aircraft didn't respond. I don't know why their IFF wasn't working. All of us feel just sick about it."

"Are you reviewing your procedures to see if anything should have been done differently?"

"Oh, yes, ma'am. At the battery level and on up. I don't think any of us are going to rest until we're certain we don't get caught like this with our pants down again." Whitman looked over at his regimental commander, who nodded approval and dismissal at the same time.

Tonnelli said, "That's fine, Captain. Thank you for letting me take up some of your time."

At the 92nd Aviation Company, Congresswoman Tonnelli talked to unit members who had known CW2 Driver, WO1 Rodriquez, and Sergeant Abraham. She grasped that Driver knew the training area very well and never would have flown in or too close to the DMZ unless something was wrong with her equipment. Tonnelli also learned that Rodriquez was new to the unit and, therefore, could possibly have taken control of the helicopter and maneuvered it dangerously close to the DMZ, but only if Driver had not been cognizant of what was going on, which was deemed by most members of the 92nd to be so unlikely as to be nonsensical. Nevertheless, Tonnelli did catch undercurrents or rumblings that Driver had made some mistakes and that the accident would boil down to that catchall—pilot error. Highly regarded as a crew chief, Abraham wouldn't have gone up in a helicopter without all systems functioning properly, so the IFF had to have been working when the UH-60 took off. Tonnelli had also spoken with all maintenance personnel who had worked on the helicopter the last time it had been in the hangar and they were firmly convinced nothing was wrong with its electronics or radios, raising the confusing point—why had its IFF stopped working?

Something was nagging at Congresswoman Tonnelli and she couldn't put her finger on it. She felt it was just there in the background of her mind, swimming around in a vacuum, and if she could only take hold and grab it, she could make sense of these strange and various happenings. She had an extraordinarily logical mind, and her brain synapses were constantly firing away subconsciously on the one helicopter accident in Germany with three women, and then another in Korea, and forged records for female flight students at Fort Rucker. She hadn't yet begun to consciously think a pattern existed between them all, but the dots were beginning to connect without her help.

CHAPTER 76

FORT RUCKER, ALABAMA
4:45 P.M., MONDAY, JUNE 2

By Monday afternoon, Stefania was exhausted. She had run her fingers through her rolodex and come up with the names and phone numbers of the most significant contacts she could think of—people she had met during her racing career and her father's diplomatic years, and through her Italian vintner and restaurateur family. The journalists and politicians were particularly interested in what she had to impart on someone forging records at Fort Rucker and sending female flight students back or washing them out altogether. The question on everyone's lips was why and, of course, who. She didn't have an answer for either and hoped that by casting the net widely enough someone would be able to dig the hole deep enough for the Army to have to explain itself.

She had started her forays with Melinda Tonnelli on Saturday afternoon and continued them incessantly, whenever Bill wasn't around. It wasn't that she was afraid of him knowing what she was doing—she just wanted him to be able to honestly look his superiors in the eye and say he hadn't leaked the information. In case her actions ever came to light. Which she doubted they would.

Stefania knew the first stories would probably break on Tuesday, maybe on Wednesday. And then the maelstrom would begin. She hoped her husband was prepared. He would be in the thick of it with General Eckling.

"Bill," she began that night. "Have you found anything out for that young lieutenant who called here the other day?"

"No, not yet," Bill replied.

"What if anyone else gets wind of what's going on here?" Stefania asked.

"We'd be in deep trouble."

"I don't imagine General Eckling would take it very well, would he?"

"God, that's the understatement of the year. He would have a cardiac arrest."

"You realize, don't you, that Lieutenant Tucker might have gone to other individuals as well?"

"What do you mean?" Bill asked sharply.

"It's very possible she might have gone to the press."

"Why in the hell would she do that? She doesn't even have all the information yet. For pete's sake, she asked me to find out who was forging the information."

"Well, if I were her, that's what I would do."

Bill gaped at Stefania, who sat innocently flipping through a woman's magazine. "That would put enormous pressure on Fort Rucker."

"I can imagine," Stefania murmured.

"If the press got the idea that someone was forging records here of just female students—I can't even begin to think of the full-scale pandemonium that would ensue."

Stefania turned to him with widened eyes and said with her voice raised, "Bill, you would practically have a riot on your hands! The number of people who would be upset would be astounding!"

"I hope to God she hasn't done that," Bill said.

"Well, didn't you say she was in league with a bunch of the other women whose records had been forged, too?"

Bill groaned. "My God, you're right! There's any number of them that could have decided to spill their sour grapes. Not that I blame them, mind you."

Stefania gave him a sympathetic look. "Just in case, you know, it might be a good idea to have some answers on the back burner."

Already light-years away, Bill said, "What? Yes, yes. You're right. We've got to be prepared. And I have really got to push to find out who this person is who has forged these records. You may very well have something there, Stefania. People may start breathing down our necks very shortly and we may have less time to lose than we think."

"Whatever you say, dear." Stefania smiled inwardly to herself.

CHAPTER 77

FORT WAINWRIGHT, ALASKA
6:50 P.M., MONDAY, JUNE 2

Captain Earl Thornton and Vanessa Robison were eating dinner at the Officers' Club. The main restaurant was closed on Monday evenings, but they were able to order burgers and fries from the bar. Earl enjoyed a nice cold beer while Vanessa decided that ginger ale would be fine.

"Here's to returning to normal," Earl said, holding up his beer for a toast. They clinked glasses and he took a long drink. "It was a hellish week. First the unbelievable snowstorm, then Congresswoman Tonnelli's visit, and then Major Petrovich."

"I know." Vanessa shook her head in disbelief. "I can't believe it either. And, of course, you've been in the thick of it all. So, I gather you liked Congresswoman Tonnelli alright?"

"Yeah. I thought she was pretty okay. She always took the time to chat a couple of minutes with everyone she came in contact with. You know—the technicians, the clerks, the food service people. They all ate it up. Once they got over their nervousness."

"That was me. You know I met her on Friday right before my ARL exam. I was already a bundle of nerves because I was going up with Nelson. But then—boom—there she was—Congresswoman Tonnelli right in my doorway."

"Yeah. We showed up like that all over the post. Everywhere we went was on the itinerary, though, including the maintenance hangar." Earl sounded a little defensive.

"I guess with everything that was going on, I never got that memo. Showed up today, though! Mysteriously in my in-box. Lot of good that did me after the fact!"

"Well, I wasn't in your office when you were talking to her. She liked to be one-on-one with everyone as much as possible."

"That did make it easier for me. She was really very personable, I have to admit," Vanessa said.

"What did she talk about?" Earl asked.

"She asked me what was on my agenda for the day, which was really easy to talk about Friday, and she wished me luck."

"Maybe she was your guardian angel during your checkride." Earl laughed. "I'm only kidding. I'm sure you would have done fine anyway."

Vanessa punched Earl in the shoulder. "Actually, it gave my confidence a real boost to have a congresswoman giving me a pat on the back. It didn't hurt any—that's for sure!"

"So, you said you needed to talk to me about something, Vanessa. What's up?"

"I got the strangest letter from my cousin in Korea the other day." Vanessa proceeded to fill Earl in on what she had heard from Lindley. When she was finally through, she asked, "What do you make of all that?"

"It sounds clear to me that your cousin is afraid the friendly-fire accident wasn't a result of friendly fire," Earl said.

"But he's also very certain there was nothing wrong with the equipment."

"That's true, but only up to the point where it remained under his observation."

Vanessa was startled. "You can't possibly be thinking someone planned this!"

"I am a military intelligence officer, Vanessa, and that's where my mind logically goes. Obviously, your cousin left the helicopter at a particular point and someone with ulterior motives and access to the aircraft could have done something to the equipment that was then undetected. It could even have occurred at the very last minute. I'm not an aviator, but it would seem to me that there's always an opportunity, especially on an open flight line, to sabotage a helicopter."

"I would say you're right about that, Earl. Most of the time we're not concerned about that, although I would think that in Korea they have more safeguards against sabotage, just because of being so close to the DMZ and North Korea. But still, there are so many moving parts and always a number of people with access to a helicopter—" Vanessa thought about the possibilities. "That still begs the question of why, though?"

"True," Earl replied. He raised his eyebrows. "So what are you going to write your cousin?"

"That's my dilemma. I thought you might have some suggestions for me. He seems to think that as a maintenance officer I can give him good advice as to what to tell the investigating officers, but all I can think to tell him is to go with the truth."

"I think that's the only thing he can do. Listen, if it will help, I'll talk to General Tucker for you. I know he's keenly interested in this accident. His daughter is a flight student at Fort Rucker."

"Oh, really?"

"Yes, and she was one of those involved in that flap about being set back."

Vanessa's mouth tightened. "Oh, God, that has been so upsetting."

"Believe me, I've heard a lot about it from him. He's one ticked-off dad. But Lieutenant Tucker actually didn't allow herself to be set back."

Earl filled Vanessa in on Iris's adventures and findings at Fort Rucker, raising Vanessa's blood pressure to the boiling point, although she managed to calm down slightly when she heard that Congresswoman Tonnelli had promised to look into the matter.

At the end of the evening, Earl said, "I'll let you know if General Tucker has any special thoughts for your cousin. Otherwise, it's been a great night."

CHAPTER 78

SOMEWHERE IN EAST GERMANY
9:30 A.M., TUESDAY, JUNE 3

Ever since Tina first realized her predicament, she had struggled to figure a way out. It seemed that her only option was to physically overcome her guards. During three days in captivity, Tina had keenly examined every inch of her small cell and had a reluctant admiration for her captors. The cement floor and plaster walls did not appear conducive to permitting her to escape easily. The boarded-up window could not be thrust open with the chair. When Tina had attempted it on Saturday, she had not only wrenched her back, she had made such a racket trying to slam the steel legs of the chair into the window glass, shattering it onto the floor, that the guard outside the door rushed in. Immediately taking in what she was trying to do, he grabbed the chair, tossed it outside and threw Tina onto the bed, slamming her up against the hard wall and cursing at her all the while. Tina was in agony for the next two days. Although her captors considered tying Tina to the bed, each time they came into the room to leave a tray of food and tea, they found her lying in a fetal position and presumed she wouldn't try anything so reckless again.

On Tuesday morning, the man with the Russian accent reappeared. He brought the chair in with him and had a seat.

"I trust you've learned your lesson, Frau Loyola," he said, leaning back and crossing one sharply creased trouser leg over the other. His freshly shined brown Oxfords gleamed, even in the shadowy depths of the cell. To ensure that Tina neither hurt herself nor used it as a tool, her captors had removed the overhead light fixture and the only light available in the room was what came through the door whenever the guards opened it. "I was sorely disappointed to learn of your escapade this weekend. I see you may have seriously injured yourself."

Tina lay with her face to the wall, and her back to the man. Although her mind cried to know why she was there, and she would have made any number of sacrifices to leave, she was determined not to give this man or her other captors the satisfaction of knowing how badly she hurt or how desperately she wanted out. It was the only card she could play.

"I can assure you no one is looking for you. After all, you have no family. Your sister is dead, and you have no parents."

Tina listened, in spite of herself, with a sense of dread.

"I feel sorry for you, Frau Loyola, really I do. I believe you had the best of intentions. But you were so misguided. As is often the case in your capitalist society."

Up to this point, even though the guards had threatened her with AK-47s and the man had come in on Saturday speaking English with a Russian accent, the thought had simply not occurred to Tina that she might have been taken out of West Germany. The possibility was too completely absurd. Although she had been told some group was keeping her indefinitely, she presumed it was a terrorist organization in West Germany. It would have made perfect sense for it to have AK-47s and a leader with a Russian accent.

All of a sudden, though, something clicked and the frightening thought came into her head that she could just as easily have been transported out of West Germany. As she lay staring at the wall, Tina willed herself not to panic. Her breathing became labored and the man's voice began to drone endlessly in her ears. If she were behind the Iron Curtain, how would she get out? Why would she have been taken behind the Iron Curtain? Bile started rising in her throat as she began to think she might never go home again.

"You see, Frau Loyola," the man continued. "You are of no use to the U.S. Army. They will scarcely notice you are gone. You are of great use to us, however, and we will keep you here as long as we need you."

Tina involuntarily shivered.

"Cold, Frau Loyola? Perhaps you're coming down with something. These summer bugs can be nasty. We'll keep a close watch over you, though. Don't you worry about that." The man smiled. He stood up from his chair and leaned over Tina's breakfast tray. "Oh, tsk-tsk. I see you haven't enjoyed your refreshment. And we have taken such pains to provide you with American food."

He swooped the tray off the ground and walked towards the door, quite pleased with the fact that his prisoner was choosing to ignore what little nourishment he felt morally obligated to provide.

CHAPTER 79

CAMP VANGCHON, SOUTH KOREA
12:10 A.M., WEDNESDAY, JUNE 4

Ever since he had spoken with Congresswoman Tonnelli, Lindley Ochiotto had been wondering about the IFF and why it had failed. The destroyed pieces of the UH-60 had been airlifted from where they had been strewn over the countryside and placed in a section of the 92nd Aviation Company's maintenance hangar. They had been cordoned off inside a general-purpose medium tent with yellow tape, police barriers, and hanging plastic, all in an attempt to keep out unauthorized individuals. Over the past several days, the area had been swarming with the accident investigation and safety hierarchy from Fort Rucker.

Although Lindley knew he wasn't considered one of the authorized personnel, he felt a compulsion to examine the IFF. Realizing he wouldn't be allowed access to the investigation area during the working day without a good explanation or without coming under suspicion, Lindley decided to try to sneak into the grounds after everyone had gone for the night. Due to the high-level interest in the case, it was one in the morning before the last inspector had closed up shop.

Lindley entered the tent through its back entrance from the rear of the hangar, keeping his movements slight and quick. With the lights still burning, he had no difficulty locating the IFF that was tagged and sitting on one of the tables lining the tent wall. Although it was slightly bent from the crash, its rugged durability had ensured that it survived relatively intact. Examining it closely, Lindley noticed when he opened it that it was no longer set for the same pulse settings that he had established. He couldn't imagine how they had been changed, for he knew exactly what he had set the pulse settings at and what they needed to be for the transponder to respond to ground control radar and to appear correctly on radar screens. Even slight variances in one direction or the other could cause the transponder to fail.

Thinking back to the day of the accident, Lindley remembered climbing out of the UH-60 after he and Driver had completed the test flight of the repaired IFF. She had been totally satisfied with its performance and said so. There was no doubt about it. He could clearly see in his mind's eye her giving him a thumb's up through the cockpit window as he walked away into the maintenance hangar.

Something made Lindley's memory bank come to a screeching halt. After the test flight, Driver had gone to lunch before she took Rodriquez on the orientation flight. While out on the flight line, Lindley recalled noticing Lieutenant John Datterly making a special trip to Driver's aircraft, remaining out of sight for just a few moments, and then returning to the hangar. Since pilots were always on the flight line and in and out of helicopters, Lindley hadn't thought anything special about it until now. But knowing, however, that he had left the IFF in perfect working order, that the artillery unit claimed the IFF wasn't operating properly, and seeing evidence that someone had tampered with his equipment had jarred his memory.

Moreover, now Lindley could understand why Lieutenant Datterly had committed suicide. If he was responsible for the deaths of three members of the 92nd, for whatever reason, he must have been carrying a terrible burden. Lindley hadn't been terribly close to Lieutenant Datterly and hadn't observed him in any particular fashion after the shootdown, but if anything, he would have said the lieutenant had hid his feelings well.

Wasn't it often said that bottled-up feelings sometimes exploded? Apparently the lieutenant could no longer contain his guilt over what he had done, and, therefore, killed himself.

It made perfect sense and Lindley needed to get to a phone to call Vanessa. He knew there was an Autovon line in his platoon sergeant's office and, at this hour of the morning, no one would be around. He hated to wake her, but he knew she would understand.

Slipping quietly out the back of the tent, Lindley only needed to walk a few feet to his platoon sergeant's office. Although the door was locked, the platoon sergeant had given him a key a few months ago so that Lindley could have access anytime. Tonight it came in particularly handy. Shutting and locking the door with its opaque glass window behind him, Lindley sat down in the gray plastic chair at the scarred wooden desk and picked up the old black telephone. Opening his wallet, he pulled out Vanessa's phone number and carefully dialed the Autovon number to her BOQ room.

"Hello?" Vanessa's voice sounded very tinny and far away.

"Vanessa? It's me. Lindley." Even to himself, Lindley's voice echoed and bounced against the high walls of the room.

"Lindley! How are you? What are you doing calling me? It's so great to hear from you!" At seven-thirty in the morning, Vanessa had been preparing to dash out the door to work, but she wouldn't have missed his call for the world.

"Did you get my letter?" he asked impatiently.

"Yes, I—"

"Never mind. I've got more to tell you. The IFF wasn't working, Vanessa. I've just taken a look at it. Someone tampered with it. Deliberately. And it caused me to remember seeing someone near the helicopter that day after my test flight."

"Who?"

"The same lieutenant who killed himself. Lieutenant John Datterly. Did you hear about that?"

"No."

"That doesn't matter. I don't know why he did it—tampered with my IFF, I mean. I can imagine why he killed himself. Even if he meant to cause their deaths, apparently he couldn't live with it after all."

"Lindley, are you trying to tell me you think a lieutenant in your company did something to the IFF—on purpose?" Vanessa was incredulous.

"Vanessa, connect the dots. I've had longer to think about it than you. I've got to get off the phone and get out of here. I just wanted to let you know. This wasn't any friendly-fire accident. In fact, this wasn't any kind of accident at all."

"But at least the perpetrator is dead now," Vanessa said, trying to make sense out of the news she'd just been bombarded with.

"Yes, thank goodness," Lindley agreed.

"Did he have anything specific against one of those women or some beef against your unit?"

"Not that I know of. He was a nice guy. A great officer. Everybody liked him."

"I guess you just never know about people, do you, Lindley?"

"No, cuz, you never do. Say, take it easy, okay?"

"Sure thing. Love ya."

"Love you, too,"

As Lindley unlocked the door and turned off the light to his platoon sergeant's office, he came face to face with Colonel John Buehlankamp, who, as the commander of the training brigade at Fort Rucker, had deemed it worth his while to visit the UH-60 investigation site in Korea. While inspecting the IFF, Lindley had not been as alone as he had thought—the last inspector, Buehlankamp, had heard a movement in the building behind him as he was departing and had stealthily returned to oversee what was going on. In addition, he had eavesdropped on Lindley's conversation with Vanessa through the locked door.

Lindley had no opportunity to express surprise or fear before Buehlankamp, a burly man six feet six inches tall and weighing two hundred and forty pounds, clamped one hand on Lindley's mouth, the other on the back of his head, and broke his neck. Buehlankamp let Lindley's limp, lifeless body drop to the hangar floor as he swiftly departed, secure in the knowledge that he had stopped one leaky gap.

CHAPTER 80

WATERTOWN, NEW YORK
9:15 A.M, TUESDAY, JUNE 3

Lying on the guest bed in Tina's house, Frank watched the lengthening and shortening of shadows as they played on the walls and ceiling of the room, as much as they were able to peek in from behind the drawn curtains and closed blinds of the one window. As day turned to night and back again, Frank knew there were things he needed to do—foremost of which was to get up and take care of himself, but he couldn't find the energy to do so. It took nearly all of his willpower to turn his head slightly and look at the changing shadows, which he found endlessly fascinating.

For two days, the constant coughing and spitting of sputum prevented him from obtaining any useful or restful sleep. Whenever he did achieve sleep, he usually awakened to find himself hot and feverish, gasping for air, with his chest hurting. Sometimes he woke chattering in a freezing chill and wrapped himself in the blankets he had thrown off in his fevered state. His hot, dry eyes could barely make out the room and he kept the lights off because only the darkness felt comfortable.

When he felt thirsty and up to the effort, Frank stumbled to the bathroom in the hall, cupped his hands, and slurped a drink of water. It was so much trouble, though, that he didn't do it too often. He wasn't hungry and didn't even think about going downstairs. After a fruitless search for medicine in Tina's bathrooms upstairs during a couple of his upright lurches, he gave up. He didn't have the strength to go downstairs and back up again and felt it wasn't that important. In his mind, all he had was a cold and just needed to sleep it off.

Whether conscious or asleep, Frank's delirious state of mind deceived him into thinking he was involved in purposeful action. He was mixing up the past, present, and future—forgetting that Crystal was dead, that he and Crystal were divorced, but continuing to plan his vengeful quest against her murderers. In his sickbed, he railed against the conspirators and devised all sorts of deaths for them, not remembering that he had already killed John and Chad. He did feel an urgency to warn someone about something, but he couldn't remember who. It tickled at the back of his mind, but each time a vision of Crystal would appear, erasing the bad and he would be flooded with warm memories of their life together as if they were still going on.

CHAPTER 81

FORT WAINWRIGHT, ALASKA
6:55 A.M., TUESDAY, JUNE 3

As General Tucker's aide, Earl usually tried to get into the office as early in the morning as possible. One of his tasks was to peruse the morning newspapers and read *The Early Bird*—the compilation of published newspaper articles that the Pentagon put together and distributed around the world. He highlighted anything he felt General Tucker should take note of immediately even though he knew the general would read it all at his leisure later.

On Tuesday morning, one of the items that caught Earl's eye in *The Washington Post* on an inner page was a small piece asking a rhetorical question about whether the Army knew of a cover-up going on at Fort Rucker. Earl's heart skipped a beat and he looked at the article more closely. Anonymous sources were alleging that records of female flight students—who had been succeeding to this point—were being forged and the women, for some unknown reason, were being pushed back to another class or thrown out of flight school altogether. Although the item was very short, Earl felt certain that other reporters, other newspapers, and other media would pick up on it quickly. Circling the article with a red felt-tip pen and drawing an arrow towards it, Earl set the newspaper aside to take into the general's office when he had completed going through the stack.

Fifteen minutes later, Earl grabbed *The Washington Post*—opened to the page with the Fort Rucker article—and the other papers, and knocked on the door to General Tucker's office. Invited in, he said, "Sir, I think there's something you might like to know about right away."

"What's that, Earl?" Tucker, relaxing on the sofa by the fireplace and surrounded by papers, looked up from his morning coffee.

"The situation your daughter was telling you about at Fort Rucker—"

"Yes?" Tucker said expectantly.

Earl held out *The Washington Post*. "It's hit the paper."

Tucker briefly closed his eyes, then opened them, grimacing slightly. "How bad is it?"

"Well, it didn't make the front page."

Quickly scanning the article, Tucker said, "Whew! The commanding general down there is going to have his hands full. I don't envy him."

"No, sir."

"Thank God Iris's name isn't in here."

"Since it's such a short article and in the middle of the paper, perhaps no one will notice it."

"You don't really think that, do you, Earl?"

Earl shook his head. "I think this might be just the start of something really bad."

"If I were—who's that general down there, Earl?"

"Eckling, sir."

"Yes, that's right. Eckling. If I were him, I'd get on the ball right now and start figuring out my answers. If there's any truth at all to these allegations, I sure wouldn't try to cover it up, that's for sure. Heaven help him if he does. The press will eat him alive if he tries to do that. But sometimes we military guys think we're so much smarter than civilians and we don't have to give out any information. Reporters are able to sniff out inconsistencies and lies, and they know how to ferret out the truth. If he thinks he can fool them, he'll be digging his own grave."

Before Tucker had an opportunity to look through the other newspapers, Earl said, "Sir? I wonder if I could have a moment of your time about another matter."

"Sure thing, Earl."

"A friend of mine here has a cousin in Korea who was the electronics technician on that Blackhawk that went down. You know, the one hit by friendly fire?"

Tucker nodded.

"Well, her cousin doesn't see how it could have been friendly fire because he says the IFF was working up until the time of the flight, and he would know because that's his job. So he's worried about what to tell the investigators."

Seeming impatient, Tucker said, "I don't understand, Earl. What's his problem?"

"The guy's afraid he's going to get blamed because they're saying the IFF wasn't working."

"So he tells the truth. It's as simple as that. I don't understand the difficulty."

"Apparently he's feeling there's going to be a lot of pressure from the artillery unit to blame the aviation unit."

"I don't get it, Earl. It doesn't sound like a hard decision to me."

"Okay, sir. Thanks."

A little later that morning, Earl received a phone call from Vanessa. She said, "I tried to reach you before you left for work this morning, but you'd already gone."

"Yeah, I'm usually in by six. I have to beat General Tucker in, you know."

"Right, I forgot. Say, Earl, my cousin called me this morning from Korea."

"You don't say!" Earl was intrigued.

"Earl, he's had a chance to examine the IFF from the Blackhawk that crashed and now he's thinking that perhaps it wasn't working."

"Really? What makes him think that?"

"He said something about the equipment made it look like it had been tampered with."

"Oh, Jesus."

"And, Earl, he thinks he knows who did it."

"You're kidding! How could he possibly know that?"

"He remembered seeing someone near the helicopter that day—after the test flight, but before the crash. He said something about a guy who committed suicide a few days later."

"I remember that!" Earl exclaimed. "I've got that casualty report here on my desk. Just a second!" He rummaged through the papers to his left. "I found it! First Lieutenant John Datterly. Does that sound familiar? Did your cousin tell you his name?"

"I think that's it. Yes, yes—I'm sure of it. I knew you were going to talk to General Tucker for me anyway, but this changes everything. It's no longer an investigation with someone's career on the line, but the fact that someone tried to commit murder. Even though he's dead. I think the Army needs to try to find out what happened."

"I'm sure General Tucker will help put things into the right channels. I already had a chance to talk to him about your cousin, by the way, and his advice was for your cousin to tell the truth. I'm sure that's what he'll still say. Your cousin should probably go straight to the authorities in Korea—the CID, his commander, etc. I don't know why he hasn't done that yet."

"Lindley hasn't always been strictly logical. It's often been frustrating."

"Well, I'll let you know what General Tucker says."

Earl put the phone down and immediately went to the general's office. "Sir," he said. "You're not going to believe this."

After Earl had relayed Vanessa's news, Tucker said, "Get Congresswoman Tonnelli on the phone for me. She has to hear about this."

CHAPTER 82

SEOUL, SOUTH KOREA
5:15 P.M., TUESDAY, JUNE 3

Congresswoman Tonnelli was departing Seoul, Korea, for Japan when General Tucker's phone call finally caught up with her.

"You're a hard woman to find, Melinda!" he complained. "I've had Captain Thornton searching high and low for you."

"I know," she replied. "It's always like this when I'm out on a junket. I've spent my two full days in Korea and now I'm off for three days to Japan. I'll be exhausted when I finally get back home. You're surely not calling because I left clothes in your dryer?"

"What?" Tucker's heart skipped a beat, remembering back to their Sunday afternoon. "No, this is serious. There's a young aviation maintenance officer here who's confided to my aide that her cousin, who worked on that downed Blackhawk, said it might not have been friendly fire."

"I can see where people might be conflicted, Sherman. I talked to the people at the artillery unit, and they say the IFF wasn't working, which was why they fired, but I also talked to everyone at the aviation company and most of them feel it had to be friendly fire."

"No, no, Melinda. That's not it at all. I've got more information."

Melinda was puzzled. "How could you possibly have more information than the people here?"

"My young officer got a phone call from her cousin this morning. It seems he was examining his IFF that everyone says wasn't working. He had been convinced it was working and didn't understand how the artillery unit could say it had quit working. Apparently he had just tested it before the crash."

"Oh, my God, Sherman!"

"What?"

"You don't know, do you?"

"I have no idea."

"I know exactly who you're talking about. I chatted with him yesterday. A young guy with an Italian name. Very confident, intelligent."

"I don't know, Melinda. I've never met him."

"He was found dead this morning."

A slight pause ensued. Finally, Tucker responded. "That's not possible. Earl said Vanessa had just spoken to him."

"I know it's true, Sherman. It delayed my departure out of the post. There was a huge commotion everywhere."

"This is unbelievable. How did he die?"

"They're still determining the cause, but it appears to have been murder. His neck was broken. He was found in the maintenance hangar outside his platoon sergeant's office."

"Melinda," Tucker asked slowly, "do you think there's any connection between his death and his phone call to his cousin?"

"It seems too coincidental to be a coincidence, doesn't it? And the platoon sergeant's office is just a few feet away from where the Blackhawk is being stored."

"You mean that's where he had gone to find the IFF?"

"I have no idea what an IFF looks like or if it was there, but I'm guessing it was. Since it was supposedly the faulty piece of equipment, it must have been there, don't you think?"

"Melinda, this has blown my mind so much that I've almost forgotten to tell you the rest."

"You mean there's more?"

"Vanessa's cousin told her that the person who sabotaged his IFF was an Army officer who had committed suicide there last week."

"What is going on in the Army, Sherman?"

"I don't know, Melinda. There's the suicide or accident on my post, this suicide in Korea, the murder in Korea, several fatal helicopter accidents, and forged records at Fort Rucker—every single thing involving aviation."

"Maybe there's some common thread that we're not seeing yet."

"That's why I'm calling you. You're the most brilliant woman I've ever met." Tucker uttered the comment without thinking.

Melinda said softly, "Plus, I feel quite certain that you're very concerned about a young second lieutenant, in addition to the responsibility you must feel for all your other personnel."

"Yes," he said simply. "I feel quite helpless actually. I can sense something taking place that shouldn't be, but it's swirling around me and I can't catch it. I need your help."

"You have it, Sherman. I promise you, I'll do everything I can. For Iris and everyone else."

CHAPTER 83

NEAR WOLFGANG KASERNE, WEST GERMANY
12:40 P.M., TUESDAY, JUNE 3

Damrow and Gunter were having lunch on Tuesday at the gaststube near the Kaserne where they had met for the first time.

"What kind of luck did you have finding Frau Loyola's female colleagues?" Gunter asked, stabbing his pommes frites with a fork and dragging them through mayonnaise. The aroma of burned sausages wafted through the air.

Damrow took a long swig of mineral water and said, "Guess what. It wasn't her address book. It was her sister's."

Gunter raised his eyebrows. "Na ja? What do you mean?"

"Apparently Tina brought her twin sister's address book with her." Damrow shrugged. "I don't know why."

"So, you could not find anything out about her colleagues?"

"Not without calling up her unit and asking around. I don't think we're ready to do that, are you?"

Tearing off a piece of brötchen, Gunter put it in his mouth with a chunk of bratwurst loaded with mustard and chewed steadily. "Nein. Not yet. I think that would be too risky."

"I did find something else in there, though."

"Ja? What's that?"

"A phone number for Lambert."

Piercing blue eyes met their match across the table.

"And? I suppose you like building up the suspense. Did you find this brother-in-law?"

"Not exactly. It wasn't his phone number. But I did talk to his mother. Seems she still thinks he's in Hawaii."

"Ahh. The parents are always the last to know."

"Well, I noticed that there was a penciled entry next to it, that said "Dad—work"—so I called it. Obviously Frank hadn't clued the mother in on his whereabouts, so I thought I'd give the dad a try since he had a separate number."

"What is it you Americans say, Herr Major? You are killing me. Please, get on with it! Do you know where he is?"

"You know, Gunter, I kind of like doing this detective work. Takes me away from the humdrum Army work. A bit exciting for a while."

Gunter laughingly raised his fist and shook it.

"Alright, alright!" Damrow said. "I talked to Mr. Lambert at work. Seems his son called him from Alaska, so he was there. The next plan was to head to Fort Drum. As far as Dad knows, Frank should be there now."

"Does he know anything about this conspiracy?"

"If he did, he didn't act like it. Didn't say a word."

"Would you? I know I would not say anything to a stranger who called on the phone about my son."

"No, I wouldn't, either. Nevertheless, although he sounded like he knew he was protecting his son's secrets, it wasn't as if he thought his son was doing anything illegal. You know, maybe his son just wanted a holiday but not coming home to see mom—that sort of thing."

"And Dad did not think that was strange?" Gunter asked.

"He went on a bit about his boy, so I got the idea his son could do no wrong. It probably wouldn't be any stranger if his son went to India to live for five years, came back, and didn't say boo. He sounded like that kind of dad."

"Now the question is, what is going to happen at Fort Drum? We have no inside track for warning anyone about him."

"Do you really think he might kill someone?"

"Good question. Did he kill a conspirator in Alaska? Have you heard of any murders in the Army in the last few days up there?"

Damrow shook his head. "No. It would have been in the *Army Times*, I'm sure."

"That's good to hear."

"Perhaps it was all talk by an angry ex-husband and blown out of proportion," Damrow suggested.

"The only problem with that, my friend, is that Frau Loyola is missing. I don't believe that's a coincidence. I think she's missing only because of what she knows. We have to find her."

"And Frank."

"And Frank. And find out who the two conspirators are at Fort Drum."

"I did find out something else interesting," Damrow commented.

"What's that?"

"Crystal Lambert had an organization listed in her address book called the Women Military Pilots. It had a president's name and phone number and I tried calling it a couple of times but didn't get an answer. I'll give it another try tonight."

"What do you think it is?"

"I have no idea, but it's worth finding out. Maybe they can help us get in touch with female pilots."

"Great idea, Herr Major! Great idea!"

CHAPTER 84

WATERTOWN, NEW YORK
8:15 A.M., THURSDAY, JUNE 5

On a wet, rainy Thursday morning, Claire Diderot parked her car in Tina Loyola's driveway, and, huddled under an umbrella, gathered her cleaning materials from the trunk. Rushing to the house with a bucket of supplies in one hand and umbrella and keys in the other, avoiding the drenching downpour was difficult. Standing under the roof of the front porch, Claire shook the rain off her umbrella, left it beside the door, and went inside.

Claire wasn't surprised by the musty smell. She knew Tina had been gone for a week. The place had that closed-up odor of a house that hadn't been opened up in a number of days, particularly in summertime. Claire popped open the windows in the living room a few inches to let in some fresh air. Even though it was raining, the porch roof would protect those windows from bringing in water, but having some air circulating was essential, she thought.

As Claire went into the kitchen, she puzzled over the things she saw. Tina was meticulous about leaving her house spotless when she left on a trip, but this time, there were glasses on the counter, in the sink, on the kitchen table. In addition, there were a couple of plates in the sink and bowls on the counter, with a smattering of silverware lying around. It made absolutely no sense at all. Claire shook her head and quickly made short work of it all, rinsing everything off, putting it in the dishwasher, and starting a light load. She figured she could empty the dishwasher before she left.

Claire had been a house cleaner for a long time, and the quirks of the people whose houses she cleaned had long ceased to amaze her, so she didn't concern herself too long over the change in patterns in Tina's kitchen. She simply figured Tina had had too much on her mind, had become involved with a fella and refused to clean up after him, or something else that Claire just couldn't be bothered to come up with a reason for.

Nevertheless, as Claire continued to clean around the house on the bottom floor, she noticed a man's t-shirt and a pair of men's athletic shoes. She thought these were strange and raised her eyebrows, for Tina hadn't told her she had a boyfriend or that anyone was living with her. But any number of Claire's clients suddenly acquired new and interesting living arrangements, and who was Claire to judge? She needed the income her employers provided and Tina Loyola was one of her weeklies. No way was she going to upset that apple cart by asking any probing questions that were none of her business. By folding the t-shirt and setting it on top of the shoes at the foot of the stairs in an unobtrusive, neat, and out-of-the-way pile, Claire was still doing her job without seeming as though she were being nosy.

Finished with the downstairs, Claire gathered her materials and the vacuum cleaner and trudged up the stairs. She always cleaned the master bedroom and bath first to ensure she kept her energy up for those most important rooms. That wasn't to say she slighted the other rooms, but just in case she found her physical energy slacking, or something interrupted her—say, an emergency phone call, or the owners returning home unexpectedly—at least the best parts of the home would be completed.

Once satisfied with Tina's room, Claire opened the door to the guest room and flipped on the light. Her eyes immediately lighted on the tousled bed and the unkempt man in it.

"I'm sorry!" she exclaimed. "I didn't know anyone was staying here."

Frank didn't stir. The sour smell of the room suddenly hit her nose and forced her to take several steps backwards into the hallway.

"What—?" Claire tentatively poked her head back into the room. She could see tissues covering the floor like snowflakes after a blizzard. A thermometer was dangling from the edge of the nightstand. Several empty glasses perched precariously nearby.

Claire slowly walked over to the edge of the bed and picked up the thermometer. The last reading said a hundred and four. Oh my God, she said to herself, as she turned to look at the man in the bed. This man has been lying here sick. Perhaps for days. I've got to do something.

"Sir?" she said. Claire leaned over and felt his forehead. He was still burning up. He didn't move. Claire rushed to the bathroom in the hallway and grabbed a washcloth, ran cool water over it, wrung it out, and placed it over his forehead. She whipped the tangled bedcovers off his body, ran to grab a clean towel from the linen closet, doused it with tepid water, wrapped him in the towel, and covered him back up with the bedcovers.

For a third time, Claire dashed to the bathroom, this time with a glass, filled it with water, and, upon returning, attempted to shake Frank awake. Moaning slightly, he never opened his eyes. Claire sat on the bed, put one arm behind him, and coaxed him to swallow a couple of sips of water. Then she let him fall to sleep again and called 911.

By the time the ambulance arrived, Claire had found his wallet and knew who he was. She had heard Tina talk about her sister, and even knew why Tina had gone to Germany, so she knew Frank was Crystal's ex-husband. Frank, however, was barely hanging on. From the looks the ambulance personnel were giving each other when they picked him up, Claire wouldn't give anyone odds that Frank would make it. Claire figured Tina would want to know, and grabbed Tina's contact number in Germany.

As Claire watched the ambulance depart, however, she decided that she had enough to do to finish cleaning up the house. She was already behind schedule in getting to her next job, and having a sick man in the guest room meant she had tons of work to do before she could leave Tina's place. And, after all, she had already done her good Samaritan deed for the day by calling the ambulance. Salving her conscience, Claire bounded up the stairs and promptly forgot about Frank.

CHAPTER 85

ENTERPRISE, ALABAMA
7:45 P.M., THURSDAY, JUNE 5

Iris and her friends were once more sitting around her apartment. The tiny news article in the *Montgomery Advertiser* about the forgeries and throwing women out of flight school had caught Samantha Ellison's eye. Although some women were in the middle of night flying, ten had gathered at short notice to discuss the next steps they should take.

"Did you leak this, Iris?" Samantha demanded.

"Me?" Iris asked in bewilderment. "No! Why would I do that?"

"You do manage to go off and do your own thing without considering how it might affect the rest of us."

Iris was stunned. "Samantha, I'm sorry you feel that way, but I guess you're right. When push came to shove, I felt my back was up against a wall. I came up with the brilliant idea of breaking and entering into a government facility—on my own, need I remind you—and I didn't think in advance of calling a conference to ask permission of a group of women. I could have been in serious trouble. As it turns out, I was very lucky. Things worked out for me, and–" Iris raised her voice as she noted Samantha about to interject something. "—hopefully, they'll work out for the rest of you in the end, too. We did go back, altogether, and get your records, too, didn't we?"

Samantha nodded. "Yes, but I'm still set back."

"I know that, Samantha. We're working on that. But because we've put new white slips in your file, you can go in and ask to have that reversed. Why haven't you done that yet?"

The room fell into a silence while Samantha looked at her feet. "I suppose because I just don't have quite the chutzpah you do to march in there and demand what's rightfully mine."

"Then don't be jealous of me for something you can't do." Samantha's face reddened. "Sorry to be so blunt, Samantha, but we've each got to do it. We can't let this guy—this forger—get away with this. Now can we?"

Raising her eyes to look at Iris, Samantha suddenly realized, "You're right. I'm letting his false opinions of me keep me down. I have to stop that. I wish I'd had your conviction from the beginning."

"Atta girl, Samantha. I'll give you some pointers, okay? I know you can do it." Iris grinned and everyone clapped their approval. "Now, what do we think is going to happen here?"

"Have you heard anything yet about the forger?" Mary Ann Tate asked.

"No," Iris said. "Colonel Brannon hasn't gotten back to me yet. I'm sure he's working on it. He seemed quite distressed when I told him about it. And now that this is in the paper, the whole hierarchy here's going to be under the gun to explain what's happening."

"I wonder if he'll feel any loyalty to you or to us to clue us in," someone else said.

"Yeah, that's a good question," another voice threw in from close to the kitchen.

Iris sighed and shook her head. "I had a good vibe from him, that's all I can tell you. Until we hear from him, we can all keep our eyes and ears open for other information. Maybe we'll find something else out somehow."

"Bloody unlikely!" the first unidentified woman shouted. Everyone shifted uncomfortably in their seats and murmured amongst themselves.

Then Tatum Richards spoke up. "I'll tell you what I think we need to do. We need to involve the Women Military Pilots."

"What the hell can they do?" the angry woman asked. "All those people did was come here, give us a speech, and try to get our membership dues."

"I think they're a bit more than that," Tatum said to the group. "When I listened to Captain Moore, I understood that they intend to be a number of things—a networking group, a lobbying organization, and a group that gets information about women in aviation out to the public."

"It's an awfully new organization," Samantha said doubtfully. "What could it possibly do for us?"

"True, it is new," Tatum agreed. "But it was founded on top of the Women Airforce Service Pilots, so there's that basis of experience. Now, I don't know how many of you are really aware of their politicking experience, but those ladies worked hard to get Congress to recognize their World War II efforts and, in the end, they got veteran's benefits. That's been through this organization."

"But what exactly could they do for us in this situation?" Iris asked.

"Granted, it's not that big an organization, but one of their goals is certainly to protect women in aviation and I would think that means to correct injustices. It seems to me they would go to bat for us. Perhaps we could get their members to call their congressmen?" Tatum suggested.

"That's a good idea!" Mary Ann was excited. "It doesn't take many phone calls or letters before members of Congress get the message that the public is upset about something. Something like one phone call or one letter represents thirty or forty people with the same view, I've heard."

"There's another advantage to getting in touch with the organization, because I think there are a couple of female flight instructors on the post. And if they're a member of Women Military Pilots, it would make it easier for someone from the organization to approach them for information about the forger than a flight student. Don't you think?" Tatum asked the group. She saw heads bobbing. "It might be a little awkward for one of us."

"Okay, then. Agreed." Iris said. "We'll be contacting the Women Military Pilots, Captain Georgina Moore, president, for their help. I'll get in touch with her since I know all the details about the forgeries, or would you prefer to do that, Tatum?"

"No, by all means, Iris, you go right ahead. We're quite happy with your leadership, aren't we, girls?" They all nodded their assent and the meeting broke up as everyone had studying to do or a flying class to get to.

CHAPTER 86

ARLINGTON, VIRGINIA
7:10 P.M., THURSDAY, JUNE 5

Secretary of the Army Reginald Maloney stormed off the golf course at the Army Navy Country Club. He had gone to play eighteen holes at the end of the day, hoping to take his mind off the unrelenting events of the past few weeks, but he couldn't stop thinking about *The Washington Post* accusation that the Army had some scam going on at Fort Rucker to throw women out of flight school.

He threw his putting iron into his golf bag, jumped in the golf cart, and peeled off towards the clubhouse. Kaneesha had come along for the ride. She didn't play golf, but loved watching her husband play and it was a fabulous opportunity for the two of them to just be together and enjoy the outdoors. With the weather slightly misty today, however, Kaneesha pulled her cardigan tightly around her and braced herself against the sides of the golf cart as it careened along the path.

"Honey! I thought this outing was supposed to calm you down," she said.

"Yes, well. It's also given me a lot of time to think."

"That's dangerous."

Maloney wasn't paying attention to his wife. Parking the golf cart, he indicated to the valet that he didn't need his services. Grabbing his bag, he motioned to Kaneesha to go to the car.

"Reg, honey? Aren't we going to go in and have a drink?" They always stopped in the clubhouse after a round of golf, where conversation with friends and high-powered Washington colleagues filled an entertaining hour or so before going home.

"I can't, Neesha. Not today."

Noting the grim expression on her husband's face, Kaneesha took a last, longing look at the clubhouse and walked briskly behind him towards her Jaguar. Since a chauffeur normally picked Maloney up from home and took him to the Pentagon, Kaneesha had met her husband at the country club.

After they deposited his clubs in the trunk and settled into the white leather seats, Kaneesha started up the engine and said, "Okay, Reg, what's on your mind?"

"I'm so upset about that *Washington Post* article. You know, there weren't any facts to back it up. And it was an anonymous source to begin with. I can't let it stand without some kind of response."

"But don't you think that if you make a big deal out of it, that sends the opposite message—that the Army's trying to hide something?"

"We've been down that road before. Where we waited too long and it came back to bite us. No, this time I want to squash any hint of impropriety before it rears its ugly head. But I have to be sure first, so I'm going to go down to see General Eckling."

"That's the commander at Fort Rucker?"

"Yes." Maloney nodded.

Kaneesha put on her blinker to turn onto the highway. "Don't you think you're overreacting?"

"What do you think? If you were just John Q. Public, and you read that article in *The Washington Post,* what would have been your first reaction?"

"Frankly, Reg, I don't think I would have made too much of it. The average citizen isn't all that interested in a tiny article about what goes on at an Army post. And besides, there weren't that many details and what details there were seemed rather obscure."

Maloney remained silent for a while, looking out at the Virginia countryside rushing by.

"You know, I can kind of see what you're doing, Reg," Kaneesha said gently.

"What's that?" Maloney asked gruffly.

"You want to protect those women just like you protected black soldiers in the early days. You can't help but be their knight in shining armor. That's who you are, and I love you for that." She looked over at him and smiled. Maloney smiled back. "But I really think you need to hold back just a tad."

"Why would you say that, Neesha? I'm the Secretary of the Army. I can make things happen."

"That's just exactly it, Reg. That's like a bull in a china shop. Right now it's like a mosquito bite, isn't it? Swat it and it goes away. But if you bring in the entire DDT truck, all of a sudden, everyone believes there's an infestation. I don't know if that's a good analogy or not—"

"I get your point. There's no need yet for the heavy guns. As much as I'd like to go in and take charge, I need to lay off and wait and see."

"Because there may be nothing to this," Kaneesha said reassuringly, patting his arm.

"I hope to God you're right."

"Aren't I always?" Kaneesha laughed.

CHAPTER 87

WOLFGANG KASERNE, WEST GERMANY
10:05 P.M., THURSDAY, JUNE 5

Erika Stohlmann did not appreciate the fact that Major Damrow had dumped upon her the task of calling this—who was this anyway?—a Georgina Moore, who was listed in Crystal Lambert's address book as the president of some organization called Women Military Pilots.

Sitting at her desk as twilight tumbled across the sky, Erika felt the annoyance creep back as she muttered the things in a low voice that she hadn't dared to say out loud to Damrow.

"Why do I have to call someone just because she's a woman? And what is this Women Military Pilots anyway? I never heard of this organization. Dardanelli might be coarse and insensitive, but at least she has it right in one respect. We need to be treated as pilots first, and women second. I get so irritated every time another news reporter wants to come here and get a story on the 'women pilots.'" Erika shuddered.

The last time it happened, one of the highest-level reporters in the national media had arrived at the unit. All of the women had had prior knowledge of her arrival and, although Damrow had asked them to make themselves available, they all knew how much their male colleagues hated the attention they got whenever a reporter or TV crew came to town, so they each made sure they had a flight mission or doctor's appointment or something else to do that day that made them completely unavailable. Damrow was absolutely pissed but there had been nothing he could do about it. The widely-acclaimed reporter could only interview the male pilots, who, of course, ate it up and buzzed around the hangar and flight line like the peacocks they thought they were.

Giving a huge sigh, Erika braced herself, called the Autovon operator and provided the unit's authorization code to call Georgina Moore's home phone number. That in itself was a pain in the neck to do—trying to dial someone's commercial telephone number from Germany. Erika prided herself on being a good XO, but sometimes, like tonight, she did feel put upon, especially when she had to stay in the office late at night in order to reach someone in the States at their home, due to the time difference.

As the call was going through, Erika wondered what this Georgina Moore could even do. She didn't have a clue as to whether the woman was in the military. Crystal hadn't put any additional information in her address book.

Before Erika could wonder further, however, the tinny clicks ended and a voice at the other end said, "Hello?"

"Hello, I'm Captain Erika Stohlmann calling from Germany. I'm trying to reach Georgina Moore."

"Yes, that's me. How can I help you, Erika?"

"I got your number from the address book of one of our unit members here—Crystal Lambert—who was killed a few months ago in a helicopter crash."

"Oh, yes, I remember that accident. Three women killed at once in Germany. That was your unit? I'm so sorry," Georgina said.

"I was hoping you could tell me about your organization—Women Military Pilots. My boss suggested I call."

"Well, the organization was founded in 1978 by the Women Airforce Service Pilots as a way to get new military pilots involved. The older ladies were concerned that their organization needed some rejuvenation. The first presidents were WASPS. I'm the first military president."

"What exactly does your organization do?"

"Well, the WASPs helped get themselves veteran status. You might have heard about that. Now they want to be sure that, through this organization, women in military aviation are protected and promoted."

"It sounds reasonable enough. It must be a pretty small organization, though, because I've been an Army pilot for several years now and never heard of it."

"The WASP presidents did try periodically to get to the military training bases to talk to female flight students, but it was usually catch-as-catch can. We're getting better at it, but it's mostly word of mouth." Georgina paused a moment. "So why the twenty questions?"

Hesitating, Erika continued. "Crystal's sister is also a helicopter pilot. Tina Loyola. I don't know if she's a member—"

After riffling through the pages, Georgina said, "No, it doesn't look like it."

"Okay, well that doesn't matter. I'm not even sure which part to go with first. Crystal's ex-husband has told Tina that her sister was killed by a conspiracy of men who sabotaged the helicopter."

"Oh my God!" Georgina exclaimed. "That's not what I heard!"

"And it's not what you're going to hear, either, because apparently it's being covered up. Moreover, Crystal's ex-husband is on a rampage to kill these conspirators and says two of them are at Fort Drum. We don't know how many others exist, who their leader is, or how many other accidents they've planned."

"I still don't understand why you're calling me."

"We thought of calling Fort Drum ourselves, but we don't want to tip off the conspirators there, and we don't know who to trust in the Army here in Germany. You see, someone had to doctor the investigation report to say it was pilot error."

"Although I understand what you're saying, it's incomprehensible to me to not be involving the military authorities."

Erika barged on. "And Tina's sister was going to alert women that she knew about the conspiracy, at least we think she was going to, but she's disappeared."

"What?" Georgina was obviously shocked.

"She went out to use a German phone here and now she's missing. That was nearly a week ago."

"And what's been done to find her?"

"We're working with the German authorities. She came from Fort Drum and was here on leave, so she isn't technically our responsibility. She was trying to look into her sister's accident on her own and we think she stepped on someone's toes. At least that's the German police theory."

"Alright, Erika. You have my undivided attention and complete cooperation. What do you want me to do?"

"What my boss was thinking was that perhaps your organization could call all of your members and let them know what's going on, at least what we suspect is going on, so that women are warned there's a conspiracy out there in the Army to kill off female pilots. But ask them to especially try to find any female pilots at Fort Drum. Right away."

"Will do. But why are these guys trying to kill female pilots? What's their reasoning?"

"They want us out of the cockpits," Erika replied scornfully.

Georgina felt a shudder go up her spine.

Minutes after hanging up with Erika, Georgina received a second phone call, this time from Iris Tucker. Outraged over the treatment the young flight students had been receiving at Mother Rucker, Georgina promised to intercede on their behalf. The Women Military Pilots were going to be busy! Warning female Army aviators about the conspiracy was an urgent task that needed to begin as soon as possible. Georgina would make a few calls to female flight instructors at Fort Rucker to ask discreet questions and nose around among the permanent party staff to see what they could find out about the forger. And, finally, the organization would begin to lobby Congress on behalf of the flight students who had been so wronged.

CHAPTER 88

DOVER AIR FORCE BASE, DELAWARE
11:30 A.M., FRIDAY, JUNE 6

Lindley's coffin had been loaded into the body of the C-5 and Vanessa boarded the metal steps to the upper deck with a heavy heart. So much had happened in the last week, but this was personal. Petrovich's accident had shocked her along with everyone else, and caused a little nervousness about aircraft safety in the unit. But Chad's death following right on the heels of the crash had started the rumor mill to really flow, as no one could be certain whether it was a pure accident from alcoholic stupor or a suicide. Knowing Chad, though, Vanessa couldn't imagine he would kill himself. He was too cocky and self-righteous, so it had to be accidental.

The murder of her cousin had completely sapped her strength. Because Congresswoman Melinda Tonnelli had known the circumstances of the death and had relayed those to General Tucker, he had personally called Vanessa into his office and given her the devastating news. She would have crumpled to the floor had she not already been sitting on the couch before the fireplace. Earl Thornton sat beside her and, after she had heard as many details as Tucker knew, Thornton led her away to her BOQ room in a daze. While the next day passed in a blur of phone calls to her family and to Lindley's unit in Korea, she made plans to accompany his body home, flying to Korea Thursday morning. After a short memorial service at his unit, Lindley's body was released and they were on their way.

During the long, exhausting overnight flight, Vanessa dozed intermittently, thinking about what Lindley had told her over the phone and wondering why he had been killed. The plane stopped in Hawaii to refuel, and a soft perfume of plumeria and hibiscus sailed on the cool night breeze from the trees growing in profusion alongside the passenger terminal. When Vanessa walked back onto the tarmac, the sight of the huge C-5, a lumbering beast, and the thought of its cargo filled her again with despair, despite the heady sensuality surrounding her. The plane refueled again at Travis Air Force Base and arrived at its final destination—Dover Air Force Base, Delaware—early Friday morning.

Vanessa was extremely exhausted and therefore extraordinarily grateful to find out how smoothly the operation went at Dover and how kind everyone was. The dignity with which Lindley's body was handled impressed her greatly. His family had been told that no one was authorized to come onboard the aircraft and receive the body, and so they were all doubly thankful that Vanessa would be the military escort for Lindley. It made Vanessa feel useful and Lindley's family reassured.

Standing outside the C-5 on the tarmac as the rear loading ramp opened, Vanessa watched as Dover Air Force Base personnel withdrew the coffin and loaded it onto a hearse. She, along with the others, saluted as Lindley's body was removed and placed on the next leg of his journey towards home. Vanessa followed the hearse in a rental car to Philadelphia, where she supervised the loading of the coffin into the cargo area of a commercial airliner heading for John F. Kennedy International Airport. The cargo handlers conducted themselves with utmost respect and delicacy, and the ticket agent behind the counter upgraded Vanessa to first class. Without her saying a word, everyone involved in the flight knew she was a military escort and sympathized with her loss. She felt it even more deeply since Lindley was her cousin.

Upon arrival at JFK, the funeral director was waiting on the tarmac with his hearse, and Vanessa turned Lindley's body over to him, draping the American flag over the casket. She followed him to the funeral home, completed the necessary paperwork, and then headed to her parents' house just a few blocks away. She needed her mother's courage to help her face the sorrow she knew she would see in Lindley's mother's eyes when she crossed the street.

CHAPTER 89

SOMEWHERE IN EAST GERMANY
11:25 A.M., FRIDAY, JUNE 6

The door to Tina's prison burst open, guarded by the usual hulk with his AK-47. Standing at the far end of the room, searching along the wall for any crevice she could grasp that would allow her to peel her way out to freedom, Tina had immediately spun around. Blinded by the initial blast of sunshine that flooded the room, Tina shielded her eyes. Although her watch had been taken from her, and her hunger pains had long subsided to a constant rumble, she didn't think it was mealtime. The only other time someone came in was when the Russian man, who had still never identified himself, came to visit.

Because of the sun behind him, the man at the door was still in shadow, but she recognized his voice. It was the Russian man. "So, good afternoon, Miss Loyola. How are you today? Are my men treating you well?"

Tina disdained to answer.

"I have a treat for you today," he said. "A colonel in the U.S. Army has come to see you."

Tina's heart skipped a thousand beats. She was going to be saved! She was going to get out of here. At last! Someone knew where she was. It was all over! Oh, thank God! How did they find her? And where was she? Why had she been here, anyway? It didn't matter. She was going home! Hallelujah!!

"Come in, Colonel, please," the Russian man motioned.

A large man blocked the door and the sunlight fell away. He was in civilian clothes, however, but the military haircut was clear enough.

"This, Miss Loyola, is Colonel Buehlankamp. You might remember him from your days at Fort Rucker." The Russian man smiled.

"Hello, Tina." Colonel Buehlankamp reached out his hand. "I'm so sorry to see you under these conditions. Yes, I'm the aviation training brigade commander at Fort Rucker. I might have been there when you went through."

"I don't know, sir—" Tina stumbled, as she shook his hand.

"I'm sure she was," the Russian man said reassuringly. "Now, Colonel, perhaps you'll be so good as to tell Miss Loyola what you're doing here." He crossed his arms and waited expectantly.

"Sir, thank you so much for coming," Tina said in a rush. "I haven't any idea why I'm here. But I'm so grateful to you for coming to get me."

"Yes, well—" Buehlankamp said.

"This is so touching," the Russian man offered. "I love to see happy endings and I'm so glad to be a part of it."

Tina grew angry. "Go to hell! You never told me what you brought me for here in the first place. All I am is a pilot. I'm just a warrant officer. It isn't as if I'm a high-ranking officer or anything. I don't have a fancy job in the Pentagon or anything!"

"Tina! Tina!" Buehlankamp admonished. "Don't you remember that you're not supposed to say much to the people holding you hostage?"

"Yes," Tina said, chastened. "But you're here now, and I'm getting out of this dump."

"I wouldn't be so hasty with my assumptions if I were you," the Russian man advised.

Tina rushed towards the door. "I'm not staying here a second longer! Not now that my government has sent someone here to take me away."

The Russian man reached out and grabbed her wrist. Holding her so tightly that she couldn't move forward another inch, he barked out in Russian and the guard aimed the AK-47 at her chest.

"Now, Tina, calm down and stay still. I wanted the colonel here to tell you right away so you didn't get false hopes, but it hasn't turned out that way. Don't move another inch or you're going to get hurt. We haven't hurt you yet, but trust me, we will if you test me."

Tina could see the glimmer of cold steel in his eyes and, in that moment, knew something had gone terribly wrong. She looked at Buehlankamp and quickly glimpsed a smirk leaving his face.

The Russian man continued. "Now, Colonel, if you please. Tell the young lady what she wishes to know."

"Tina," Buehlankamp began, "I didn't come here to take you away. I came here to warn you. Leave the investigation of your sister's accident alone."

"What?" Tina could scarcely breathe. "What do you have to do with that? And what do you have to do with him?" She motioned in scorn to the Russian man.

"There are things here you couldn't possibly understand," Buehlankamp warned.

"That's what I'm trying to do!" Tina yelled in frustration. "I'm trying to find out how she died."

"We know how she died," Buehlankamp said. "She was killed, and if you don't leave it alone, you'll be killed, too."

With that, he turned around and walked out, leaving Tina feeling more alone and confused than she had felt since the day she had learned of Crystal's death.

CHAPTER 90

FORT DRUM, NEW YORK
9:15 A.M., FRIDAY, JUNE 6

Deirdre Holloway walked out of Operations with her helmet bag slung over her shoulder, exchanging quips with Lieutenant Mark Andreasen. They were scheduled to fly support missions for a light infantry battalion out in the field over the next few days, and their field gear had already been loaded onto the helicopter.

They both looked forward to getting in some good training and racking up a lot of flying time, at least theoretically. Sometimes these support missions ended up with a lot of sitting on the ground. It just depended on the imagination of the ground commander as to how they put their aviation assets to use.

"Okay, Deirdre," Andreasen said. "I know you're the pilot-in-command, but don't embarrass me alright?"

"I don't know what you mean, sir," Deirdre replied coquettishly.

"I don't want any of those ridiculous questions about how many rivets on the horizontal stabilizer, or that kind of nonsense."

"Just doing my job, sir. You know that." Deirdre smiled. She and all the other warrant officers loved to give commissioned officers a hard time when they went out flying, especially the ones who didn't take it so well and especially because they knew commissioned officers didn't get much time to practice flying. The warrant officers had a severe advantage and they pressed it every chance they got, making their superior officers squirm, particularly since, when warrant officers were pilots-in-command of the helicopter, they were in charge and commissioned officers had to do their bidding and everyone knew it. It made the commissioned officers extraordinarily uncomfortable because they desperately wanted to be in charge, desperately wanted to be the pilot-in-command, and desperately wanted to be the better and more experienced pilot, but the very nature of their rank and position ensured it would rarely happen and everyone knew it. The job of a commissioned officer aviator was, first, to be the unit commander, executive officer, platoon leader, operations officer, maintenance officer or to fill some leadership role that required hours and hours of time undevoted to flying, and flying became a secondary skill. For a warrant officer aviator, flying a helicopter was the primary responsibility and filling other roles in the unit, such as supply officer or postal officer, were secondary and, naturally, totally burdensome.

Andreasen, however, was a natural pilot and one of the few commissioned officers likely to pass the rigorous requirements to become a pilot-in-command in addition to his primary responsibilities in the unit. So Deirdre knew that, unlike some commissioned officers, who could easily disassociate their subservient role on the flightline with their superior role off the flightline, it would irk Andreasen too much to have his knowledge tested too far, particularly since she'd have to go deep anyway.

As they were walking, they heard Lieutenant Cecil Boniface, the assistant operations officer, call out, "Hey, Andreasen and Holloway—hold up! There's been a change of plans."

Deirdre and Andreasen turned around to see Boniface walking swiftly from Operations.

"What's up?" Andreasen asked quizzically.

"Well, I was going through the flight training records, and Lieutenant Wright has got to get in a bunch of hours before the end of the month or she turns into a turnip. I pointed it out to the commander, and he said that since she could probably pick up ten during this exercise, she needs to take the place of one of you."

Deirdre and Andreasen looked at each other in exasperation. Andreasen said, "We're loaded up and ready to go, Cecil. All we have to do is the preflight. This is ridiculous."

"Mark, you understand about getting your hours. Lieutenant Wright has been under the gun lately as the XO."

"That's not my problem. That's not her problem, either." Andreasen jerked his thumb towards Deirdre.

Deirdre shrugged her shoulder. "Well, I don't mind giving up my spot. I've got a son at home, anyway."

"What a great sport, Holloway!" Andreasen exclaimed.

Boniface smacked his head. "What am I thinking? Andreasen! You have to be the one to give up your seat—you're not a pilot-in-command. Only Deirdre can fly with Lieutenant Wright."

"Oh, Christ!" Andreasen moaned. "You're right."

"Oh, well," Deirdre smiled. "We'll do it again some other time, sir."

"Alright, then. That's settled," Boniface said. "Lieutenant Wright is just grabbing her things. Her alert bag was already packed so she'll be out in a jif. I'll change the aircraft manifest for you."

"Great," Deirdre said.

"I guess I'll get my junk off the helo," Andreasen said. "I know when I'm not wanted."

When he and Deirdre arrived at the helicopter, they informed Sergeant Marjorie Clearwater that there had been a change in plans and that she could rest her heels for a few moments until Lieutenant Wright appeared. Marjorie was accustomed to the sudden whims of officers, so it didn't surprise her in the least. She was secretly pleased at the thought of flying in an all-female crew.

CHAPTER 91

FORT RUCKER, ALABAMA
1:35 P.M., FRIDAY, JUNE 6

Lieutenant Colonel Bill Brannon felt stymied. He hadn't forgotten his promise to help Iris Tucker, but he didn't know how he could figure out who on the permanent party list of Fort Rucker could possibly have worked for the FBI without going through their personnel records, and there were thousands of people on the post. That posed an impractical, impossible task. He'd pondered it for several days and, truly, was just hoping it would go away.

Unfortunately, each evening, Stefania asked, "Bill, did you find out anything today to help that poor lieutenant?" When he said no, Stefania looked at him with such disappointment that his resolve was renewed to figure out a new plan of attack.

By Friday afternoon, Brannon suddenly remembered that he had an old college friend who worked for the FBI, who might be able to get into their files, and maybe there was some kind of cross-referencing system. Nah, he thought. That would be way too easy.

After listening to Brannon's explanation, Rob Wilkens said, "Send the names of anyone at the post who has access to student records."

"So you don't think it's a ridiculous idea?" Brannon asked.

"No," Wilkens said. "It can be done, but it will take a few days to run everything through the databases and come up with something."

Brannon spent the rest of that afternoon putting together a list to send to the FBI, in the hope that his friend's results would generate a smaller list of individuals who had worked for the FBI and now were resident at Fort Rucker.

Walking through the corridor, en route to an appointment with Eckling while Brannon was on the phone to Wilkins, Buehlankamp had paused in the hallway, eavesdropping on the conversation, and had overheard every detail about Iris Tucker, the forged documents, and the search for the forger. Pretending to peruse the division photos hanging on the walls, Buehlankamp readjusted his mental strategy of what needed to happen over the next few days.

CHAPTER 92

FORT DRUM, NEW YORK
8:25 P.M., FRIDAY, JUNE 6

After a successful afternoon of flying missions for the infantry unit, Deirdre and her crew took a short dinner break, grabbing some hot food from the mobile kitchen set up in the field, and ate from the confines of their helicopter, perched on the metal floor plates, legs dangling over the sides. Men from the unit they were supporting constantly came by to joke and flirt, so they rarely had a moment's peace, but after they finished eating Deirdre amusedly told the last stragglers to disappear so the women could preflight the aircraft for the night missions they were scheduled to do.

"Yes, ma'am," the men all chorused as they trooped away.

Deirdre smiled as she climbed atop the helicopter to inspect the rotorhead. Young enlisted guys never changed. Sergeant Clearwater was a magnet to these men—that was clear. Despite a Native American background, she was short, impish, with blue eyes and blond curls. There must have been a lot of intermixing on the prairies.

Tonight they would be sling-loading a jeep from one location to another. Not Deirdre's favorite thing to do at night, particularly in a mountainous area like upstate New York, but it would give her and her aircrew the opportunity to sign off on a few aviator tasks, so that would be good.

Satisfied that everything looked kosher up top the helicopter, Deirdre got back down. Lieutenant Yolanda Wright had gone through the preflight checklist down below. Since they'd already flown earlier in the day and just interrupted their flight, this was simply a secondary preflight—required, but not as thorough as the first one of the day.

"Alright, let's get this show on the road, ladies," Deirdre said.

As they flew along the treetops to where they needed to pick up the jeep, a multitude of stars shone brightly to guide their way, causing them all to gasp with wonder and delight. The serenity of the night created in each of them a stillness that lasted until their destination, with the only conversation in the helicopter being phrases necessary for safe flight.

After arriving at the landing zone, Lieutenant Wright maintained the helicopter at a high hover while Army Rangers on the ground, who were conducting their own training, busied themselves with hooking up the quarter-ton jeep. Deirdre and her crew were accustomed to the hubbub on the ground during a sling-load operation. The most difficult part for the aircrew was keeping the helicopter as stable as possible at a hover for as long as it took for the ground crew to get the sling load hooked up. Sometimes it seemed to take forever. And since the action was taking place right beneath the helicopter, the aircrew couldn't see what was going on, which was why it was so important to have a guide out front.

At long last, the jeep was securely attached, and those below indicated thumb's up. Deirdre had been watching the people on the ground closely, while Lieutenant Wright had been flying and watching the instrument panel even more minutely.

"Okay, time to go, ma'am," Deirdre urged. "Take her on up."

Lieutenant Wright slowly maneuvered the helicopter out of its high hover and transitioned to flight. She could feel the sling load begin to swing and adjusted the controls ever so slightly, but tried not to overcompensate.

The Huey flew through the night towards its destination, skimming the treetops, with its load casting darting shadows on the ground as it flashed by. Having picked up their load, the women were now much more voluble.

"This is a gorgeous night, isn't it?" Deirdre mused as she looked up at the stars.

Lieutenant Wright was too busy concentrating on her flying to talk, but she clicked her mike twice.

Sergeant Clearwater said, "I love flying at night. Back on the reservation, I used to go out and ride horses at night. I especially love it in the winter when the stars are all out and the air is biting cold and you can see your breath in front of you. At those moments, you feel like there's no one else in the world."

Deirdre turned her head around to her crew chief and murmured assent, putting her thumb up to show she agreed.

They were half-way to their landing zone, about fifty miles from where they had taken off, when everyone in the helicopter heard a loud snap like a car backfiring, then felt the aircraft shake violently to one side. Lieutenant Wright tried to right the aircraft, but it continued to shudder uncontrollably.

Sergeant Clearwater leaned out one of the open cockpit doors. "The jeep's come off one of its tethers!" she yelled into her intercom. "It's swinging back and forth!"

The helicopter began to move wildly from one side to the other, and the treetops that had been at a level distance now loomed extremely close, as if on a roller coaster ride, as the nose of the aircraft pitched up and down and rolled back and forth. Lieutenant Wright gripped the cyclic and collective and tried to stabilize the Huey, but her motions tended to overcontrol the helicopter and put it in a worse condition.

"Oh my god!" Deirdre yelled. "We've got to jettison the sling load. Quick."

Deirdre and Lieutenant Wright summoned all their willpower to keep the aircraft level and stable, and to follow the emergency procedures for jettisoning a sling load, but before they could accomplish that task, the sling load became hopelessly tangled in the trees, forcing the unstable aircraft to almost simultaneously smash into a seventy-foot-tall red pine.

CHAPTER 93

THE PENTAGON, WASHINGTON, D.C.
11:52 P.M., FRIDAY, JUNE 6

Secretary of the Army Reginald Maloney entered the conference room from the back door and strode towards the podium. Camera lights flashed as news photographers whipped off as many pictures of him as they could. Gripping the side of the wooden lectern, embossed with the seal of the United States, Maloney stood erect and silent until he had everyone's attention.

"Ladies and gentlemen," he began. "I know you've all heard of the tragic helicopter accident in New York State. There have been some unfounded rumors that this is a conspiracy. I want to lay this to rest. We have absolutely no evidence to indicate that such a thing is true. The helicopter accidents that have recently occurred in the Army have no relationship to each other. We have had our investigation board examining the accident sites, the aircraft, the pilots, and the events surrounding the accidents and have not uncovered anything to suggest that they have been in any way related."

"You've now had three accidents with all female crewmembers. Doesn't that suggest something suspicious to you?" asked the reporter from *The Washington Times*.

"Not at all." Maloney shook his head. "It's purely coincidental. First of all, the accident in Germany was clearly determined to be pilot error. The investigation report for the Blackhawk accident in Korea hasn't been made public yet, but

I'll tell you the gist of it—the pilot apparently didn't turn on her transponder and then flew in and out of the demilitarized zone. So she was mistaken for a North Korean aircraft and shot down by friendly fire. We don't know yet why this third accident happened. We just know they were carrying a sling load at night, which is always a dangerous operation, and the helicopter crashed into some trees."

Although Maloney noticed reporters waving their hands in the audience, he decided to go on. "Let me give you another reason why I think it's all a coincidence. We have a lot more women flying helicopters these days. We're very proud of that. Far more women have become pilots-in-command, so they're taking the aircraft out on the missions and training other pilots in their units, including other women. We have more female technicians—crew chiefs. So it stands to reason that we'll have more crews made up of all women. The days of all male crews are in the past."

"Following up on that, sir," the *Post* reporter continued, waving her pencil in the air. "So you just see it as another form of integration, but this time with women instead of blacks?"

Maloney smiled. "I suppose you could say I do." Turning serious again, he added, "I'd also like to point out that we had another fatal accident in Alaska where the sole occupant was male. The theory about a conspiracy doesn't hold water in my book."

Looking out at the audience, Maloney pointed to the CNN reporter, who asked, "The women in the first two accidents were all killed. What about the crewmembers on this Huey? Were they all killed as well?"

"I can't comment on that at this time," Maloney said tersely. "It's too soon to say."

"I have an unnamed source who says there were no bodies at the crash site," said a reporter from *The Washington Post.* "Can you comment on that?"

"No, I can't."

"Do you know the cause of the accident yet?" asked the Channel 9 reporter.

"We're looking into it."

"Can you identify the aircrewmembers?" the same reporter pressed.

"You know I can't do that at this time. It's barely been an hour since we got the word." Maloney shook his head and left the podium,

Leaving the conference room through the back entrance, Maloney walked only a few steps around the E-ring until he came to an unmarked door with an exit sign above it that led to the basement where he could walk unfettered and unnoticed for a few moments to clear his head. Despite the fact that it was very late on Friday night, he knew that he would have innumerable messages and phone calls waiting for him when he returned to his office, requiring his attention and response. And some of those might involve talking to the loved ones of dead young women. Maloney had to brace himself for that dreaded, horrific moment.

CHAPTER 94

SOMEWHERE IN EAST GERMANY
12:45 A.M., SATURDAY, JUNE 7

Ever since Tina had learned that an American Army officer was, for some reason, in league with a Russian officer, she had been beside herself with wondering anew why she was being held hostage. Moreover, she found herself sifting through all the pieces of information about Crystal's accident and the conspiracy to try and figure out where she fit into the picture or to determine the overall scope. Try as she might, she couldn't wrap her mind around what the Russian and Buehlankamp were trying to accomplish.

On Friday night, Tina was awakened from a light sleep when the guard outside her door, tipsy from alcohol, burst inside the room with a bosomy and slatternly woman hanging onto his arm. While his paramour attempted to plant wet kisses on his face and neck, the listing guard drunkenly swept Tina from her bed and motioned her to a corner.

Startled from her slumber, it didn't take Tina long to realize what was taking place and she wasn't looking forward to being a peeping tom. The woman fell backwards heavily onto the bed and the guard heaved himself on top of her, but then he turned his head towards the door, slowly got up, took a few unsteady steps, locked the door, and returned to resume his lovemaking. After a few grunts and groans, he was done, and presumably, so was his partner.

Tina waited for them both to get up and leave, but, instead, could distinctly hear two separate snores. Both the guard and his woman had fallen asleep. Tina was dismayed to think she might have to sit there on the cold concrete all night. She hadn't had much sleep before these disgusting creatures had come in and stolen her bed. She might have to lie down on the floor and sleep, and that would be the worst night she'd had yet in this dump.

Her eyes having adjusted to the dark, Tina looked over at the pair occupying her bed. The guard's shiny white buttocks shone like a beacon in the night. Despite his haste, he had obviously taken the time to take off his pants. Tina wasn't a prude, but she averted her eyes.

In the next second, she realized—his pants! The key to the door was in his pants! Trying not to get too excited, Tina very stealthily and quietly moved across the floor, crawling as low as she could and keeping an eye on the guard's back, hoping he wouldn't roll over or wake up. Listening for the sound of their continued snores, Tina almost couldn't keep breathing herself. When one of the snores nearly stopped because one of them was taking a deep breath, Tina nearly died of fright.

She reached the pants and put her hands into the right pocket, where she thought she had seen him put the key. It wasn't there! Now she frantically searched all of the other pockets, but couldn't find the key.

Perhaps it was on the floor. Tina began to move her fingers rapidly along the floor of the room, hoping to find the key, when, suddenly, the guard did roll over. He mumbled something out loud, and Tina was afraid he'd woken up. She froze, but the woman partially woke up as well, grabbed the guard by the shoulder, and coaxed him to turn back around towards her. Tina relaxed, but only slightly.

Where was the damn key? As her fingers fumbled against the floor, Tina's hand suddenly brushed against another pair of pants. She must have had the woman's pants the first time. Tina feverishly put her hand in the right pocket and was rewarded with a key.

Slowly, Tina moved along the floor to the door, keeping her ears cocked for any change in movement or noise from the sleeping couple. As she passed by the foot of her bed, she gathered her shoes. She tenderly unlocked the door and crept out of the cell where she had been held captive for the past week, locking it behind her just as quietly. Holding the key tightly in her hand, Tina waited until she was safely a hundred yards away before she stopped to put on her shoes.

Assessing her surroundings, Tina discovered she was in a wooded area and needed to find her way out as soon as possible. At the same time, she knew it provided her a certain measure of cover and concealment from her captors and she intended to make full use of it until she found a safe haven.

CHAPTER 95

ADIRONDACK STATE PARK, NEW YORK
12:04 A.M., SATURDAY, JUNE 7

Although Sergeant Marjorie Clearwater found herself still tethered to the seatbelt of the Huey as it creaked in the wind, she was nearly dangling over the skids. The aircraft was slipping sideways down the huge pine it had hit, and Marjorie had a birds-eye view out the cockpit doors, straight down to the pine-needle-covered ground.

Deirdre looked back at her crew chief. She yelled, "Get back in here!"

"I can't!" Marjorie screamed with fright. She clutched with both hands at the metal plates of the cabin floor. She tried to grab part of the door to hold onto for stability, but her swaying only made her swing out further.

"Watch what you're doing, you're only going to make things worse," Deirdre warned.

"I know!" Marjorie yelled. "I'm trying to get back in."

"Let me help her," Lieutenant Wright suggested, starting to undo her seatbelt.

"No!" Deirdre said sharply. She motioned with a movement of her forehead towards the front of the helicopter. Lieutenant Wright immediately understood that if she had climbed out of her seat, the helicopter would have instantly plummeted to the ground and they all would have died. As it was, they were in a slow, albeit precarious, fall to the ground and it was best not to interrupt it.

The tree's voluminous branches had initially created a soft landing spot for the helicopter, until its enormous weight had begun to overpower the branches one by one, creating a skidding motion as the Huey stopped and started on its dizzying descent to the bottom, with its tail rotor constantly getting hung up in neighboring trees.

All of a sudden, though, the slow fall began to accelerate.

"Oh my God!" Deirdre exclaimed. "Brace yourselves!"

In the front seats, she and Lieutenant Wright folded their heads into their laps as best they could, hoping their heavy flight helmets would protect them from the imminent crash. Just as they did so, a dead limb protruding from another tree stabbed the windshield of the rotating helicopter, missing both women by mere inches, but putting the aircraft into a new trajectory, pushing it off of its slide down the tree and into a free fall. In horror, Marjorie watched the ground come up closer, closer, closer, certain she was seeing her last views of the world. At the last possible moment, she shut her eyes and said a prayer, asking God to look after her parents and grandmother back on the reservation and resigned herself to her fate.

With a shattering thud, the Huey crashed into the smallest of clearings, with its landing softened by decades of pine needles and spongy earth. Marjorie opened her eyes in disbelief. She was now looking up at a slope—the helicopter had landed perpendicular to it and rolled slightly backwards, which was why she had managed to not get crushed, although she found she couldn't walk.

"Ma'am?" she called out to either of the two pilots. "Are you okay up there?"

Deirdre was the first to rouse herself. She patted herself all over. "I'm not sure yet, Marjorie. I think I'm okay. How are you? How are you, ma'am?" she asked Lieutenant Wright.

"I might have broken my leg," Marjorie said. "It might only be sprained. I'm not sure yet."

"Don't move, Marjorie. Let me get out and help you." In the moonlight, Deirdre took a quick look at Lieutenant Wright, who still hadn't said a word, and whose face was abnormally pale. "Lieutenant Wright! Wake up! Are you alright?"

Deirdre gently patted Lieutenant Wright's arm, then patted her on the cheek. When her copilot didn't respond, Deirdre first searched for a flashlight, then grabbed the first aid kit on the helicopter and found the smelling salt, waving it under Lieutenant Wright's nose. After waving it a few times, Deirdre realized her copilot had been more seriously injured than smelling salts could revive.

Extricating herself from the helicopter and wrenching open her copilot's door, Deirdre ripped off Lieutenant Wright's flight helmet and proceeded to drag her from the aircraft to a level spot on the ground where she quickly applied CPR.

"Come on, ma'am," she implored, as she worked on Lieutenant Wright's chest. "Don't die on us." Marjorie was sitting on the skid and watching helplessly.

After three tries, Lieutenant Wright's eyes fluttered open. "Did we make it?" she asked. Tears rolled down Deirdre's and Marjorie's cheeks, the tension of the last few minutes overwhelming them.

"Yes, ma'am," Deirdre said. "We made it. Now just rest here a second. I've got to see to Sergeant Clearwater."

She rushed over to Marjorie, who was now wincing from the pain and clutching at her right leg. "Let me see it, Marjorie." Deirdre rolled up the torn flight suit and could see the ugly gash along the shinbone. If she wasn't mistaken, Deirdre thought she could glimpse some white bone through an upper part of the gash. This was going to get a lot worse before it got better. It hadn't started to bleed yet, but it would.

Deirdre jumped into the helicopter, racing around grabbing supplies, anything that could make a tourniquet and then a splint. "I'm going to fix you up and then call out on the radio to get us out of here, Marjorie. We don't want you to go into shock."

Using the first aid kit, her medical knowledge gleaned from being married to an Army nurse, and improvised supplies in the helicopter, Deirdre stanched the blood and tried to splint the leg.

When Deirdre was done, Marjorie looked as pale as Lieutenant Wright had before she had been pulled out of the helicopter and regained consciousness. Deirdre shook her head in dismay, looking at both women sitting on the ground. It was pitch black and getting colder as the night drew on.

"I've got to try and raise someone on the radio," she told them both.

Going to the highest ground possible, Deirdre took her survival radio out of her vest and tried to make a mayday call. Most of what she heard was static. After a few minutes, she returned to her crewmembers and said, "I'm sorry, guys. No luck. I think we're out of range here in this valley."

"I'm sure someone will be out looking for us before long," Marjorie said reassuringly.

Lieutenant Wright had fallen asleep. "Luckily," Deirdre said, "we have our sleeping bags with us, so at least we're going to be able to stay warm through the night." She crawled back into the helicopter, grabbed their gear and threw it out onto the clearing. As she tossed one of the flight kits, she felt a sharp pain shooting up her shoulder. Although she'd felt it ever since they'd crashed, she had been so busy she'd ignored it, but this stopped her dead in her tracks. Turning the flashlight on herself, Deirdre could see a dark stain on her flight suit near her elbow. Touching it, she felt a stickiness that she knew could only be blood. Once she rolled up her sleeve, she could see she had been injured in the accident and hadn't realized it. She had very likely broken her arm and kept using it without realizing it. Luckily, it was her left arm, and she could keep working once she got it splinted. But it would make everything much more difficult.

Deirdre tried to raise anyone on her survival radio, to no avail. From time to time, she ministered to her crewmembers—checking their pulses, their temperatures, giving them water, keeping them warm and comfortable, and trying to think of ways to either attract attention for rescue or how to get the three of them out of there. She pored over her map of the Adirondack State Park and soon she had come up with a plan.

CHAPTER 96

ENTERPRISE, ALABAMA
2:04 A.M., SATURDAY, JUNE 7

Iris Tucker awoke with a start. She felt a presence by her bed. Before she could move a muscle, a large hand encased in an oily leather glove clamped down on her mouth, shoving her into the mattress, while another gripped both arms in one swift move and clasped them together. At the same time, she felt a knee across her groin, immobilizing her legs completely.

"Wha—?" she feebly mumbled, half asleep but still frightened out of her wits, hopelessly fighting to get out of the person's clutches.

Against the backdrop of the patio drapes leading to the balcony off the bedroom of her second-floor apartment, Iris could make out the looming outline of the shadowy figure—probably a man, considering the size and the intense hold he had on her. Struggle though she might, she was unable to loosen his tenacious embrace.

He leaned close, and Iris caught a whiff of cigar smoke. It momentarily whisked her back to her grandfather sitting on the porch in his rocking chair. The words that the man whispered, however, quickly knocked her back to reality.

"I don't like killing little girls, but you've made me do this," he said so slowly and quietly, that Iris thought she was mistaken. She tried to jerk her head to see his face, but, being prepared, he riveted her head into the pillow more firmly, ensuring she couldn't turn her face a single inch.

"I'm sorry, Iris, really I am. But I have a higher mission than you, and I have to follow it. You and your female friends are standing in our way."

Iris's eyes grew wide with fear. Was this the forger? It couldn't be possible. But who else could it be? How could he possibly have known what she had found out? Well, enough people knew about it—all the female flight students, Cynthia Hailey, Colonel Brannon—Colonel Brannon wouldn't have betrayed her, would he? No, he couldn't have. He wouldn't have. But who else was this man, threatening to kill her? And why else was he saying he was going to kill her?

All these thoughts ran through Iris's mind in a split second, an interminably long split second. By the time she had noticed that the man had let her hands go for an instant, he had already covered them with another part of his body, and had jabbed a syringe filled with a sleeping agent into her arm. Her arms, eyes, mouth, and neck immediately went slack as the narcotic took effect. Taking a last look at his victim, Buehlankamp was satisfied and set to work on finishing her off.

First he stashed a couple of cartons of cigarettes in her pantry, ensured there were batches of matches in kitchen drawers, placed ashtrays in the living room and bedroom, opened up a box of cigarettes in the living room and threw it on the coffee table. He removed several cigarettes, which he put in his pocket, and took out several stubs and a longer cigarette from a baggie. These he took into Iris's bedroom, placed between her lips and fingers, and then arranged in the ashtrays. The longer cigarette was strategically placed in the bedroom as the crowning glory—it would be the one suspected as starting the fire. As the final touch, he added the cigarette ashes from the baggie to the ashtrays.

Buehlankamp had wrestled with whether or not to slosh kerosene around the apartment and finally decided to do so. He had to get rid of the girl. The mission was too important and she was jeopardizing it. Even though he knew fire inspectors would most likely, in the end, determine it was a case of arson, it might take them longer with the diversions he put up, and, maybe, just maybe, the idea of arson might elude them anyway. At any rate, he thought he had been clever enough not to leave any clues and he wanted to be sure he left a dead Iris Tucker.

Still, he didn't think he needed to overdo the kerosene, so Buehlankamp quickly tossed it underneath the bed. A conflagration there would take care of what needed to be taken care of, and that was all that mattered.

Buehlankamp lit a match, threw it under the bed, and watched the flames begin to leap and sizzle along the carpet towards the overhanging bedspread. He would have liked to stay to ensure that Iris died, but there was no doubt she wasn't moving, and no doubt that this fire would consume her. He swiftly opened the sliding balcony door, looking back one last time, as the flames started licking up over the top of the bed. The air that rushed in from the outside gave the fire an extra boost. Buehlankamp, extremely satisfied with his night's work, climbed down off the balcony, brushed himself off, and drove home.

CHAPTER 97

SOMEWHERE IN EAST GERMANY
1:12 A.M., SATURDAY, JUNE 7

As Tina stumbled through the woods, she knew the odds of finding her way out alone were not very good, especially at night. She shivered in the chill night air, and drew her thin blouse tighter against her chest. Her captors had never given her anything additional to wear, so she was still wearing what she had on when she'd gone out to dinner with Gunter a week earlier.

Although the little building where she had been kept had been isolated, a dirt road led up to it, and a couple of trails led off into the woods. In the dark, Tina knew of none of these, but she had instinctively taken off and run around behind the building, sensing it was much safer to be as far away from the road her captors' vehicles would travel on as possible.

Suddenly, Tina slowed her forward motion. She clutched the keys in her hand. What if one of them was a vehicle key, she thought. Do I dare go back? She turned slightly around and hesitated. She couldn't even see the building anymore at this point. The guard might have woken up and noticed I'm missing. It's too risky. She shook her head. I should just keep going. But if I can get in a car, I can get miles away from here. She thought some more. That's only if they don't hear the engine making a noise. That's if there's enough gas in the car.

Tina deliberated only seconds more and then bolted back silently, noiselessly, towards the building, pausing at the back to listen for any movement inside. She could definitely hear the deep rumble of the guard's snoring and the soft whisper of the woman's. Tiptoeing along the side of the building, guided by her hand along the wall, she reached the dirt road, where she saw two vehicles parked one behind the other.

At the second car, she crept to the driver's window, which was rolled down, and nearly wept for joy when she saw the car keys hanging from the ignition and the woman's purse casually slung into the passenger's seat.

"Sorry, sister," Tina savagely said under her breath. She inched the door open and winced when the seat creaked as she sat down. Holding her breath and watching the door of the building, even though she'd locked it behind her, she started the motor, put the car in reverse, and more silently than she could have imagined, escaped for good.

As soon as she reached a spot where she could safely turn around, Tina put the car in forward, and raced ahead, sometimes spinning the tires on dirt curves. For the next half-hour, the roads she was on seemed to lead in a rational direction. As a helicopter pilot with good navigator skills, she was able to determine which way to turn when she had to make a choice. At long last, she broke out of the woods onto a small country road. The road signs didn't help her at night, but she turned towards what she thought was west.

She passed through several small towns, dead asleep at this hour. A closed-up gas station reminded her she might be living on borrowed time. Checking the fuel gauge, Tina found she had half a tank of gas, but she also realized the guard and his companion might wake up and sound an alarm before she could use it up. She had to think of a strategy before she became surrounded with polizei stopping her for stealing a car or before she ran out of gas. But she wanted to get as close to the border as she could until then. The main question was—where was it?

Her eyes accustomed to the dark, Tina located the glove compartment and yanked everything out, holding each piece up to the tiny bits of moonlight to see if anything looked like a road map. Once done, she tossed everything into the back seat. Groping around in the pockets in the driver's door and passenger's door—nothing. Contorting her body, Tina reached her arm behind the driver's seat and there it was—a dog-eared map of East Germany. Now the only thing was to figure out where she was.

Pulling over at the edge of the next town under a street light to take a look at the map, Tina encountered another stroke of luck. The guard's lover had used the map to find her way to their tryst. She had drawn a red circle around a spot in the woods at the end of a dirt road, and identified it with a big red arrow. On top of that, in girlish letters off to the side, she had written "Freitag!" Tina had no doubt this was where she had been held. Now all she had to do was backtrack her route out of there.

As it turned out, Tina didn't need to do that because, in starting to look at her route, she spotted the name of the town she had just arrived in—Nieberg—on the map. So she knew exactly where she was. She'd been headed north and needed to adjust her route. Once she had determined some country roads to travel on in a westerly direction, Tina threw the map on the passenger's seat and continued on her way. She intended to drive for another hour, ditch the car, and then look for help.

The next hour passed agonizingly slowly in some respects, as Tina wanted more than anything to get off the road and out of public view, to get out of the car that was her savior by putting miles between her and the captors and bringing her closer to the border. At the same time, the hour sped by as she recognized that she only had so much time before she might be caught and she willed the car to get her as far as it could.

Luck was with her, however, insofar as her plan went. Either the guard and his lover had not awoken, or they had no way to communicate their captivity to anyone, or they didn't know the woman's car was gone. At any rate, Tina drove the car a couple of miles down a dirt road to a small lake she had seen on the map, set the brakes, wedged the accelerator with a piece of wood, revved the engine, and when she removed the parking brake, watched with amazement at how quickly the car sank into the deserted lake.

Having kept the woman's ID, what little bit of money was in her purse, and the map, Tina set out to walk the seven miles to the tiny farming village beyond the lake. Daylight had not yet dawned, so it was easy to step off the road when she saw approaching headlights and remain unnoticed.

Tina wasn't exactly sure what she was going to do next, but she didn't think going to the authorities would be particularly helpful. It struck her that perhaps someone in the citizenry might be who she should turn to. Her best bet, she thought, would be a loner, someone who didn't care what the rest of the community thought. Someone, perhaps, who lived on the edge of the community, a recluse. That was what she was on the lookout for.

As she walked along the edge of the country road, careful to stay ten feet away so she wasn't easily visible, Tina noticed smoke rising out of the woods to her right. Unless someone arose before dawn, it was too early for a fire. Since it was June, it seemed strange for someone to be having a fire anyway.

Pondering these thoughts, Tina was a bit startled when a golden hue appeared, broken by the shadow of a man. The man stood still, and Tina felt he must have seen her, but she believed she was too far away.

"*Hallo!*" he called. "*Was tun Sie?*"

Completely startled, Tina turned around. Could this apparition be talking to her? And what was he saying?

"*Hallo! Hallo!*" he called again.

Tina shook her head. "*Ich spreche kein Deutsch.*"

The man clambered out of his doorway and came a hundred yards closer. "*Ach, ja. Was, dann? Russische?*"

"*Nein.*" Tina wasn't certain how forthcoming she should be.

"*Das Auto*—" the man motioned back in the direction towards the lake and raised an eyebrow. "*Sehr interessant.* Whoosh!" He dipped a hand up and down in the air to indicate the car being sucked into the lake.

Tina didn't understand much German, but she understood perfectly that he knew what she had done. Her mouth went dry.

"I . . . I . . . I didn't want the car anymore," she feebly said.

"Ahh, American," he said with satisfaction. "I haven't helped one of you in a long time. And you do need help, don't you?" he asked.

Tina stood there dazed.

"I was at the lake, getting ready for some early morning fishing, when I saw what you had done. I followed you back here. It's just convenient that you were passing by my house." He shrugged. "I ducked inside for a moment." He handed her a sweater. "You looked quite cold."

"Thank you," she said. "But you don't know anything about me."

"You're obviously in trouble. That's all I need to know. My name's André, by the way," he said as he led the way to a small cabin nestled in the trees that looked cozier with every step they took.

CHAPTER 98

WATERTOWN, NEW YORK
2:15 A.M., SATURDAY, JUNE 7

Lying in the Watertown hospital, Frank saw the television news report that a helicopter from Fort Drum had gone down in the Adirondacks. Although no one knew whether the crew onboard had lived or died, the presumption was that they had all been killed. What sent chills up and down his spine was the announcement that all crewmembers, even though their names couldn't be released, were female.

"Shit!" he exclaimed, balling his fist up and slamming it down hard on the hospital bed. "Don't they realize they're practically telling the families who was on that helicopter? There aren't that many females in a unit. What fucking idiots!"

Of course, the immediate family members had already suspected their loved ones were involved, knowing they were supporting an infantry unit in the middle of the Adirondacks. Since the make-up of the crew had changed at the last minute to all-female, that wasn't the clue—just knowing that one member of the crew was female raised their antenna.

It had been thirty-six hours since Claire Diderot had found Frank at Tina's house and arranged for an ambulance to rush him to the hospital. In that time, he'd been pumped full of antibiotics and his fever had broken. He felt like a new man. In fact, truth be told, he was bored to death. Staring at the news anchor, who had gone on to another story, Frank couldn't believe he was lying in bed, doing nothing when he still had a mission to fulfill.

"I've been lying here on my lazy butt, getting shot full of medicines, when those crazy assholes have tried to kill someone else!"

A nurse appeared at Frank's side and sharply asked, "What did you say?"

He mumbled, "Nothing."

She handed him a small paper cup filled with pills and a glass of water. "Take these."

"What are all these for?" he asked suspiciously.

"Mostly antibiotics, but also to help you sleep. I'm taking the IV out now. The doctor doesn't think you need that anymore."

"I'll take them when you're done," Frank said.

"No, I have to watch, so I can write it in my notes."

Frank tossed the contents of the paper cup in his mouth, added some water, threw his head back, and swallowed.

"Good boy," the nurse said, smiling. "Now, let me get this IV out of you."

For the next few moments, the nurse patiently removed the IV needles, placed a bandage over the entry point on Frank's arm, patted him down, and then rolled the IV station out of his room, turning off his light as she did so. "Sweet dreams, hon."

As soon as she left, Frank unrolled his tongue and removed the pills from where he'd let them slide. He figured it wouldn't hurt to swallow the antibiotics, but he wasn't sure which ones they were, so he tossed them all in the wastebasket. Grabbing his wallet from the bedside drawer and searching around for his shoes, which had not come with him from Tina's house, he threw on some hospital slippers and slipped out of the hospital room.

Although the corridor was bright, very little activity was taking place along the corridor between his room, the nurses' station to the left, and the stairway to the right. Frank silently made his way from the third floor to the ground floor and out the door.

Several blocks away from the hospital, Frank found a pay phone. Calling information, he got the phone number for Deirdre and Wayne's house. One of the things he'd failed to do was warn Deirdre, which he'd never forgive himself for, but at least now, perhaps, he could help Wayne find her, or her body. He had to call collect since he had no cash.

"Hey, Wayne, this is Frank Lambert. I'm sorry, man. I just heard the news. I'd like to help."

Wayne's voice sounded dead. "Frank. I don't know what kind of help you could be. Say, I need to get off the line in case someone's calling me about Deirdre."

"I want to go help look for her."

Wayne laughed derisively. "Where in the world are you, Frank? No one knows where you are."

"I'm right here, Wayne. In New York."

"What are you doing here?"

"I came here to warn Deirdre—" Frank's voice trailed off.

"To warn her about what?" Wayne's voice asked sharply.

"Two guys in her unit are involved in a conspiracy to kill female pilots."

"What?" Wayne nearly jumped through the telephone in an attempt to throttle Frank. "Why didn't you say something sooner? Who are these guys?"

"Mark Andreason and Cecil Boniface."

"Omigod! I know those guys! Deirdre flies with those guys!"

"I know. I came here to get rid of them."

"What do you mean?"

"What do you think I mean?" Frank asked bitterly. "The world doesn't need scum like them. But I ended up in the hospital before I could do anything."

"I work in the hospital, Frank. I didn't see you there."

"Not at Fort Drum, Wayne. I was taken to the Watertown Hospital."

"Oh." Wayne was silent for a moment. "Where are you now, Frank?"

"I'm at a pay phone a few blocks from the hospital. As soon as I saw that the helicopter went down, I skipped out."

"What's wrong with you?"

"A bad case of pneumonia, but I think I'm over it now."

"I wouldn't be so hasty, Frank. I'll come pick you up."

"That would be nice, Wayne, since I'm standing here in a hospital gown with wind flapping up my rear end and any minute I'm sure a police car will roll by and take me to the loony bin."

"I've got to gather up Zach. Just give me some landmarks and I'll be there in a few minutes."

Wayne took Frank first to Tina's to collect a few items of clothing. Then they returned to Wayne's home, where Frank filled him in on all that he knew about the conspiracy.

"You're telling me you told Tina about Mark and Cecil, but she left here without saying anything to Deirdre?" Wayne was furious. "How could she do that?"

Frank shrugged his shoulder. "I don't think it's as easy as it sounds, man. Tina didn't believe me. She thinks those are great guys, plus she was flying to Germany that day."

"But she could have prevented it by calling Deirdre and warning her—"

Suddenly, something clicked in Wayne's memory. "Goddamn it, Frank. I think she did call to warn Deirdre, but something happened."

Frank leaned forward in his armchair. "What are you talking about?"

Wayne searched backwards to remember what had happened in those few seconds. "I was in the emergency room and got a phone call. It was Tina calling from Germany. All she said was that she'd found out something more about Crystal's accident and that I had to tell Deirdre something that you had told her. Then the line went dead. At least I thought it did."

"What do you mean?" Frank asked.

"Well, she never called back. And I got busy and forgot about it. The phone call only lasted a few seconds."

"Shit, Wayne!" Frank exclaimed. "Why didn't you call her back?"

"I told you, Frank. I was in the emergency room, and it happened in a split second. You know how those overseas calls go. I figured if it was important, she'd call back."

"But she didn't."

Wayne shook his head.

"Did you tell Deirdre Tina called?" Frank asked. "Maybe she tried to get in touch with her."

"No, I wish I had. It just totally slipped my mind. And I don't know why she didn't call us at home. She's got our number there. Or if she wanted to talk to Deirdre, why she didn't call her at work."

"Think about it, Wayne. She couldn't chance Mark or Cecil picking up the phone at the unit. What would she have said to them?"

"All she would have had to say is that she wanted to talk to Deirdre," Wayne commented.

"True, but I also told her to keep away from the unit as much as possible."

"I don't think Tina would have avoided warning Deirdre if she knew someone in the unit was out to get them, Frank." Wayne looked across the room at a family photo of himself, his wife, and their infant son. "I'm certain Tina would have called Deirdre at home at the earliest opportunity. But she didn't. So the next question is why?"

Frank grimaced and nodded in agreement. "Unless she couldn't," Frank said.

"Unless she couldn't," Wayne agreed.

"We've got to find out that she's alright."

Wayne nodded. "Right before she left on her trip, the Germans told her that Crystal's helicopter had been sabotaged, so you were right all along. They've got some sort of proof, Tina said."

"God almighty."

At that moment, Wayne's phone rang. When he hung up, he turned to Frank and said, "The search party is getting underway now. I'm sure you gathered that they told me my place is to remain here by the phone."

"Yeah, that's tough. I know you'd rather be out there doing something."

Frank gathered up his windbreaker. "What are you doing?" Wayne asked.

"I'm going to hitch a ride out to Fort Drum and offer myself up to the search party."

"But you're too weak from your pneumonia," Wayne protested. "You just got out of the hospital!"

"I'll be fine." Frank waved aside Wayne's concerns. "I'll be doing this for me and you, okay, bud? It won't make up for my earlier mistakes, but at least I'll do what I can now."

"Take my jeep, Frank. I've got another car out there for when they call me to go to the post."

Wayne walked Frank to the side door of the house, lifting a set of car keys off a rack hanging nearby. "Thanks, Frank. You really don't have to do this."

"No, I really do. After all, Deirdre is one of the best pilots I know." Their eyes locked and Wayne gave Frank a nod and slight smile. As Frank walked to the car, Wayne hoped that Deirdre would still be alive to learn that Frank really did have a high opinion of her and her flying ability. With a catch in his throat, Wayne turned to go back in the house and wait by the phone.

CHAPTER 99

ENTERPRISE, ALABAMA
2:17 A.M., SATURDAY, JUNE 7

Iris dreamed she was lost in a forest, trying to get through a thicket of brush, searching for a way out, but every time she pushed aside some dangling vines or branches, they would snap back at her, dripping with fire. She would scream and turn in another direction, only to find herself stopped by more fiery obstacles. Dripping with sweat from her nightmarish exertions, she awoke with a start and screamed aloud. A fire was consuming her bed!

Iris jumped up into the middle of the bed closest to the headboard and grabbed her pillow. The fire had started up the edges of the bedspread and had curled around the foot of the bed. It was just now beginning to race down the middle. Iris had pulled her feet away from the edge of the bed just in time.

"Oh, shit!" she exclaimed. Knocking over the lamp on her nightstand, Iris jumped off the bed and ran out of the bedroom. Grabbing a phone, she called 911, then yanked a fire extinguisher out from under her sink and began to extinguish the flames. When the firefighters arrived, they admonished her severely for not getting out of the apartment, but Iris brushed them off and told them she wasn't going to let all her things go up in smoke while she waited for them to arrive. She didn't tell them that she knew their method of blasting the entire apartment with high-pressure water hoses would ruin everything, especially since the fire would have been allowed to go on for a lot longer by the time they got there. With her method, the damage was relatively minor.

Upon questioning, Iris wasn't able to tell the firefighters or police much other than that an unidentified man had held her captive, threatened her, shot her up with an apparent narcotic, and set the place on fire. She didn't tell them that she thought he was the forger of the female student flight records. That was a piece of information Iris was saving for herself and Lieutenant Colonel Brannon. She figured it wouldn't mean anything to the Enterprise town authorities anyway, and, besides, she still didn't know the forger's identity so she wasn't exactly keeping anything from them.

Iris was taken to the hospital emergency room where she was treated for smoke inhalation and minor burns, but she was released within a few hours. Shortly after arriving home, she called her dad. She had considered whether or not to disturb him in the middle of the night, but also knew he would be quite upset with her later when he found out what had happened and if she hadn't called right away, so she did.

"Hey, pumpkin, what's wrong?" Tucker asked warily, with a trace of sleep still in his voice.

"Dad, I'm okay now, I want you to know that."

"Why? What do you mean? What's happened?" All of Tucker's antennae were on alert.

"It's been a bad night. Someone broke in my apartment and set it on fire."

Although Iris tried to underplay what had happened, her dad was sharp and extracted everything that had happened out of her.

"My God, Iris! You're playing a dangerous game! That man tried to kill you!"

"I don't know how he knew about me, Dad, although there were enough of us involved in getting our records."

Tucker helplessly wiped his forehead and sat down on a footstool. "What do you want to do now, Iris?"

"What do you think's going to happen when this man, whoever he is, finds out I'm not dead?"

Sighing, Tucker said, "Your life is in severe danger, Iris. This is exactly what I was worried about. You've got to tell the authorities."

"Tell them what, Dad? I don't know anything. That someone—I don't know who—altered the records? I don't have any proof. I have to get this guy."

"You can't do that by yourself, Iris."

"Dad, you taught me I can do anything I want to."

"I didn't mean this, Iris!" Tucker cried in frustration. "There are limits!"

"Not in my book, Dad. This guy tried to take me out, and I'm going to find out who he was. This has gone beyond some idiot or idiots trying to keep us females back in flight school for some obscure reason. I could deal with that because it was so nonsensical and we found out there was no basis for it. I thought that was just some guy with a beef. And we were going to find him out and unveil him. But now there's something evil out there and he's pinpointed me. I can't live with that, Dad. I'm sorry."

"Iris! Wait! Think what you're saying! You can't just go kill someone! Is that what you're saying?"

"Dad," Iris sounded like someone trying to be inordinately patient. "I'm not going to seek him out, as if I were an assassin or something, if that's what you mean. But I'm going to be prepared. If this guy comes at me again, he better watch out. That's all I'm saying. He's going down."

Tucker was stunned. This was his little girl? Iris of the blond curls? He couldn't believe it. He held the receiver away from him for a second to look at it, hoping that when he put it back to his ear the familiar Iris would have returned.

And, in a sense, she had. "So, okay, Dad? Don't worry about me. I'll be fine. After all, you're the greatest teacher I ever had, right? Love ya, peaches!"

Tucker only had a second to reply, "Love you, too, Iris," before he heard the fast click of the telephone and was left standing in the gloom of his living room while his mind remained thousands of miles away with his vivacious daughter.

CHAPTER 100

FORT DRUM, NEW YORK
3:58 A.M., SATURDAY, JUNE 7

"All systems go, then," Cecil said, looking down at the checklist in his hand and scanning the cockpit panel.

"Right you are," Mark replied, keeping an eye out around the airfield as the rotor blades whirred to be sure no one ran into them. He talked to the control tower and said, "We're ready to taxi."

Cecil clicked his mike in response, lifted the helicopter off the ground, and began taxiing to the runway. Once in position, Mark called the tower again and received permission for takeoff.

Just before Cecil put the helicopter into translational lift, Mark said, "Did you feel that?"

Cecil looked out over the dark field at the end of the runway, illuminated only by runway lights. "Feel what?"

"I felt a jolt of some sort, just as you were taking off." Mark turned his head back around to look into the pitch blackness of the helicopter. He shrugged. "I guess I imagined it."

"Okay, so direct me, maestro," Cecil demanded.

"We've got to find that aircraft before anyone else," Mark said.

"I know that, Mark," was the impatient response. "Why else do you think we got our butts out here so fast? We were supposed to be flying in formation. We're going to get reamed by the commander for taking off early. What excuse are we going to use?"

"We couldn't bear to think of those poor women being out there all alone?" Mark suggested.

Cecil laughed. "That might work. So what's our sector? It would have helped if their damn locator had been working," he complained.

"Yeah, well, that would have made it too easy, now wouldn't it? Of course, we wouldn't be in this fix if other people had done their job right in the first place," Mark glared.

"What's that supposed to mean?"

"You know damn well what that's supposed to mean. You arranged the job with the Ranger at the infantry location. I thought you were there supervising."

"I couldn't risk being there, Mark. That's crazy! I set it up, yes, but I couldn't very well stand by and watch while he severed the chain close to breaking point. Someone would have recognized me, and what excuse would I have had for being there?"

"Yeah, well—" Mark's voice trailed off. "You just better hope we find these women."

"And are we hoping they're dead or alive?"

"Buehlankamp wants them dead."

"Wanting them dead and wanting us to kill them are two different things. He's not expecting us to outright kill them if we find them, is he?" Cecil asked.

"Why? What's the difference between killing them on the ground or killing them in a helicopter? Are you getting squeamish on me, Cecil?" Mark asked with disdain.

"I mean, Mark, hand-to-hand combat with a woman? What our group's been doing so far has been pretty removed. We've been getting rid of them, true, and Buehlankamp's plan has been working. But I don't know if I can hunt some girl down in the woods and kill her in cold blood." Cecil looked worried.

Mark threw a glance over at Cecil. "Well, buddy. Tonight that's your mission. But only if they're alive. If you're lucky, they'll already be dead. So cross your fingers, okay?" He slapped Cecil on the shoulder.

A movement from the back of the helicopter caused Cecil to turn his head around suddenly, but not before a gun was pressed up against the right side of his neck.

"Don't move, buddy," Frank Lambert hissed. "Or I'll blow this bullet right through your skinny little neck and you'll never find out what you can do in cold blood."

Cecil's hands involuntarily shook on the cyclic and collective, causing the helicopter to dip and lose altitude, as well as drop off to one side.

"Keep control of the aircraft, Cecil!" Mark admonished sharply. "Or give it to me!"

"I've got it," Cecil said quietly as he made slow adjustments and stabilized the helicopter.

"What do you want, Frank?" Mark asked. "To what do we owe this unexpected pleasure in the middle of the night on our helicopter? I don't recall seeing you on the manifest."

"I didn't think I'd be invited," Frank said. "I'm along to make sure you don't harm those women, assuming they're alive."

"What do you care?" Mark asked. "You were with us from the beginning. We all had the same goal, to get women out of the cockpits."

"I told you, asshole," Frank said in a controlled voice, "you and your merry band took things way too far. I don't know what came over you or who this Buehlankamp guy is, but the minute you decided to start killing female pilots, you crossed the line."

"Says who, Frank? You? That's laughable. We've got the support of lots of guys." Mark said.

"I doubt it," Frank scoffed. "You're living in a fantasy world. A sick, fantasy world. One in which only you and your white, male aviator friends occupy the positions and you're deathly afraid of everyone else who isn't like you. Who's next on your list? Black aviators? Single aviators? Warrant officer aviators? Commissioned officers have never liked us, remember that? Will you start killing us off, too?"

"Don't be ridiculous, Frank." Mark said scornfully.

"Ridiculous, the man says. And yet he talks about killing female pilots as if they are a group of mosquitoes."

Mark turned around and said with a vengeance, "They are taking our spots, Frank. They can't go into combat. They are ruining our morale and esprit de corps. Everyone knows they don't have the same talent we do and that most of them probably slept with their flight instructors just to graduate. We have to get rid of them. I don't know why you can't see that."

"Oh, grow up, Mark." Frank pulled the gun away from Cecil's neck, pointed it directly at Mark's face and pulled the trigger.

"Oh, God! Oh, Christ!" Cecil screamed as blood and tissue spattered on his hands, his arms, his helmet and all over the cockpit window. "What did you do that for?"

During the blast, as Mark's body was thrust backwards against the pilot's seatbelt, Cecil momentarily lost his grip on the cyclic and the Huey dropped a couple of hundred feet. Swiping the slimy mixture off his visor with the back of his glove, Cecil steeled his nerves, grabbing the cyclic at the same time, and regained altitude.

Frank placed the muzzle of the gun back against Cecil's neck. "So that you know I mean business, Cecil. Now, let's find that downed helicopter. And if those women are alive, we're rescuing them. Kapice? If you have any ideas like your friend here, speak now or forever hold your peace."

Cecil remained silent.

"I didn't think so. Listening to you talk, I figured you were the one I could convince to see things my way. I'm glad I made the right choice. I bet you're pretty glad, too, huh, buddy?"

Frank dug the pistol muzzle deeper into Cecil's neck. "Oh, and just for reassurance, I'm turning off these radios so you don't get any ideas."

CHAPTER 101

SOMEWHERE IN EAST GERMANY
4:07 A.M., SATURDAY, JUNE 7

After André had led the way back to his cabin, he hustled Tina to a cozy kitchen where he made a pot of coffee. While it was brewing, he quickly scrambled her some eggs, fried some sausage, and buttered some thick slices of homemade bread, placing some strawberry preserves on the scarred wooden table.

"Eat up," he said. "You look like you haven't had a good meal in a while."

Tina stared at the food momentarily, wondering what she was doing in this strange man's house in the middle of nowhere, and then thanked herself for her good fortune and began to eat ravenously. Hot food right off the griddle tasted fabulous, especially after not having had any for so long.

"This tastes fantastic!" she gasped, when she could finally come up for air and took a gulp of hot, black coffee.

Leaning against the kitchen counter, André grinned. "Thanks. Now, do you feel like telling me why you ditched your car in the lake, or do we not know each other well enough yet?"

Tina blanched, and put her fork down momentarily.

"Obviously, you're running away from something," André said. "That's clear. You got rid of your car. You were walking in the middle of the night. You're an American in East Germany—that's the biggest red flag of all. You weren't dressed at all for the weather. I don't see a purse of any sort. Shall I go on?"

"You said you're used to helping people," Tina said. "What do you mean?"

"I don't normally go around blurting it out, but it seemed pretty safe to tell you. Are you done eating?" André motioned to her plate. Tina nodded. "I've got something to show you. Come on." Tina pushed away from the table and followed him.

André opened the door to his pantry and slid the pantry shelves out on a hidden sliding mechanism, revealing creaking wooden stairs that led to a small room beneath the cabin.

"Stand still while I turn on the lightbulb," André said, "and then you can go down while I shut everything behind me."

A small office with radios and electronic equipment greeted Tina at the foot of the stairs, along with a cot, a hot stove, a coffeepot, cans upon cans of food, and many bottles of water.

"It looks like you're prepared to live here if you have to," Tina remarked when André joined her.

"This is my safe room."

"So it appears," Tina said approvingly, looking around. "Do you come down here often?"

"Well, when a refugee turns up, or someone who needs help—" André looked pointedly at Tina—" this is where I come to make contact. In East Germany—I don't know if you've heard—but it isn't often safe to use the telephones," he said wryly.

"Why do you do this?" Tina asked. "Isn't this dangerous for you?"

"My parents and grandparents were both in the Holocaust. My parents survived—they were only children. My grandparents all died, as did a lot of my aunts and uncles. It traumatized my family for decades. I don't think my mother ever got over it. I vowed that I wouldn't turn my back on people who needed help, like a lot of Germans did during the war."

"But you're risking a lot, aren't you? Do people in the village know what you do?"

"Yes, but we're a close-knit bunch. We're all Jews here and we hate the East German authorities." André shrugged. "I have to live my conscience or what good is my life? Now, enough about me. Let's talk about you. Why are you here?"

"God, that's a great question. I have no idea why I'm here. I can tell you how I got here, but it's going to sound crazy."

"Try me. I've heard it all."

Tina took a deep breath. "I was in a small town in West Germany looking into my twin sister's death when I was kidnapped, thrown into a van, and brought here. I've been held captive in some small place in the woods for about a week. I escaped in the middle of the night, grabbed a car that was there—the keys were in it—and that's the car I ditched."

"Okay, who was holding you captive?" André asked.

"I don't know. An East German guard was always at the door, and a Russian man would come in from time to time."

"Did you know their names?"

"No, they never said."

"Well, that was clever. And no one else?" André asked.

"Just the guard's lover. She came the night I escaped. Oh! And then one day, an American colonel, named Buehlankamp, came to see me."

"What was an American colonel doing here, and why was he in cahoots with a Russian man?"

"I don't know. It didn't make sense."

André shook his head. "Did they give you any idea why they kidnapped you?"

"Apparently they were upset because I was investigating my sister's helicopter accident. You see, my sister, Crystal, died in March with two other women and I didn't believe it was pilot error as the accident report said, so I've been looking into it. Then, my ex-brother-in-law told me it was actually a conspiracy to kill female helicopter pilots."

"What?" André looked confused.

"Yes, that's what Frank told me. I thought it was outrageous at first, too. And then Frank told me he actually killed one of the conspirators in Korea and was going to kill another one in Alaska. He warned me that two more were at my unit in New York."

"Wait a minute. Are you in the military?"

"What? Yes, yes," Tina said impatiently. "I'm a helicopter pilot, too, just like my sister."

"So what were you doing in Germany?"

"I was working with the West German police office that had initially investigated the crash site because they had supposedly gotten evidence of sabotage."

"But didn't you say the accident report said it was pilot error?"

"Yes, which means that the Army must have been covering it up, which confirms what my brother-in-law was saying—that there was a conspiracy. But I had no proof. I was also, at first reluctantly, working with the commander of the unit where my sister was killed."

"So how did you get kidnapped?"

"I went out at night to call one of my female friends at my unit in New York to warn her about the two conspirators there, and while I was at the pay phone, someone grabbed me."

"And here you are."

"And here I am."

"Alright," André said. "Now we have to make some decisions. First and foremost, we have to figure out how to get you out of here, and that requires making some contact. Who do you trust most at the moment?"

Without hesitation, Tina said, "Karl Gunter."

André replied, "Okay, tell me what city he's in, and I can take care of the rest. The next order of business for you is to lie down on that cot and get some sleep."

CHAPTER 102

ADIRONDACK STATE PARK, NEW YORK
4:16 A.M., SATURDAY, JUNE 7

Deirdre stumbled out of the woods after her three-hour long hike, peering down the silvery concrete lane and listening intently for the rumble of welcoming traffic. The darkness of the night had severely hindered her progress; her arm ached and throbbed. Scratched by branches on every part of her body because she could scarcely see where she was going, Deirdre wearily lifted a limp hand to wave some straggly strings of hair away from her forehead. The exertion of walking so many miles had caused beads of sweat to drip down her back, around her waistband, inside her bra, along her ears, down her nose, and in every uncomfortable spot. Now that she could stand still, the chill of the night air reversed the process and she hugged her damp flight suit as closely to her body as she could, hoping to create some warmth while wishing more cars would drive by than one every twenty minutes.

The first two cars refused to stop, nearly blinding Deirdre as they came around the curve with their brights on. When the third car arrived, Deirdre decided she'd had it with being patient and stepped out from the side of the highway.

The car veered to the left to avoid missing her, but, unfortunately, the curve in the road continued to the right. Leaving the road, the car bumped over some gravel and screeched to a halt, wedged between two small saplings.

Deirdre ran across the road and tapped on the window.

"Are you alright?" she exclaimed. "I'm really sorry."

After gingerly moving his limbs, the driver opened the door. "I think so," he said. "What the hell were you doing out there on the road? You scared the living daylights out of me."

"I need help," Deirdre said.

"I might need help getting my car out of here, but tell me about you first. What kind of help could you possibly need out here in the middle of nowhere in the middle of the night?"

"My helicopter crashed in the woods back there—"

The man looked to where Deirdre was pointing. "You've got to be kidding me."

"No. Two of my colleagues are back there. Both are hurt. One of them has a broken leg and needs medical help to get out."

"You don't look so great yourself," the man nodded his head towards Deirdre's arm.

"Yeah, well, I've felt better," she admitted wryly.

Looking at his car, the man commented, "If I push on the car and you put it in reverse, I suppose we can get it out of here."

"Let's give it a try," Deirdre said.

After fifteen minutes of strenuous pushing, gravel-spinning, and motor-squealing, his car was finally free.

"Alright, time for introductions. I'm Steven Crawford. I live up around Cranberry Lake."

"I'm Deirdre Holloway. If you could take these map coordinates and let someone know where we are, then I can go back to my colleagues and tell them help is on the way."

"Okay, now look, Deirdre, I understand you wanting to help out your friends and all, but it appears to me you need medical attention yourself."

"That can wait until my friends get medical attention," Deirdre said stalwartly.

"That's very noble of you. But what if you go back into those deep, dark woods—and, Deirdre, I'm a veteran Adirondack hiker—you can't find your way? The rescue team is now searching for an accident site with two hurt people and a lost hiker who needs medical attention. Does that seem like a good idea?"

Deirdre laughed. "No, I guess it doesn't. I wish to hell our radios had been working."

"I bet you do," Steven replied. "I bet you wish your helicopter hadn't crashed, either. Come on and jump in. You can tell me all about it."

CHAPTER 103

SOMEWHERE IN EAST GERMANY
9:58 A.M., SATURDAY, JUNE 7

Tina felt a gentle hand shake her awake as the man said quietly, "I've got the police captain on the ham radio for you." She shook the cobwebs out of her head and looked up fuzzily at André.

"Have I been out long?"

He smiled and nodded his head. "Yes, a few hours. It took me a while to raise someone. They weren't in this early on a Saturday morning. I think you needed the sleep."

André gave Tina a hand out of the cot and motioned her over to the black and gray radio set sitting on his wooden table. He placed the headset over her ears, showed her the microphone, and said, "Now say 'over' when you want Gunter to talk, and 'out' when you're completely done."

Tina didn't feel like reminding him that she was a military pilot and knew the rules of radio communication. She simply sat in front of the radio and said, "Hello? Hauptmann Gunter? Are you there? Over."

She stared at the radio in front of her, waiting, while the wires sizzled. Suddenly, Gunter's voice came booming back, "Hallo, Frau Loyola! Es freut mich—I'm so happy to talk with you! We've been so worried about you! All of us! My assistant—Polizeimeister; Herr Major, Frau Hauptmann. We've tried to find out what happened to you!! Gott sei dank that you're okay! You are okay, aren't you? Over."

Tina felt tears welling in her eyes. "Yes, I'm okay. Thank you. I—I—don't really know what happened. One minute I was there, and the next I was here. Over."

"André has told me a little bit about what happened to you, so you don't have to talk about it now if you don't want to. What we really need to do is figure out how to get you back. Over."

"Trust me, I'm ready to come back. I don't want to be here any longer than I need to. Over."

"I can understand that, Frau Loyola."

"I thought you were going to call me Tina," she said.

"That's right. And you're supposed to call me Karl. So, Tina, why didn't you call the U.S. Army? Over."

"From the very beginning, you and Marthe have been the only ones to shoot completely straight with me. You don't have any kind of an agenda at all."

"I really don't think Herr Major has anything to do with your sister's death or your disappearance, Tina. He and I have spent a lot of time together this past week, and he's probably a lot more on your side than you can imagine."

"Okay," Tina said a bit gruffly. "But, still, it's you I wanted. I mean, it's you I trust."

Gunter laughed. "Perhaps you meant a little more in that comment than you intended, Tina."

Tina was silent a moment. "Well, maybe I did. Over."

"It will be nice to see you again, Tina. I'm extremely glad to hear from you and know that you're safe. Now, we need to discuss the details of your return. André has volunteered to drive you to the border of East Germany, and Frau Hauptmann and Herr Major have volunteered to fly a helicopter there to pick you up. Since Damrow is the commander of his unit, he figures he can authorize a mission without a lot of fanfare just in case there is something nefarious going on in his unit. What do you say?"

"Will they let you come?"

"I beg your pardon?" Gunter asked.

"If they let you and your assistant on the helicopter, then perhaps I'll feel they can truly be trusted."

"You are a distrustful sort, aren't you? But I don't blame you after what you've been through."

"Let me explain something else," Tina said, her tone becoming even more serious. "An American full-bird colonel came to visit me in my imprisonment. He said he was the aviation training brigade commander at Fort Rucker. Now what in hell was an American officer doing in East Germany and why was he helping these people keep me kidnapped? Over!"

"Tina, I can't even begin to answer that for you. But from the very beginning, this all smelled fishy. Now it smells absolutely rotten. Let's get you out of there, get you safe, and see how all of the pieces line up. Okay? I'm sure we can figure it out together." Gunter's voice was warm and reassuring, and Tina felt herself begin to calm down slightly.

"Alright," she said. "When do I leave?"

André spoke up from beside her. "In the middle of the night. That's the best chance to avoid the border guards."

Gunter spoke at the same time. "André and I have worked out the mechanics. He's apparently done this sort of thing before. You really lucked out falling into his hands. We owe him a big one."

Tina looked up at André, who smiled and shrugged modestly.

"Okay, so we'll see you soon. Take care of yourself, Tina. Out." And Gunter was gone.

Drained of emotion, Tina sat in the chair for a few moments longer until the last vestiges of the conversation had faded away. Then she slowly removed the headset, rose from the chair, and faced André. "So," she brightly said, "tell me about yourself. I might as well have one East German friend before I get carted out of here."

CHAPTER 104

ADIRONDACK STATE PARK, NEW YORK
4:22 A.M., SATURDAY, JUNE 7

"Set the helicopter down in that clearing," Frank said sharply.

"What clearing?" Cecil asked, straining to see in the dark. Any glimmer of light had faded away by the clouds that had rolled in, threatening a thunderstorm.

"At one o'clock."

"I don't see it."

"Look harder, numbskull. Or will a bullet in your brain help you see better?"

Frank waved his pistol in front of Cecil's face in the direction of the clearing. "There—can you see it now? Dimwit."

Cecil gripped the collective and cyclic harder and nodded his head. "Yeah, I see it. Just barely. But I don't think we can make it into that. That's too small an LZ."

Emitting a sarcastic laugh, Frank said, "And you call yourself a pilot? I could land this thing down there with my eyes closed."

"Maybe you should do it then," Cecil muttered.

"That's where you're wrong, Cecil, my friend. Because you're going to be extra-careful getting this bird down on the ground, aren't you? Or I'm going to blow you to smithereens like your buddy here." He motioned to Mark, slumped over in a bloody pile against the cockpit door. "Now, Cecil! Get it down, now!"

Cecil abruptly began the motions of bringing the helicopter out of its low altitude and into a landing, descending at a rapid rate over the tall pine trees that ringed the small clearing. The aircraft came to a shuddering stop just inches away from trees on the far side.

As the rotor blades whirred to a standstill, Cecil complained, "We're never going to find them out here in the wilderness anyway. This makes absolutely no sense, landing like this in the middle of nowhere."

"You did check your fuel gauge, didn't you, Mr. Pilot?" Frank asked scornfully.

Cecil reddened. "Obviously, we should have gone back for fuel. We shouldn't be wasting our time here on a wild goose chase."

In a falsetto voice, Frank repeated, "'Obviously, we should have gone back for fuel. We shouldn't be wasting our time here on a wild goose chase.'" Lowering his voice to his natural tone, he said, "You really are as dumb as you look, Cecil. Did you forget about your pal here?"

Cecil looked at Mark and back at Frank.

"No way could we go back to civilization now, Cecil. Haven't you realized that?"

True fear flashed across Cecil's face.

"Ahh," Frank said. "You have realized it. Good boy. Now, let's go find those girls, shall we? Perhaps you'll do at least one decent thing before you die."

"What the fuck are you talking about?" Cecil screamed.

Frank sighed impatiently. "We're going to find that helicopter that you and Mark caused to go down. I don't care how long it takes. If the women are dead, we're going to get the bodies back to their families. If they're alive, we're going to bring them home. Or at least I am. I'm only using you to help me find them. Somewhere along the way, I'll kill you just as I killed Mark. You can be sure of that."

"What makes you think I won't kill you first?" Cecil demanded.

"This." Frank whipped out a pair of police handcuffs and slapped them on Cecil faster than his brain's activity could register. "Now, get out of the cockpit and let's start walking."

Stumbling through the Adirondack woods in the deepest, blackest night, they had no concept of where they were going or where the downed helicopter was. Frank, however, had been right in that they could not return to Fort Drum or anywhere else to refuel and they had been about to crash because of low fuel, so they had had to land somewhere. Where better but in the middle of the woods? Moreover, Frank would be a hunted man once a murdered body was found in the helicopter, but he was past the point of caring. Nevertheless, it wouldn't help to give anyone a head start in finding him. They knew that Deirdre and her crew had flown a certain distance into the Adirondacks and, according to Frank's calculations from what he'd seen on the news and what he'd overheard from Mark and Cecil, they were at least in the general vicinity. But even being in the general vicinity meant that the wreckage could be in the next valley and they would never see it.

There was so much brush and foliage that it took a great deal of time just pushing through it. Frank made Cecil cut a path through it first, holding his handcuffed hands in front of his face, and they quickly become scratched despite being covered with his flight gloves. Allowing Cecil to keep his flight gloves made Frank feel he was being pretty soft.

After about an hour of trudging up and down hills, across boulders, over ravines, past streams, and over fallen trees, they finally found a hiking trail. Although they had no idea whether this would lead them any closer to Deirdre's helicopter or not, Frank opted to follow it for a while and see how it panned out.

Suddenly, the threatening thunderstorm erupted and water cascaded from above. Claps of thunder startled them in their tracks, and lightning lit up the skies momentarily. The muddied trail became more difficult to walk, particularly the protruding slippery rocks that were impossible to see in the dark, catching the hikers unawares and propelling them headlong into falls on the ground so that they ended up wet, dirty, and bruised.

After one particularly nasty spill, Frank yelled out, "Can't you watch out where you're walking, you stupid shit!"

"It's the damn combat boots! They keep sliding on these rocks. If I were wearing better shoes like you—"

"Oh, God! Listen to the complainer. Just keep walking, Cecil. And try to not keep falling down on top of me, would you?" He shoved Cecil in the back with the muzzle of the gun.

"Is this fun now, Frank? How long are we going to wander around in here, just the two of us?" Cecil laughed bitterly.

"Well, it won't be too long, will it? Without food or water. I didn't bring any. Did you?"

Cecil remained silent. The storm's waters continued to drip down trees' leaves and down their faces, arms, and necks. Not only were they soaked, they were now shivering and the night air was cooling their bodies to an uncomfortable level. Their feet squished in pools of water with almost every step.

But then, Frank tripped over a tree root on the ground, losing his grip on the gun. It spiraled away from him, landing several feet in front of Cecil. Frank fell to the ground, watching Cecil lunge for the gun with both hands, pick it up, turn, and fire. The first bullet hit Frank in the left shoulder, and left a gaping, bleeding wound.

"You're going to have to do better than that, Cecil," Frank taunted, as he grabbed Cecil's pants leg and pulled him to the ground. The two men tussled in the mud, with rain streaming down their faces. Grunting with every breath, Frank strained to pin Cecil beneath him and grab the gun back. Cecil twisted his body to the side, wrenching the gun out of Frank's reach and, then, to Frank's utter surprise, butted his head against Frank's. Frank howled in pain, sat up, and, in that moment, Cecil staggered to his feet, dashing away a safe distance.

Cecil took aim and shot Frank in the left lung, and again in the heart. Frank thought one last time of Crystal, whom he hoped he'd see soon, and wished Tina well. He sorrowed over not being able to save Deirdre, and cursed himself over not killing the last of the conspirators. His vengeance quest was over. As Frank slumped and died, the only thing of him that continued to move were his wet strands of hair lying in the dirty water that flowed downhill.

Walking slowly towards Frank, keeping the gun pointed at his body, Cecil searched his pockets until he found the key for the handcuffs. After removing the steel bands, he took off his flight gloves, and tossed both deep into the woods. Deciding he would offer up a version of self-defense, Cecil left Frank's body where it was and continued on his way. He now had a renewed mission—back to keeping Colonel Buehlankamp's plan—find the girls and kill them. Perhaps it wasn't impossible after all.

CHAPTER 105

ADIRONDACK STATE PARK, NEW YORK
5:13 A.M., SATURDAY, JUNE 7

Lieutenant Wright and Sergeant Clearwater had awakened and, despite the rain, managed to start a small fire. As the women sipped their fragrant tea, the rain began to come to an end. The slight curls of smoke from their fire had attracted another visitor. From another part of the Adirondack State Park, Cecil had also smelled the odor of burning wood despite the wetness of the rain, and had kept his nose turned in that direction. Emerging from the forest into the crash site, Cecil immediately saw the helicopter in front of him and the women seated at the edge of the woods around a tiny fire.

Patting the gun in his right pocket, Cecil stepped around the helo wreckage and said as he walked forwards, "Well, looks like you ladies are basically okay."

Cups clattered and the women shrieked. "Cecil!" Lieutenant Wright exclaimed. "My God, you gave us a fright. How did you find us?"

"Trust me, it hasn't been easy. So, how's everyone doing? It looks like there's a couple of broken limbs here. Is that right, Sergeant?" Cecil motioned to Marjorie's leg.

"I think it might be broken, yes, sir."

Cecil knelt down and inspected the job Deirdre had done with the splint. "Looks like a pretty fine job of setting a broken leg for out in the field."

"Deirdre did that," Lieutenant Wright said. "Once it started to rain, I tried to move her into the helicopter, but it was so excruciating for her, we just couldn't do it. So I strung a couple of ponchos here for shelter."

"I'm fine, really I am," Marjorie said. "Lieutenant Wright has been great. We're on a bit of high ground. She dug a little trench around us and you can see the water is swirling past us. We're really quite alright." Marjorie smiled brightly.

"How about you, Yolanda?" Cecil asked Lieutenant Wright solicitously. "That helicopter looks pretty banged up. How'd you make out?"

"I seem to have had a concussion. I'll probably have to be checked out. I don't remember a thing before the accident or for about an hour afterwards. Otherwise, I'm fine," Lieutenant Wright said.

"Glad to hear it. So now we're down to the pilot-in-command, right?" Cecil asked, looking around.

"We think Deirdre's got a broken arm. She splinted that herself, too, and now she's gone off for help."

Cecil stiffened. "Yes … yes … I know that. That's why I'm here. As I said, it wasn't easy finding you. How long ago did she leave?"

Lieutenant Wright looked at Marjorie. "I'm not sure, are you?" Marjorie shook her head. "Hours ago. She said she was going to be back. She was going to give our coordinates to someone to get help and then she'd come back."

"I was told to tell you not to expect her back. She's getting medical attention as we speak."

"Oh," Lieutenant Wright said. "Of course, that makes perfect sense. Why in the world should she come back here? We weren't even thinking. I suppose our thought process was that we could help each other until more help arrived."

"Sure," Cecil agreed, "but now you've got me and we can all leave."

"But how?" Marjorie piped up.

Cecil looked perplexed. "What do you mean, how?"

"I mean, I can't walk on my leg. It's broken. I need a stretcher to get me out of here. I don't mean to be a bother, but …" Marjorie's voice trailed off. She and Lieutenant Wright both looked expectantly at Cecil.

"Where's your co-pilot?" Lieutenant Wright asked.

"My what?"

"Your co-pilot. And where's the medical equipment or medical personnel? Do you have a stretcher? Are you prepared to help us get out of here? I know Deirdre would have passed on what our situation here was like. This is really going to piss me off if Fort Drum sent you out here unprepared."

"Actually, that's a long story, and we don't have time to talk about that right now," Cecil said. He suddenly realized that Lieutenant Wright might not capitulate easily and he needed to gain control over the situation quickly. "What we need to do is get out of here."

"What do you mean, get out of here?" Lieutenant Wright asked. "We can't leave this place unless you have a stretcher because Sergeant Clearwater can't walk. You can see for yourself that she has a broken leg."

"My helicopter isn't too far back, and I can fly you out of here in a jif. So, let's go. I can help the sergeant."

"What's your rush, Cecil?" Lieutenant Wright asked. "I don't understand. This doesn't make sense. And your co-pilot had to have known we were injured and needed help, so I can't figure out why he isn't here with you."

Cecil's eyes narrowed. "I said, get up and get moving."

"This is some way of helping us, Cecil," Lieutenant Wright said. "You seem to have some agenda of your own. But guess what, we're not leaving. I'm not going to allow a person with a broken leg to be dragged through the woods, particularly when I have no idea how far it is she has to go. Do I make myself clear?"

Cecil pulled out the gun and pointed it at Lieutenant Wright. "Do I make myself clear? You're right, Yolanda. I do have my own agenda. And that includes vacating this area. Now get up off your butts and get moving."

Lieutenant Wright had no time to think, only to react. She threw herself at Cecil, knocking him off-balance and sideways into the fire. He screamed and lost control of the gun. Seizing the gun, Lieutenant Wright pointed it at Cecil, then transferred guard over him to Marjorie while she hurriedly grabbed some rope from the aircraft, marched him to a pine tree where she tied him fast, arms stretched overhead, writhing in pain all the while.

Cecil had failed in his mission to Colonel John Buehlankamp.

CHAPTER 106

FORT WAINWRIGHT, ALASKA
10:08 A.M., SATURDAY, JUNE 7

General Tucker and Captain Thornton stared in amazement at the television screen as Secretary of the Army Maloney's press conference of the evening before was replayed on the Saturday morning news.

Earl turned to his boss. "General, he's lying!"

Tucker frowned. "Wait a minute, Earl. I just can't believe the Secretary of the Army would deliberately tell an untruth on national television. Maloney is a man of integrity. It isn't in him to prevaricate. If he's got something to hide, he would find another way to do so than tell a lie, trust me."

"But, General, you heard what Lieutenant Robison said. Her cousin told her that Blackhawk was sabotaged!"

Tucker scratched his head. "I know. And his being killed right after telling Robison lends credence to his account."

"So why didn't the Secretary put that information out on the air?"

"It could be because that's still part of the homicide investigation and the detectives don't want that piece of information out there," Tucker suggested.

"Okay," Earl unwillingly agreed. "I suppose that could be possible, sir." He looked back at the television set, where the anchors had now skipped on to another story. "Something doesn't sit right with me."

"I'm with you, Earl. I think it wouldn't hurt if I called up the Secretary and told him what I know. I seem to have become a conduit of information from several sources here—all informally—and I want to be sure that info is being passed along somewhere."

"Congresswoman Tonnelli said she would be following up on the Blackhawk accident and Robison's cousin's murder, as well as what was going on with the female flight students at Fort Rucker. She's really concerned with the aviation community at the moment."

"Yes, I've talked to her off and on during her trip to Japan and now that she's back in the States," Tucker said automatically.

"I beg your pardon, sir?"

Tucker looked up and tried to backtrack . "Oh, it was nothing. We've just stayed in touch. A number of loose ends from her visit."

"Oh, yes, sir. Of course. If you say so." Earl looked amused. Tucker rearranged some paper files on his desk. "If I'd known you'd needed to be in touch with the congresswoman, I would have been happy to arrange the phone calls."

"Get out, Earl!" Earl turned to leave, trying unsuccessfully to stifle a grin. "And when you get to your crummy little desk out there, connect me to Secretary of the Army Maloney. I need to have a chat with him."

"Yes, sir!"

Within minutes, Tucker was talking to Reginald Maloney on the secure phone in the Secretary's study.

"Sir, I caught your press conference this morning up here in Alaska—"

"I know you didn't call to congratulate me on my sterling acting abilities, General Tucker, so there must be something more to this call."

"Yes, well." Tucker arranged his thoughts for a few seconds and then continued. "I was especially struck by your emphasis that there was no conspiracy to kill female pilots. I don't know if that's true or not, but I don't know if you're privy to all the information that I have."

"What do you mean?" Maloney asked.

"The young soldier who was murdered in Korea—"

"Ochiotto. I remember him. Terrible tragedy. Neck snapped off in his supervisor's office. Still no leads. His cousin just arrived in New York with his body. The funeral's Monday. Yes, what about him?"

Tucker was suitably impressed with Maloney's recall of the details. "He called his cousin right before he was killed. She works here at Fort Wainwright. A maintenance officer. He was one of the electronics technicians on that Blackhawk that went down in Korea."

"The friendly-fire fiasco. Right."

"Except he told his cousin he'd just examined the IFF and that someone had deliberately sabotaged it. He suspected Lieutenant John Datterly, an officer in the unit who later committed suicide."

"Did he say why?" Maloney asked.

"No idea."

"Is this in the accident report?"

"I don't know. I bet it didn't make it in. Once Ochiotto was killed, information on the accident died with him, except for those of us who knew of it second- or third-hand. We reported what we knew to the homicide investigators, but I'm not certain they passed it on to the accident investigation team. Two different sets of people."

Maloney mused. "And two different sets of protocol, rules, and procedures."

"I know this doesn't give any credence to a conspiracy theory, but it shoots the dickens out of the friendly-fire position on the Blackhawk," Tucker commented. "I knew it was conceivable that you had information you weren't sharing with the press or the public, but I couldn't keep silent with what I knew."

"I'm glad you didn't, Tucker. I don't mind telling you, I didn't know this. And if it's true, it's not only upsetting, it's extremely alarming. One episode of sabotage against an Army helicopter is bad enough, if founded. Now, if we find out that it was done because there were female pilots aboard, we're in big trouble."

"I hadn't really made that connection yet, but you're right, sir, that would be an absolute disaster."

"Three helicopter accidents each with three female flight crewmembers onboard—how much of a coincidence is that? Especially when we find out that one of those accidents was not an accident but a planned killing?" Maloney's measured voice crisply moved forward. "Each one has taken place in a different country and under decidedly unique circumstances. Each one looks like pilot error. My God, Tucker, what do the police say? There is no such thing as a coincidence! I've watched three of our Army helicopters filled with women crash and I steadfastly maintained in the face of them that there is no conspiracy. How blind could I possibly be?"

At the other end of the phone, Tucker remained calm. "Secretary Maloney, none of us knew. We still don't know. But I agree with you. It seems as though there is a conspiracy. Especially with the helicopter accident last night."

Maloney drew a deep breath. "We've got to change course. Something dark and evil is coursing its way deep inside the Army. I don't know what it is, where it is, or who is leading it. But we're going to find it."

"I'm with you, sir," Tucker said immediately. "Even if I didn't have aviation units under me, or female pilots serving under my command."

"Or a young daughter in flight school," Maloney said softly.

"That, too," Tucker said, with a catch in his throat.

CHAPTER 107

ADIRONDACK STATE PARK, NEW YORK
5:35 A.M., SATURDAY, JUNE 7

A weak sunrise was just beginning to break through the trees when the women heard the rotors of a helicopter overhead. Lieutenant Wright jumped up and stood in the tiny clearing created by the wrecked Huey, waving the orange cloths they were given as part of their survival gear, hoping the flight crew above could see them despite the foliage canopy. Almost as suddenly as the sound had appeared, it dissipated.

With Cecil's appearance, the two women had realized he certainly wasn't the help Deirdre was sending for them, so they had been on the lookout for something else.

"No, no!" Lieutenant Wright yelled. "Come back!" She threw her orange cloth down in frustration. "They should have found us by now."

She looked longingly in the direction of the helicopter and then added, "Yes, well. When you think of the time it takes to rouse a helicopter crew in the middle of the night in the Adirondacks … I mean, how many do they have just sitting around for rescue missions?"

"Good point, ma'am," Marjorie said. "For all we know, they called back to Fort Drum. That would have taken some time. Wait, look! Look! It's coming back!"

Lieutenant Wright picked up her orange cloth and started waving it crazily. The helicopter came to a high hover and someone leaning out of the helicopter waved in response and started talking on a megaphone.

"What are they saying?" Marjorie asked.

"I can only catch a few words," Lieutenant Wright said. "The noise of the helicopter is drowning out most everything. It looks like they're pointing over there." Lieutenant Wright motioned to the other side of the hill.

The aircraft veered off to the right and the women were left with a disquieting stillness.

"Where did it go?" Marjorie asked. "I thought they'd come to get us out of here."

"I'm sure they have," Lieutenant Wright said reassuringly. "They have to find a safe place to land. I imagine that's what they were trying to tell us. They probably wanted to get as close to us as possible."

For the next few minutes, the women remained poised, listening intently to the sounds of the forest and for any unusual noises. Their efforts were rewarded when a small group burst upon them from the direction in which the helicopter had flown. Vanessa Robison was in the lead. She stopped in her tracks as soon as she saw the women.

"Yolanda!" Vanessa gave her friend a big bear hug. "Once I knew you were up here, I begged your unit to let me come." Lieutenant Wright made the introductions. "We were in flight school together. Then Lieutenant Robison went off to her maintenance test pilot program. How did you get to be in New York? I thought you were in Alaska?"

Vanessa briefly explained the sad news about Lindley. "Thank God we've found you all. Everyone worried so much about you during that thunderstorm. How are you doing? We brought some blankets for you." Vanessa draped blankets over each of the women's shoulders. The women were still cold and the blankets made a huge difference to their comfort level.

"What about Ms. Holloway?" Lieutenant Wright asked. "She was our pilot-in-command. She's the one who went off to get help."

"She's being taken by ambulance to Fort Drum. That's about all I know at the moment," Vanessa said. "Apparently, she got the information through to a police station in Cranberry Lake, which patched it through to Fort Drum, and here we are. Fort Drum decided to send out a medevac helicopter, but because of the thunderstorm, it couldn't depart until that was over. With your broken leg, Sergeant, they decided it would be better to lift you out by helicopter than try to carry you out several hours on the park trails."

"I appreciate that, ma'am," Marjorie said. "It wasn't so bad waiting. We knew someone was coming."

In a brisk but cheerful tone, Vanessa said, "Okay, let's get this show on the road." She looked over at the medic, who had already re-bandaged Marjorie's leg in a more professional manner. "Is she ready to go yet, boss?"

"Yes, ma'am," he said. The crew chief helped him put Marjorie on the gurney and the two set off down the trail to the helicopter.

"The rest of the crew and I can help you carry whatever you need," Vanessa said. "You obviously can't take all of your things." All of a sudden, Vanessa noticed Cecil in the shadows of the forest. "Who's that?" she asked sharply, taking a few steps forward.

"That," Lieutenant Wright said bitterly, "is someone from my unit who theoretically came to help us but pulled a gun on us instead."

"How did he get here?" Vanessa asked quizzically.

"Says he flew in and left his helicopter nearby, but you would have thought his co-pilot would have come looking for him by now." Lieutenant Wright said.

"He sounds like a matter for the MPs to handle. We've got the coordinates of this place. It was easy enough to find. If his buddy is out there, and he's got a helo to fly him out of here, then good for him. I'm not inclined to untie someone who held a gun to people's heads and put him on a medevac helicopter. But then, again, I'm not the PIC, either." Vanessa looked over at the medevac pilots, who nodded in agreement. "Alright then, looks like he's staying here."

Cecil yelled, "You can't leave me here!"

"Watch us," Vanessa said. And the women picked up the last of their belongings, followed the flight crew, and walked the fifteen minutes over an easy trail to a flat clearing where the medevac helicopter was waiting, rotors turning, to lift off for Fort Drum.

CHAPTER 108

ENTERPRISE, ALABAMA
5:45 A.M., SATURDAY, JUNE 7

After the phone conversation with her dad, Iris felt restless. She didn't feel up to cleaning her apartment after the fire, though she knew she needed to tackle that pronto. The stench inside was overwhelming and she was going to have to sleep on the couch until her bed was replaced. Calling her insurance company seemed like a lost cause on a Saturday, although Iris would have even less time and energy once she was in classes during the week. After surveying her bedroom for a few minutes and thinking it over, she grabbed her car keys and headed out the door for a country breakfast at the diner frequented by locals on the highway.

Not too many of the Fort Rucker crowd ate at the diner, particularly since it was more of a distance from the post than the fast food joints, and because it was a sit-down restaurant that required a bit more time than the hurry-up-and-eat military types could usually afford. Whenever Iris had the time, she loved to luxuriate in reading the paper, drinking coffee out of white ceramic mugs, hearing the hubbub of good old boys, and being called "hon" by the waitresses while she partook of an enormous breakfast.

Iris bought a Dothan newspaper from the stand outside the diner, pushed open the door, and went in. Seeing that the diner was fairly full, she took a booth close to the front door, sliding into the seat with the best view of the entrance. After placing her order and getting a cup of steaming, hot coffee, Iris gave her complete attention to the fairly dull happenings reported in the local paper. This, for her, was comfort. Some people liked bubble baths. Other people liked wine. Iris liked grits and home fries. It reminded her of her mother's Southern roots and all her visits back to her grandparents' house, whenever her dad could take her home to Georgia for a couple of weeks each summer. If he couldn't go, due to military commitments, he always made sure Iris could go spend time with her grandparents.

Those had been special times. The swimming hole in the river that ran past their property, the tire swing in the front yard, learning to make biscuits, the attic filled with treasures, the long dirt driveway that filled with dust when it hadn't rained for a long spell. Plus, Grandma's brothers and sisters all lived nearby, and Iris had an instant family of aunts, uncles, and cousins for those couple of weeks every single year. Although she loved her dad madly, theirs was a quiet house, and being around Grandma Jasper, even though Grandpa Jasper had been dead for years, was a busy, hectic lifestyle filled with friends and family. Iris loved it and yearned for it all year long. Grandma was still alive, and Iris spent part of her leave going back to see her each year, just as she had when she was growing up.

Iris's breakfast arrived and, after buttering a fat, flaky biscuit, she bit into it with deep pleasure. As a man departed the diner, Iris caught a whiff of what seemed a familiar scent, but wrapped up in her delicious meal, newspaper, and thoughts, it initially triggered no reaction. She paused, trying to trace that smell in her memory banks, and remembered that Grandpa Jasper had smoked cigars that smelled almost exactly like that.

Suddenly, Iris froze as she recalled a more recent recollection. A man in her bedroom with his hand over her mouth. And, although her sleep had been abruptly interrupted and she had been terrified, she knew without a shadow of a doubt that he had smoked the same kind of cigar as her grandfather. And the man who had just walked out of the diner also smoked the same cigar. The coincidence couldn't be a coincidence. That had to be the man who tried to kill her!

Remembering that the man in her bedroom knew who she was, Iris watched him as he walked to his car, keeping her face shielded from sight with the newspaper. Her Corvette was so conspicuous, she was afraid the culprit might recognize it, but luckily, she had parked in the diner's side lot. From her vantage point, Iris had an excellent view of the man as he turned around to get into the driver's seat.

"My God," she said under her breath, as chills ran up her spine. "I don't believe it. Colonel Buehlankamp."

CHAPTER 109

THE PENTAGON, WASHINGTON, D.C.
2:35 P.M., SATURDAY, JUNE 7

The return of Deirdre and her colleagues to Fort Drum caused quite a stir, particularly with their report about Cecil brandishing a gun and his being left behind in the Adirondacks. A team of military police was dispatched immediately to fetch him and, upon interrogation, his insistence that he had only meant to help the women and was trying to hurry them up didn't hold water. Towards the afternoon, some hikers in the woods found the abandoned helicopter with Mark's dead body inside and blood splattered all over. With New York police descending on Fort Drum and military police pressuring Cecil to confess to that murder, he was spilling the beans about the entire night, spinning Frank's death into an act of self-defense. It was only a matter of time before police could get far enough into the woods to bring Frank's body out. Until then, Cecil was in custody and under deep suspicion and observation.

The women were in amazingly good spirits considering their frightfully dangerous adventure. Even having learned that Army mates had attempted to kill them by sabotaging their helicopter had not managed to push them over the edge. All three were ecstatic to be alive, and none had life-threatening injuries. The incident they had just gone through had been traumatic and they wouldn't forget it, but each realized that they were extraordinarily lucky to have escaped the fate of the women in the helicopter accidents in Germany and Korea. For, although they hadn't heard any official announcement of a conspiracy yet, each one feared that if their helicopter had been sabotaged, then perhaps those others had been as well for they had seen the accusations in the media and, just like everyone else, had discounted them as pure nonsense. Now they knew they couldn't do that for they had seen the face of evil and it resided in the face next door.

The news that their helicopter had been sabotaged made the rounds at lightning speed—to Fort Rucker, to the Secretary of the Army, across the air waves courtesy of the news media. Speculation of a conspiracy was again rife, and the Army was announcing a press conference for later that afternoon.

Secretary of the Army Reginald Maloney sat in his office, pondering his dilemma. Did he raise the specter of a conspiracy to worldwide scrutiny, which would also perhaps alert innumerable people to be suspicious and report what they knew but might also create unbelievable panic as well as send the hoodlums under cover? Or did he keep the whole concept under wraps as long as possible until the Army had more information, hoping to find the culprits, thereby risking accusations of a cover-up later and maybe more deaths if the Army wasn't fast enough?

He blew out a frustrated sigh and punched his intercom. "Sally, I want you to get General Eckling at Fort Rucker on the phone."

"Yes, sir," she replied.

While waiting, Maloney leaned back in his chair, cupping his long fingers behind his head, thinking back to the first helicopter accident and wondering what signs there were and what he could possibly have done differently to have prevented the others. He only had two minutes before Sally was back on the intercom telling him to pick up the phone and, in that amount of time, he hadn't picked out any identifiable red flags that he or the Army should have picked up on.

"General Eckling, hello. How are you, today, sir?" Maloney said cordially. "I'm sorry to be bothering you on a Saturday afternoon."

"No problem, sir. It was pretty easy to find me. These days I've been spending a lot of time in the office."

"I hear you, General. I'm calling you because I think we have an extremely serious problem in our ranks with these helicopter accidents."

"I know that, sir. I'm on top of that. We seem to have had a rash of them lately and we're going to get to the bottom of it. I sent a request to review the unit training records of all female pilots in the Army up to the DCSOPS since several of the recent accidents have all involved female pilots."

"That's not going to happen, General, and I'll tell you why."

Eckling sputtered, "Secretary Maloney, I understand that you believe in fairness and I'm all for that, but I've got to protect my people and my machines. Somehow we're sending female pilots out of here and they don't seem to be getting the same training as the males. Now, when we reviewed their training records here, we found that nearly half of them should have failed or been set back."

"You know, General, that's another thing I've been meaning to talk to you about. You created an enormous flap by doing that. You were expressly ordered by the DCSOPS not to do that, but you did it anyway, and I can't begin to tell you the problems that's created for us with Congress."

"Oh, Congress!" Eckling laughed. "They're just a bunch of pompous—"

"I know what you guys in the trenches think, but those of us in the Pentagon, and particularly those of us who have to ask for money for those of you in the trenches, have to be concerned with what they think. And our fine men and women in Congress have been extremely upset on behalf of their constituents by what they think is going on at Fort Rucker. But we're going to talk about that some other time. The important thing right now is this—I have reason to believe that these three helicopter accidents involving female pilots—in Germany, Korea, and now New York—are the result of a conspiracy."

"What?" Eckling asked. "You've got to be kidding me. Don't tell me you're starting to believe the old liberal rags?"

"No, I've got inside information. It seems that one of the technicians on the Blackhawk that went down in Korea knew that it had been sabotaged, and right after he reported it, he was killed."

Eckling vaguely remembered seeing the casualty report about someone being killed in Korea. "That doesn't make a conspiracy, though."

"You're right, it doesn't. But you're the commanding general of the finest aviation school in the world. Doesn't it make more sense to you that you're putting out the best aviators in the world—male and female—rather than assuming that the females are somehow slipping by unprepared? What does that say for your curriculum, your instructors, your oversight? After all, General, it wouldn't be the fault of the females if they weren't adequately taught, now would it? The responsibility is totally on your shoulders. Have you looked at it that way?"

Eckling was indignant. "My instructors here are top-notch, and the curriculum is admired and respected around the world. I would put this institution up against any other anytime."

"Then why, General, could you possibly think that some students, simply because of their gender, aren't making it? Did your instructors fake the records? Did your instructors pass them along without regard to their abilities? Did your instructors give the women special advantages in exchange for favors? In the end, really, doesn't it come down to what your instructors did and not what the women students did? Because, after all, the students have no power. It's the instructors who decide who passes and who fails."

"My instructors have absolute integrity," Eckling boomed. "They would never pass a student who needed to be set back. They understand that an Army aviator is flying an expensive piece of equipment that carries the Army's most important cargo—the soldier—and that safety is paramount. If a student isn't safe, the student keeps learning until the student gets it, or the student doesn't graduate. There's no such thing here as special favors. My instructors aren't gigolos and I totally resent the implication. They are decent, hardworking men—and women, I'll have you know, sir. I do have a couple of female flight instructors as well," he said proudly.

"Then, why," Maloney asked, "do you persist in thinking that the women who have been involved in these accidents must have been faulty pilots?"

"First of all, the internal report we did of their training records alarmed me. Secondly, I suppose accident investigation reports can always find some element of pilot error."

"I think something fishy went on about their training records, but I'll concede the latter point. There's something else going on here, though, Eckling. And I need you to keep an open mind. We've got to come together as a community and figure out how to approach this and what to do about it."

"It's pretty hard when I have the evidence in front of me that so many female students were failing and needed to be washed out or set back. Who knows what it's been like in the past? I was told that this was the way it was, to pass them on, but my instructors assure me they haven't been doing that, so I have been getting a little suspicious myself about what has been happening. At the same time, sir, as I said, I've got documents in front of me that say these women aren't doing the work. Based on what you say, though, I'll look into this some more. On the other matter, though, the conspiracy thing, I'll talk to my people and we'll brainstorm a bit."

Maloney cautioned, "Don't talk to too many people. I don't want the word to get out. I'm only calling a select few Army leaders that can make a difference. Get back to me as soon as you can with some ideas or if you've got information. We've got to be on the same team. I don't need for us to be at cross-purposes."

"Right, sir. Believe me, if what you're saying is true, I'll jump on your bandwagon in a New York minute and help uncover the conspiracy in a heartbeat."

"I know you will, Horace. You're a good man. It just takes a while to get through that thick head of yours."

"Yeah. Stubborn as a mule, my grandma used to say. Thanks for keeping me informed, sir."

When Eckling hung up the phone, he picked it up again to dial Colonel Buehlankamp and let him know what was happening.

CHAPTER 110

FORT RUCKER, ALABAMA
2:40 P.M., SATURDAY, JUNE 7

It had taken Iris most of the day to locate Brannon, but when she did, she filled him in on her certainty that Buehlankamp was the forger of the student records and the man who had tried to kill her.

"My God, Iris! You are one lucky young woman. And you're quite alright?"

"Yes, sir," she said. "More angry than anything else."

"Thank goodness for small miracles. Now, how can you be so sure it was Colonel Buehlankamp who set the fire?" he asked.

"That odor was pervasive. I'd know it anywhere, and when I smelled it again this morning—"

"Not to be argumentative, but I just can't believe Colonel Buehlankamp tried to kill you," Brannon said in disbelief. "He could have retired years ago. If this is true, he's put his whole career in jeopardy. Why would someone with such an exemplary career do such a thing?"

"I have no idea, sir. But I know it was him. I recognized that smell when he was leaning on me, talking to me. He smelled just like my grandfather. That's what I remembered. The cigar my grandfather smoked. And when he walked by me this morning, it was the same exact smell. It was him. And from what he said to me, I believe he was the forger. He said he was sorry, but he had to kill me, because I was in the way of his mission."

"You'd better come with me. I think you need to tell this straight to General Eckling," he said.

"I'll follow you in my car," Iris said.

Eckling was still at the headquarters. It had been a long day. He'd been getting reports in periodically about the New York accident and sending off investigation teams. It was particularly perturbing now that he'd received a confidential call from the commanding general up there that sabotage on that helicopter was confirmed. Luckily, it was all over the news that the young women had been recovered and were back at home base, albeit some with injuries, nevertheless alive. The gruesome part of the story was the apparent murder of one of the pilots and the as-yet-missing whereabouts of a presumed murdered stowaway pilot. That part of the tale hadn't been completely unraveled, but Eckling's head was bursting at the seams from the ramifications and ugliness to Army aviation that were going to occur over the weeks to come as all the details were picked apart one by one and blame was laid where it rightfully belonged.

"Sir?" Brannon knocked on the door to Eckling's office. Milly wasn't in the outer room. Eckling didn't see any need to keep her away from her grandchildren on weekends just because he might have extra obligations that kept him busy.

"Come on, Bill. I've got a dozen irons in the fire. Who's that you've got with you?"

"General Eckling, this is Lieutenant Iris Tucker. Her father is General Sherman Tucker, commanding general at Fort Wainwright."

"Nice to meet you, young lady, come on in. I don't imagine this is a social call, Bill, and, as I said, I'm up to my eyeballs in alligators, so I need you to get to the point, if I may be so blunt."

"Sir, we've got a serious problem on our hands, deadly serious." As he spoke, Brannon got up and shut the office door.

"We believe that Colonel Buehlankamp forged the student records of the female flight students here to make it look as if many of them were failing, forcing them to be washed out or set back. We also believe that he then also tried to kill the young lieutenant here last night in her apartment by setting fire to her bed while she was asleep, because she was trying to discover who the forger was."

Eckling leaned back in his chair and drummed his fingers on the desk. He swiveled around and looked out the window at the parade field. He remained silent a long moment, all the while staring at the peace of the outdoors. Without turning around, Eckling said,

"I'm in a real pickle, here. It seems as if the whole aviation world is going to hell in a hand basket. And I don't have a hell of a lot of time to make decisions. I don't have the luxury to dilly-dally over whether to believe you and this young lieutenant here—whom I've never met before—or Colonel Buehlankamp. But I've always trusted my gut. And you know what? I've never trusted that son of a bitch. There's just something about him I don't like. Something that's a little off-kilter. I don't know what it is. I wasn't really copasetic with his results about the women's student records, but I trusted him because he'd been here a while. It just didn't sit right with me, especially considering that all of a sudden we had this huge national flap and women had been graduating alright up until then. We looked like fools. I didn't get it. I still don't get it. But if you're telling me he tried to kill someone—you, Lieutenant Tucker—well, that's beyond the pale. He's definitely going to answer to me for that, and I'm putting him on my radar screen. There's too much going on right now to take chances. There are things going on that I can't even talk about. So, Bill, I want you to get the phone number for the military police for me."

"Sir?"

"I'm going to have them bring Colonel Buehlankamp in."

Brannon went to his desk, dialed the number, and handed the phone to Eckling, who grudgingly turned away from his picture window.

"This is General Eckling. I want Colonel Buehlankamp picked up immediately and arrested on suspicion of murder. Notify me as soon as possible." He slammed down the phone.

CHAPTER 111

FORT RUCKER, ALABAMA
3:05 P.M., SATURDAY, JUNE 7

Within minutes, General Eckling's phone rang, and a nervous military policeman on the other end informed him that Colonel Buehlankamp's wife said her husband had left the house to escort Congresswoman Melissa Tonnelli to the flightline on a special mission.

"Goddamn it all to hell!" Eckling exploded as he threw the receiver back in the cradle. "I don't like the sound of this."

"I don't either, sir," Brannon said. "Yesterday, when she arrived, we believed Colonel Buehlankamp was a fine, upstanding officer. That was one thing. But now that we have these suspicions, he shouldn't be allowed to be alone with anyone, let alone such a high-level individual. We don't have any idea what he's got up his sleeve."

"She's investigating this slew of female students being set back. You listened in on Buehlankamp's briefing yesterday," Eckling said, getting ready for a tirade. "He was all butter and cream, running her through the paces."

Blood drained from Eckling's face. "Goddamn it! Goddamn it! He's going to kill her!"

Brannon and Iris looked confused. "What are you talking about, sir?"

"Come with me. I'll explain on the way, but first, call the MPs and tell them to meet us at the flightline, in full force, ready to apply deadly force if necessary against Colonel Buehlankamp."

As soon as that task was accomplished, the three dashed out of the headquarters. "We'll get more respect in my car," the general said, "and allowed onto the airfield faster. Let's go," as he ushered the other two into his vehicle.

On the way to the flightline, Eckling explained that the New York helicopter accident had been deemed an act of sabotage and two conspirators had been found, one murdered and one under suspicion of murder. The Secretary of the Army was still in the process of holding a press conference linking the three helicopter accidents around the world as an act of conspiracy.

"But what does that have to do with Colonel Buehlankamp?" Brannon asked.

"Congresswoman Tonnelli is flying today with an all-woman crew," Eckling muttered with an angry frown. "It was Buehlankamp's idea to prove to her that our training was sound and, that once we had scoured all the records and determined which young women needed to be retrained, their quality of flying had been significantly enhanced. I don't know that she bought that argument, but she was still eager to go up in the helicopter."

"So you think Colonel Buehlankamp is involved with this conspiracy of sabotaging helicopters?" Iris asked.

Eckling turned around to look at Iris in the back seat. "Lieutenant Tucker, I'm sure your father taught you that the Army is filled with noble men and women. But I also know your father didn't get where he is without realizing there are bad apples every now and then. It appears that Colonel Buehlankamp, based on what you've told me and what Secretary Maloney has told me, is one of the worst. I wouldn't put anything past him right now. I just don't know why he's doing it. And right now, we have to stop him."

Eckling's car screamed past the gate guard at the airfield and screeched to a stop near one of the aircraft hangars. As the group piled out of the car, they saw Buehlankamp a few hundred feet away leading Tonnelli towards a helicopter with rotor blades turning.

"Congresswoman Tonnelli," Eckling shouted. "I need a word with you."

Buehlankamp turned and stared. Tonnelli made a movement to turn back, but Buehlankamp leaned in towards her and motioned towards the helicopter, shaking his head. As Tonnelli started to walk towards Eckling, Buehlankamp put an arm on her shoulder and pressed her forwards towards the helicopter. Irritated, Tonnelli shook him off and began walking towards the hangar where Eckling and his small band were standing.

At that moment, the flightline became surrounded by military police cars with sirens flashing and wailing. The noise was overwhelming. Policemen were swarming out of their cars with guns drawn, and Tonnelli was right in the middle of their aim.

"Ma'am, move out of the range of fire!" they warned.

Tonnelli looked back at the helicopter. Buehlankamp had suddenly disappeared. The pilot in the front left seat was frantically pointing to a figure running down the runway. The MPs looked at Eckling for the signal to fire.

"No, not yet," he exclaimed. "We've got too many other people out here in the open. It's too risky. As much as I'd like to take that guy down, I can't give that order. I don't know what level of violence he's ready to inflict and Congresswoman Tonnelli is my responsibility, as well as everyone else out here who's unarmed."

Eckling and the others watched helplessly as, within seconds, Buehlankamp jumped into a helicopter, lifted the helicopter off of its parking pad, and burst through translational lift. He was gone. It was a drizzly, gray day and the helicopter could barely be seen after it had flown a few hundred feet.

"Get to the tower!" Eckling ordered Brannon. "Track that son-of-a-bitch! We've got to know where he's going. This isn't over yet, not by a long shot."

When Brannon returned, he said, "The control tower reports that it appears Buehlankamp is heading to the Gulf Coast."

"Tell them to contact the FAA and the Coast Guard," Eckling said. "We've got to put up some fighters to escort him back. We have no idea what he's up to, but I suspect he's running. He's gone too far to come back now. His game is up. And get me a radio so I can stay in contact with the tower."

Brannon returned from the control tower within a few moments and reported, "Fighters will be up in the air momentarily, sir. He can't outrun them. The tower's got him locked in their sights."

Eckling looked impatiently towards the tower. He barked into his radio. "What the hell's going on up there? What's taking so long? Why haven't those fighters brought Buehlankamp back yet?"

The crackling response wasn't positive. "Sir, it looks like he's heading out towards the Gulf of Mexico."

Eckling bit his lip. Even he tried to control his temper in front of a U.S. congresswoman. The general spoke slowly and with great deliberation. "Where, I ask you, could he possibly land a helicopter in the middle of the Gulf of Mexico?"

"The Coast Guard has reported a small ship in the Gulf that he seems to be making a beeline for. They're heading there now to try to board the ship, but it's outside of our national waters."

"Tower, when you have new information like this, kindly pass it on as soon as you get it, not when I call up there and ask for it, would you please?"

"Uh, yes, sir." The nervous quake in the voice was evident.

Eckling looked out at the sky from which Buehlankamp had disappeared. "Jesus H. Christ. I never thought I'd live to see the day when an Army colonel would steal an Army helicopter and fly away with it. What was he thinking? What is this all about? I'm totally flummoxed." Eckling rubbed the top of his bald pate.

The radio in Eckling's hand sprang to life again as the tower voice, trying to regain credibility, said, "General, sir? The fighters are still trying to get authority to shoot the helicopter down, but they've not gotten that yet. We just wanted to keep you apprised, as you asked."

"Thank you, Tower," Eckling said.

As Eckling's explosive comments eased, Tonnelli asked, "What the hell just happened here, General?"

"You weren't just investigating, Congresswoman. You were about to become part of an investigation report yourself. Colonel Buehlankamp appears to have been at the bottom of forging female student records here, he tried to kill Lieutenant Tucker the other night, and we think he's part of a widespread conspiracy to sabotage helicopters with female pilots. We don't know why."

"Well, a heartfelt thanks for saving my life, General. And to think I used to think nasty things about you."

Conversation was at a standstill. The flightcrew in the UH-1 helicopter had shut down the engine, closed up the helicopter, and were standing off to one side. They didn't particularly want to be too closely associated with the visiting congresswoman or the commanding general if they could help it, but they now knew how close they had come to being killed. One of the pilots was friends with Iris, who filled them in on what was happening. The three women were shaken at their close call and aghast at the vast conspiracy that was seemingly rooted in the very man responsible for their flight training.

CHAPTER 112

OVER THE GULF OF MEXICO
5:10 P.M., SATURDAY, JUNE 7

As Buehlankamp flew along in the UH-1, he exulted in the fact that he had made his getaway despite the fact that dozens of policemen were actually at the flightline. He had been ready for this eventuality for a long time. This particular helicopter was never assigned to a student. It was always the one he flew as the aviation brigade training commander—fueled, maintained, and ready to go. If, by chance, it was redlined or under repair, then he had another helicopter at his disposal. He always knew exactly where it was parked and, long ago, he had had duplicate aircraft keys made. And, although he knew the value of a good preflight, in an emergency such as this one, that was unimportant. Getting off the ground and into the air before the vigilantes got him was essential.

What Buehlankamp regretted was not having succeeded at his coup de grace—the last accident at Fort Rucker, with a high-level politico onboard and several flight students. That would have sent a message to the U.S. Army that their flight school training program, despite the revamping they had done, had completely failed.

He didn't think too much about leaving his family. That had always been in the cards.

Due to the poor visibility, Buehlankamp wasn't able to see the two U.S. Navy fighters sent to accompany him, but he knew they were there. Skimming low over the waters of the Gulf of Mexico, Buehlankamp knew he didn't have much further to go. If the military had received orders to shoot him down, he would be dead by now. Since he wasn't, Buehlankamp felt home free. Away from shore, a stronger wind was whipping the waves into ten-foot-tall whitecaps, and Buehlankamp had to fly higher to prevent the frothy foam from splashing his windscreen. Due to the high winds, he had to maintain significant left pedal to keep from sliding off course and was constantly fighting with the controls to keep the helicopter from pitching into the water.

Approaching the stern of the huge white yacht, Buehlankamp felt an immense sense of relief. Crewmembers onboard guided his landing to the helipad at the stern. Buehlankamp realized he needed to adjust his altitude higher to clear the stern. As he went to increase collective, a rogue wave rolled and hit the port side of the stern, causing it to rise up and smack the underside of the tail assembly.

The crew rushed to the stern and watched in horror as the helicopter plummeted into the water and sank instantly beneath the waves. From the bridge, their captain said in Russian, "Our mission has changed. Instead of picking our comrade up, we're leaving without him. The Americans will be here momentarily. Prepare for immediate departure."

Within five minutes, the yacht was steaming for parts unknown.

CHAPTER 113

THE PENTAGON, WASHINGTON, D.C.
7:20 P.M., SATURDAY, JUNE 7

Secretary Maloney braced himself for the onslaught of media inquiries that would attack the Army after he gave this press conference. He didn't look forward to it. He stepped into the briefing room, and waited for all the camera flashes to cease before he began to speak. Usually the reporters were patient, but today an excited buzz ran rampant through the room. Maloney held up his hand.

"If I could have your attention, please." He scanned the men and women, poised with their pens and notebooks, ready to devour his every word and regurgitate it back to the public, albeit with their own twist and connotation. He hated to give them anything they could interpret to the Army's disadvantage and they were going to have a field day with this.

Maloney continued. "First, the good news. The women involved in the helicopter accident in New York are in relatively good shape, barring minor injuries. They were rescued earlier today and were returned to Fort Drum. Now, for the bad news." He looked up. "And I don't say this lightly. There is a conspiracy in the Army to sabotage our helicopters."

Chairs scraped against each other as reporters tried to be the first ones out of the door with the story. Most individuals, however, remained, as Maloney went on. "I take full responsibility for the Army not recognizing this in time and for putting our aviators at risk. I know you all recall the earlier press conference at which I categorically denied that such a conspiracy existed. Unfortunately, we now have undeniable proof in the form of conspirators. Two were Army officers stationed at Fort Drum who sabotaged the helicopter in an effort to kill these young women. One of those men is in custody, and one of those is dead. That's all I'll say about that incident at this time.

"I also have unofficial information that leads me to believe the accident in Korea was sabotage and not friendly fire. All three accidents involving female crews will be thoroughly researched. Moreover, a fourth accident nearly occurred today but was prevented by the quick action of Major General Horace C. Eckling, the commanding general of Fort Rucker. For reasons that remain unclear, one of the Army's top officers and a highly-ranked aviator, Colonel John Buehlankamp, seems to have had a pivotal role in this conspiracy. However, the Coast Guard reports he was killed in a helicopter crash in the Gulf of Mexico earlier today as he was fleeing.

"Ladies and gentlemen, that's all I have. I'll entertain your questions now."

Although the reporters threw questions at him fast and furiously, Maloney drew his breath, and answered them as best he could. At this point in time, it was important to get information to the public rather than keep cards close to the chest. The Army never liked to air its dirty linen, but this was going to come out regardless, so it might as well be done right and truthfully.

When one of the reporters asked Maloney why a conspiracy existed to sabotage Army helicopters and, as a follow-up, why Buehlankamp participated, the Secretary of the Army's shoulders sagged. "I don't know," he said. "That's the million-dollar question. But we'll find out. The American people can trust us on this one."

CHAPTER 114

SOMEWHERE IN EAST GERMANY
1:00 A.M., SUNDAY, JUNE 8

Tina and André had spent the day talking, eating, walking through the woods, and, finally, taking a nap in the evening. Without any clothes or possessions, Tina really had nothing to pack and she wasn't going far. Nevertheless, André did insist on filling a small backpack for her with a light jacket and a few necessities, in the event their car broke down on the way or the helicopter didn't come as it was supposed to. In addition, he included some food and East German money in case she ended up on her own.

"That's a scary thought," Tina said with surprise. "You said you were handing me over at the border."

"I am," André said. "But I can't hang around for long. It's quick in and quick out. And if your friends are delayed—because of weather or some other reason—I might have to leave you. I'll try not to, but—"

Tina looked alarmed. "Whew! Just what I've always wished for. To be stranded on the East German border."

"Really, Tina, I don't expect it to happen. Everyone I've ever driven to the border before has been met by the people who've said they will be there. I just like to be ready for contingencies."

Tina breathed a sigh of relief and smiled. "Well, alright then. I'm a tough cookie. I can handle it."

"Ahh," he said. "This is an American expression I've heard before. Tough cookie. Yes, I can see that you are." André smiled in return.

At one in the morning, they quietly left the back door of André's cabin and got into his car and began to drive west on back roads. André had long ago determined the best route to the border and practiced it a number of times at night. Tina sat beside him with rising anticipation, wondering if, along the way, they would be stopped by East German police or if, at the border, East German guards would impede her crossing.

After two hours, they reached a thicket of woods from which André promised Tina that crossing the border would be relatively easy. Switching off the headlights and driving in complete night blindness, André guided the car down several dirt paths and then parked.

"This is it," he said in a low voice. "There's a small stream nearby that goes over into West Germany. The stream has cut away the soil enough so that you can wiggle under the fence. But as you're following the stream, try to stay as low as possible and follow the bank. Remember there are guards out there and they make rounds every hour or so. We're going to wait and watch until we see them come by and then I'm going to let you go. Remember that the helicopter coming to get you is going to be a mile away on the other side. It's supposed to be there at 4 a.m., so you don't have much time."

"And other people have gone through here?" Tina asked quietly.

"Most assuredly," André said, "although we only use each place a couple of times. We don't want to give ourselves away."

Tina looked out into the dark night. Luckily, there was no moonlight tonight to cast shadows or give her away. It seemed as though the plan would work. "Okay, André. It sounds like a great plan. If I don't have another chance to tell you, thanks for everything. It was the greatest stroke of luck, running into you. I don't know what I would have done if I hadn't."

"Tina, you broke out of your captivity by yourself and made your way through part of East Germany alone. I have no doubt you would have gotten here and across the border somehow. I'm just making it a bit easier for you, and maybe doing it a bit faster than you might have. Trust me, you really are one tough cookie!"

Tina impulsively hugged André and he hugged her back tightly. "Take care of yourself, Tina, and I hope you find out all the answers. If you get a chance to let me know, I'd love to hear how it all turns out."

"You bet, André."

The two left the car and positioned themselves closer to the stream, sitting among shrubbery, camouflaged where they could have a better view of the guards as they appeared. Fifteen minutes later, they saw two guards walk towards each other from opposite directions. After exchanging a few words, the guards turned around and walked back to their unseen posts.

André held Tina back for another ten minutes and then whispered to her, "Okay, Tina, here you go." Standing, he held out his hand and helped her up. "So long, soldier," he said, with a snappy salute.

"So long, André." And Tina was off without a backward glance, rustling through the ferns and tall weeds lining the bank of the stream, trying to make as little sound as possible and crouching as low to the ground as she could.

A manmade clearing had been created in the middle of the woods, right along the border fence, approximately fifty yards wide. As soon as Tina left the safe cover of the woods and burst into the clearing, she felt quite vulnerable, but the pitch black of the night and knowing that the guards would probably not return for at least another forty-five minutes helped to steel her nerves. Moreover, she could see the border fence directly in front of her.

Tina stealthily dropped down the steep bank into the running water, surprised at how cool it was in July. The depth of the stream was about two feet and its width about five feet. Now that she was actually in the stream, she felt much more unobtrusive and less visible, but her motions were certainly noisier although she tried to keep the water from splashing. Nevertheless, she had to keep reminding herself that no one except André was nearby.

As soon as she reached the fence, Tina grabbed hold and felt underneath it to ensure that there was an opening for her to go under. The stream's waters covered part of the fence bottom, so Tina definitely had to go underwater. No problem, even though the water was churning through a little rapidly at that point, as the stream had narrowed due to a turn in its course.

Tina removed the small backpack and wrapped one of the straps around her left arm so that she wouldn't get entangled on the fence by the pack on her back. Then she gulped a breath of air, dropped down horizontally, and pulled herself forward under the fence. On the other side, she raised her head out of the water and slowly began to crouch forward, but the backpack wouldn't budge.

"Crap!" she muttered. She tugged a little harder but it had become snagged underwater on the fence. She turned around and bent back to undo it.

Just then, she heard the footsteps of the guards again. Either it had taken her a lot longer to get through the stream and to the border fence than she thought or the guards had altered their routine. Her heart began to pound furiously. Tina stayed exactly where she was, head down, not moving, body pressed against the fence. She knew she was on the other side of the border fence, but she also knew that technically she wasn't yet out of East Germany. The fence was still in East Germany and she had to make it to the "1-k zone." West Germany didn't really begin until one kilometer past the border fence. If the guards saw her now, they could shoot her.

Tina didn't even breathe. Through the reflection of the water she could see the play of their flashlights. Luckily, the guards were bored. They had done this routine so many times tonight and would do it so many more. Nothing ever happened out here and they didn't expect it to tonight. They called out something indecipherable to each other and were gone again in minutes.

Tina waited, hanging onto the fence for at least five minutes after they had left, before she moved a single muscle. Then she rapidly whisked the unruly backpack off the fence, and, despite her violent desire to flee the area, forced herself to control her movements so they remained calm and unnoticeable. Within fifty yards, she was on the opposite side of the clearing but didn't stop to open her backpack to grab the jacket to get warm, no matter that she was now wet and shivering. Her primary goal now was to reach the helicopter.

And, within twenty minutes of leaving the border fence, Tina found her way through the dark woods to the designated spot where Gunter, Marthe, Damrow, and Erika were all waiting beside a UH-I helicopter, its rotor blades stopped.

As Tina stepped out into the clearing, Erika was the first to spot her. "There she is!" The rest jumped up from where they'd been waiting.

Gunter walked over quickly and stood in front of Tina. Tina and Gunter stared at each other, then Gunter wrapped his arms around her and said, "Welcome back, Tina."

Marthe noticed an undercurrent of emotion between her boss and Tina, but pretended not to. She bustled about grabbing the blankets and clothes they had brought for Tina and handing them to her. "Here, Frau Loyola," she said. "You're cold now and when we get up in the air, it will be even worse. These will help."

"Thank you so much, Marthe," Tina said. "I can't thank all of you enough. You don't know what it means to me, first of all, to be back here, and then to see such familiar faces."

"We've also got some hot coffee and some food, if you're interested," Damrow offered.

"I'd love some coffee, but I don't need anything to eat just yet. My stomach's a bit unsettled from all the excitement."

As Damrow poured her a cup of coffee, Erika settled Tina into the helicopter. "I imagine you're anxious to get out of here and back home," she said.

"Not until I get the answers about Crystal that I came for," she said. "Now that this has happened, I'm even more determined. I'll use up all the leave my unit will let me take to stay here if you'll just take me back to your part of the world."

"Will do, Tina," Erika said. And with that, Erika started up the rotor blades, and Tina watched the ground fall away.

CHAPTER 115

ETLINGEN, WEST GERMANY
9:30 A.M., SUNDAY, JUNE 8

After Tina had been able to get a few hours of sleep, her phone rang. Gunter was on the other line.

"Tina, there's a report on BBC right now about another U.S. Army helicopter accident—"

Tina flipped on the television set. "Oh my God," she said. This is unbelievable."

"They're calling it sabotage," he said.

Tina shook her head in amazement. "What's going on, Karl? These were all women?"

"They said this was a helicopter from New York." Gunter said. "Could this have been your unit?" he asked.

"Frank tried to tell me someone would try to do this. Oh no!" Tina gasped, as Deirdre's face came into view on the screen. She increased the volume and listened intently.

Deirdre said, "My co-pilot, crew chief, and I want to thank all the rescuers who helped us through this harrowing ordeal and want to reassure everyone that we're quite alright. There might be some individuals who wished us harm, but overall, the Army remains one big family."

Tina lowered the volume and said to Gunter, "That was my friend, Deirdre, who I tried to warn when I went to the phone booth. If I'd only gotten to her—"

"They probably would have tried some other time, some other way. It seems these people are bent on getting rid of you women pilots. Luckily for your friend, it didn't work this time."

Her eyes riveted to the screen, Tina agreed. "Yes, Deirdre was lucky. Still, I wish I'd been able to warn her. She must have been scared to death."

"Tina, you tried and you suffered some horrible consequences for that, so you needn't beat yourself up. Okay?" Gunter sounded a little irritated.

"Did she ever know I was kidnapped?" Tina asked.

"I reported it to Herr Major. I know he was leery of who to trust, but whether he would retain that kind of information, I don't know. As he said, you didn't belong to him. And you told us Frank Lambert said people in your unit were part of the conspirators. We didn't know where to turn. We tried to find Deirdre but couldn't locate her, and tried to find Frank, but that didn't work, either."

Tina sighed. "I guess this lends credence to the whole sabotage theory behind Crystal's accident, doesn't it?"

"Absolutely, and it was your corroboration here that made the difference."

"Well, Karl, I'm going to call Deirdre so we can exchange war stories."

Abruptly, Gunter said, "Don't go out to the pay phone again. Use the one in your room and charge the call to the hotel."

"Thanks for your concern, Karl. I'll do that." Tina hung up, called the hotel operator, and waited for her connection to New York. As soon as she and Deirdre heard each other's voices, the two women had a good long cry. Deirdre hadn't known a thing about Tina's kidnapping, and was appalled to hear about Tina's ordeal, despite the fact that she had come through it unscathed. Likewise, Tina felt so guilty about not having warned Deirdre about Mark and Cecil, that she couldn't apologize enough, but Deirdre told Tina the same thing Gunter had. Those guys would have found some other means, and Tina had paid a high enough price for getting involved.

"And, Tina," Deirdre said. "I have some other really bad news. It hasn't been confirmed yet, but it seems as though Frank is dead. I'm really sorry to have to tell you."

Tina caught her breath. She'd often felt irritated with her brash, sentimental, drunk ex-brother-in-law, but he had loved Crystal as much or more than she had. And he had apparently gone to extraordinary lengths to avenge her death.

"What happened?"

"No one really knows, but it seems that he jumped on Mark and Cecil's helicopter right before they took off, then, realizing they planned to finish us off if we were still alive, he killed Mark right in the cockpit. Apparently, according to Cecil, if he can be believed, they had a scuffle out in the woods, and it came down to self-defense and Cecil shot him. Cecil claims he was hand-cuffed and somehow got hold of the gun."

Tina scoffed, "I don't believe that. I'm sure he shot Frank in cold blood."

"I don't believe it, either, but once they find Frank, if he is dead, I'm sure the police will figure it all out. I'm sorry, Tina."

"Thanks, Deirdre. It's been a rough time for all of us."

"Yeah, and the worst part is, I don't get why they want to get rid of us."

"Me, neither, Deirdre. Me, neither."

"Did you see the Secretary of the Army's press conference?" Deirdre asked.

"No, why?"

"He's finally admitting there is a conspiracy to sabotage Army helicopters."

"And to kill female helicopter pilots?" Tina demanded.

"He didn't say that directly, but he's putting two and two together. Now that Colonel Buehlankamp is killed—"

"What!"

"You didn't know that, either?"

"All I saw was the news report about your accident. What happened to Buehlankamp?"

Deirdre told her what she'd gleaned from the news media and the rumor mill. "Why do you sound so shocked?"

"I don't know why it completely left my mind, Deirdre, but Buehlankamp came to East Germany while I was being held hostage there. Now why did he come there and why didn't he help me? He specifically came to see me. I know that without a doubt."

"You've got to tell someone, Tina. This could help crack the case," Deirdre urged.

"Yeah, I've just got to figure out who exactly," Tina mused.

CHAPTER 116

FORT RUCKER, ALABAMA
8:10 P.M., SUNDAY, JUNE 8

Vivian Buehlankamp was totally beyond distraught. She couldn't believe that the man she had been married to for thirty-two years would up and leave her without a word of farewell. She knew she had loved him far more than he had ever loved her, but this stabbed her deep beyond where any wound could be repaired. When he had walked out the door Saturday afternoon, giving her the usual peck on the cheek and a careless wave, she had suspected nothing. This had been their pattern. He went to work, and she stayed home. He made the rules, and she complied. He came and went as he pleased, and she asked few questions.

All Vivian had ever wanted from her husband was a sign of affection now and then, and those she did receive. He acted the part of a southern gentleman when he wanted to. When they first got married, she had hoped to have a lot of children, and then some children, and then at least one child. When all those hopes ran dry, because John constantly kept saying the timing wasn't right, Vivian eventually gave up and concentrated all her efforts on him. As a military officer's wife, she could find plenty to do—entertaining, being a member of clubs, playing golf, keeping herself fit and attractive, and maintaining a nice home. She often reminded herself it was a nice life.

But the moment that the military policemen arrived on her doorstep telling her that John was dead, all that had changed.

She was stupefied. First of all, she had to accept that her beloved husband would never walk through that door again. Secondly, it was clear from the expression on the face of the policemen giving her the news that her husband was already being branded a common criminal. And, third, even she couldn't grasp why her husband had grabbed an Army helicopter and flown it out to the Gulf of Mexico.

More than anything else, however, she was angry that he had apparently had a secret life that didn't involve her. He didn't trust her enough to confide in her, or he didn't care enough about her to tell her what he was doing.

"That bastard!" she cried through her hot tears, as she searched through her house for any clue as to what he had been up to.

Hours later, exhausted, with dusk approaching, Vivian sat with red-rimmed eyes in her bathroom, ready to take a hot bath. She thought about all the trips that John took out to the garden shed, when he didn't like to garden. She jumped up and raced out back, carrying a flashlight. The dinginess of the shed was spooky.

Vivian splayed the flashlight's rays around the wooden walls, looking for what, she had no idea. She started pushing bags of mulch, tools, and plant pots around, and then, underneath the potting table, saw something in the wooden floor that looked slightly irregular, as though it could be lifted up. She searched for a screwdriver, placed the tip in, and leveraged upward. The wooden area was only a foot square and six inches deep, lined with plastic. Inside was a small metal box, locked. Grabbing a hammer, Vivian knocked off the lock and tore open the lid. Inside were a few vials of microfilm.

As Vivian reached in to take them out, a voice behind her said, "I'll take those, Vivian, if you don't mind."

A chill went up her spine as she slowly turned around. She swallowed. "And if I say no?"

"That wouldn't be wise."

"I know you from somewhere," she said, frowning. "And how do you know me? What do you want with my husband's things?"

"Actually, they really belong to me," he said. "You see, your husband was in my employ."

Recognition dawned on Vivian's face. "You're the Russian ambassador! What are you doing here at my house?"

"I've already told you, Vivian. Coming to collect what's ours."

"What did my husband have to do with you?"

"A great deal, Vivian. You must realize by now that he wasn't at all what you thought he was, I'm sorry to say."

Tears slipped down Vivian's cheeks as she struggled to control her emotions. "Get out! Get out! He's dead! That's enough, isn't it!"

"I'm afraid not, Vivian dear. Now hand over the box."

"No!"

"Then I'm afraid I'll have to take it from you." The ambassador pulled out a gun and pointed it at Vivian. Before he could shoot, however, he was suddenly surrounded by military police cars, sirens blaring and flashing, and an officer behind a megaphone ordering him to put down his weapon.

CHAPTER 117

FORT RUCKER, ALABAMA
7:45 A.M., THURSDAY, JUNE 12

Eckling placed a call to Tina as soon as the microfilm had been developed. "Well, young lady," he said, "I can't thank you enough for calling me when you did. Our MPs were going to go over and search his house, but we had to get a warrant and, being the weekend, we hadn't gotten it yet. You saved Mrs. Buehlankamp's life." Eckling recounted the circumstances of what had happened.

"There are even more amazing things here in this situation that neither you nor I could have imagined, Miss Loyola, and I'll try to be brief, or we'll never get off the phone. But I know you've gone to extraordinary lengths to determine the cause of your sister's death, never being satisfied it was pilot error and I want to commend you for that. I think we can all accept now that it was a vile conspiracy, perpetrated by Buehlankamp and a few of his henchmen."

"But why—"

"I'll get to that. I think we know the reason why now. Another thing I wanted to say is that you've suffered some incredible personal losses throughout all of this, and you have my personal condolences. Your sister, your brother-in-law, and being kidnapped yourself. I just want to get that out of the way."

"Thank you, sir."

"Now, you told me that there was a Russian man who visited you several times while you were kidnapped, but you never knew his name. Is that right?"

"Yes."

"He's the Russian ambassador to the United States. The Soviet Union is recalling him under pretext of a family emergency."

"Are you sure?"

"You gave us a physical description of him that matches. He was threatening to kill Mrs. Buehlankamp in her own backyard. That isn't normal behavior for a diplomat. Now, for the mind-numbing information. Have you ever heard of Soviet moles?"

"No, sir. I have no idea what that is."

"Most people who aren't in intelligence don't know what they are. The Soviet Union has spent millions of dollars and decades of training preparing people as intelligence operatives to live in other countries under deep, deep cover, to be awakened one day when the right moment comes. Their cover is so deep that no one in the country in which they live knows that they came from the Soviet Union. They have a completely new identity with flawless accents that match the country they live in right down to regional parochialisms. They blend in with the locals and don't draw attention to themselves, and they go about their daily lives and careers just like ordinary people. They marry, they have children, they participate in the community. To all intents and purposes, they are citizens of the country in which they have been placed, except for one glaring problem—they aren't. Their loyalty always remains with the Soviet Union. That is their sole purpose—to lie dormant in their new country until they receive marching orders to conduct a mission."

"Are you saying, General, that Colonel Buehlankamp was a spy for the Soviet Union?" Tina asked incredulously.

"More than that, Miss Loyola. He was a Soviet, through and through. He only appeared to be an American on the surface. Once you peel back the layers of his American culture, education, family, and even the military, apparently he has a Soviet soul that none of us ever knew about."

"And how did you find out about this?"

"The ambassador's last task was to retrieve some microfilm left behind by Buehlankamp, which we were able to recover and develop. It appears that the ambassador directed this conspiracy to sabotage Army helicopters."

"I still don't understand why," Tina said.

"It will all sound very clear once you know it's coming from the Russian bear," Eckling said. "The Soviet Union, as you know, is terrified of our military might, despite their rumblings in Red Square every May Day. As soon as we began to put women into military cockpits, Soviet leaders, remembering the fear that Soviet female pilots put into Germans during World War II, became afraid that our military prowess would improve even more with this new force multiplier. They concocted a scheme to deprive us of our new tool by feeding into our basest fears—men not wanting women in their cockpits, and finding individuals who believed it was in the Army's best interest to ultimately kill those women."

"Wait, sir. I'm not sure I'm following you. First of all, you're saying that the Soviets used to have female pilots in World War II?"

"Yes, they had three regiments of fighter and fighter-bomber pilots, and they were so respected by their own country and feared by the Germans that they were known as the Night Witches. They had many kills. A great many of these Heroes of the Soviet Union are still alive today."

"Wow. I had no idea." Tina whistled out loud. "And the Soviets' idea was that if our female pilots got to be this good, we could be a real threat to them?"

"That seems to be the general idea."

"And from the Russian ambassador on down, right through to a—what did you call him?—a Soviet mole?—and some yahoos who wanted us dead, they had a pretty good conspiracy going."

"We think we've got it wrapped up now, though."

"I'm glad, sir. It's been a long time."

"I'd like to ask you a favor, Miss Loyola. I've been one of those male aviators who was pretty entrenched in my views about female aviators, and it took me a long time to get my ostrich neck out of the sand. I wonder how you'd feel going around to the different installations and being a talking head about this conspiracy, how to avoid sabotage, what to look for in investigations, that sort of thing."

"I'd be honored, sir."

"I'll work it out with your boss. Until then, you've done one hell of a job."

Acknowledgments

My husband, Cliff, remains my number-one fan and biggest supporter. In addition, he has read the manuscript of *The Elimination Game* too many times to count, always providing strokes of reassurance and delight as well as constructive comments. Then, too, he is also my life partner and shares in all my dreams, successes, and near-misses. After thirty-one years of marriage, the Army, raising children, and settling down in Maryland, we're still not through with life's adventures.

My two children, Derek and Jessica, remain continually and constantly enthusiastic about my work, my writing, and now my publishing, always with kudos and "awesome" and introducing my first novel, *Hawthorne's Cottage,* to friends and co-workers. They have both lived away at different times, from home and Maryland and me, but our family of four now lives within a five-mile radius of each other, and for that, too, I'm very grateful. It's an amazing honor to get to know your adult children as friends and to come to rely on them for things you can't do yourself, and certainly proves the point that we all have our own special talents.

I learned an enormous amount from writing, revising, editing, and publishing *Hawthorne's Cottage,* one of which was to be sure I sent my manuscript for *The Elimination Game* to readers for their comments and suggestions, and, in some cases, technical advice. For the latter, I especially owe grateful thanks to a dear and old friend, Brad Lupien, one of the Army's first CW5 aviators, and my compadre in German language class at the Defense Language Institute in Monterey, CA, from 1987 to 1988. Brad took my manuscript and, because I have such enormous respect for his knowledge and experience, his suggestions helped ensure that this book is as technically accurate as it can be.

Other readers who offered me valuable advice upon reading the manuscript include my dad, Calvin Reeves, who did a wonderful job of catching the tiniest things that puzzled him or needed to be changed. Another is Susi Haywood, who cast a particularly keen eye on my use of the German language and urged several changes that I did incorporate. Michele Trumbull, one of the first to ask to read the manuscript, offered a valued perspective as a non-military reader.

Diana Davis, my classmate at Fort Rucker, Alabama, from 1979 to 1980, when we were both two of the early pioneers in Army aviation, has shouted long and hard for me to publish *The Elimination Game,* offering numerous suggestions for marketing and publicizing, and, at last, it is available. I have so many friends from my membership in The Whirly-Girls: International Women Helicopter Pilots, as well as in Women Military Aviators (which used to be called Women Military Pilots), and I admire them and their involvement in persisting to highlight women in military aviation as a career. If I started to name any of them, I wouldn't be able to quit, but they are all remarkable in many and varied ways. This country has been served well by women military aviators, whether part of the formal organization or not, and I'm proud to be a member of WMA that helped change the law so women could finally fly in combat. In addition, I would be remiss for not mentioning the inspiring Women Airforce Service Pilots who helped provide a guidepost for women in military aviation beginning in the 1970s. The WASP were our valiant foremothers who flew every known military plane in World War II, freeing men to fly "over there," and just this year were recognized with Congress's highest honor, the Congressional Gold Medal.

I met Linda Maloney, however, through WMA and her book, *My Mom Flies.* Through the years of emailing and phone calls and providing information and feedback on her fabulous idea about mothers who also fly, we became friends. Her immense work ethic and dedication to an all-consuming project provided me often with the invigorating jump I needed to get cracking, whether on a website, blog, the work itself, or finding someone totally reliable (Susan Briggs) to clean my house and remove that temptation from me as an excuse for not writing.

I can't think of a single friend or family member who doesn't know that I'm a writer or doesn't support my writing and my books. To every single one of them, most of whom were individually acknowledged in *Hawthorne's Cottage*, I give another hearty thank-you. As all writers know, writing is a lonely profession, but it helps the ego when others remember what we're doing and take the time to ask about a project under way. Although, if no progress has been made since the last query, guilt is an easy visitor to this writer!

My writer's group in St. Mary's County, MD, under the vigilant tutelage of Page Faust, has continued to offer support and constructive criticism for this novel, and I can't express enough how much this has meant to me over the years. Both Page Faust and Helen Carson read the manuscript in its entirety and offered me valuable advice, as well as the always desired dose of praise.

So many readers of *Hawthorne's Cottage* told me they were eagerly looking forward to my next book. That was balm to a writer's ears! *The Elimination Game* is a totally different style of book, but I trust it will meet with its own advocates.

I'm also very grateful to all the booksellers that offered me an opportunity to sell and sign my book. I gained a lot of confidence in marketing and publicizing, and in selling. I felt deeply honored to have been selected for the Baltimore Book Festival in 2008 and for a book-signing at Barnes and Noble in Annapolis, MD, in 2009.

I wouldn't be here today to see this book published if it weren't for my gynecological oncologist, Dr. Teresa

Diaz-Montes, and all the staff at Johns Hopkins Hospital in Baltimore. There is no gratitude sufficient to express my thanks to Dr. Diaz for saving my life. And to Barb Patterson, my health care provider, who believed me when I told her I thought I had ovarian cancer and ordered all the right tests immediately, more gratefulness and appreciation is owed. In addition, Barb read *Hawthorne's Cottage,* invited me to speak on it at her book club where it had been the month's chosen book, and I now belong to a cherished book club and have a new set of friends.

I no longer feel guilty about not writing or not working, because, since I am now three years cancer-free, I am so delighted to be here, present, and living and traveling and loving and lazing around and reading and eating, etc., that I place less stress on myself to accomplish something. One of my main goals these days is raising awareness about ovarian cancer and participating in fundraisers to improve research on this deadly disease. Moreover, I have another new network of friends—all my cancer buddies. We belong to a club none of us wanted to join, but the fellowship and understanding found there, as well as the ability to guide and mentor others walking down the same path, became a new life's direction for me. One of my future projects is to write a book, along with Dr. Diaz, on ovarian cancer from the perspective of a number of survivors.

I'm pleased to have more energy than the year of my chemo drain (2007), and delirious to have gone on several "celebrations of life" trips. But I do still have a desire to produce some tangible work, and, to that end, published *The Kapellmeister's Daughter* by Helen Carson, a novel of historical fiction set in the decades immediately before, during, and after World War I, focusing on a family from Romania traveling the exotic Far East with a hotel orchestra. It has been my deep pleasure to work on this book with Helen, and I hope you, my reader, will look for her book.

I expect my third novel, *Betrayed in Antarctica,* to be available in 2012. But I have some serious writing to do first! Thank you for spending your valuable resources and time on my book, *The Elimination Game.*

Connie Reeves
August 2010

www.ingramcontent.com/pod-product-compliance
Lightning Source LLC
LaVergne TN
LVHW050915080826
845145LV00001B/96